Pentecost Island
Books 7-10

Odessa

Sienna

Tess

Isla

Also available in print
Pentecost Island 1-3
Pippa
Eliza
Nell

Pentecost Island Books 4-6
Tamsin
Evie
Cherry

Cover Design: Annie Seaton
Editing: Susanne Bellamy, R.L. Aiken, Kristen Woolgar.
Copyright © 2021 Annie Seaton

DEDICATION

To girlfriends all over the world.

A note from Annie

I have really enjoyed writing this series, and I will miss my Pentecost Island girls.

I hope you enjoy spending time with them too.

Have you read the Augathella Girls?
Now available in four boxed sets

Odessa

Pentecost Island 7

Be yourself. Everyone else is taken.

Oscar Wilde

Prologue

Pippa - Pentecost Island – October

The night before our wedding, I moved out of Rafe's house and slept at Aunty Vi's with Nell and Tam. Funnily enough, I still thought of the old house as Aunty Vi's, even though she had passed away a couple of years ago, and the 1930s house and half the island had been left to me.

Nat and Gabe, Nell and Tam's partners had gone to Rafe's for the night, so we were indulging in a girls-only night. Like old times, if we could call a year ago, old times. We stayed up late, chatting and reminiscing. Much laughter and giggling fuelled by champagne—for Nell and I, anyway—filled our night, and there was no talk about work or the resort.

'Might as well act like teenagers again for a while. You're going to be an old married woman this time tomorrow,' Nell said.

'Seriously, Pip, are you sure this is right for you? Are you happy?' Tamsin asked. Nell was usually the worrier for all of us, but Tam was drinking soda water and wasn't tiddly like Nell and I were. Since she'd become pregnant, she seemed more serious and worried more.

'I am. Absolutely, unequivocally, damn straight sure. And I'm in lurve.' I spread my arms wide and knocked Nell's shoulder. 'I wouldn't change tomorrow for the world.'

Nell nudged me in retaliation, and champagne slopped from my glass onto the threadbare but comfy sofa.

'Whoops.'

We both giggled, and Tam did her famous eye roll. 'No Darren or Eric regrets?' she persisted.

'Ooh, wash your mouth out, Tamsin Jones,' I protested.

'With soda water,' Nell snorted.

'At least one of us is sober,' Tam said with a smile.

'Remember what Aunty Vi used to say to me?' I said, mopping at the damp sofa. 'Positivity, Pip. Well, you know what? I'm so certain of Rafe, I don't ever need to say or think that anymore. I've found the love of my life. And I trust him implicitly. Rafe would never hurt me.' My voice softened, and I gazed dreamily up to the hill where the lights of my partner's house glowed softly in the dark.

'Okay, it was just a last-minute check.' Tam lifted her glass and sipped her soda water. 'I never dreamed in a million years that the resort would grow like it has. I remember when we met you in Solaris last year, and you read the letter from that solicitor, Mr Morton. We imagined we'd be letting out rooms in Aunty Vi's old house to kayaking backpackers but, holy shit, girls, look at us now!' Her grin matched ours.

'We've done good,' Nell said. 'Really, really good.'

'And don't forget we've worked hard too.' I grinned at Tam. 'But it's just as well you saved Eliza from drowning. What a difference that's made to us.'

'And just as well, Sienna came to visit,' Tam replied.

Nell giggled again. 'And just as well, you didn't turn Evie back when you saw that pink sail.'

'I could have, couldn't I? But I've got over my pink phobia. Those days are long gone. The memories, the reminders of sad times. All gone.'

'Please don't tell us your top secret wedding dress is pink!' Nell wagged her finger at me, and I laughed when she almost slid sideways off the sofa.

'It's all right for you pair on the bubbles and giggling.' Tam yawned. 'If I drink any more soda water, I'll be up to the loo all night. I'm going to bed. I can't get over how much more sleep I need now.'

Nell hiccupped. 'Well, you're sleeping for two now.'

'Not sleeping for two, you airhead.'

Nell and I must have been tiddly to earn a second eye roll from Tam.

'That's eating for two, and boy, I'm doing that,' she said.

'Airhead?' Nell managed to sit up straight. 'I am not an airhead. I am a resort manager.'

'Hey, gals?' I pushed myself up off the sofa. 'Before you go to bed, come down to the beach with me and look at the moon. My last moonrise as a single woman.' A strange feeling fluttered through me. Maybe it was the champagne, or maybe it was the thought of the new direction my life was about to take.

Married. Who would ever have believed it?

'A group hug by moonlight,' Nell said as we left the house.

Together, we made our way carefully along the path without speaking and crossed the beach to the rock where we always sat. The full moon had risen and hung heavy above the horizon. The night sky held a tinge of pink, and the brisk wind had whipped up small waves on the usually calm passage. The water was grey and ominous, and I shivered, hoping it wasn't a premonition.

We sat quietly side-by-side on the edge of the wide, flat rock as we had done many times over the past twelve months.

'Everything's changing, isn't it?' I said, with a break in my voice.

'But would you really want things to stay the same or go back to the way it was before we came to Pentecost Island?' Nell asked.

'No, but just for one hour, I'd like to go back and see Aunty Vi in her house and tell her how it was going to be.' I swallowed the emotion. 'Tell her how happy I am, and how it was meant to be that she sold half of the island to Rafe.'

'I know she'd be happy, Pip, and that's what you have to remember and hold close in your heart,' Nell said.

I was sitting in the middle, and Tam reached over and put her arm around my shoulder, and then Nell did from the other side.

'Make me a promise, girls. No matter what happens, we're still—'

'All for one, and one for all,' we chanted together.

'I love you pair. Ever since you were kind to me at primary school. Friends for life,' I said, hugging them back.

'We'll still come down here to watch the moon rise when we're old and grey,' Tam said.

'Nah.' Nell shook her head. 'We won't get our walkers over the rocks.' She snorted again, and I joined in with a giggle.

'Come on, you two.' Tam stood and pulled us to our feet. 'It's time we were in bed. There's a wedding tomorrow, and you need your beauty sleep.'

***

Surprisingly, I slept well. Being back in the old house with Nell and Tam had been an excellent decision for the night before my wedding. Their constant chatter and our laughter kept me calm. We had breakfast together, and then Nell asked me to keep her company in the office. Tam went across to the new kitchen to see if Angus and Cherry needed any help. There was no sign of the other girls, but each time I suggested going to find them, Nell found something to keep me occupied. I narrowed my eyes and wondered what they were up to. I knew these girls well.

The morning passed quickly, and Tam prepared lunch for us. We sat on the veranda and could hear the chatter and clatter from the kitchen as the casual chefs prepared lunch for the resort guests seated on the side veranda. The inhouse guests would be served dinner here tonight while our wedding reception was in the new restaurant and bar.

'Cold drink? Champagne? Coffee?' Nell asked when she came out of the office.

'No champagne until we go down to Sienna and the day spa,' I said as Tam put a platter of cold meat and cheese on the table. 'I can't wait. She is so talented. I was floating when she did the practice run on Thursday.'

'Is your dress down there already?' Tam asked.

I nodded. 'Sienna and Evie had a sneak peek so they could get my makeup and hair right.'

'Ooh, I can't wait to see it,' Nell said. 'Is it a white wedding dress? Come on, give us a clue.'

'Nope. Not long to wait now.' I fanned my hand in front of my face. 'I'm getting more excited by the minute.'

'That's why I kept you busy, so the nerves couldn't kick in.'

When we'd finished lunch, Tam headed for her shower, and Nell went to tell Tess, the part-time office assistant, it was time for her to man reception.

I waited on the veranda for Tam and Nell to walk down to the day spa with me. On the way down, when we reached the small glade, I stopped, and Tam bumped into me.

'What's wrong? Nell asked. 'Did you forget something?'

'You haven't changed your mind, have you?' Tam's brow wrinkled in a frown.

'No, of course not. I just want to tell you both something I forgot to say last night. You know, me being married isn't going to change our friendship.'

'Of course it's not. And me being a mum won't either,' Tam said, looking relieved.

Nell nodded slowly. 'Things will change, but one thing I do know is that our friendship is strong enough to take change.'

'Good. That's sorted then.' The soft, warm breeze caressed my skin as we began walking again. It was a brilliant Whitsunday afternoon; the sky and the water were both such a deep blue that you could barely see the horizon where they met. I couldn't have asked for a better day for our wedding. Serenity filled me and I let out a soft sigh.

The noise of a boat motor easing back caught my attention as we passed the beach on the way to the day spa. I turned to look at our bay. Jiminy's boat was approaching the wharf and I frowned. He and his wife, Sarah, were guests at the wedding, but they were arriving very early. The ceremony wasn't until three o'clock, and it was just past noon.

I was further surprised when Rafe hurried down the steps from his house, but I let my eyes take my fill.

He must be coming down to see why they were early, I thought.

His dark hair glinted in the midday sun as he headed towards the jetty. Even though I'd enjoyed the girls' company last night, and slept well in my old bed, I'd missed having Rafe beside me. As I woke at first light, I'd reached out for him, before I remembered where I was and that it was our wedding day.

Rafe jumped down to the wharf and ran towards the boat as Jiminy secured it. The gate at the side of the deck opened and I stared as a tall slim woman in white stepped onto the jetty. It wasn't Sarah, and to my knowledge there were no new guests arriving today. We'd cleared the bookings calendar for the wedding day. The only guests in-house were those who were already on the island.

Rafe held his arms wide open as he reached the woman.

Clutching her broad-brimmed white hat with one hand she fell into his arms and clung to him with the other. He embraced her and my fiancé's dark head rested against the woman's for a long time.

A very long time.

A moment later, an older couple stepped off the boat and joined them.

Then it hit me. These were Rafe's publisher friends and their daughter, Odessa. I thought they had cancelled because of the accident. Why hadn't Rafe told me they were coming?

'What are you looking so worried about?' Tam asked.

I pointed to the boat. 'We have unexpected guests.'

Tam peered past me. 'Who?'

'I know I'm being a bitch, but why the hell did she have to arrive today of all days? On our wedding day!'

'Who? Who is it, Pip?' Tam put her hand on my shoulder, and I took a deep breath.

'A friend of Rafe's from England. We were expecting her for a visit, but not yet. Or at least I wasn't. She's had a horrible tragedy in her life, and she was coming here in a few weeks to help her That's her parents with her. They own the company that publishes Rafe's books. He invited them to the wedding, but they had to say no, because she was still in hospital. And I didn't think she was invited.'

'Maybe they decided to come after all, and travel with her.' Tam frowned. 'But now that they're here, where will they stay?'

I shrugged and tried not to sound worried. 'I don't know. I'm right out of the English friend loop.'

'Nell, we're not full, are we?' Tam asked.

'No, but the vacant huts haven't been serviced, because the cleaners haven't come over today. I'll go and see Tess right now, and get it sorted, because they can't stay with you and Rafe tonight. It's your wedding night, for goodness sake.'

'I know,' I said glumly as Nell took off back to the office.

And more to the point, why hadn't Rafe told me she was arriving? I thought. He must have known that she, I mean, they were on the way, I told myself. All I could think of was the way that Odessa had clung to him, and he had held her close.

'If the worst comes to the worst, I'll make up your bed here with clean sheets, and Gabe and I can give up our room too, and go to a single bed for the night,' Tam said.

'Thanks, sweets, but it'll be fine. Tess has cleaned the rooms before. If she needs to, we'll pay her extra.' I forced a calm smile to my face. 'I'm really happy that Rafe has some friends here for him today too.'

'Are you ready, girls? Where's Nell hurried off to?'

I jumped. I hadn't seen Sienna coming along the path.

I turned to her as she stood beside Tam and I. 'Nell won't be long.'

Sienna took my hand. 'Hebe Day Spa awaits you. We have just over two hours to make the three of you even more beautiful. Evie's waiting down there. She's set up a mini-hair salon in the other treatment room. Are you excited, ma cherie?'

'I'm happy.' I forced myself not to look at the jetty or the group heading for the steps leading up the cliff to Rafe's house.

As I walked through the dim forest with Sienna and Tam to get ready for my wedding, my serenity was tainted by a growing doubt. My past rushed through my thoughts. I should have known that things wouldn't work out perfectly.

I also knew I shouldn't doubt Rafe because of my past. I couldn't do that.

But all I could see was him holding that woman close to him. Their heads together as though they were a couple.

Was it too late to change my mind?

Chapter 1

Odessa - August - London

'Come on, Han. It won't make us too late. There's a sale on, and we could get some new dresses and shoes for the weekend. I really need a dress for your Gran's birthday tomorrow night.' Odessa Walker reached over and tugged her friend Hannah's arm as Hannah gripped the steering wheel of the Aston Martin. 'Harrods is only a few blocks from where we join the motorway.'

'Careful, Essie, Daddy will kill me if I so much as put a scratch on his car.' Hannah shrugged Odessa's hand off as she focused on the road ahead. 'Driving through those narrow country lanes is enough of a worry, let alone trying to find a park in Knightsbridge.'

'You need to be a more confident driver, sweets. If you didn't worry as much about other drivers and just focused on the road and drove at a decent speed, it would be much easier. Let me drive, we'll get there faster.'

'Says the woman who lost her license for speeding last month.' Hannah chuckled as she slowed the car to a crawl as they approached the turnoff. 'Of course you're not going to drive my father's car. God in heaven, I'd be cut out of the will.'

'My father's publishing office is there, and we can park at the side. Come on, please?' Odessa was well-practised in getting her own way. 'I saw the most gorgeous sun dress that would be perfect for you for drinks at the river this afternoon.'

'What label was it?' Hannah threw her a glance, and Odessa knew she had her hooked. Now, to reel her in.

'It was a Minko. A patchwork maxi. It was just you, darling.'

'Ooh, you're bad. I suppose we'd have time for a quick champers at the wine bar across the road from Harrods too. Just one, of course.'

'Of course. But honestly, I'd be fine to drive too. Who's going to pull us up in the hedgerows of Berkshire? We can open the top once we get off the motorway.'

'How much was the dress?' Hannah asked as she took one hand off the steering wheel to smooth her already perfect hair. 'I had two flat tyres yesterday, and Daddy took them out of my allowance. And no to driving, and no to the top down. I paid out a fortune at the hair salon this morning.'

'You can afford it. If you're short, I can loan you. Now turn left at the next street. Daddy's office is on the left, halfway down.'

'Are you telling me you haven't packed a formal dress in one of those three suitcases in the boot?' Hannah grinned and did as she was bid. 'Okay, I guess another couple of dresses won't hurt. Gran does like everyone to dress formally for dinner. Tonight too.'

'I've already worn both the dresses I've packed. I need a buzz, and a new dress or two will give me that.'

'I thought coming to the estate for the weekend would cheer you up. I had noticed you've been a bit quiet lately.' Hannah flicked the left indicator on, and Odessa smiled. Although they'd been friends since boarding school, Hannah's family were higher up the social ladder than Odessa's.

Nouveau riche, Odessa had been called. She'd overheard Clarissa, one of the women in their group, talking about her father's company one night. Clarissa was a bitch, so Odessa hadn't let it bother her.

'I'm so excited that you managed to get me invited to your gran's party. Such a great group of people will be there.'

'I asked Gran if I could invite our whole set. She was happy to have the young crowd there.'

'That's good. It's hard to believe she's going to be seventy,' Odessa said. 'She's still gorgeous.'

'She is. I hope I have her genes.'

Odessa rolled her eyes. 'There's no doubt of that.'

'I might look like her, but I'm not driven like she is. Gran has no need to work, but she's still running her PR company, you know.' Hannah laughed. 'She keeps telling me I need to get a job. I'm sure I'll get another lecture this weekend about work or study.' She shook her head. 'Now, why would I need to do that?'

'I remember when we both got suspended from Mayhew, and we got sent down to your gran for a serious talking to.' Odessa giggled as she remembered. 'She told us every young woman has particular talents, and the staff at Mayhew see it as their job to help her find and develop them.'

'You've discovered yours, Essie darling. I'm still looking.'

'What work skills have I got?'

Hannah shot a laughing glance her way as she turned into the narrow street. 'You have a talent for drinking champagne, looking gorgeous, and attracting the best-looking men in London. I'm surprised you haven't nabbed one by now.'

'Turn at the building with the black wrought iron gates open on the left.' Odessa ignored her friend's frivolous summing up of her talents. It rankled; maybe it was time she did something with her life. The one thing she had taken away from school was the discovery that she had a talent for jewellery design. Working with fine silver and designing unique pieces had appealed until she'd tried to find work in the field. Everywhere she'd tried had suggested starting out as a sales assistant. Serving in the store and making coffee for the designers.

Not for her. Maybe one day she'd start her own business. But while she was young, there was too much fun to be had. One day, she'd make use of the knowledge she'd learned in the silversmith course she'd done. She was sure Daddy would help; he'd be pleased to see her doing something. Both her parents would.

Odessa couldn't see the point in working, and she'd never mentioned her creative interest in jewellery to her friends. Her family had enough money to keep her in the style to which she had become accustomed to. Occasionally she made a token effort and worked for a while, but it always interfered with the things she wanted to do. Since her best friend, Rafe, had moved away to some tiny island off Australia, she'd lost focus.

Rafe had given her a talking to before he left. 'It's time you grew up, Odessa. Your father spoils you rotten, but one day you'll get bored with swanning around looking beautiful, and not doing anything useful,' he'd said.

'You think I'm beautiful?' she'd asked with what she hoped was a coquettish look from beneath her lashes.

'You know you are. I don't need to tell you that.'

'Well, why are you going away? Don't you love me?' Odessa had pouted.

'Of course I love you, like a little sister. And I worry about you as much as your parents do.'

'But why are you moving away? I need you.'

Rafe stared past her, and she saw a dark despair in his eyes, a despair that she didn't understand. Odessa had met his ex-wife and knew Rafe was better off without her. He should know that too.

'Because I must.'

'And you won't get bored away from here? Living on a tiny speck in the ocean? Sorry, darling, but I disagree.' Odessa knew it was Rafe's divorce that was making him run away. She knew she had to wait until he got over it, and came back to England, and then he'd realise that she was the best woman for him. She knew she was; he just had to realise that fact. Absence makes the heart grow fonder and all that.

Hannah parked the luxury car very carefully and checked it was locked when they were standing in the small parking area. 'I won't get booked here, will I?'

'No, I'll sort it with Daddy if there's a problem. I don't want to go in now, though. He'll think I've listened to him. He's been trying to put me to work in the family business for a couple of months.'

'Let's go shopping.' Hannah looked down at the Cartier watch on her wrist. 'We have forty-five minutes to shop and have one quick drink. There's a wine bar on the corner across from Harrods.'

Odessa's grin was cheeky. 'We can be a teensy bit late and make an entrance at Swallowfield House, can't we?'

'We can, and I'll be in my new Minko dress. That's an excellent idea, Essie. Maybe we'll have time for two drinks!'

##

An hour and a half later, Hannah tugged at Odessa's arm as she talked to the barman in the Green Vine Wine bar.

'Sweetie, we really have to leave, or we'll miss the pre-dinner drinks by the river at Gran's.'

Odessa smiled across the bar. 'We'll come back in for a drink on the way home on Sunday, Oliver.'

Odessa's smile grew as he reached over and took her hand. 'I'll look forward to it.'

Hannah was waiting by the door as Odessa tucked Oliver's card into her pocket.

She curled her lip. 'A barman? Your standards are slipping, darling.'

'He was an interesting guy. He's doing a law degree, and it's only a part-time job.'

'If he needs to work while he's at university he's not the man for you. And'—Hannah's smile was sly—'he was a teensy bit young too.'

Odessa lifted her chin. 'Don't be a bitch.'

'Well, we are almost thirty, and he looked like he was just out of school.'

Depression settled over Odessa like a wet blanket and her interest in the weekend ahead sank like a stone in the Thames. She should have stayed home. 'Let me drive, Han? We'll never get there at the rate you drive. And you can look at all your shopping.' She watched as Hannah stowed a dozen shopping bags on the back seat.

Hannah shook her head. 'No. Daddy would kill me if I let you.'

'Come on, how will he know?'

Hannah stared at her as she considered the offer, but finally shook her head again. 'No, he'll be at Gran's when we drive in or he might pass us on the way. I'll drive. I can't afford to lose my allowance, and he's been threatening more often lately. Daddy wants me to get a job too.'

'What is it with our parents?' Odessa opened the passenger door.

'They simply don't know what's important when you're young.' Hannah started the car and pulled out onto the A4 and headed towards Hammersmith.

'Shite, Han. Look out. You pulled out in front of a lorry.'

'He stopped,' Hannah replied, but her voice shook a little. 'I hate driving in the peak hour traffic and Friday afternoons are the worst.'

'Well, you know the solution. I can have us in Swallowfield in an hour, and you can relax.'

'Oh, all right, you win. I'll pull up after the Chiswick flyover and you can take over.'

Odessa smiled. It never took much to get Hannah to give in.

The two young women were lost in their own thoughts as they headed towards the M4. Odessa tried to shake off the strange blackness that had descended on her. Once she was driving, she would be able to focus on the road, and chase those dark thoughts away.

Hannah pulled over as promised and they swapped sides. Odessa took over, and the Aston Martin surged along the M4.

'I wish I had your confidence. If I drove that fast, I'd run off the road,' Hannah said.

'I'll teach you how to drive properly on the way home.'

'No, I'm not game,' Hannah said as she reached across to the back seat and pulled some of the shopping bags onto her lap. 'Oh, I adore these earrings. They'll match the dress perfectly. I'm so pleased you spotted them.'

'I love the shoes. The colours are gorgeous. How much did you end up spending?' Odessa changed back a gear and the car roared past two lorries.

'Oh, Essie. I'm not game to add it up. Probably over a thousand pounds. Thank God for credit cards.'

'And fathers,' Odessa said drily. 'Anyway, you'll look gorgeous. Now remind me where to turn off to Swallowfield.'

'You take the left exit off the junction after Whitely Wood. I'll tell you when we get there.'

'Ha, fat chance. You'll have your nose stuck in those shopping bags. I think I remember.' She reached over and flicked on the screen of the Sat Nav.

Half an hour later they turned off the motorway.

'Yes, I remember now. Three Mile Cross is where I head to your Gran's.' Odessa slowed the speed as the road narrowed.

'Don't go too close to the hedgerows. We can't turn up with scratches on the car.'

'Just chill, sweetie. Trust me.'

'Oh and I forgot to mention, don't call Gran, "Gran". Now that she's seventy she's decided she wants to be called Vivian.' Hannah put her head back and closed her eyes as they travelled the last few miles.

'Oh shit,' Odessa exclaimed as they turned into the narrow lane that led to Swallowfield Hall.

'What's wrong. Did you scratch the car?'

'No, worse than that. Look!'

'Oh, fuckety-fuck. I'm dead.' Hannah groaned as she spotted her father walking along the side of the lane with two black Labradors bounding ahead.

Odessa gulped. 'Is it too late to swap seats?'

'Yep, he's already seen us. Oh shit.' Hannah shoved as many of the shopping bags as she could beneath the seat. 'I know, I'll say we swapped over in the lane because I wanted to get changed.'

'Good luck with that.'

They both waved as they passed him, and by the look of his face, Odessa knew Hannah was going to have to sweet-talk her way out of this one.

It didn't bother Odessa. She'd loved driving the Aston Martin down the motorway. Hannah hadn't realised, because she'd been dozing, but Odessa had clocked over a hundred and ten miles per hour when she'd overtaken a couple of cars travelling slowly in the middle lane. Speed gave her a better rush than alcohol did. And you didn't end up with a hangover.

'Pull over at the carriage house before we go up to the main house, and we can freshen up. I want to put my new dress and earrings on.'

'Don't forget the shoes.' Odessa stood beside the car while Hannah went inside. She brushed her fingers through her hair and pulled out her lipstick. Even though she'd said she was excited to be here, Odessa really wasn't looking forward to the weekend anymore, and she couldn't be bothered getting changed for drinks and then again for dinner.

But maybe it was better than the alternative of being home alone in her flat.

Same old crowd, drinking too much in the early evening spent by the river, sharing all the latest gossip. Champagne. She'd probably end up sleeping with Charlie Cochrane, because it was the easiest way to get him to stop nagging her to marry him.

God, we're a shallow bunch, Odessa thought. Even though Hannah was a friend, she still wouldn't trust her to be there if she ever really needed support.

None of the girls in the group were close. Most of them were worried about being the prettiest, looking the best and snaffling the best-looking guy. Scrap that, the richest guy, she thought with a grin. And that was Charlie.

With a sigh Odessa walked around to the passenger side when Hannah came out of the house.

'Well?' she asked, twirling around to show off the new dress.

'Gorgeous,' Odessa replied. 'You'll have them all salivating over you, even Charlie with a bit of luck.'

'Oh no, Charlie's all yours.'

'I don't want him. Come on let's get this to-do with your father over and then we can go and have a drink.'

Chapter 2

Pippa and Rafe's wedding - Pentecost Island

The music that Sienna had playing on low volume in the day spa went a little way to calming me. I lay back and closed my eyes as Evie massaged my scalp over the basin; the scent of coconut shampoo surrounded me. Sienna had a schedule for the afternoon; she ran Hebe, the day spa like an army general.

I was with Evie for my hair first while Sienna did Tam and Nell's makeup. Then Sienna had insisted that when they were finished, makeup and hair done, they would leave and not see me until I was dressed and they walked me through the rainforest to my wedding.

My thoughts turned to what was ahead today. Not having any family to see me married or a father to give me away left a little corner of my heart sad. Losing my parents at a young age had come at an emotional cost that I had only recently learned to cope with. I had adored my dad, and although I was sad that he wasn't here to give me away today, I had no sense that he or my mother were watching down on me, but in my heart, I knew Aunty Vi was.

'Are you a little nervous, Pip?' Evie asked as she rinsed off my hair. 'I could feel the tension through your scalp.'

'No, just a little bit sad. Thinking about my parents and my aunt. No family to cheer me along on my wedding day.' I didn't want to say anything about the doubts that had surfaced before. I'd done my best to push them aside.

Evie walked around to the front of the basin. 'Jed and I didn't have any family there either. We were married in a registry office in a country town, and we had one friend each as a witness.' She laughed as she towelled my hair and then wound it around in a turban. 'And we went to the pub for our reception. Look at you and your wedding! Getting married on your own tropical island and being pampered in a day spa.'

I nodded and the towel around my hair wobbled as I sat up. 'I know. I am so lucky. And it's going to be a wonderful day.'

'It is. And remember you're surrounded by friends who love you like a sister.' She nodded to the schedule that Sienna had written up on a small whiteboard. 'I'll dry your hair, and then after Sienna does your makeup, I'll style it. Then we'll help you into your dress.'

As I walked into the other treatment room, a cork popped. Bubbles cascaded from the bottle of Moët that Tam held up.

'Don't waste it!' I said with a laugh. 'Moët!'

'Nothing but the best for your wedding day.' Tam handed me a crystal flute, and I smiled. 'You look gorgeous, Tam.'

Tam nodded. 'Sienna is a magician.' She poured four more glasses and handed them around to the girls. 'Just a little bit for me. After all, it's a very special day.'

Laughter filled the room as we chatted, and Sienna finished Nell's makeup. Nell and Sienna picked up their glasses, and we sipped our drinks.

'Where's Eliza?' I asked. 'She should be here too.'

Tam and Nell looked at each other with a smile. 'She's busy. Overseeing the organisation while we get pampered.'

'What's going on?'

'A wedding, silly!' Tam widened her eyes, trying to look innocent.

Hmm, I knew her well.

'Don't you worry about anything,' she said. 'We have it all under control.'

'I'm sure you do. I trust my team.' Laughing with the girls had eased my tension, and I finally let go of my worries. 'It's not every day a girl gets married.'

Tam and Nell came over to me before they left.

'How long do we have, Sienna?' Nell asked.

Sienna glanced at her watch. 'It's a quarter to two now, so come back in an hour. Evie and I have our clothes here, so once Pippa is ready, we'll get dressed and head over to the restaurant, ready for you two to walk her over.'

My fingers tingled with excitement and I put the glass down as I held my arms open. 'A hug please, before you go.'

I blinked away tears as my two best friends in the whole world hugged me one at a time.

'Love you, Pippa,' Nell said with a sniff.

'Me too, girlfriend. See you soon.' Tam brushed a tear away before it could spill over.

I swallowed as they left the day spa, and Sienna led me over to the mirror.

##

An hour later, my makeup was done, and Evie had finished my hair, but I remained in the chair as Sienna instructed.

'Just to relax you, not to put you to sleep,' she said as her gentle fingers kneaded my shoulders and neck in a light massage.

'Between that and a glass of bubbles, I probably will go to sleep.' I smiled as serenity and anticipation filled me.

'No, you will not. I will not let you.' Sienna's lilting accent kicked in. She gently wiped the oil from my shoulders. 'It's time to put on the dress. Evie, can you please put that silk scarf over Pippa's hair while we get the dress over her head.'

Sienna crossed the room to where my wedding dress hung beneath a cover on a dress rack. She pulled the cover off and I let out a small gasp.

'I'd forgotten just how beautiful that dress is,' I said staring at it.

'And it will look even more beautiful when you have it on. Come on, my sweet, it's time.'

Chapter 3

Odessa - Berkshire - August

By the time Hannah's father had ranted about his precious car and they made their way down to the river where evening drinks were being held, Odessa was over it.

'It's a car, for fu— for God's sake,' she said to a very contrite Hannah as they opened the gate to the lawn edging the River Blackwater that ran past Hannah's family estate. In the distance Odessa could see the five-arched brick bridge that crossed the river to Swallowfield Park, the seventeenth-century country house next door. Voices and laughter drifted up from the river.

'Yes, but it's Daddy's car. At one point he said he would drive us back to London on Sunday, but then he remembered he had an estate meeting here on Monday, thank God.'

'So we're fine to go back in the Aston Martin?' Odessa asked.

'Yes, but I have to drive.' Hannah shook her head. 'For goodness sake, warn the others not to let on to him that you lost your licence.'

Odessa yawned. 'You know, I think I'll see if I can get a lift back to London tomorrow. I don't fancy spending the whole weekend with the crowd.'

'Don't be silly, Essie. You'll have fun. You always do, and you'll be the life of the party by tomorrow night.'

The friends who'd already arrived were sitting on the lawn outside the small pavilion at the back of the estate. Odessa's mood began to mellow as she inhaled the fresh country air and took the glass of champagne that Charlie held out and sat in the chair that he vacated for her. It was a perfect August afternoon, and the air was warm as the sun lowered to the horizon in a dramatic splash of gold and violet. As Odessa sat back and looked up, a flock of geese flew over low enough that the flap of their wings moved the still air and the flurry reached her bare shoulders. To the east, parkland dotted with ancient oaks and silver-trunked beeches climbed to the crest of the hills surrounding the estate. It was so different from the city.

Odessa took a long sip of her champagne and let out a sigh as relaxation began to seep in. Charlie sat at her feet and leaned his head back on her knees.

'Happy, Ess?' he asked with a sweet smile.

She reached forward and ran her hand over his hair. He wasn't as bad as she'd made out. 'I am, Charlie.'

'I could tell you were in a mood, so I was giving you some space.'

'You know me very well.'

'I do.'

If Odessa said the word, Charlie would marry her tomorrow; he'd proposed a few times and been hurt when she'd laughed at him. He'd also been the one to console her when Rafe had left for his tropical island. But she didn't love Charlie that way, and she never would. In the meantime, being friends with benefits suited her fine.

The weekend turned out to be enjoyable, but the dark feeling stayed with Odessa. Maybe it was because Rafe wasn't around anymore, or maybe it was because of the glum face that Charlie wore most of Saturday because she'd opted not to share her bed with him the night before.

On Saturday evening before the birthday celebration, they all congregated down by the river. Odessa put her head back and settled into the chair enjoying the warmth of the midsummer sunshine. It wouldn't be long before the leaves were flushed with the gold of autumn.

And another year had passed. It was time to think about her future. Maybe she should just give in and marry Charlie, but she wanted more than that. Her parents had a happy marriage and she knew how much in love they still were. Odessa wanted a marriage like that, and Charlie—as sweet as he was—was only a friend.

A boat puttered past the end of the garden where Hannah's young cousins were playing on the riverbank, their laughter adding to the happy mood as everyone anticipated the party.

Her mother had come back from visiting Rafe a few months ago, raving about the warmth of his island even in the southern winter. Maybe she'd go and visit him soon. She really hadn't thought Rafe would stay there as long as he had; once he'd got over his writer's block and delivered his next book, she'd expected to hear he was coming home.

He hadn't called her for ages, and she was unhappy about that too. Her phone buzzed in the pocket of her summer dress, and Odessa pulled it out and glanced at the caller ID.

'Hello, Mummy,' she said.

'Hi, sweetie, I thought I'd call before the party started.'

Odessa grinned. The party hadn't stopped; it had actually been one nonstop drinking session since they'd arrived last night. That was probably why she was feeling down; too much alcohol had depressed her system.

'What's happening? Is everything okay?' This constant sense of doom sent her into a panic. 'Is Dad okay?'

'Yes, everything's fine. We've had some lovely news and I wanted to share it with you.'

'Someone's hit the Sunday Times bestseller list?'

'No. It's better than that.'

'Wow, you have me guessing. I didn't think there was anything in the publishing world better than that.'

'One of our authors is getting married. And we are very happy about it. And we've been invited to the wedding.'

A cold prickly feeling ran up the back of Odessa's neck. 'Who?'

'Who do you think? There's only one person in our stable of authors who's close enough to be almost family.'

How strange that she'd just been thinking about him. 'Rafe,' Odessa said dully.

'Yes. Isn't it wonderful? After all he's been through, and now he's getting married to an Australian girl. Apparently she owns the other half of the island he lives on.'

'Very convenient. Maybe she just wants him for his land.'

'Odessa! That's not a very nice thing to say. I thought we'd taught you better manners than that. Can't you be happy for him, sweetheart? Daddy and I are delighted for him. He sounds so happy.'

'When's the wedding? Have I been invited too?' She felt like a bitch, but how could she be happy when Rafe was marrying someone else? Just when she'd been thinking about going to see him.

A long silence. 'Ah, it's the first of November. You're not on our invitation, but I don't expect you would be. Ours arrived yesterday, and I expect yours could be there when you get home.'

'I don't want Rafe to get married. And if I did get invited, I'm not going. I don't want to see him marry some long-legged tanned Aussie bimbo with long blonde hair.'

'Odessa.' Her mother's voice held a warning note. 'You sound about twelve-years-old.'

'Well, I'm not, and I'm not going. I have to go and get ready for the dinner.' She jammed her thumb on the phone with much more pressure than was necessary and disconnected the call.

So that's why she'd been feeling so strange; she must have known. A premonition.

Odessa stood staring at the river as a small sailboat drifted past. When a hand touched her elbow gently, she jumped.

'Are you okay, sweets?' Charlie asked.

'Oh, sod off, Charlie,' she hissed. 'Just leave me in peace.' With that, Odessa turned on her heel and hurried back to her room.

Maybe she wouldn't even go to the formal birthday dinner.

Chapter 4

Rafe - Pentecost Island

Rafe was cleaning up his kitchen after a huge breakfast with Nat and Gabe.

'You'll need energy to get through the day,' Gabe had said as he handed Rafe a plate overloaded with bacon, eggs and sausages with three hash browns on the side. 'How about a beer to wash it down?'

'God, no.' He shook his head. 'I had enough beer last night to do me for a while.'

Gabe and Nat had left to help Eliza, Phillipe and Jed prepare the lawn area for the ceremony this afternoon. As they left, he knew he was grinning like a loon, but the day he'd been waiting for had finally arrived.

Today he was marrying Phillipa, the love of his life. He realised now why his first marriage had never stood a chance. The love that he held for Pippa was the first time he'd ever loved a woman with his heart and soul. He and Rebecca had been too young, and they'd had different ideas about what they wanted out of life, but it had taken Rafe a long time to get over it. Not that she'd left him, but the fact that he'd failed. It had affected his work for a year or more and delayed his publication schedule.

Rafe's phone buzzed on the countertop and his grin widened. He'd known Pippa wouldn't be able to help herself, even though she'd only moved down to the old house yesterday.

Last night had been fun—some light-hearted teasing about losing his freedom, and a few beers, had cemented the friendship with the guys. Phillipe and Jed had come up for the barbeque too but had left before midnight. He'd also invited the new landscape gardener, Dylan, and it had been interesting talking to him about his time in Cornwall.

As Dylan had left last night, he'd offered to help out however he could at the wedding.

'That would be excellent,' Phillipe had said. 'The girls are spreading rose petals along the path through the glade to the lawn, and we want to keep it private for the day and get the guests to use the other path.'

Nat chimed in. 'We didn't want to put up signs, so if you could just hang around the path that leads to the spa hut at the restaurant end from about two o'clock, and redirect anyone who comes that way, that'd be a great help.'

'Consider it done,' Dylan said.

'And if you want to help in the bar, I'm sure they'd appreciate another pair of hands. Just clearing glasses and the like,' Gabe said.

'Not a problem. I've done bar work before.'

Rafe was impressed with Dylan; he was obviously an intelligent guy as well as a hard worker. He'd fitted in well as they'd laughed over a few beers last night. Even though he had only just started work on the island last week, he had the resort looking good, and had mowed the lawns yesterday ready for the wedding. Rafe knew Pippa was pleased with him too. The team on the island was great, and now that Cherry and Angus had sorted out their misunderstanding, everything was going smoothly. For a while there, it had looked as though they might have lost a chef.

Rafe picked up his phone and eyebrows lifted as he read the message.

Surprise!

The message was from his publishers and great friends, Jenny and Bryant; he'd been disappointed when they couldn't come to the wedding.

Jenny and Bryant had been there for him during his divorce. The residual bitterness had drilled a huge hole in Rafe's self-confidence when Rebecca had walked out on him. The move to Australia—to Pentecost Island—had been worthwhile in many ways. His writer's block had gone and he'd produced his next two novels for them. But best of all, he'd met and fallen in love with Phillipa. His smile grew as he scanned the text.

I hope a surprise is okay. We've just landed on Hamilton Island and will be at your wedding. If there's no

room on your island, we will find accommodation here. See you at the wedding. xxx Jenny. P.S. Odessa is with us.

Rafe replied immediately. **Very happy to hear that. Welcome! We will find accommodation.**

He'd call down to Nell as soon as he'd finished cleaning the kitchen. Even if the huts were full—but he was sure they weren't—Bryant, and Jenny and Odessa could stay in the house tonight, Rafe was sure Pippa wouldn't mind. He'd also let Angus know there would be three extras in the restaurant. Rafe was smiling as he went back to the kitchen and finished his chores.

Chapter 5

Dylan - Pentecost Island

Just before two o'clock, Dylan Nash had a quick shower, and dressed in clean shorts and pulled a *Ma Carmichael's Resort* polo shirt over his head. He hummed beneath his breath as he hurried from the bathroom that he shared in the building at the back of the original house with Angus, one of the chefs. Being offered the job on Pentecost Island had made him very happy. So far, he'd liked everyone he'd met in his first week, and everyone had been very welcoming. The island had a great vibe to it.

Being invited up for a barbeque at Rafe's last night had been unexpected, but he'd soon found acceptance as one of the guys and not just a staff member. Nat and Gabe explained their relationship to the partners on the island, as did Phillipe, the Frenchman, who pointed out his yacht riding at anchor out in the bay.

The handover of the landscaping role from Evie had gone smoothly, and Dylan already had some new ideas for the resort gardens. He'd walked around the island on his second day and had been impressed. What Evie had achieved in a few months was admirable.

'I'll be over on the mainland, just north of Mackay,' Evie had said as she showed him where the equipment was kept in a building adjacent to his accommodation. 'Jed and I have bought a property near Calen, so it's not far to come over here for a day occasionally if you ever need a hand.'

'I'll be taking you up on that,' he said. 'I've seen the order for the outdoor furniture that Jed is making for the bar, so I'm sure you'll need to come over here.'

'Don't hesitate to call if you need to know anything either. Jed and I will be here until the day after the wedding, and then we're back to Brisbane to get packed up for the move.' She handed him a card with her mobile and email. 'I love Pentecost Island, and I'll be back as often as I can.'

As Dylan walked the back path, he stopped a few times and moved a couple of small branches from the glade where seats wrapped around the trunk of one of the large hoop pines. This was a lesser-used path to the bay, but the guests would be using it for the rest of the day. Once he reached the day spa, he took the right fork and headed to the reception area, smiling at what the girls had done.

The path was strewn with red rose petals, and luckily, so far, the breeze hadn't come up and blown them off the path, but he was sure that would happen later in the afternoon. The wedding would be in full swing by then and he'd be helping in the bar. Tealight candles flickered beneath glass covers on both sides of the path; he knew Tam and Nell had done it as a surprise for Pippa. He walked along checking that all the candles were still alight. As he reached the end of the path where it led to the restaurant, a couple in swimming costumes were about to head that way down to the beach.

'Hi there,' he said. 'If you don't mind, I'll ask you to take the other path. This one is closed for the wedding party to use for an hour or so.'

'Certainly.' The man nodded and Dylan directed them to the other path.

Dylan went back to pick up a couple of large twigs that he'd noticed as he'd heard the couple coming. As he approached the curve in the path, he bent to pick up a branch and was about to straighten when someone barrelled into him, almost knocking him off his feet.

Before he could speak, he was subjected to a mouthful of vitriol delivered in a shrill voice, at odds with the plummy English accent.

'What the hell do you think you're doing? I almost fell and that's the last thing I need.'

'I'm sorry, madam, but this path is closed for the wedding.' He kept his tone pleasant, despite her attitude. 'I'm sorry you didn't see me.'

'Are you blaming me?' She looked at the logo on his shirt. 'I'm assuming you're staff?'

He stared at the woman as she attempted to push past him. 'This path is closed, madam.'

'How dare you. I'll go where I please. Move.'

Dylan gently took her arms and turned her to face back the way she had come, still keeping his voice civil. 'The path is closed as there is a wedding this afternoon. The other one there will take you to the beach.'

'How dare you touch me. I'll report you to Rafe. And of course I know there's a bloody wedding.'

'I've been instructed to keep this path clear for the bridal party.' Dylan let go of her and stood in the centre of the path with his arms folded. Even though she was tall, he towered over her.

She lifted her chin and stared at him. 'I am a guest at this bloody wedding, and I need to speak to the bride, so step aside. Now.'

'No.' Dylan wondered if he was doing the right thing, but he didn't like her attitude or her 'bloody wedding' comment. Something was wrong here.

'Odessa!' Dylan looked past the woman when he heard Rafe's voice. As he looked back at her, her expression had changed, and tears now welled in her eyes. 'Oh, Rafe. Thank goodness you're here. This man just assaulted me.' Her voice held a contrived shake that hadn't been evident a moment ago.

Rafe took the woman's arm. 'Come back to the house, please. You're not to bother Pippa.'

Dylan couldn't believe it when she stamped her foot. He'd never witnessed such a performance from a grown woman. He'd had his own problems with Siobhan, but his ex had been able to manipulate without resorting to tantrums, and he'd fallen for it every time. He'd learned a lot about women in the six months before his wife had left, and judging by her behaviour this one had an impressive range of tactics in her repertoire

He watched, fascinated as the woman looked up at Rafe and her whole demeanour changed. Along with her voice, her expression softened. She was a very attractive woman, pale skin and dark hair, her large blue eyes were framed with thick lashes.

'I just wanted to meet her and tell her how happy I am for her, darling.'

'I'm sure you do.' Rafe's voice was dry as he glanced at Dylan and took the woman's arm. 'Thanks, Dylan. I appreciate your work.'

'Are you taking his side? That . . . that gorilla? He manhandled me.'

'I'm sure he didn't. He was doing his job. Now you have one more chance. Come to the house and be reasonable or I will have no hesitation in putting you on a boat and sending you straight back to Hamilton Island.'

'No,' she said in a childlike voice.

'For fuck's sake, this is the very reason why you didn't get an invitation to the wedding.

Dylan widened his eyes when Rafe lost his cool.

'And don't go hiding behind what happened.' Rafe's voice was cold. 'You've always been a spoilt brat, Odessa. Look, I'm sorry for what you've been through. It's awful, and I'm more than happy for you to stay here and recover, but on one condition. I am not going to let you hurt Pippa. I am not going to let you ruin our wedding day. Is that clear?'

'You're a bully, and I hate you.' Again, the foot stamp, but this time the woman called Odessa started to cry.

Dylan was surprised when Rafe put his arms around her. As he gently patted her back, Rafe caught Dylan's eye.

'Thanks, mate. I'll get you to keep an eye on the path. If you see anything untoward'—he inclined his head towards the woman in his arms—'do what you have to do. I'll deal with the consequences. Now I have to go and get ready. Can't be late for my wedding. Not a good look. Especially now.'

Dylan nodded, watching as Rafe led her away.

All he could hope was that she didn't come back.

Chapter 6

Odessa – Berkshire - August

Odessa's mood had improved after a couple of glasses of champagne. She caught sight of herself in the large mirror on the southern wall of the ballroom. The red figure-hugging dress that she'd bought at Harrods on their stop yesterday afternoon had been worth every penny, even if it meant she'd have to hit Dad up for another loan to get her through the month. The sequins along the edge of each shoulder sparkled as she moved closer to the group of her friends who were sitting on a curved seat in the corner. Clarissa sent her a sweet smile and she gave an equally false one in return.

Charlie jumped up to make a space for her and she reached up and kissed his cheek. 'Sorry I was such a cow this afternoon, sweets.' Her temper had only lasted a few minutes and then she'd felt bad for being mean to Charlie. As long as Rafe was truly happy, that was all that mattered. She'd just have to get used to it and hope he wasn't making another mistake. Men, they never knew what was good for them.

Charlie's fingers brushed her cheek. 'You're forgiven. You do look ravishing, Odessa.'

'Ravishing? Now that's a word with connotations.'

He grinned and put his arm around her, and she leaned against Charlie, and whispered, 'Rafe's getting married.'

'Is that good news?' he asked carefully.

'I guess it is for him,' she said. 'But as long as he's happy, I suppose I can be happy for him.'

'I'm pleased, if you are,' he said carefully.

'I'm happy.' She nudged him. 'Now are you going to get me another drink?'

Even though the night was lively, and the music was geared more to their generation than Hannah's grandmother, Odessa felt apart and on edge. She was thoughtful and realised it was because she was tired of this partying, drinking never-ending champagne, constant gossip and laughing at things that really held no amusement for her. Hearing Rafe's news had been a wake-up call; her reaction had been immature. She knew full well that there was no romance between them, but she had let herself dream.

But when she finally chose a man, he would be like Rafe. A gentleman, and steady and true. But first, she was going to get her career sorted. It was past time that she settled down.

##

Breakfast the next morning was more of the same. A huge table was set in the conservatory, and the buffet was loaded with English breakfast food. Odessa turned her nose up at the black pudding and mushrooms that Charlie was loading onto his plate as she reached for a piece of toast.

Taking a seat opposite Hannah, Odessa shook her head when a white-jacketed waiter offered to add champagne to her orange juice. 'No, thank you, just juice for me.'

'What time do you want to go back to the city?' she asked Hannah.

'This morning,' Hannah said sipping her champagne. 'I'll only have the one drink and it's watered down anyway, so it won't take long to wear off.'

'Can I cadge a lift too?' Charlie sat beside Odessa, his plate holding scrambled eggs and bacon, two grilled sausages, hash browns, black pudding, mushrooms and tomatoes all covered with a layer of baked beans.

'Charlie, that is just gross,' she said nibbling on her toast. 'Talk about clogging your arteries.'

He laughed as he shovelled a forkful of food up. 'Hey, this is what my grandfather has every day, and he's almost ninety. A breakfast like this every day should see me live to a hundred.'

Odessa finished her orange juice and stood. 'Well, I'm going for a walk along the river and then I'm going to pack. What time, Han?'

'Say ten-thirty?' Hannah lifted her glass for a refill as the waiter hovered.

Odessa raised her eyebrows. 'Looks like I'm driving back to London.'

Hannah glanced at her father three seats along, but he was talking. 'Ssh. And no.'

'I can drive,' Charlie said.

'Would you two please be quiet,' Hannah grumbled in a low voice.

Odessa grinned and headed outside. She was surprised to see Hannah's grandmother sitting on a deck chair on the grass. She crossed over and knelt beside her. 'Everything okay? Have you had a lovely party?'

'Hello, darling.' Vivian's hand reached out to Odessa's arm, her diamond rings sparkling in the sunlight. 'We haven't had a chance to catch up yet. What are you doing?'

'I was going to take a stroll along the river.'

'May I join you or would you prefer solitude?' Vivian's eyes were shrewd.

'Please come.'

They strolled past the pavilion and stood together on the riverbank without speaking. The clear water below babbled over the rocks and small fish darted about the rocks. A couple of dragonflies hovered over the water and their green bodies glinted in the sunlight.

Vivian linked her arm through Odessa's. 'So, tell me what you've been doing lately.'

'Not a lot.'

'I've noticed you seemed extra quiet this weekend.' Vivian's soft hand squeezed Odessa's.

'I know it was your birthday celebration, but this weekend has made me realise that I need to do something. Han and I were talking about our talents on the way down, and we remembered that talking to you gave us when we were at Mayhew.'

'And what have you decided?'

'I'm going to do what I know I'm good at. I'm going to try to start a career in silversmithing. Making jewellery.'

'That's a career that takes skill, as well as time and patience.'

'I know, but I'm sure I can do it, if I apply myself. And it's time I did.'

'I have a friend who has a son in jewellery production. Do you have your phone with you?'

Odessa nodded.

'Text me your number and I'll send the contact to you. And I'll have a word to my friend.'

'Thank you, Vivian.' Odessa took out her phone and texted her contact details to the number that Vivian recited. 'Thank you so much.'

'Dedication, darling. That's what it takes.' She tapped her nose with an elegant finger. 'And the right contacts.'

##

After she and Vivian had returned to the house, Odessa hurried up to her room, and packed her bag. This was a weekend for tying up loose ends. On the way back to London she would tell Charlie they were finished. Or to be fair, tell him to go and find a girl who would value him, and not use him for her own ends.

Hannah and Charlie were waiting at the car when she went downstairs. Hannah's eyes were glittering, and her cheeks were flushed.

'How many champagnes have you had?' Odessa asked suspiciously.

'Only two. Watered down with juice.' Hannah's gaze slid away.

'I think I should drive,' Odessa said with a frown.

'No, Daddy's watching from upstairs. Don't look up.'

'Okay. Maybe we can change over.' Odessa handed the first of her suitcases to Charlie who hoisted it into the boot. 'The other two are in the foyer. I'll go and get them.'

'I'll go.' Charlie said and loped up the drive.

When he came back, Odessa offered to sit in the back. 'There'll be more leg room for you in the front,' she said.

'Thanks, but no,' Charlie said. 'I'm going to have a kip in the back seat. You can talk to Han and keep her awake.'

The motorway was busy, and Odessa was a nervous passenger as Hannah constantly changed from the left lane to the middle lane.

'Just be careful. If you're going to stay in the middle lane, you need to go a bit faster.

Hannah turned her head. 'No, I'd rather be in the left, and go slow. I can't concentrate when there are cars and lorries on both sides of the car.' She swung back the car back into the middle lane.

'Shit, Han, watch the traffic. You nearly ran up the back of that lorry.'

'Sorry, but he's spooking me. He keeps changing lanes and tooting at me because I'm going slow.'

'Pull up at the next service area, and I'll take over. Unless you want to drive, Charlie?' Odessa glanced over to the back seat. Charlie was asleep, his mouth open and he was snoring softly. As Odessa turned back to the front, Hannah let out a piercing scream. The Aston Martin drifted into the left lane and as she wrenched the steering wheel to the right, there was a sudden loud bang, followed by the terrifying sound of grinding metal.

Odessa looked past Hannah as she tried to control the car. Her eyes were wide, and her fingers were white where she gripped the wheel. The car was heading back towards the lorry that had clipped the driver's side. There was another loud bang and Odessa's head whipped back and hit the head rest as the Aston Martin slammed into the lorry. Pain seared through her neck and her vision blurred, and then the world went black.

Chapter 7

Odessa - August - London

The pillow was firm beneath Odessa's head, harder than her pillow at home. She'd have to tell Vivian about the hard pillows. Or was she somewhere else? She knew she'd been at Swallowfields, but her head was heavy, and she couldn't open her eyes. And her neck was hurting.

The traffic past the house was very loud and Odessa couldn't figure out why. The estate was a long way from the motorway. Random thoughts flitted in and out of her head as she tried to wake up. Forcing her eyes open was impossible, and she lifted her hands to her face. Her fingers came away wet and sticky, but she still couldn't see anything.

Maybe she'd drunk too much last night?

I must wake up, she tried to say but no words came out.

Time was of the essence because they were going back to London today, and she was going to start her new life like she'd told Vivian.

She was going to help me, Odessa thought. She gave me something. But she couldn't remember what it was.

She frowned and tried to lift her head, and then remembered she'd already been out of bed once. She'd had breakfast, and then she'd talked to Hannah's grandmother after that.

Gritting her teeth Odessa forced her eyes open and was relieved to see Hannah next to her. Her eyes were wide, and she was staring at Odessa. Cold trickled through her and her vision blurred but she kept looking back at Hannah.

'Why are you looking at me like that, Han? What's wrong?'

Panic built in her chest as the events of the past few minutes came back and she stared at Hannah, but her friend didn't move, and her eyes stayed wide.

A sob rose in Odessa's chest and voices reached her. 'Two deceased. One in and out of consciousness. Second ambulance is two minutes away.'

'Don't move, love. Close your eyes.' Gentle gloved hands held her arms. 'We just have to check you over and then we'll get you out.'

'Out of where?' she whispered 'Let me go back to bed. I don't want to wake up.' Her voice rose shrilly. 'Why is Hannah here? Where's Charlie.' The sob broke in her throat, and she drew in deep, gasping breaths.

The lorry.

Hannah's lane changing. Charlie's snoring Her yelling at Hannah.

She'd been in an accident. They had said that there were two deceased, and she knew she wasn't one of them.

'No, no.' Odessa put her hands on either side of her head and tried to move it from side to side in denial, but excruciating pain shot up her neck and into her head.

Maybe I'm dying too.

When Odessa woke next, Hannah wasn't staring at her. She would never forget that as long as she lived. There was silence now and the bed was soft beneath her back. She could smell that awful hospital smell that she'd hated. Ever since Daddy had taken her to see his father—her granddad—when he was dying, she'd hated that smell and had never visited anyone in hospital since. Not even for new babies when her friends delivered.

I wasn't interested in babies anyway, she thought vaguely. Or parties, anymore.

'Odessa?' The familiar voice calmed her as her thoughts took a dive.

'Daddy,' she murmured but no sound came out. Odessa lifted her hand, and immediately, it was engulfed in her father's smooth grasp.

She knew it was Daddy. His hands were soft from working in the office all day.

'It's okay, sweetheart.'

'Am I going to die too?'

His voice caught and she heard him swallow. 'No, you're going to be fine. You have a neck injury. We can probably take you home tomorrow.'

'Yes, please.' She drifted back to sleep but when she woke up a while later, her father was still holding my hand. 'Is it true, Daddy? Or are Han and Charlie in hospital too? Did I dream that . . . that . . . that they died in the car?' She managed to open her eyes and was distressed to see his mouth working, and his eyes were wet with tears.

'We'll talk about it when you're better.'

Odessa knew then that she hadn't dreamed any of it.

Hannah and Charlie were dead, and it was her fault.

I should never have let Hannah drive, she thought, as huge wracking sobs rose in her chest.

Chapter 8

Pippa- Pentecost Island-the wedding

Sienna and Evie slipped my wedding dress over my head, and I laughed as the silk scarf tickled my neck when Evie whipped it off with a "ta-da".

'Oh my God, look at you,' Evie said with her hand on her chest. 'Absolutely stunning.'

Sienna let out a soft sigh as she stared at me. 'You are exquisite, ma cherie.'

I stood there feeling almost surreal as Tam and Nell came through the door, each carrying a small posy of yellow-centred frangipani. Nell lifted one hand up to her mouth, and as Tam stared at me, tears welled in her eyes.

'So beautiful,' she mouthed, shaking her head. 'Oh Pippa, it's just perfect.'

When I'd found the dress on Hamilton Island, I knew it was the one before I even tried it on. It was one of those moments when I just knew it was meant to be. The plain white silk clung to me like a second skin. I'd lost a little bit of weight since we'd been on the island and my olive skin now had a permanent glowing tan. The only embellishment on the dress was Spanish lace around the fitted bodice and the low-cut back that plunged to just below my waist. The bare skin of my back was crisscrossed by fine narrow straps.

My smile was shaky as I acknowledged Tam and Nell resplendent in matching ivory silk dresses. With her other hand Tam held out a single white cattleya orchid to me. The strong spicy aroma filled the room.

In the absence of any family—no, I wasn't going to feel sorry for myself—Tam and Nell were doubling up as my attendants as well as giving me away.

'Look at you pair. You both look gorgeous.' My voice didn't sound like me.

'Evie and I will be very fast to get changed and then we all are ready,' Sienna said, her words formal as she quickly poured us a glass of champagne. 'You must not be late.'

I smiled but my hand was shaking as I lifted the glass to my lips. The warmth of the emotion in the room settled over me like a soft cloak.

'Don't wreck your lipstick,' Tam said, her voice husky.

Nell brushed the back of her hand over her eyes. 'I thought you'd like to know that the English guests are in two huts. Luckily we had three empty, due to a late cancellation. Dylan helped move their luggage down from the house about half an hour ago.'

'So you and Rafe will have the house to yourselves tonight,' Tam added.

I couldn't help the giggle that escaped. I'm sure it was relief. 'No different to every night for the past few months, since I moved in with him.'

'Yes, but this is your wedding night. Anyway, it's all sorted,' Nell added.

'Thanks for that.'

After Sienna and Evie got changed and headed off, it wasn't long before we were ready to walk through the forest to the restaurant. The ceremony was being held on the lawn outside the new building.

'Where's Eliza?'

'She's making sure everything is right.' Tam grinned. 'She didn't trust any of the guys to do it properly.'

'So, are you ready to go get married?' Nell drew a deep breath and put her glass on the small table near the door. She and Tam picked up their posies, and Tam passed me the orchid that had been placed on the table.

'I am.' I caught sight of myself in the mirrored wall behind the counter where Sienna took the bookings. I wasn't wearing a headpiece. My pale auburn hair had grown over the past year and Evie had curled it into long ringlets and then caught them up high on the back of my head so that the curls fell down past my shoulders.

Sienna had worked her magic with my makeup. My green eyes looked larger and were tipped at the corners with the skilful use of a pale eyeliner. My cheeks were slightly flushed, and I knew that wasn't makeup, but from the anticipation curling in my stomach.

'Let's go to a wedding,' I said.

Tam led the way, and Nell was behind me as we stepped out onto the veranda at the front of the hut. If it was possible the morning's weather had improved from perfect to magical. There wasn't a breath of wind and the water in our bay shone like a roll of blue silk. To the west, cumulonimbus clouds rose high in the sky, and white fragments of clouds drifted lazily in the sky high above us.

Eliza waited at the bottom of the two steps holding a basket full of rose petals. 'Beautiful, Pippa.' She blinked away tears.

'Thank you.'

Eliza led the way, and Tam and Nell put their arms through mine.

I let out a tiny gasp as we stepped onto the path. The narrow walkway that led to the glade was covered in red rose petals, and candles on each side of the path flickered in the dim light. The faint sound of classical music drifted through the forest—Rafe had asked that the music be his choice—and I wasn't surprised by the gentle violin music that hovered in the glade. He'd introduced me to his favourite music over the year, and I was learning to love it.

'I hope Rafe's there,' I said nervously.

'He is, and looking just as stunning as you, m'dear.' Eliza put on her Cockney accent.

I shook my head as we walked from the glade to the lawn outside the new restaurant. We were only having a small wedding, so there was no need for the nerves that began to tingle in my limbs as we got closer and the music filled the air around us.

Tam and Nell let go of my hands as we stood on the edge of the lawn, and Sienna and Evie fussed with my dress. Eliza gestured to Philippe in the bar and the music changed to the bridal march.

Goose bumps rose on my arms and my throat closed with emotion as the music swelled.

Rafe turned to look at me, his brilliant blue eyes holding mine as I stood there. I remembered the first time I had seen him in the restaurant at Hamilton Island. It was only a year ago, but it felt like a lifetime. Now I couldn't imagine a life without Rafe in it.

My God. What a beautiful face, I'd thought that night.

Nothing had changed in those months, but I now knew every inch of his skin and loved tracing those features with my fingers each morning as I woke beside him.

Rafe was so good-looking he could have been a movie star. Jet-black hair hung over eyes set wide above chiselled cheekbones. A five o'clock shadow on his olive skin gave him a rakish look. I smiled as I saw the long-sleeved pirate-like shirt he wore tucked into dark trousers. The lacing at the front matched the back of my dress. His full lips tilted in a smile as I walked slowly across the emerald green lawn.

There were only two rows of white chairs on each side of the lawn as the gathering was small. Our friends from the island, and their partners, plus Jiminy—who I'd gone to high school with—and his wife, Sarah, and some friends who'd come over from Hamilton Island. The Riccardo brothers were there, each with a partner; Rafe and I had got to know them well while they worked on our new buildings.

Everyone stood as I followed Tam and Nell down the aisle between the rows of chairs to where Rafe was waiting for me. Several of the guests who were currently at the resort, and the kitchen staff, including Angus and Cherry, stood to one side near the path. Dylan, the new landscaper, was beside them.

I glanced up to the azure-blue sky and sent a silent message. Thank you for bringing me here, Aunty Vi.

I glanced left and right and returned the smiles of our friends as Tam and Nell led me to where Rafe and the celebrant were standing at the front. Three unfamiliar faces looked at me as I looked to the left, two with kind smiles and one pale-faced without a smile.

Rafe's friends. The young woman—Odessa, I assumed—was flanked by her parents and each of them held her arm. A fleeting glimmer of sympathy replaced my happiness briefly as I noticed her pallor and gauntness. She wore a clinging dress and it was easy to see how thin she was.

But I forgot about them as I looked up and saw Rafe's tender smile.

The celebrant gestured to his side and I stepped beside him.

'I love you,' he whispered to me before the celebrant began the ceremony.

Rafe took my hand and held it gently. An exquisite feeling ran through me as I prepared to promise my life and love to this man.

'Good afternoon, everyone, on this glorious Whitsunday afternoon. My name is Catherine Shaw and I am authorised to solemnise marriages according to law. Before Phillipa and Rafe are joined in marriage in my presence and in the presence of these witnesses, I am bound to remind you of the solemn and binding nature of the relationship into which you are now about to enter. Marriage, according to the law in Australia, is the union of two people to the exclusion of all others, voluntarily entered into for life.'

Tam held her hand out for my single orchid before the celebrant spoke the words Rafe had penned and I had chuckled over. Having a world-famous author for a husband was sure to mean he would always have the final word. I blinked away tears when Tam and Nell both kissed my cheek before they left me standing with Rafe.

Catherine smiled at both of us. 'I like to get to know the couples I marry, but I can honestly say this is the first wedding I have officiated at where the couple fell in love in a tree during a rescue from a feral goat.'

A wave of chuckles rippled through the gathering, and I couldn't help wondering if Odessa was smiling too.

'As I've spoken to Rafe and Pippa over the past weeks, I have no doubt that this couple have a deep and abiding love for each other. Now before we get to the formal vows, I would like to ask for an affirmation of support from everyone present.'

I froze as Rafe tensed beside me, and I wondered if something was going to happen. Not being able to turn was frustrating, but I refused to let myself be brought down. I squeezed his fingers and looked up at him and held his gaze steadily as murmurs of assent came from behind us.

As Catherine smiled, one lone cloud crossed the sun, and we were cast in shadow. 'Shall we begin?'

We both nodded, and as she spoke, I forgot about the people behind us. I forgot about my past, and I forgot about Rafe's previous marriage. I let my love for Rafe fill me as I prepared to pledge myself to him for the rest of my life.

My eyes stayed on his as Rafe spoke the vows that we had written together.

'Pippa Carmichael, today, I take you as my life partner. From this day, I give to you my heart and my life. My everlasting love and devotion are yours. I promise to cherish you and pledge myself truthfully to you and with all my heart. Forever. Let us share our dreams, thoughts, and lives. Knowing that from this moment, I will have you as my wife fills me with joy. I love you and I will love you forever.'

I blinked away happy tears as joy surged through me and I repeated the words as I made my vow to him. 'Rafe Rendell, today, I take you as my life partner.' I repeated the words that Rafe had written. My voice shook when I came to the final sentence. 'I love you and I will love you forever.'

We exchanged rings and then Rafe's hand gripped mine tightly as Catherine declared us to be husband and wife.

'Now I invite you to share your first kiss as a married couple.'

I lifted my face to his as Rafe's arms went around me and his warm fingers rested on my bare back. The whistles and cheers behind us faded as his lips took mine and he whispered against them.

'Hello, my beautiful wife.'

I lifted my arms and put them around his neck. 'Hello, my gorgeous husband.'

As we kissed, the cloud cleared the sun and we were bathed in a shaft of golden sunlight.

Chapter 9

Odessa – Pentecost Island - November

Odessa sat on the hard plastic chair and wished that she'd taken a couple of painkillers as her mother had suggested.

'Just in case, sweetheart,' Jenny had said before they headed from the huts to the lawn. Odessa had been quietly impressed with the accommodation. When the term "hut" had been bandied about when Rafe had explained there was alternative accommodation for them, her expectation had been of something like she'd stayed in on one of those awful school camps in the Lakes District when she was at boarding school. But when they'd been shown to their huts by a woman called Nell, Odessa had been impressed by the unexpected size and quality furnishings, not to mention the incredible view of the bluest water she had ever seen.

If she had to recover somewhere, maybe this was the place to do it. Far away from the memories, and the familiar places, an island where she wouldn't see anyone from her past. Or anyone who had known Hannah and Charlie.

As she thought of them, the ever-present nausea rose, and she put her hand to her mouth.

Her mother leaned over and whispered. 'Are you alright, darling?'

Odessa nodded as her mother pressed a handkerchief into her hand. Despite the threatening tears, she was as "alright" as she could expect to be.

Ever.

She was breathing, and she was alive, and could still function despite the depression that gripped her when she thought of what had passed.

The last minute rush to get to this island in time for Rafe's wedding had been a result of Dr Ennis giving her the all clear to fly. The flight had been exhausting, despite the overnight stop in Singapore.

Maybe coming to Australia to Rafe's island had been stupid, but Odessa knew that her parents had been disappointed when they had told Rafe they couldn't come to his wedding because of the accident. When she'd got the all clear from her doctor, their reaction had convinced her to agree to the trip. She thought if she saw Rafe that everything would switch back to being alright. Even if he was getting married.

Odessa's neck ached and she wriggled in the seat as her darling Rafe stood on the lawn promising to love another woman. She could see why he'd fallen for her—Philippa—she was very beautiful, and her dress would have done justice to one of the exclusive London boutiques that Odessa frequented with Hannah.

Had frequented. Tears welled in her eyes as she corrected herself. Even though it had been eight weeks since the accident, the pain and guilt remained, and she doubted that they would ever leave her.

Her neck pain had eased—it had before that horrendous long flight—but the sadness and the black days would not go away. Her thoughts were chaotic filled with "what ifs". She should have insisted on driving, and then Hannah and Charlie would still be alive. Each time she thought that if she'd been in the back seat instead of Charlie, she would be dead instead of him, her mind would go blank and faintness would overtake her.

The funerals had been horrendous, but Odessa had insisted on attending both. It was the right thing to do. She would never forget the grief on Vivian's face as she had hugged Odessa tightly.

Her parents had organised for her to have a couple of months on the island, and she'd agreed reluctantly. If it had just been Rafe, Odessa would have jumped at the chance, but now he had—or would have in the next five minutes—a wife.

Her temper simmered as the celebrant told Rafe he could now kiss his new wife. Odessa had wanted to check Philippa out before the wedding, and she'd slipped away while her parents were getting dressed. She'd gone looking but had been stopped by that rude guy on the path.

Who needed a bodyguard before a wedding? There was something strange there. It was as though this Phillipa was doing everything she could to make sure that Rafe didn't get away.

Odessa suspected that Rafe had made another poor choice.

If he had, she would be doing something about that.

Odessa looked down as Rafe took his new wife in his arms and kissed her.

Chapter 10

Dylan – Pentecost Island - November

Dylan stood at the edge of the lawn next to the kitchen staff. As soon as the ceremony was over, he would head across to the bar and help out where he could. The wedding ceremony had been pretty good; Rafe and Pippa were obviously in love, and the excitement of their friends around them had been very obvious and contributed to the happy mood.

The atmosphere on Pentecost island was very different to anywhere Dylan had worked before. There seemed to be close relationships and friendships between everyone, and there was a cooperative mood to the place with no obvious hierarchy.

Pippa was the owner and the boss of the resort, but she seemed to work as hard as everyone else did—even last week with the wedding coming up.

Maybe things in his life would change now.

As Pippa and Rafe exchanged their vows, Dylan's gaze shifted to the English woman he'd encountered on the path today. She was obviously a friend, rather than a resort guest since she was at the wedding.

But that didn't matter. He didn't care who she was, he had taken an instant dislike to her, and that surprised him. Dylan was usually easy-going and went with the flow wherever he was, getting on with most people, but that woman and her attitude had fired him up. He'd remained calm with her, but it had made no difference, and he wasn't sure what would have happened if Rafe hadn't come along when he did. She'd got under his skin and he'd felt his temper building when she'd refused to co-operate.

Now his gaze lingered on her where she sat as Rafe and Pippa sat at a small table covered with a white cloth and signed the wedding certificate.

An emerald green dress left the woman's slim shoulders bare and her fair skin translucent. Her dark hair was pulled back in some sort of roll on the back of her head, and her swan-like neck added to the elegance of her appearance. Her eyes were hooded as she stared ahead, and as he watched, she dropped her head and put one hand to her face. The older woman beside her leaned across, obviously comforting her.

So not only rude and ill-mannered, she was not happy about the wedding. It took all kinds, he guessed. He'd had a hard enough time in his life, and it had taught him to not get involved with the crap that some people carried on with. They thought they had it hard, but these days it seemed easier to give in and plead that you couldn't cope, instead of putting your head down and getting on with life.

Dylan well knew what life could throw at you, and you had to move on. There was no point dwelling on the past; it just brought you down.

If he could survive a wedding without falling to pieces, anyone could. He pushed the forbidden memories away and stood straight. He'd left that life behind him, and he planned on making a success of the opportunities on offer here on Pentecost Island. He turned back to look at the woman and scowled as she looked around to see if anyone was paying her attention and then dabbed at her eyes with a lace handkerchief.

An attention seeker too.

No matter how beautiful she was, she held no appeal for him whatsoever; she'd done her dash in the glade this afternoon.

Dylan shrugged and headed for the bar. He had better things to do than wonder what her problem was. And he was annoyed with himself that he'd paid her attention. Hopefully, she wasn't staying on the island for long, and he wouldn't run into her again.

##

Odessa

Odessa took the handkerchief that her mother handed her and looked around to make sure no one had seen her cry. She hated showing emotion like she had been constantly for the past two months; everyone she encountered knew what had happened and wanted to show their sympathy, and when she couldn't stop crying, embarrassment consumed her.

That was one of the best things about being on an island. Rafe—and her parents—were the only ones who knew. Or she hoped that was the case.

A tall woman with curly blonde hair—one of the two who had escorted the bride to the lawn—stepped to the front and spoke above the murmur of conversation. 'Hey everyone, if you'd like to stand, in a couple of minutes we'll clap Mr and Mrs Rendell out as they head down to the beach with the photographer, and then if you'll make your way across to the bar, we'll be serving drinks and canapés on the lawn for the next couple of hours. Dinner will be served at six p.m. in the restaurant over there'—she gestured to a newish looking building on the other side of the lawn—'and then the party starts.' She turned as Rafe and his new wife stood and embraced.

'Woo hoo, everyone, let's show our best to Rafe and Pippa,' the blonde called out. The Australian accent grated on Odessa, but she stood along with the rest of the guests.

She stood back as the bridal couple crossed the lawn, and most of the guests—not that there were many—walked across and hugged them as they offered their congratulations. Her parents stood and joined the throng and she sat back down on the chair. She had all night to meet this Phillipa. Odessa wasn't too keen on spending the next two hours socialising. It was too late to check Phillipa out and get Rafe to change his mind now that they were married. But if she was honest, he did seem to be in love, and he did look really happy.

'Oh, she's lovely,' her mother exclaimed when her parents returned to where Odessa remained sitting.

'That's good. I'll meet her later.'

'Are you okay, love?' Her father leaned down and put his finger under her chin. 'That trip's taken a lot out of you, hasn't it?'

She nodded. 'I think I might go and have a bit of a rest before dinner. I won't be missed. This is *their* day.'

'It is. And it's so good to see Rafe looking so well and happy. He's a different man to the one who left the UK a couple of years ago.'

Odessa covered a pretend yawn, so she didn't have to comment. 'I'm going to go back to the hut. I'll set my alarm so I'm not late for dinner. Okay?'

'Do you want me to come and sit with you?' her mother asked.

Odessa shook her head. 'I'm fine, Mummy. Honestly. Don't worry. I'm just tired from that long trip, and if I have a rest, I'll make it through dinner.'

'All right then. Bryant, you walk Odessa back to her hut.'

'There's no need, Daddy. It's not far.'

'Don't take a sleeping pill, will you? You won't make dinner if you do.'

'I don't particularly want to come to the dinner,' Odessa thought, but she kept her tone sweet. 'I'll have a cup of tea and a nap, and then I'll come back over.' She stood and put her hand up to her aching neck. 'You two go and have some fun.' She gave them a gentle push in the direction of the bar. 'I'm fine. You deserve a break after how you've looked after me for the past two months.'

'Of course we did, sweetheart. And we want to see you recover,' her father said. 'Isn't this the most beautiful setting for healing?'

With a smile, her parents left her. As much as they meant well—and to be honest, they had supported her without a break since the accident—she felt stifled. It would be good when they went home and left her on the island.

She needed space, and she knew she needed time alone to process what had happened.

The noise of the conversations around her were getting louder, and before anyone could talk to her, Odessa put her head down and turned towards the path that led back to the hut she was staying in.

Chapter 11

Pippa - Pentecost Island-the wedding

As the sun set, the light breeze picked up and the fragrance of rose petals filled the air. I still couldn't believe what the girls had done for me, and I wondered how on earth they'd managed to get so many roses over to the island.

My body was light, and the love that surrounded me made me feel like I was walking on air. Rafe's love fulfilled me, but the love of my friends and their determination to give us a memorable wedding day meant so much to me too. It might sound strange, but the happiness that filled me was so strong it almost hurt.

The whole hour we were on the beach having our photos taken Rafe didn't let me go once, and by the look on his face, I knew he was feeling the same as I was.

A bit stupefied, and a little bit disbelieving.

We were married!

As we left the beach to walk back to the restaurant, Rafe's whisper brushed my ear and goose bumps rose on my skin.

'Are you happy, Mrs Rendell?'

'Blissfully so. I don't know if I can take much more.' I put my hand to my chest and reached up to kiss his cheek. 'I'm so happy it hurts.'

'I'll kiss you better.' He turned his head and our lips connected and held.

'Did you know about the roses?' I asked.

He shook his head, but it only increased the movement of his lips on mine. 'I didn't.'

We walked back to the restaurant along the rose-strewn path where the breeze was sending the petals into the air in a flurry. When we reached the lawn, we paused and looked at each other.

'I don't know if I can cope with feeling so happy,' I said.

'Get used to it, babe. This is our life from now on.'

I smiled as my husband's lips brushed mine again.

The guests had broken into small groups and my smile widened as I saw Nat and Nell working together behind the bar. Tam and Gabe were talking to the Riccardos and Gabe's arm was around Tam's shoulder. For the first time I noticed the slight swell of her stomach.

'We probably should mingle, do you think?' I said.

'I'd like you to meet Jenny and Bryant first.' Rafe looked across at the couple who were standing with Eliza and Phillipe. Sienna was standing away to the side by herself.

'I'd like to. I know how much you think of them.'

Rafe took my hand and we joined the four who were chatting. 'Jenny, Bryant, I'd like to introduce Philippa, my wife.' His voice was full of pride.

As Jenny leaned forward and hugged me, I was surrounded by the sweet fragrance of a floral perfume. 'It's wonderful to meet you, Pippa. May I call you that? Congratulations, you have got yourself a fine man.'

'I have.'

'And this is Bryant,' Rafe said.

The tall dark man leaned over and kissed my cheek, and Rafe looked around.

'Where's Odessa?'

'She's gone for a rest, but she'll be back for dinner,' Jenny said.

'I'm sorry to hear she's been through a difficult time,' I said.

Jenny reached out and squeezed my hand. 'We appreciate you allowing her to spend some time here. We had to talk her into coming, but I know it will do her the world of good to get away for a while.'

'We'll look after her,' Rafe promised.

'We know you will, but let's not talk about that tonight,' Bryant said.

'Yes,' said Jenny. 'It's your special day and it's a time for celebration. Oh, here comes Odessa now.'

We stood quietly as Odessa crossed the lawn towards us. I was struck by how thin she was. Her emerald green dress was obviously a designer label, but you could see her hip bones through the clinging fabric.

Rafe held one hand out as he held me close with the other. 'Odessa, come and meet Pippa. I hope that you two will become friends.'

When Odessa lifted her head and our eyes connected, I knew immediately that she wanted no friendship with me. Her eyes were cold and empty as they met mine, but when she turned to Rafe, her lips tilted in a smile and her voice was full of warmth. I knew she was here to recover, but I didn't think for one minute that the way she'd looked at me had anything to do with the tragedy.

'That would be lovely. Pippa, I'm so pleased to finally meet you. Rafe kept you a secret from all of us.'

Tam caught my eye, and I could tell she'd seen the look, but I was on my best behaviour.

'I'm pleased that you could get here for the wedding, Odessa. I'm looking forward to getting to know you too. It's so good to meet Rafe's friends. Please make yourself at home on our island.' I kept my voice and smile sweet. I was not going to let a spoilt miss ruin my happy mood or my wedding day. 'Rafe, look. The Riccardos are calling us over.'

As we walked away, I could feel her eyes boring into my back.

I didn't care what was wrong with Odessa Walker. I was holding onto my husband, and I knew I looked good.

I was not going to let one English woman with no manners spoil my wedding.

Chapter 12

Dylan

'Dylan, do you mind if I take Nat off for a quick dance?' Nell, the office manager and one of the bridesmaids, asked as she stood at the bar.

'Of course not. I'm fine here. Go and dance with your lady.' Dylan nodded with a smile. 'I'm happy to take over here. Everyone's right for drinks and it's not busy now that the speeches are done.'

'Did you get something to eat, Dylan?' Nell asked.

'I did. Angus insisted I sat in the kitchen and I had the same meal as you guys did.'

'It was amazing, wasn't it?' Nat opened the half door and walked around to where Nell was waiting.

'Sure was.'

'That dessert that Cherry created was to die for, but I'll need to dance all night to work it off.'

'Thanks, mate, appreciate it.' Nat took Nell's hand and crossed to the small dance floor. Dylan had helped move some of the tables after the meal was cleared away.

Pippa and Rafe had taken to the dance floor for the bridal waltz and after they had done one circuit of the small dance floor, most of the other couples were joining them. After Dylan had helped with bringing the meals out from the kitchen and clearing plates he moved to the bar. A few groups remained chatting at the tables as guests danced, but most glasses were full or half-full.

Dylan was beginning to get a handle on the relationships on Pentecost Island. He frowned as Sienna, the cute woman from the day spa walked over to the bar and climbed up on a stool. She appeared to be the only unattached female on the island, so he would keep himself a bit distant. He had no intention of getting involved in a relationship while he was on the island.

Ever.

This island was so small, it was going to be hard to keep to himself. And there was the fact that it seemed to be perceived as a romantic place. Dylan held a snort back. If you believed in that sort of thing. He had once, but sadly life had shown him the truth.

Sienna sat at the end of the bar looking out over the water. Dylan frowned as he pulled a tray of clean wine glasses from the washer, hoping that she didn't suggest he dance with her.

He'd use the excuse that he wasn't a guest if she did. Her fingers gripped a straw and she stirred the drink that she'd brought over from the table. He kept himself busy cleaning up the bar and rearranging the wine bottles in the fridge.

Eventually he realised how stupid he was being, and his good nature kicked in. He turned and made his way to the end of the bar and was surprised to see the expression on Sienna's face. He'd only spoken to her twice since they'd been introduced when Evie had shown him around the island, but Sienna always had a smile and looked calm and serene. Now as she sat there with her still full glass in front of her, her lips were turned down, and he saw how sad she looked.

'All good for a drink here, Sienna?' he asked quietly as sympathy kicked in.

Her eyes were shimmery as she turned with a tremulous smile, and he'd swear that she was on the verge of tears.

'I have gin and tonic as you can see, but I would appreciate a glass of iced water. I would prefer not to have a headache in the morning. There will be much to do.'

'Cleaning up, you mean? I'm happy to help out.' He filled a glass with ice and topped it up with bottled water from the fridge.

'Thank you, Dylan. Yes, cleaning up after tonight, but mainly for me, I have guests booked into the day spa all day.' Her hand shook as she lifted the glass to her lips. She tilted her head, and her pretty hair fell forward, hiding her expression. 'It's good of you to offer, and to help out tonight and let Nat have some time at the wedding. I hear that the casual barman didn't get here.'

'Yes, he missed the boat, apparently, but it's all good. I'm happy to help out.'

Sienna lifted her head and held his gaze and her eyes were sad. 'You'll fit in well here. Everyone helps wherever it's needed.

What do you think of the island so far?' She had a soft voice and her words were slightly accented.

'I'm very impressed.' He put his hands behind him and leaned back on the opposite counter. 'Everything seems to run well. It's going to be quite a big place when all the new buildings are finished. How long are you here for?'

Stupid question, man. Sounds like you're interested.

'I'm on a working visa, but I'd like to stay here for as long as I can.' She dropped her head again. 'Maybe.'

'From Italy? I'm trying to pick your accent.'

There was no harm in being friendly.

'No. Switzerland. Lucerne. My family are still there in the house I grew up in. On the lake.'

'Really? I did some work in Lucerne before I went to Cornwall.'

She put her glass down on the bar. 'So you've travelled?'

'Yes, my work has taken me to a few countries, but I'm happy to be home in Australia.' He lifted his arms and gestured to the water and the forest. 'And what a beautiful setting to do my work in.'

'Maybe you'd do it better if you'd stop talking and get me a drink.'

Dylan turned and fought a scowl. It was the woman he'd been watching before, the one he'd had to stop on the path this afternoon. He could feel his temper building, and that was way out of character; it took a lot to get him cross. Siobhan had told him that was half his problem. He could still hear her voice now.

'You're nothing but a big teddy bear, Dylan. And that gets boring. If you'd been more of a man like Tommy, we wouldn't have ended up like this.'

Like this? Divorced less than a year after his wedding when his wife decided she'd rather live with the best man than the groom. A wedding that had been nothing like this one.

'Hello? I said perhaps you could get me a drink.' The woman spread her hands, and her shoulders lifted in an eloquent shrug. 'Looks like you make a better security guard than you do a barman. I can't see Rafe giving you a job on his island.'

Dylan kept his expression bland. 'What would you like to drink, madam?'

Her eyes narrowed, obviously at his lack of reaction.

What a piece of work.

'Are you able to make a cocktail?' She turned to Sienna before he could answer. 'Nothing worse than drinking alone, is there? Will you join me?'

'Just one.' Sienna's smile was sweet, and Dylan thought what a contrast there was between the two women.

'So, Mr Jack-of-all-Trades, do you know how to make a Cosmopolitan?' Her fingers tapped impatiently on the bar.

'If there's cranberry juice in the fridge, I can accommodate that, madam,' he said politely. The time working in bars when he was at university in Brisbane had taught him his cocktails.

'I'm impressed. With your knowledge, not to mention your vocabulary, I thought I'd have you there.' With a dismissive glance, she turned to Sienna and held out her hand. 'Hello, I'm Rafe's friend, Odessa. Where do you fit into this wedding?'

Sienna looked ill-at-ease, but she smiled. 'I'm Sienna. Like Dylan here, I'm an employee. Long story, short: I came here to visit my friend, Eliza—that's her dancing with the guy in the white jacket, he's Phillipe—Pippa offered me a job in *Hebe*, the day spa.'

'Oh, a day spa. I must come and book an appointment,' Odessa said.

'How long will you be here?' Sienna asked. 'The resort fills up again from tomorrow, I believe.'

Dylan could hear the bored tone in Odessa's voice, but her reply dismayed him. 'Oh, I'm here for a month or two, unfortunately.'

If she had to say "unfortunately", why didn't she just go back to where she came from, he wondered. The ruder she got, the more "la-de-da" her accent sounded.

'Why unfortunately?' Sienna asked with a frown.

Dylan's ears pricked up as he opened the fridge and spotted a bottle of cranberry juice. Along with two limes, he carried it to the chopping board beside the sink and deftly sliced the limes. He kept listening as he pulled down two cocktail glasses, the vodka and he scanned the shelf for Cointreau. The bottle was at the far end, and he was aware that Odessa was still watching him as she spoke. Her voice was very cultured, and she enunciated each word slowly. Very different to the tirade of words he'd copped from her earlier.

'Oh, my parents thought I needed a break, so they organised for me to come over to Rafe.'

Lucky Pippa, Dylan thought.

'A break from your job?' Sienna asked. 'What do you do?'

As Dylan turned with the two cocktails, he noticed the colour stain Odessa's cheekbones.

'No, a break from my normal.' Her reply was enigmatic, and she didn't elaborate. Odessa picked up the cocktail he had placed in front of them, and she held it up to Sienna's glass. 'So, here's cheers and it really is nice to meet you.'

Dylan was pleased when a group of guests came to the other end of the bar to order, and he was kept busy with a couple of beers, a bottle of wine and another Cosmopolitan. Once he had filled the orders, they went back to the tables and only two men remained.

The taller man held his hand out across the counter. 'Hey there, You're the new landscaper, I hear. I'm Renzo Riccardo—it's my company that's doing the building works. I'd like to sit down and go over some plans with you in the next few days. There's a couple of trees up on the hill where we're pegging out the site, but I think we can work around them, if you think they're worth keeping.'

'What kind of trees are they?' Dylan glanced to the other end of the bar but the two women were in a conversation and had barely touched their cocktails.

'Just a couple of hoop pines, but they're two of the biggest on the island, and the first that you see as you approach the island from the west. I haven't had a chance to talk to Pippa about it yet, but I thought I'd get your advice first.'

'I think I know the two you mean. I've been for a walk up that hill. Where the staff housing is going to be built?'

'Yep, that's right.'

Dylan felt in his pocket, but he didn't have a business card on him. 'Next time you're over on the island let Nell know and she can give me a message.'

Renzo chuckled. 'We'll be back tomorrow.' He gestured to the guy beside him. 'This is Danny, my brother. He's my right-hand man.'

Dylan shook Danny's hand, but he seemed preoccupied. He was staring over to where Sienna and Odessa were still talking.

'Danny.' Renzo's voice held a note of warning. 'Take the wine over to the girls while I chat to Dylan. I think Rowena is waiting for a dance.'

Dylan looked across to the table the two men had left. A plump woman with curly black hair sat back glaring over towards the bar, her arms folded. Her voluptuous breasts were almost spilling out of the top of a very tight low-cut red dress.

'When I finish my beer.' Danny picked up his glass and drained it in one hit, his gaze heading immediately back to Odessa and Sienna.

Dylan wondered if he was going to have to go into security mode as he caught Sienna looking over, and then she frowned at the attention the younger guy was giving her.

He'd never been in a place where there were so many undercurrents. Shame, because on the whole it was a happy wedding, and he hoped that none of this tension boiled over into an ugly scene.

'Danny.' This time Renzo's tone held more authority, and Danny shrugged, deferred to his older brother's request, put his glass down and went back to their table.

'Women,' Renzo said, and shook his head. 'You can't live with 'em, and you can't live without 'em.'

I can live quite well without them, Dylan thought, but he gave a non-committal nod, and glanced back at Sienna. She was watching the young builder as he held his hand out, inviting the woman in the red dress to dance.

Sienna's lips were slightly parted in a smile until the woman took Danny's hand and they moved to the dance floor. Dylan's gaze shifted to Odessa and he was surprised to see her watching him. She lifted her glass, and he wasn't sure what she meant.

He moved closer. 'Would you like another cocktail?' he asked politely.

'No, I was raising my glass to thank you. It's an excellent Cosmopolitan.'

'I'm pleased it meets your standards. I'm sure you've been to some very good cocktail bars.' Dylan's words were polite but all he received in return was an eyebrow raise while she sipped, keeping her eyes on him.

He moved to pick up the cloth to wipe the countertop, but she stopped him. 'Wait. Look, I'm sorry I was rude to you this afternoon. I hadn't realised that Rafe had asked that the path be kept clear.'

He nodded, and wiped the counter.

'I thought you were security. But Sienna just told me you're the gardener.'

'Gardener? I'm the landscape architect, yes,' he said not impressed with her tone. Obviously wherever she came from, a security man or a gardener didn't make the grade.

'Well, whatever you are. I'm sorry I was rude.'

'Apology accepted. I was doing my job, so it's no big deal.' Despite his words, he did appreciate the apology. Maybe she wasn't as much of a bitch as she'd first seemed.

'If you're the landscape architect, why are you working the bar tonight?' she fired another question, and he thought he caught a sense of sarcasm.

He raised his eyebrow and briefly considered telling her it was none of her business, but the gentleman in him won. It was hard; it had been a while since he's encountered anyone like her.

'I'm helping out.'

'Paid overtime?'

'No. Now if you've finished with the twenty questions, I have some customers waiting.'

There was a break in the music, and a small group of guests had gathered at the end of the bar closest to the dance floor. Dylan began to fill the orders. When he next looked to the other end of the bar, there were two empty cocktail glasses and two vacant stools. He looked around the restaurant, but there was no sign of the two women.

With a shrug, he picked up the cloth and wiped down the spotless counter top. Despite the snarky Odessa he was enjoying the bar work. If they needed anyone to fill in occasionally, he'd be happy to step in.

Chapter 13

Odessa

One thing Odessa had found about female friendship as she'd navigated her teens and then her twenties was that alcohol always loosened tongues quickly, allowing the establishment of a friendship to bypass the usual social niceties and the getting-to-know-you process.

None of the "What school did you go to" or "What does your father do", but straight to "Why are you looking so pissed off? Let's have another drink" stage.

That was the case with Sienna. As soon as that Italian guy gave her the eye and then asked the gross woman in the skin-tight dress to dance with him, Sienna's mood had plummeted.

'Can I buy you another drink?' Odessa asked, one eye still on the good-looking gardener.

'No, thanks,' Sienna said. 'I think I'll go for a walk down to the bay. It'll be a while before Rafe and Pippa leave, and I won't be missed anyway.'

'You're sounding very sorry for yourself. Want some company?'

'That would be very welcome if you would like to come for a walk.'

They both kicked their shoes off before they stepped onto the sand, and then walked along the shore towards the jetty. The water shimmered silver from the waxing moon above, and a fairyland of lights glimmered in the bay.

'What are those lights?' Odessa asked.

'Sailing boats. Some of the yachties are regulars in the bar. We didn't see them tonight because there was a temporary bar open on the veranda of the house where the guests were served dinner.'

'So, there's often different people here?'

'Oh yes. Between the guests, the yachties, and the builders and their crew, there are people coming and going all the time. Pippa's talking about opening up the day spa to day visitors soon, but she has to see if Jiminy can bring them over before she starts advertising.'

'What's Pippa like?' Odessa took a step closer to the water and went to paddle her feet.

'Stop.' Sienna's call was shrill. 'Don't go in the water.

Odessa jumped.

'Why not? I'm used to cold water. I'm English, remember?'

Sienna took her arm and guided her back up the sand. 'I know you are, and I'm Swiss, and I'd never heard of stingers and box jellyfish and Irukandji. Plus, there can be crocodiles too. That's why we don't go in the water here.'

'What? I'd heard about snakes and spiders but not those other things. They're out here in the ocean? They swim?'

Sienna chuckled. 'They do.'

'And they are really dangerous?'

'Deadly. That's all you need to know. In the daytime, you'll see the warning signs Pippa's put on the beach.'

'So,' Odessa said thoughtfully. 'If I go for a swim or put my feet in the water, I could end up dead.'

'There's always a risk of being stung, yes.'

Odessa filed that fact away to think about later.

'Apparently, it's worse in the summer,' Sienna continued. 'It might be low risk, but it's always there. I haven't seen any crocodiles. I think they're more on the mainland from what I've heard. But if you get hot and want a swim or a snorkel there are stinger suits you can wear.'

'Sounds wonderful.' Odessa pulled a face. 'Not.'

Sienna laughed again. 'Don't worry, there's a pool going in soon.'

'I won't be here that long. And I'm not much of a swimmer anyway.'

'I'm not either.' Sienna was quiet as they strolled along to the jetty where the boat had delivered Odessa and her parents to the resort.

'You didn't answer my question about Pippa. What's she like?' Odessa persisted.

'She's a fabulous boss. She's handed over the day spa to me to manage how I want. She trusts me, and she knew nothing about me, apart from Eliza's recommendation.'

'As a person?'

Sienna shot her an intense look. 'That sounds more than curiosity to me. I can't really comment as we all have different opinions of people.'

'So you don't like her.'

The small flare of satisfaction was soon gone.

'Oh no. Don't get me wrong. She's a lovely person. Good and kind, and a fabulous boss. Everyone loves Pippa. I'm sure you will too.'

'We'll see,' Odessa said drily. 'Okay, so tell me why you looked so upset at the bar?'

Sienna lifted her head quickly and stared at her. She stopped walking and sighed. 'Oh no, was I that obvious?'

'Obvious that you were mooning over that chap? Yes, my sweet, it was obvious to me—and to our perceptive gardener who doesn't seem to miss a trick. He looked quite concerned too.'

Odessa followed Sienna as she took the steps up to the jetty and walked to the end. Sienna sat on the edge of the jetty staring out over the water.

Odessa took a deep breath; the air was clean and pure, and the only sound was the soft sigh of the waves and the occasional call of an unfamiliar bird. As much as she hadn't wanted to come across to the other side of the world, she was beginning to think it might have been what she needed. It was very different to what she'd expected, and quite pleasant.

She sat beside Sienna. 'So?'

'Danny and I have been talking a lot over the past few weeks. I really like him, and I guess when I heard he and his brother were coming to the wedding, I got my hopes up.'

'How?'

Sienna shrugged. 'I guess I was daydreaming a bit. All the other girls on the island have got partners now and I don't want to feel like . . . what's the word? Blueberry? That's what Eliza said when I said she didn't want me around when she met Rocco.'

'You mean gooseberry, and who's Rocco?' Odessa asked with a frown. 'I thought her partner was Phillipe. I can't keep track of everyone here, it must be jet lag.'

Sienna shook her head. 'It is Phillipe. Rocco was Eliza's husband. I still feel guilty that I didn't stop her marrying Rocco. We were together in Florence on a holiday when she met him.'

'So they're not together now.'

'No. He's dead. It's not a nice story.'

Odessa swallowed.

Dead. Like Hannah and Charlie. The darkness swirled in her chest again, rose up into her throat and she knew that she had to breathe evenly to get her breath past that hard lump in her throat. She didn't speak, but she clenched her fists against her sides and focused on her breathing. Maybe she would faint and fall into the water and let it close over her head.

'Anyway,' Sienna said, not noticing Odessa's distress. 'I was hoping to dance with Danny tonight, but I had no idea he was bringing a partner to the wedding with him.' She let out a soft sigh. 'I was reading too much into our talks. The last two weeks he put the finishing touches on the day spa and we talked a lot. He lived in Italy for a while before he started his building trade with his brother. I just really liked him, and I was reading too much into him talking to me.'

The music coming from the restaurant stopped and Sienna pushed herself to her feet gracefully.

'We'd better go back. Pippa and Rafe will probably leave soon.'

'Where are they going? I haven't even had a chance to talk to Rafe yet,' Odessa managed to say. The lump was easing but the darkness was still there.

'They're going to stay on the island for a few months until the building work is done and then I think they plan on going to England for the northern summer.'

Odessa nodded as Sienna waited for her. She turned and looked up at her. 'You go back. I'll stay here for a while. It's very soothing looking out over the water.'

'Are you sure?'

'Yes. I'll be fine.' Her breath hitched again, and she was aware of Sienna's curiosity as she stared down at her. 'Go on, I'll be fine. Really.'

'Okay, I'll see you back there.'

When Odessa was sure Sienna had gone, she lay back on the wooden planks and stared up at the sky. The stars were brighter than she had ever seen them in the city. The velvet black sky over the ocean was not tainted by light pollution. Thousands upon thousands of pinpricks of light twinkled above her, and made her feel very, very small in the universe.

Her presence on the planet was insignificant. Really, who would miss her, apart from her parents, if she wasn't here?

If she had been in the back seat instead of Charlie, her parents would have grieved, but they would have got over it.

The counsellor at the hospital in London told her that what she was feeling was called survivor guilt. Every day she reassured her that it would pass and gave Odessa strategies to deal with it. *Time heals* was her quiet mantra.

She had to hold onto that thought when these dark feelings took hold of her. She would get over it, she had to; she couldn't spend the rest of her life feeling like this.

The accident hadn't been her fault; in her mind Odessa knew that, but emotionally she had to convince herself that it wasn't her fault.

But it was hard.

So bloody hard.

Too bloody hard.

Chapter 14

Pippa

Today, our wedding day, had been the most wonderful day of my life. The lack of any family there for me didn't take away from the joy; the presence of my friends had made up for that. We danced and laughed and enjoyed celebrating with people we loved and loved us in return.

We'd cut the wedding cake—an incredible concoction that Cherry had created. Cherry was our trainee chef, and partner of Angus, who was taking over as head chef now that Tamsin was pregnant.

I stood and stretched as Rafe went over to the bar to get a glass of water for me—I was determined not to be hungover from my wedding, I didn't want to miss one minute of it by drinking too much.

Jiminy, my friend from high school, who was now bringing the resort guests over on his boat, stood beside me. He put his arm around my waist and his lips brushed my cheek.

'Congratulations, Pippa. You look gorgeous. Sarah and I are really happy for both of you. You don't look anything like that wild schoolgirl who used to get the boat across to school with me all those years ago.'

'A lot's happened since then,' I said.

Jiminy nodded and looked around. 'Whoever would have thought that this resort would be on your Aunty Vi's island. God, she'd be proud of you, Pip.'

'She would be happy, wouldn't she? She'd be out on the dance floor dancing nonstop if she was still with us. She sure knew how to have fun.' I looked up as Rafe joined us and passed me a glass of iced water.

'Pippa, would you mind if I asked Odessa to dance? Just a quick one?' Rafe looked across at Jiminy and put on a mock-stern face. 'There is duty to be done.'

'You are a true gentleman, Rafe,' Jiminy said as Rafe looked at me with his eyebrows raised.

'Of course I don't mind. Go ahead,' I assured him.

'Dance with me, Pippa? If you want to, that is.' Jiminy's cheeks flushed red.

'Oh, yes.' I grinned at him as Rafe left us. 'I'll step on your toes and pay you back for all those times you pulled my braids on the bus when we were at high school.'

'I never did,' he said indignantly and then grinned back at me. 'Not more than once anyway.' Jiminy held his arms wide and I stepped into them.

The music swelled as Jiminy led me onto the dance floor and I was surprised by how well he danced. We did two circuits of the small floor passing Rafe and Odessa each time.

'Shocked you, didn't I? Thought I was a boatie who knew nothing else,' he said with a cheeky grin. 'Sarah made me do ballroom dancing before our wedding.'

'Ha ha. Now why would I think that? And good on Sarah. Who's minding the kids tonight? I'm sorry we couldn't invite them.' My words were all over the place as I tried, and failed, to focus on our conversation. I really didn't want to see Rafe dancing with his English friend. I could just imagine the gloating expression on her face if she saw me looking. In the end I couldn't help myself, but strangely, I felt sorry for her when I glanced across the dance floor. She held my eye for a brief moment, and there was no gloating there, just sadness.

'Don't be sorry.' Jiminy's voice pulled me back. 'A wedding's no place for kids. Besides, they were quite happy to see us leave this afternoon. Sarah's parents came over from Airlie Beach, and the kids will be spoiled rotten tonight. New toys, eat whatever they want, and stay up watching movies all night.'

'Sounds good to me.' I kept my eyes on Jiminy's when I heard Rafe talking to Odessa near us. 'Nothing like grandparents to spoil them,' I said.

There was a break in the music before the chorus began, and the words that I heard Rafe say were imprinted on my mind. 'No, Odessa. I'm sorry. I cannot and I will not.'

Before I could hear any more, the volume increased and Jiminy twirled me across the dance floor.

##

Could not what? I wondered.

I quickly got over my brief surge of jealousy and a glass of wine helped me chill. Rafe sitting close to me with his arm loosely around my shoulder as we talked to Tam and Gabe, and Nell and Nat, helped.

There was no sign of Odessa, and I noticed Sienna had disappeared too. I'd kept an eye out for her earlier because she was sitting by herself after the dinner. She'd sat at the table with Eliza and Phillipe, and Evie and Jed while the meal was served, but she hadn't looked happy. I don't know what was wrong because she'd been fine when she and Evie had helped me get ready for the wedding.

I looked up as I heard chairs being moved. Eliza and Phillipe, and Evie and Jed were joining our table and we all moved along to fit them in.

Eliza squeezed into the space on my left. 'Happy?'

'I am,' I replied.

'The ceremony was beautiful, and the dinner was amazing.'

'The meal was incredible,' I said. 'Angus excelled himself. I told the kitchen staff to call in for a drink when they finished, but I think they've all gone back to the house.'

'They have. They're over there having a few staff drinks on the veranda. They didn't want to impose on the wedding.'

'Oh, that was thoughtful, but they would have been welcome.'

I looked around the restaurant again. Small groups of guests were sitting together talking. Catherine, the wedding celebrant, was deep in conversation with Jenny and Bryant, and loud laughter carried across from the table where the Riccardos were sitting. Jiminy and Sarah were the only ones left on the dance floor and seemed oblivious to anyone else. There was still no sign of Sienna.

'Where's Sienna gone?' I asked with a frown. 'I noticed she looked a bit lost earlier.'

'She's palled up with Rafe's friend. I think they've gone for a walk down to the beach together.'

'Odessa?'

'Yes.'

'Oh,' I said.

Eliza's eyes narrowed. 'Oh, what?'

'I'm surprised, that's all.' I kept my voice low. 'I just didn't think she seemed very friendly.'

'Really? We had a good chat before. She seems nice, but I don't know how impressed she is with the island. I think she might get bored here.'

I shrugged. 'We'll see.'

The next hour passed very happily as Rafe and I moved around and talked to everyone, thanking them for coming. Renzo and Danny Riccardo both grabbed me, and each took a turn to hold me in a tight hug. I smiled as they both kissed Rafe on each cheek. A lot of back-slapping, laughter, and congratulations came our way.

Renzo introduced me to his wife, Maria, but Danny seemed to be ignoring the woman beside him. She was staring into her wine and didn't acknowledge either of us.

As we walked back to the table where we had been sitting, Jiminy called us over.

'How much longer do you want us to stay, Pip?' he asked. 'I was thinking about rounding up those who are heading back to Hamo shortly.' He glanced down at his watch. 'I got a shock when I saw what time it was. The night's gone quickly. Shows what a great time we've all had. I've danced with Sarah so much tonight I've got brownie points for weeks.' He put his arm around his wife, and she shook her head.

'You just lost them all, boyo.'

Jiminy chuckled. 'See what you've got ahead of you, Rafe?'

Rafe chuckled, and I couldn't hold back the yawn that had been threatening for a while.

'I think it's time we left too,' Rafe said. 'Jim, grab the microphone and let them all know the boat will be going in what? Say, half an hour?'

'Sounds good.' Jiminy did as Rafe asked.

Our group of island friends over at the big table—with the exception of Tamsin—looked as though they'd settled in for the night. Her head was on Gabe's shoulder and her eyelids were drooping.

I glanced over at the bar. Dylan was still there, wiping down and polishing glasses—he was a good worker. I honestly hadn't seen him stop moving since he'd arrived on the island.

'Excuse me for a minute,' I said and headed to the bar. 'Dylan, thanks so much for helping out tonight. I think you've done most of the night by yourself. We really appreciated you stepping in.'

'It was my pleasure, Pippa,' he said. His full lips lifted in a smile, and his dark eyes crinkled at the edges. He was a fine looking man. Tall and strong, but he exuded a quiet and gentle manner. I liked him.

'Well, thank you, again, and make sure you take a day off tomorrow.'

'I'm going to go for a walk up to the peak,' he said.

'Enjoy yourself.'

Jenny and Bryant were standing beside Rafe when I came back. 'We're heading to bed now,' Jenny said. 'Jet lag has finally kicked in.'

'You've done well to last this late,' Rafe said. He pulled Jenny in for a hug. 'I'm so pleased you all decided to come.'

'*We're* so pleased,' I corrected him as I hugged Jenny and then kissed Bryant's cheek. 'I'm looking forward to getting to know you both. Rafe speaks so affectionately of his time with you.' I grinned at Jenny. 'You know, Jenny, the first night I saw Rafe on Hamilton Island—before I knew he was the difficult man who owned half of my island—'

'Hey,' my husband interrupted. 'You owned half my island.'

I ignored him. 'Anyway, Jenny. Rafe was with you that night in the restaurant. Never in a trillion years did I dream that I'd meet you at our wedding a year later.'

'It was meant to be, Pippa,' she said as she hugged me back. 'And I'm looking forward to getting to know you too.'

'We'll see you both tomorrow,' Rafe said. 'But it won't be early. I think we all need a sleep in.'

His words elicited some risqué comments from the table where our friends were. I rolled my eyes.

'Come on Pip, it's your wedding night. We have to tease you,' Tamsin called out.

'Last time I looked you were asleep on Gabe's shoulder,' I said with a laugh. 'Okay, tease away, you lot. My husband and I are going to bed now. But feel free to party on. Nat, you'll have to get their drinks. I told Dylan to knock off. He's been great.'

Rafe's arm went around my shoulder, and I snuggled in.

'Come on, wife, Let's go home.' He held me close as we walked along the beach and headed towards our home up on the hill.

Our first night as a married couple.

I held his hand tightly as we walked up the steps and joy filled me. The emptiness that I had carried for such a long time was gone; it had been filled by Rafe's love. Gradually at first, and then as I learned to trust, it filled the emptiness within me in one huge rush.

We didn't speak. Words weren't necessary.

Rafe opened the gate that led to the small garden on the cliffside of our home and stopped. I let out a contented sigh as his arms went around me, and gentle lips sought mine.

My lips opened beneath his, and my husband kissed me for a long time before he murmured against my mouth.

'Are you ready to be carried over the threshold, Mrs Rendell?'

'You might tear my dress,' I said, shaking my head.

'That can be remedied.'

I laughed as his fingers searched and finally found the concealed zipper on the side of my dress. Slowly, he lowered it, and as I lifted my arms, the moonlight bathed my bare skin in a translucent glow.

Rafe carefully folded my wedding dress, and handed it to me before he scooped me into his arms and carried me towards our home.

Chapter 15

Dylan

The last two days had been full on and being on his feet in the bar for a few hours had added to Dylan's tiredness. He took a quick shower in the small bathroom near his room, and crashed into bed, sleep overtaking him immediately.

It only seemed like moments later when a loud constant knocking woke him. He lay there for a moment, but the noise continued. It seemed to be coming from the back of the house across the lawn.

Quickly pulling on a pair of jeans over his boxers, he closed the door behind him. He hurried across to the entrance of the small building and, as he pushed the outside door open, the knocking got louder.

An outside security light bathed the Englishman who was knocking on the back door of the house. His wife stood on the bottom step below him.

Dylan called out as he crossed the lawn. 'Hello, is everything all right?'

The woman—Jenny, Dylan recalled her name—put one hand to her chest, as her husband turned.

'Thank you, we couldn't raise anyone, and the door is locked,' he said.

'What's wrong?' Dylan asked. 'Are you locked out of your hut?'

Before the man could answer, the door opened and Tamsin came down the two steps to join them on the lawn.

'What's happened? Bryant, what's wrong?' she asked.

'We can't find Odessa.' Jenny's voice trembled.

'What do you mean you can't find her? Where have you looked?' Tamsin asked.

'After we left the restaurant just after midnight we went back to our hut and made a cup of tea. We sat and talked for about an hour,' Bryant said.

'Even though we were tired, we couldn't get to sleep because we haven't adjusted to the new time yet,' Jenny said. 'When we finished, I went to check on . . . to say goodnight to Odessa but she didn't answer. I went back to our hut, but I couldn't stop worrying, could I, Bry?'

'No.' Her husband reached for her hand. 'I went to the hut and knocked. When she didn't answer I opened the door, and she wasn't there.'

'We thought she left the wedding early and went to bed. She was tired from the long trip, plus her medication makes her tired anyway.'

Tamsin shook her head. 'She went for a walk with Sienna after dinner and I haven't seen either of them since they left the bar.'

'Where have you looked?' Dylan asked.

'The hut, the path to the beach, and as far as the jetty. We also went back to the restaurant, but it was in darkness.'

'Yes, we turned everything off and came to bed not long after you left.'

'We might seem as though we are overreacting,' Bryant's forehead creased in a frown, 'but Odessa hasn't been well, so we're more concerned than perhaps seems normal.'

'We didn't want to bother Rafe and Pippa, that would have been inappropriate on their wedding night,' Jenny said. 'So we came here to see if anyone could suggest where we should look, or what we should do. It's so isolated here.'

Dylan took charge. 'I'm guessing that everyone is in a pretty deep sleep in there,' he said to Tamsin, gesturing to the house.

'Yes, most of them had a few drinks. I wouldn't like to see them on the bush tracks tonight. We'd end up with a few lost out there.'

'Where are the bush tracks?' Jenny's words were high pitched, and Dylan could see she was close to panic mode. 'Where do they go to?'

'Tamsin—' Before he could finish, Dylan was interrupted.

'I can help.'

Dylan hadn't noticed Angus join them. 'Thanks, mate. Tamsin,' he continued, 'you go and see if Sienna is in her room, and then Angus and I will go out looking. Jenny and Bryant, you stay here. It's dark out there, and the paths are quite dangerous as you head up towards Red Wave Wall. If Sienna is with Odessa, and they went that far, there's a good chance that they weren't game to come down in the dark. The track goes close to the cliff edge.'

'Thank you.' Jenny took a deep breath and put a hand on Dylan's arm. 'I'm so sorry to cause this bother on our first day here.'

'Don't be silly. It's not your doing,' Tamsin said. 'I'll go and check if Sienna's back. Wait here.'

As Tamsin went into the house, Bryant put both arms around Jenny and she rested her head on his shoulder.

Dylan turned to Angus and gestured for him to move away from the couple with him as he spoke quietly. 'Have you had much to drink, mate?'

The chef shook his head. 'No, just one beer. Listen, Cherry's awake too, and she only had a Coke. If we have to go out looking, we'd be better to work in pairs. It's pretty hairy up that hill.'

'I've heard that. A favourite of rock climbers,' Dylan said. 'I haven't been up there. I intended climbing the peak tomorrow.'

'Yeah, Cherry and I walked as far as Red Wave Wall last week. There's feral goats up there too.'

The door opened and Tamsin hurried down the steps closely followed by Sienna.

Jenny drew in a loud breath. 'You're here.'

Sienna's eyes were wide. 'I'm so sorry. I left Odessa out on the jetty. She wanted to look at the stars a bit longer. I was . . . tired. I said I was going back to the restaurant but I changed my mind and came straight here and went to bed.' Sienna put her head down and looked a bit embarrassed. 'I should have gone back to the restaurant, but I knew Pippa would understand.'

Dylan frowned. "Understand" was a strange choice of word.

'It's all right, love. It's not your fault.' Jenny moved away from Bryant and reached out and touched Sienna's arm. 'Was she all right? Did she seem upset?'

Sienna shook her head. 'No, she was fine. We talked about not being able to swim in the bay, and'—she tipped her head to the side—'we talked about the island, and working here. She asked me what Pippa was like.'

Jenny and Bryant exchanged a glance and then Jenny kept firing questions. 'Did she intend coming back to the restaurant? Did she say what she was going to do. She's walked a lot since . . .'

Sienna put her hand to her face. 'I don't think she did, but I really can't remember. She was looking at the stars. I do remember she said she hadn't had much of a chance to talk to Rafe, so I guess I just assumed she'd head back to the wedding and talk to Rafe and Pippa.'

'Okay.' Dylan took control. 'Now that we know that, we need to co-ordinate what we're going to do. I was in the local volunteer search and rescue group when I was in Cornwall, and I've had experience in many searches.' He turned to Jenny. 'Look, the conditions are perfect here. A warm night and no rain. I'm sure she'll be fine.' He didn't voice his worry of drownings or falling off cliff faces. 'I'll get my phone and we can exchange numbers and that way, if she comes back, you can let us know. Angus, go grab your phone and put some sturdy shoes on. Same for Cherry, if she's happy to come with us.'

Jenny nodded, her face pale.

Dylan ran back to his room, pulled a T-shirt over his head, and grabbed his walking shoes and a pair of socks before he picked up his phone. He'd put it on the charger when he'd gone to bed and the battery was almost at full capacity.

When he returned, Angus was back with Cherry, and Gabe was there too.

'Cherry's coming with me,' Angus said.

'I'll come too. I didn't have much to drink tonight. Last night, I mean. It's after two a.m.' Gabe looked at Tamsin. 'You take Jenny and Bryant to the kitchen in the house and put some coffee on.'

'I was going to help search,' Tamsin protested. Dylan saw the look that passed between them and finally she nodded.

'Okay. Kitchen it is.' She reached up and kissed Gabe. 'You be careful, it's dark out there now that the moon's set.'

Dylan exchanged phone numbers with Bryant and Angus, and then Tamsin took the older couple to the kitchen.

'Would you prefer coffee or tea?' she asked as they walked up the stairs.

'Tea please,' Bryant said.

'We're English, after all,' Jenny said lightly but her voice hitched in a sob.

Sienna spoke quietly. 'I'd like to come and search too.'

'Okay,' Dylan said. 'You pair up with Gabe. If you two follow the shoreline from the house to the far rocks, and check the jetty, I'll head up the track. Angus and Cherry, if you could check all the paths through the rainforest, and then take the one that goes over to the bay on the other side of the island, that should cover most of where she could have walked to.'

'Right,' Angus said.

'If you find her, send a text to all of us. Did you get all the phone numbers?'

Gabe and Angus nodded, and Angus and Cherry headed off.

Dylan had a quiet word to Gabe while Sienna went to get a pair of boots. 'Keep an eye in the water. I hate to think the worst, but if she fell off that jetty . . . '

'Or worse,' Gabe said quietly. 'Tam told me that Odessa has come over here to get over some problems.'

Dylan nodded. That made sense. Both her interactions with him had been intense and he'd sensed that she had been worked up about something. Rafe had managed to settle her down on the path when she'd been insisting on finding Pippa, and when they had talked at the bar, her eyes had glittered hard and bright, and her manner had been insulting, sarcastic and dismissive despite her apology.

Dylan had met women like that before, but despite that, he'd still found himself watching her during the evening. She was a very beautiful woman, and when she wasn't trying to put on an act, she had an air of vulnerability about her. He knew what it was like to be unhappy, and he sensed that was what lay beneath her brash and cocky behaviour.

And now she was missing, and who knew what she was capable of.

Sienna ran lightly down the stairs. She now wore a pair of jeans, a long sleeved T-shirt and sturdy boots.

'I'll walk with you two until the path turns off to the peak,' Dylan said as he turned on the flashlight app on his phone. 'I wish we had some good lights.'

'It's less than two hours until first light,' Gabe said.

'True,' Dylan replied. 'I still haven't acclimatised to being back in Australia.'

'How long have you been back?' Sienna asked.

'I arrived from the UK two days before I came to Pentecost Island. I couldn't face another winter over there, and my contract was up, so I decided to come home.'

They reached the point where the path diverged, and Sienna grabbed Dylan's hand. 'I do hope we find her quickly. I feel guilty. If I'd stayed with Odessa and we'd walked back together, we wouldn't be wandering around in the dark looking for her now.'

'It's not your fault, and I'm sure it'll be fine.' Dylan tried to reassure her. Sienna had looked upset at the wedding as it was, without blaming herself for Odessa disappearing. 'I'll text you when I get to the top of the path,' he said. 'I'm sure she'll turn up quickly. It's only a small island.'

Dylan headed into the rainforest, and Sienna and Gabe walked the path that led to the beach.

Chapter 16

Odessa

Odessa had stayed on the jetty for a long time after Sienna went back to the wedding. The music started up again and as she focused her thoughts, the music drifting down from the restaurant faded into the background. Gradually the blackness had lifted, and she made herself breathe deeply as Jemima, the psychologist, had taught her.

She had been a kind woman and obviously good at her job, but even though Odessa had listened to what she had said, she had barely spoken to the woman.

Ask yourself who is truly responsible, she'd told her. If she considered that, it had been Hannah and her lack of confidence driving on the motorway.

'Dealing with the sadness and grief is the hardest,' Jemima had said. 'It might sound harsh but focusing on guilt is often a way to avoid that. In a week or two I want you to think about the intense emotion that you are experiencing, Odessa.' Jemima had put her small hand on her arm and Odessa had stared at it. 'We all process grief in different ways. Some of us internalise, and some of us scream and yell, and that's okay. Whatever works for you is okay.'

Her parents didn't know she'd stopped taking her anti-depressant medication two weeks ago. Maybe it had been the wrong decision, but that's what she'd wanted to do.

But it was hard.

Oh, God it was so hard.

Jemima had told her to find something positive to focus on. Her thoughts kept returning to Hannah's family.

Hannah's grandmother, Vivian, had come to see her when she was in the hospital. She'd held Odessa close, but she hadn't cried. Her shoulders straight and her voice steady, she had been stoic, and had talked to Odessa for two hours.

Before she left, Vivian had lifted her head and her graceful neck seemed to be more wrinkled than it had at the birthday party. 'I can be strong, darling, and I want you to be strong too. There has been a waste of two lives. Don't let your grief burden you down. I want you to promise me that you will do something with your life.' She'd held Odessa's hands so tightly it had hurt and her eyes had held hers for a full minute before she spoke again. 'My darling Hannah has gone, and you were spared. Don't waste that gift.'

In that moment, Odessa had vowed to follow her dream of making jewellery and the first pieces she made would be something for Hannah's mother and Vivian that would be a link to Hannah.

As much as she hadn't wanted to come to Pentecost Island, these few weeks would be a chance for her to regroup, recover and start planning how she would do that. Jemima had told her that, most importantly, she had to look after herself physically.

'Eat well, and sleep well, and your body will help your spirit recover, Odessa. It will take a few months, but in time you will make sense of it all.'

Maybe she would, but right now she was having trouble making sense of anything. Maybe it was the jet lag that was making her feel worse.

As Odessa walked along the jetty, she couldn't bear the thought of going back to the wedding. It was Rafe's day, and he'd chosen a wife who would now keep him here. She had to accept that her special friendship with Rafe was over, and she wouldn't see him as much as she had before he moved to Australia.

And even if Odessa didn't particularly like his wife, she knew Pippa was his choice and his life. He was part of a new group of people now and just because she was here, she didn't have to be part of that close-knit group.

It seemed no different to what she'd left behind.

And she wasn't going to waste her time like that ever again.

Odessa had intended going back to the wedding, but as she'd walked along the path, the laughter and happiness met her like a huge crushing wave, and she knew she couldn't go back there.

Indecision filled her; she was wide awake, and she didn't want to go back to the hut.

With determined steps, she turned away from the restaurant and took another path.

##

Dylan

The first part of the path wound through a dense pocket of rainforest and the leaf mulch crunched beneath Dylan's boots. A couple of times he heard creatures scurry away on the path ahead of him. He flashed his phone to the left and the right scanning the bush as he made his way along the path. Possums and rats he could deal with, but he wasn't too fussed on stepping on a snake or walking face-first into a spiderweb.

Dratted woman, he thought uncharitably as a wave of tiredness rolled over him. He'd been sleeping soundly when the knocking had woken him, and if there was one thing Dylan needed it was his eight hours sleep each night.

He wondered if he should be calling out her name, but instinct told him if she was up here, she may not want to be found. He moved as quietly as he could as the path began to ascend.

After ten minutes of a fairly steep climb, and he was beginning to puff, he reached what he first thought was the top of the hill. But looking ahead, he realised it was a false crest and he was only halfway to the top. The moon had set, and the slight wind had dropped away. The side of the island and the mountain ahead were in darkness, and the mournful horn of a ship echoed across the water. An ominous feeling prickled his neck.

She could be anywhere. It was hopeless.

Dylan paused on the flat area of rock-strewn dirt and caught his breath. He took the opportunity to flash his phone ahead, but there was no sign of anyone. A faint sound caught his attention and he cocked his head to the side and listened. It had sounded like a faint cry, but as he stood there, a flutter of wings stirred the air, and the cry was repeated as a bird dipped below the side of the hill, its mournful call hanging on the night air.

Below him he could see two pinpricks of light as Gabe and Sienna, and Angus and Cherry made their way along the beach paths and through the forest. The lights would bob for an instant and then disappear as they headed into thicker bush.

He took a deep breath and set off up the hill again, and as the path narrowed he used the flashlight on his phone more frequently to guide his way. After a couple of hundred metres, the path was barely a track, and Dylan could smell the salt tang of the sea below. He flashed his light and stepped back, shocked.

The edge of the path was less than a metre from him and beyond, a sheer cliff plunged a couple of hundred metres down to the sea. Taking a deep breath he stood and looked out over the water. To the east, a smidgeon of pink stained the sky heralding the dawn.

Despite the dangerous drop it was a beautiful sight, and he thought how spectacular it would be in full daylight. Setting off again, this time he kept the flashlight on ahead of him and kept well to the right side of the path away from the cliff edge. He shivered as he thought how close he'd gone to the edge without knowing. God forbid, Odessa had come this way in the dark.

The only sound was the one persistent, and obviously distressed, bird that kept flying over him, swooping down to the water and then soaring above the track again to return moments later. There were no trees nearby. Perhaps there was a nest on the ground that she was protecting.

After another ten minutes of climbing, Dylan spotted a fork in the track ahead and thought back to when he'd studied the map the other day. From memory, the path to the right led to the peak, the high volcanic cone that made Pentecost Island so unique and beautiful, and the path to the left led to Red Wave Wall, the escarpment that was a popular rock-climbing destination.

Dylan stood there for a moment and thought, pondering his choices. No one in their right mind would attempt to climb that towering peak in pitch darkness and without proper climbing gear. There was no way Odessa would have gone that way.

He hoped.

Huffing a breath, he took the left fork and as the path widened and moved away from the cliff edge, he strode along. Suddenly, ahead of him, he heard footsteps and the rattle of stones.

'Odessa,' he called urgently, quickening his pace. He held the phone up and the flashlight illuminated the path ahead.

'Shit,' he mouthed with disappointment as a lone goat scampered up the almost sheer rock wall ahead. He'd reached the end of the track and above him was the sheer face of Red Wave Wall.

Dylan pulled out his phone and sent a group message to those searching and waiting below.

Reached the end of the track. No sign of her. On way down. Any luck down there?

Three messages came straight back. All negative.

With a sigh, he switched his phone off. Two hours wasted and no sign of Odessa. The bad feeling stayed in his chest; he'd been involved in search and rescues where the outcome had been tragic, and this was not looking good. It was a strange time to go missing in the middle of the night on an island she had only arrived on and wasn't familiar with.

At least the sky was lighter now, and he knew what to expect on the track as he descended. Dylan turned and headed back towards the resort.

When he reached the fork where the path split, he stopped for a rest and to consider their options. He guessed once it was morning and Pippa and Rafe were informed that Odessa was missing—if she hadn't turned up by then—the police would be called and watercraft brought in to search. Maybe a helicopter. His volunteer search and rescue work had only started since he'd been in the UK and he was unsure of the local processes here; he only knew what he'd seen on news programs.

The sky was getting lighter and he could see the silhouette of a flat rock at the edge of the path away from the cliff's edge. As he walked across, the soft rose pink at the edge of the horizon deepened into apricot, and he knew dawn was not far off. The dawn of an unpleasant day that would take the happiness from Pippa and Rafe's wedding.

Maybe if he'd kept talking to Odessa at the bar last night, she wouldn't have wandered away. Her sarcasm had bugged him; he'd had enough of that from Siobhan to do him a lifetime.

Dylan turned to face the sea again and leaned back on the rock, his thoughts churning. The island was small, but there would be so many places she could be.

'Find your own rock,' came a sarcastic voice from the other side of the rock. 'I was here first.'

'Jaysus, Mary and Joseph, what the hell are you doing here?' Dylan jumped as Odessa pushed herself to her feet on the other side of the rock.

'I was tempted to stop you and ask the same thing when you strolled past me around three a.m.'

Chapter 17

Dylan

As he watched in disbelief, the woman he'd been searching for stood and moved to his side of the flat rock. She was still wearing her green dress, but her hair was now loose and covering her shoulders.

Relief flooded through him, but it was tainted with anger as he pulled his phone out. 'What? Are you telling me you were here all the time? You were here when I walked through here on my way up to that blasted wall?' He lowered the hand holding the phone, unable to take in the fact that she'd been behind this rock and he'd walked right past her, and she hadn't let him know she was there.

Not a word.

He'd climbed what seemed like another ten bloody thousand feet when he could have been tucked up in his bed.

'What's it to you where I've been? I chose not to give away my presence behind this rock. I was enjoying the solitude.'

'Enjoying the friggin' solitude! At three o'clock in the morning? Do you realise the whole island is being searched for you as we stand here and have this ridiculous conversation?' Dylan stood and gaped like a fish as she protested.

'Oh bugger! Did Mummy go to check on me in my bed? They drive me crazy, you know. I am not a child or a wild teenager on a curfew. I've been almost engaged three times, and I live in my own apartment. Honestly, they are hopeless.'

His anger grew as her laughter surrounded him and his fingers stabbed into the keys of his phone.

Found her. She's fine. We'll be back soon.

'What are you doing?' she said moving closer to him. A waft of musky—and he was sure, expensive—perfume drifted over him, and his anger exploded.

'What am I doing? I'm telling people who care about you that you're not bloody dead. Do you know what you've put your parents through tonight? How selfish and inconsiderate you are? Do you know there are people who worked hard all day to make yesterday a success who have given up their sleep to look for you?'

She drew herself up straight and stepped closer so that her face was right in his. Her words were cultured and precise. She had the hide of a bull elephant, and Dylan decided in that moment that he really didn't like her one bit.

'I called you a gorilla the other day, and I wasn't far wrong, was I? If I want to go for a walk and wait to see the sun rise, that, sir, is none of your business. Or my parents, or anyone else's, for that matter.'

Dylan held his tongue because he knew if he spoke, he'd regret the words that came out. He'd already said more than he should have.

Her tone lowered to a placatory level. 'Look it's all a fuss in a teacup. I am perfectly fine, and if it wasn't for my mother thinking I'm suicidal every time I take some time out, no one would be going without sleep. Now I'd be really grateful if you would disappear down that path, and leave me to enjoy my solitude and the sunrise.'

'No. You can come down with me.'

'I will do no such thing.'

'You will.' He stood in front of her and folded his arms.

'I won't.' She folded her arms.

'Well, then, I guess madam will just have to put up with my company until she sees the sunrise and then decides to come down.'

'It's a free world. You can do what you want. But if you do decide to stay up here, please don't talk to me. I've heard enough of your opinions to do me for a lifetime.'

Dylan pulled out his phone and lifted it. 'Smile please.'

'What the hell?'

'I'm going to explain that you are going to watch the sunrise. If your parents see you are all right, they'll go to bed and stop worrying.'

'Oh, you are such a kind and thoughtful gorilla. Take my photo, send your bloody message and then piss off.'

Before Dylan could take the photo, her eyes widened, and he was surprised when she put a shaking hand up to her face. For a moment he thought she was fixing her hair for the photo.

He waited until she lowered her hand and he clicked the photo.

'Now if I ask you politely, will you please go and leave me in peace? Please?' Her voice broke on the "please" and she lifted her hand again and this time it was to wipe her eyes.

Dylan's eyes narrowed; she wasn't as calm as she'd been making out, and the suicidal comment that she'd made stayed with him. He had thought she looked vulnerable when he'd watched her last night.

He lowered his voice and spoke gently. 'Look, let's start over. I apologise for interrupting your solitude, and I'm very sorry that I lost my temper.' He forced a grin. 'I'm usually quite a gentle gorilla, you know. You seem to bring out the worst in me.'

'Oh I'm good at that. I can bring out the worst in most people without even trying.' Bitterness laced her words. 'And it often has a very unhappy ending. I'm not a very nice person, you see, Dylan, so you really don't want to be around me.'

He stared at her and wondered what had happened to make her so bitter. He kept his voice low. 'I'd like to stay and watch the sunrise too. Especially after that climb. I'm quite happy to keep to my side of the rock, and I promise I won't break into song or rave on about the beauty of nature. I can enjoy it quietly.'

'Send that photo to my parents and they can go to bed.'

He quickly sent the photo with a short text.

All good. Staying up here to watch the sun rise. Go to bed.

She stared at him warily as he put the phone back in his pocket. and gestured to the edge of the cliff. 'I know what you're thinking and why you want to stay.' Her tone held a tiredness that obviously went bone deep. 'Look, yes, I have been depressed, and yes, I know what people are saying about me, but I came here to get away from all that. I just want to be left in peace. Can't anyone understand that. I need time and I need space. Please—'

Dylan was dismayed when Odessa suddenly bent over and put her hands over her face. A high keening wail that made goose bumps raise on his skin came from her lips. He moved to her instinctively and put his arms around her. Holding her close he was surprised by the frailty of her body against him. She was tiny; he hadn't realised just how thin she was.

*****

Odessa was horrified when she lost control, but no matter how hard she tried to compose herself, she couldn't stop crying. She sobbed and ranted as a torrent of words flowed from her lips that were pressed against a hard shoulder. Firm hands held her close; if Dylan hadn't held her, she knew she would have fallen.

. Ever since she'd left the hospital, she'd held her emotions in check; it had been easy when she had taken the medication that the doctor had insisted she continue for six months.

No matter how hard it would get, she knew she needed to be able to feel and not control and subdue her emotions with drugs if she was ever going to get over the horror of the accident. When she came out of hospital, her parents had insisted that she move in with them, and that had been her first mistake. Having her every move and every word watched and analysed had put her in a place where she'd merely said what was expected and behaved accordingly. Pretending that everything was normal had resulted in a great mass of emotion staying inside and getting darker and stronger every day.

She was tired of being watched every minute of the day, as her parents seemed to expect some awful breakdown.

Well, she'd just had it.

The freedom of walking up that hill in the middle of the night had loosened that tension within her. The words she'd exchanged with her rescuer—or rather her unexpected sympathetic companion—had breached the tight control she'd held since she'd flushed the medication down the toilet.

It was the first time Odessa had let her emotions out since the first day in the hospital after the accident. As her sobbing lessened, she realised her rescuer was holding her close, and his large hands were rubbing soothing circles on her back.

He didn't speak, and she started talking, and taking gulps of air between sobs and words.

'If I had made Hannah let me drive . . . if I'd been in the back . . .oh, poor Charlie . . . Vivian will be disappointed in me . . . and now I can't talk to Rafe anymore . . . and I know his wife hates me . . . I hate me.' She dragged in another huge gulp of air, and those gentle hands patted and soothed. 'I didn't want to come here. But I'm here and . . . I have to do something for Vivian . . . I don't know what to do.' She lifted her face away from his shoulder and didn't care that her eyes were red and her nose streaming. 'Dylan, please help me. Tell me what I should do,' she whispered.

When he lifted his hands, her back felt bare and cold, but they moved to her shoulders, and he held her in a firm but gentle grip.

'I suggest what we both do is move a little bit to the left where there is a small patch of grass, and we can lean against that rock and watch the sunrise without thinking about anything apart from how beautiful it's going to be. Then we can talk. If you want to. How does that sound?'

She nodded mutely and let him lead her to the grassy spot next to the rock. Her breath hitched as she realised that it was the place where she'd sat a couple of hours ago, but she had frightened herself when she kept looking at the drop below and moved back behind the rock. Maybe her mother was right. Maybe her thoughts had gone in that direction when the guilt had almost crushed her.

She'd been on the grass when she'd heard someone coming up the hill. At first, she'd been frightened, worrying that it was a wild creature of some sort, but as he'd come closer, he'd flicked a light on and shone it ahead, and she'd realised it was him.

Not wanting to reveal her presence or explain herself to anyone, Odessa had pressed against the rock, and he'd walked right past. She knew he'd come back but hadn't been prepared for him to stop right beside her in the dark on his way down.

Once they were seated with the rock behind them, Dylan's arm went around her, and she put her head on his shoulder. She felt drained, and her eyelids were heavy.

'Thank you, I—really—'

'Sssh. Just relax.'

Odessa closed her eyes and listened to the quiet breathing of the man holding her. Her first impression of Dylan had been wrong; he certainly wasn't the gorilla she'd accused him of being.

He was kind and gentle. Most men of her acquaintance would have left her up here if she'd talked to them like that.

Except for dear Charlie.

Her breath hitched again. Odessa tensed and sniffed as tears threatened; Charlie would have stayed with her.

The hand resting on her arm moved up and down in a soothing motion.

'Ssh, Dylan said. 'Don't think. Just enjoy the quiet. Close your eyes, and I'll tell you when the sun is about to rise.'

Odessa snuggled into his side. 'You're a nice man, Dylan. If you want to sing when the sun rises, I won't complain.' Her eyes closed, and sleep overtook her.

Chapter 18

Pippa

In that delicious moment between sleep and waking, I turned my face into the soft feather pillow, and an unfamiliar floral fragrance tickled my nose. I inhaled slowly and stretched my legs out against the cool Egyptian cotton sheets. They were soft against my bare skin, and I thought about going back to sleep. I wrinkled my nose and opened my eyes; it was the pillowcase that held the unusual sweet smell.

'I love watching you wake up.' Rafe's deep voice had me opening my eyes wide.

'Hair spray,' I said.

'Hair spray? That's a strange morning greeting for your new husband. Perhaps you're not awake yet,' Rafe teased as he bent down to kiss me. 'I need coffee, and I was trying not to wake you.'

'It's hairspray. I can smell it on the pillow from my hairdo yesterday.' I reached up and put my arms around his neck. 'There's no need to get up yet. It's only early, isn't it?' I looked across to the window and realised that the blinds were down and that was why the room was dark.

'It's after ten. We slept very late.'

'I guess I'd better get up then. Back to work today.'

'Yes, it is. And I'd like to go down and spend some time with Jenny and Bryant. They're only staying on the island for four days.'

'What about Odessa? She didn't seem to spend much time at the wedding last night.'

'Jenny said she went for a rest but she did come back for the meal. Anyway, I can spend some time with Odessa when they leave.' My husband of less than one day smoothed his hand gently over my hair and then cupped my cheek. 'You won't mind, will you, love?'

'No, of course I don't mind.'

And I meant it. Yesterday Rafe and I had promised our hearts and lives to each other, and I trusted him implicitly. 'She's been through an awful experience. Rafe, I know what loss is like, and I know how it affected me for a long time when my parents died.' Rafe knew the story of my father's death in an oil rig accident and my mother's suicide the same year.

'I'm worried about her. She seemed to be very much on the edge of breaking last night. I'd love you to get to know the Odessa of old. She was vibrant, full of life and nothing ever worried her.'

'What did she do? For a job, I mean? Was she in the family publishing company too?'

'No. She didn't do anything as far as I know.'

'No job? Uni?' I asked.

'No. I'll go and put the coffee on and then tell you more.' Rafe leaned over, and his lips brushed mine.

I put one hand behind his head and held him close.

'Are you sure you want to get out of bed?' I asked with a provocative smile.

'I don't, but don't you have a meeting with Renzo this morning?' He grinned. 'I told you to take Sunday off, and now you know why.'

'Oh, damn,' I said, letting go of him and sitting up quickly. 'Yes, he had to come over this morning because he has to fly to Brisbane this afternoon for business for the week. He'd got a few projects on the go around the state. We're taking a final look at the site for the staff accommodation at eleven before they start excavating.'

'He and his wife should have stayed the night.'

'They could have, but Maria said they had to get back because the babysitter couldn't stay. What time did you say it was now?'

'A quarter past ten.'

'How about you put the coffee on and then come and keep me company in the shower? I have to wash my hair.' I slowly ran my fingers down Rafe's bare chest, stopping at the top of his boxer shorts.

'Ah, I've married myself a wanton wench,' he said as he climbed out of the bed. He paused in the doorway. 'But I do love her.'

##

Thirty minutes later, I stood on our balcony, sipping the coffee Rafe had brewed. The sun was shining, and the water of the Whitsunday Passage was its usual brilliant blue. Being Sunday, the water was dotted with more sails than usual as local residents took advantage of the perfect spring weather. Happiness filled me as I looked down over our resort; it was growing so quickly.

'Yesterday was perfect, wasn't it?' Rafe said as he came outside to join me.

'It was. I think everyone had a good time. I wonder how long it'll be before the next wedding. Gabe and Tam are engaged, and Nat and Nell look very cosy together.'

Rafe chuckled. 'Leave them be. Now that you're a married woman, you want everyone else to follow suit. Come on, we'll have to walk down now unless you want to be late for Renzo.'

I put my cup on the table, and Rafe held the gate open for me and then took my hand as we headed down the path. 'The only one I was worried about last night was Sienna. She seemed a bit . . . I don't know . . . distracted. She wasn't her usual outgoing self.'

'I noticed that too,' Rafe said. 'She was quiet. Although I was pleased to see her sitting and talking with Odessa for a while.'

'I'll ask Eliza if Sienna's okay. I do hope she's not getting homesick just as we're ready to get the spa going.'

When we reached the path at the bottom of the hill, Rafe stopped and pulled me into his arms. 'Do you know why Ma Carmichael's is going so well?'

I looked around. 'Because it's in such a wonderful setting, and we have good people on board.'

'No, it's you, Phillipa. And I don't want you to ever doubt it. It's your dream that's being realised, and it's happening so well because of you. Because of the person you are. You care about your friends, and you care about the staff you didn't know. You put people first, and that's the special ingredient that is making this place go so well.'

A warm glow filled me as he held my gaze.

'Thank you. That means a lot to me.'

He raised my hand to his lips and as we headed towards the restaurant where I'd organised to meet Renzo, happy voices and laughter greeted us.

Chapter 19

Odessa

'Odessa.' The quiet deep voice saying her name belonged to the man in her dream. 'Wake up.'

Odessa opened her eyes and blinked as the soft cotton of a T-shirt rubbed against her nose. Dylan was still holding her close, and she assumed he had been since they had sat down on the grass.

'The sun's about to rise. I thought you wouldn't want to miss it, seeing you climbed all the way up here to see it.'

Odessa sat up, rubbed her eyes and then ran her fingers through her hair. Her voice was husky as she turned to Dylan. 'I went to sleep.'

'You did. And you've been asleep for almost an hour.'

'Thank you,' she said quietly, looking out to sea. She was too embarrassed to meet his gaze. 'I had a bit of a meltdown, didn't I?'

'Do you feel better for it?' he asked quietly.

She bit her lip and then nodded. 'I do.' The constant pressure that had been in her chest was gone.

Dylan pushed himself to his feet and held his hand out. She slid her hand into his and let him pull her up to her feet.

They stood quietly together, and she slowly let go of his hand. The first curved sliver of gold peeked above the horizon, and a low bank of cumulonimbus cloud above was edged with a deep pink rim. Odessa drew a breath as the huge golden orb slowly rose until it seemed to hover above the dark blue water before beginning its climb into the sky as the new day dawned.

'Oh my God,' she whispered. 'I have never seen anything more beautiful in my entire life.'

'Magnificent, wasn't it? I'm really happy to be living on Pentecost Island. It's a pretty special place,' Dylan said. 'Look at the colour of the mountains on the mainland.' He gently took her shoulders and turned her to face the west. In the far distance, the tops of the mountains glowed gold, and the gullies were shadowed in dark green.

'The colours are so strong. Breathtaking. At home, we have soft green fields and a watery blue sky.'

'I know. I've lived over there for the past two years.'

'I heard you telling Sienna last night you were in Cornwall.' She put her head down. 'When I was being particularly rude to you. I'm sorry. My behaviour has been awful.'

He looked at her curiously. 'Is it okay if I ask why? I sort of picked up before that you had something bad happen in your life. If you'd rather not talk about it . . .'

She held his gaze. 'I think I do need to talk about it. I've avoided talking for the past eight weeks, and it's all jammed in me and turned me into this horrible person. Are you sure? It would be a bit of a relief. I mean, you don't know me, and I can be honest.'

Dylan turned and patted the rock that was beginning to catch the warmth of the tropical sunshine. 'Jump up here next to me and talk to your heart's content, and then we'll walk back down, and you can shout me a coffee.'

'I'm sorry.' Odessa bit her lip again. 'You haven't had any sleep, have you? Do you have to work today?'

'No, it's Sunday. I can go back and sleep all day.'

'Where do the staff live?' she asked.

'The girls are in the original house and Angus, the chef and I bunk down in an old building at the back of the house.' He pointed down the hill. 'See the red roof of the old house? If you follow the bush up the hill, there're some new buildings going up there, for the staff. Pippa said when the resort is full-size, there'll be about thirty staff on the island permanently.'

'What's Pippa like?'

'So far I find her very good. I've only been on the island a short time. She's really happy to give me a free hand with the landscaping. I'm imagining something like I did in Cornwall, but with different plants of course. '

'What did you do over there?'

'I was one of the head gardeners at Nancarrow Gardens.'

'I haven't been to Cornwall.' She pulled a face. 'I'm ashamed to say I haven't been far from London. I mean I've travelled extensively in Europe, but I haven't seen much of the UK.'

'I loved it. I did a lot of travelling on weekends when I was in Cornwall. The distances are nothing like Australia.'

'So tell me about Nancarrow Gardens.' Odessa was feeling calm and was genuinely keen to listen. It was the first interest she'd felt in anything since the accident.

'It's a thirty-acre garden surrounding Nancarrow Castle in a beautiful Cornish valley.' Dylan's eyes lit up with enthusiasm as he told her about his work. 'There's over four miles of footpaths under canopies that burst with exotic blooms with colours that I've never seen in plants anywhere else. The paths lead down to the private beach below the castle. It's also got a lot of historical interest. It has its very own Smugglers' Cove.' He chuckled, and she looked up and held his gaze. 'It took me back to my Famous Five days.'

She smiled. 'So why did you leave?'

He shrugged. 'Homesick for blue skies and familiar country, I guess. Anyway, enough about me. Tell me about you.'

Odessa kept standing, but she leaned back against the rock that Dylan was sitting on. 'I was in a car accident on the way back to London. Two of my friends were killed instantly, and I got out with barely a scratch. I haven't coped well with it.'

'That's understandable,' Dylan said quietly.

'So to cut a long story short, my parents thought it would be a good idea to ship me out to stay here with Rafe to recuperate. They were coming to the wedding anyway, so they made me come.' She knew her laugh was bitter. 'At my age, imagine doing what your parents tell you. I think it's the first time in my life I ever have. I think they knew that Rafe would be good for me. He was always getting me out of trouble in my late teens.' She looked away from him out over the water. 'I always thought that Rafe would marry me, and then he married his first wife and got divorced, and hey presto, before I knew it, he's married again. So, I guess I've missed that boat.'

***

Dylan

'Are you in love with him?' Dylan waited until Odessa lifted her face and met his eyes again. Her eyes were not red or puffy anymore; they had cleared now and it was hard to tell she'd had a crying jag in his arms before she'd gone to sleep. 'Sorry, maybe that's a bit personal, but if you are, it might be a difficult situation with him only married yesterday.' Dylan knew how complicated relationships could get. Odessa was enough of an emotional mess without unrequited love being factored in.

'No. I love him, but I'm not in love with him. Don't worry, I wouldn't do anything to mess up his life. I couldn't help myself yesterday when you stopped me on the path. I guess I took it upon myself to make sure that Rafe was marrying the right person this time. I'm really sorry I was so rude to you.'

'They seem to be very happy.' Dylan had been slightly envious yesterday when he'd seen how Pippa and Rafe had looked at each other. Siobhan had never looked at him like that, even on their wedding day. 'I'd hate to see anything cause them grief,' he said carefully.

'I'll be on my best behaviour. I don't know Pippa, but I'll do nothing to hurt Rafe.'

He must have looked uncertain because she reached for his hand and squeezed it. 'I promise. Trust me.'

He nodded and gestured down the hill. 'We should probably head off before they send out another search party.'

'Dylan?' Odessa tipped her head to the side, and he thought again how beautiful she was.

'Yes?' He cleared his throat and looked away. He had no intention of getting involved with another woman.

'Can I ask that you keep this to ourselves? My parents worry about me enough without knowing I had a full-blown meltdown on a mountain in the middle of the night.'

'My lips are sealed,' he said. 'I stayed up here with you because I wanted to see the sunrise too.'

'Thank you.'

He couldn't help himself. 'If you need an ear again while you're on the island, come and talk to me. You'll find me in one of the gardens or glades. It's not a very big island.'

Odessa looked down past him. 'You can see how small it is from here. I didn't think I was going to like it here, but you know what? I'm going to give it my best shot.'

He held out his hand before they headed down the hill.

It was only because she was wearing flimsy sandals, and the track was steep, he told himself.

Chapter 20

Pippa

I was surprised to see Danny waiting in the restaurant with Renzo when Rafe and I walked in just before eleven. Jenny and Bryant were there having a late breakfast, and four of the tables were filled with guests from the huts. One of the casual kitchen hands had stayed on the island overnight and was running the coffee shop for Cherry. I'd insisted that she and Angus take the day off today. There was no sign of any of the others.

It was time we hired more staff; the problem was that they had to come over from Hamo each day until the staff quarters were built.

'You go and meet with Renzo, and then we'll have lunch with Jenny and Bryant,' Rafe said. 'Is that okay with you?'

'Of course,' I said as we headed for the table overlooking the water where Jenny and Bryant were sitting. Bryant stood and leaned over and kissed my cheek, and Jenny smiled up at both of us.

'Hi there,' I said. 'I've just got a quick meeting with the builders, and then Rafe suggested we have lunch together.'

'That sounds wonderful,' Jenny said.

'Where's Odessa?' Rafe asked, looking around.

Bryant shook his head. 'She's having a sleep-in. Would you believe she climbed the mountain this morning so she could see the sunrise!'

'What?' Rafe's eyes widened in horror. 'Not the peak?'

'No, about halfway up.'

'By herself?' I asked. 'There's wild goats up there.'

Jenny and Bryant looked at each other for a moment.

'Ah, she had company,' Bryant said. 'That gardener chap was with her.'

Rafe frowned. 'Dylan?'

'I don't know his name. He walked her back to the hut just as we were going for a walk about eight o'clock. Odessa was animated and raving about the island.'

'That's excellent. Pentecost Island is weaving its magic already by the sound of things,' Pippa said.

Rafe shook his head. 'But I can't get over that she climbed up there to see the sunrise after the wedding. It's not an easy walk.'

'Well, she's sleeping it off now,' Bryant said.

I left them chatting as I made my way across to the Riccardo brothers. Renzo had his laptop out and was typing as he waited for me. Danny—who was usually bright and full of cheek—had his head cradled in one hand as he held a huge coffee in the other.

'Morning, guys,' I said.

'Morning, Pippa.' Renzo was brisk and businesslike as usual, and he snapped his laptop shut as soon as I sat down at the table. 'I asked Danny to come over with me this morning too, because he'll be in charge of the excavating while I'm away this week. No point putting it on hold, is there? There is work to be done, and we have a schedule.'

I shook my head. Renzo fired his words out like bullets, and sometimes, with his Italian accent, it was hard to keep up. But I was pleased with their work. We were ahead of schedule by two weeks.

'I want Danny to be very clear about where the building will be located.'

Renzo had drawn up the plans for the staff quarters and a single-storey lodge that was going to be built on the hill up behind the old house. As well as sixteen small bedrooms with four large bathrooms, there was a staff kitchen, a dining room and a living area. He'd designed it so that it would blend into the rainforest on the hill, and of course, under current building standards, it had to be cyclone-safe. Thanks to Eliza coming on board as a financial partner after she had sold her ex—and dead—husband's villa in Tuscany, we were able to move ahead at a fast rate.

I reminded myself that I needed to meet with Dylan to work out how we were going to access it from the resort but make the pathway private. The description of the work—and the photos I'd seen—of the gardens he'd designed in Cornwall had given me some ideas, but I was sure he would have something suitable in mind. We'd been lucky to get him for our small island; he was very qualified and had a raft of experience in Australia and England.

The last thing we wanted was guests wandering up there inadvertently. We were getting an excellent staff group together and I wanted to keep it that way. Providing private and suitable accommodation on the island would hopefully entice more quality workers.

'Hurry up and finish your coffee, Danny,' Renzo said, a tad impatiently, interrupting my flow of thoughts. 'We need to get up that hill. Are you right to go, Pippa?'

'Yes, I'm right. I'd like to be as quick as possible too.'

Renzo stood and pushed his chair in and it scraped on the pavers.

Danny flinched.

I shot a sympathetic glance at him, noticing bloodshot eyes. 'Need a hair of the dog, Dan?' I asked. 'I can order you a bloody Mary.'

'Water will be fine, thanks. I'll grab a bottle from the fridge.' He hurried over and grabbed two bottles. 'Put it on my tab.'

I shook my head. 'As it was my wedding, I feel some responsibility for your hangover.'

'I kept drinking on the boat on the way home. Foolish move,' he said. 'Especially with an early start this morning. But we had a good night, thanks for inviting us.'

I wasn't sure who he was referring to by "us". Danny had pretty well ignored his partner all night as far as I'd noticed as Rafe and I had mingled amongst the guests.

Renzo strode ahead and as Danny and I followed him, laughter from the lawn had me turning my head. The rest of the gang were coming in for breakfast. Evie and Jed were arm in arm, Eliza and Phillipe were deep in conversation, Tamsin and Nell were giggling together, followed by Gabe and Nat. There was no sign of Sienna or Dylan, although I figured if Dylan had been up the mountain, he'd be having a sleep in too. Sienna had mentioned something about guests wanting the day spa today so at a guess, that's where she was.

'I'll be back to see you all in a short while,' I called out.

Waves and smiles followed me as we headed towards the path that led up the hill. We were almost to the forest when we met Sienna hurrying from the old house towards the day spa.

'Morning, can't stop,' she said brightly and kept going. 'Running late for an appointment.'

Danny went to speak to her, but Sienna put her head down and didn't look back. We had almost reached the bottom of the hill when Danny stopped.

'I'll meet you up there. I need to use the bathroom.'

Renzo made a noise that sounded like a disgusted grunt. 'Well, hurry up.'

Danny took off, and when I glanced back, I was surprised to see him take the path leading to the day spa.

I followed Renzo up the hill.

Chapter 21

Odessa

Hunger woke Odessa after only a couple of hours of sleep. She'd only picked at her meal at the wedding last night, and the walk up the mountain and back down again had taken all her energy. Not to mention the crying jag that filled her with embarrassment when she thought about it.

Dylan had been very kind to her, and she cringed more as she remembered their first meeting. If someone had treated her like that, she would have cut them dead. At least there was someone here she felt comfortable with now. Her parents were watching her like a hawk, and she was sure they'd told Rafe to do the same. Pippa was distant with her, and she couldn't blame her, and the others on the island seemed to be such a tight group; she really didn't want to waste time getting to know them all.

God, she'd soaked Dylan's shirt with her tears, telling him what she'd been through. Maybe if she'd been that honest with Jemima, she'd be at home and getting back to her life.

She needed to talk to Rafe. That was her focus today.

Odessa's stomach grumbled as she stepped out of the shower and reached for the thick white towel. The quality of the hut and its fittings had surprised her; it was a lot more luxurious than she'd expected. The bed was comfortable, the bathroom was small but beautifully fitted out, and if she was honest, the view from the small porch was as good as anything she'd seen in Europe.

Better actually. Being on the water's edge and watching the colours change the water helped her focus and stay calm. She dried herself and quickly wound her damp hair into a clip. As well as needing food, she didn't want to lie around wasting time; she'd thought about what she was going to do, and she intended to get started.

Today.

Odessa had made a plan, and she needed some time with Rafe to set it in motion. She pulled on a white sundress and ignored the pang of grief that shot through her when she remembered it was one she had bought in Harrods that last day shopping with Hannah.

'Block the sadness,' she told herself sternly. 'Remember instead how we laughed and how we had fun that day.'

She headed off towards the restaurant, knowing it was probably too late for breakfast but hoping that she could at least get a coffee. She frowned as she approached the outdoor restaurant, and voices and laughter met her. It sounded like there was a crowd there.

The last thing she wanted to do was get involved in conversation. Stopping, she tapped one finger against her lip, tempted to turn around.

Maybe she could go up to Rafe's house?

With another frown, she shook her head. No, she wasn't ready to talk to his wife yet.

Irritation threatened to overwhelm her. What a stupid place to live. Really! Who'd choose to live on a tiny island like this?

No shops, no coffee shops. All she wanted was a coffee and something to eat without seeing anybody before she found Rafe.

As Odessa stood there deciding what to do, footsteps approached along the path ahead.

She went to duck into the forest but paused when Dylan appeared ahead.

'Good morning,' he said with a wide smile as he approached her. 'Again.' He looked fresh and bright and had obviously had a shower. Damp hair curled onto his neck.

'Where are you going? I thought you'd be sleeping in on your day off,' she said quietly.

'I'm in search of coffee and food, in that order,' he said.

'Me too,' Odessa admitted. 'But it sounds very crowded over there, and I don't really feel like company yet.'

He stood there and looked down at her without speaking, and she stepped to the side of the path.

'Well, I'll let you go then,' she said.

Dylan shook his head and turned back the way he'd come. 'Come with me. We'll go to the kitchen in the house. That way you won't have to be sociable if you don't want to. Is the company of one suitable? There was no one else there when I walked past.'

'Is that okay?'

'Yes, there's a section at the back of the kitchen for the staff. I can get coffee and rustle us up something to eat.' He laughed, and again Odessa thought what a kind man he was. He was gentle and there was no bluff or bluster about him. Comfortable in his own skin, he obviously didn't see the need to try to impress.

'What do you fancy? I cook a mean French toast.'

'Are you sure?' she asked, and then nodded. 'I love French toast.'

Fifteen minutes later, she was sitting in a big old fashioned kitchen, and Dylan had a pan sizzling on a huge gas range. He'd brewed them both a coffee in the coffee machine in the corner, and now Odessa wrapped her hands around the mug as she watched him cook.

'How many pieces,' he asked as he deftly turned the first one over.

'Oh, only one, thank you.'

He shook his head as he looked over his shoulder at her. 'I beg to differ. Once you taste my cooking, you'll come back for more. Maple syrup or tomato sauce?'

'Um—' Before she could finish speaking, one of the bridesmaids from yesterday walked in from the veranda—the blonde one called Tamsin. Odessa put her head down and stared into her coffee.

'Morning, Dylan,' she said and then looked taken aback when she saw Odessa sitting there. 'Oh hello.' Her tone was cool. 'Back from your adventure?' she said.

Odessa sat straight. 'Adventure?'

'Last night up the mountain. I heard there were a few search parties out there in the wee small hours.

'I'm afraid I don't know about that. I walked up to see the sunrise.' She lifted her chin and stared. 'Is there a law against that on the island?' Odessa knew she was being rude, but the other woman had started it. She wasn't going to be patronised by some Aussie chick who thought she was better than anyone else.

'Fair enough.' The blonde turned to Dylan. 'They're still serving brunch over in the new restaurant. You didn't need to cook your own.' She threw a last curious glance at Odessa. 'Anyway, I just came over for some more eggs from the cool room. They've run out over there. Feeding hangovers, I think.'

'Is Rafe over there too?' Odessa butted in and received another cool considering look.

'Yes, I believe he's having breakfast with your parents.' Her tone made it sound like an accusation as though Odessa should be doing the same and not associating with the staff.

'Thank you. I'll join them after I finish here.'

Tamsin shrugged and disappeared through the door.

Dylan looked at her curiously as he placed a slice of golden crispy bread onto her plate, but he didn't say anything about her being rude again.

Again. Odessa huffed a sigh. She was going to have to try harder.

They ate quietly and when she'd finished, Odessa stood and picked up her plate.

'Leave it, I'll load the dishwasher,' Dylan said.

She nodded and put her plate and mug on the sink. 'Thank you for that, it was delicious. You are a man of many talents. Landscape gardener, psychologist, and excellent cook and cocktail maker.'

Dylan's smile was gentle. 'It's called self-sufficiency.'

'That's what I need to find,' Odessa said. She realised what he'd said. 'You could have been a counsellor. Thank you again for this morning.'

'My pleasure.' Dylan stared past her and seemed briefly distracted. 'I did a lot of reading when I went through a bit of a tough time before I went to the UK. If I was able to help you, I'm pleased.' He stood and brought his plate across to the sink. 'Come on, I'll walk you over to the restaurant and then I'll come back here and clean up.'

'There's no need.' Odessa moved towards the door. 'I can find it.'

'I insist. My mother taught me to be a gentleman.'

She smiled at him. 'She was very successful.'

'Come this way, it's quicker to join the path from the back of the house. He led her down two steps and onto a lush green lawn edged with colourful flowers. A path of pavers led across the lawn to what looked like an extra-large garden shed.

'That's where Angus and I bunk down,' Dylan said. 'There's three small rooms and a bathroom at this end, and you can't see, but it's an L-shape and my workshop is at that end. I don't spend much time in there, it's mainly to store the mowers and tools.'

'A workshop?' Odessa's interest was piqued. And you don't use it?'

'No, I'm either out on the island working, and when I plan, I use my computer in the loungeroom of the old house.'

'I haven't been able to get internet on my laptop here,' Odessa said. 'Is there any Wi-Fi on the island?'

Dylan nodded. 'I know Pippa's been talking to Nat—he's Nell, the office manager's partner and he and Gabe work in IT together. At the moment you can pick up a strong signal in the house here, because it faces Hamilton Island where the tower is, and there's a booster in the outside bar.' He chuckled. 'I think she is going to extend it to the huts, but at the moment, the guests go up to the bar.'

'Good for business there, I guess,' Odessa said. 'They buy drinks while they browse. I'll head up there later then.'

'If you'd rather come over here where it's quieter, I'll be working here this afternoon. I have some plans to draw up.'

'It's okay. I'll need to spend some time with my parents, I guess. But thank you.'

Dylan walked with her as far as a small glade near the restaurant. 'I'll leave you here. I hope you have a good day.'

Odessa couldn't help herself. She stood on her tiptoes and brushed a light kiss on his cheek. 'Thank you for being so kind to me.'

She turned and headed towards the noise and laughter.

Chapter 22

Dylan

Dylan was thoughtful as he walked back to the house. He'd enjoyed Odessa's company—even though she'd been prickly to Tamsin—but he didn't want her to get the wrong idea. The kiss—albeit on his cheek—had been a warning for him to pull back. He knew from what she'd said that she was going to stay for a couple of months on the island, and the last thing he wanted was to give her the wrong idea.

Odessa was an interesting character—not to mention beautiful—and he'd found himself drawn to her more than he should be.

Dylan reminded himself why he'd come to the island. He'd wanted to come back to Australia, and one of the reasons he'd applied for this position was because there was no chance of running into Siobhan and Tommy. If he'd gone back to Brisbane, he would have done eventually, as they shared the same group of friends. Last he'd heard, Siobhan was pregnant with their second child; she and Tommy hadn't wasted much time.

He turned off the path before he reached the house and walked down to the beach. Listening to Odessa and comforting her on the mountain had brought back many of the feelings he'd had when his marriage had broken down.

If you could call someone meeting you at the door on the way home from work with a packed suitcase a marriage breakdown.

He'd had no idea that Siobhan had been seeing someone else, and when she'd left, and then the divorce papers arrived a few weeks later, he'd been devastated.

Even more so when he'd found out it was his best mate—and best man at the wedding, Tommy Hammond.

Dylan walked across and sat on the flat rock, looking over the Whitsunday Passage. He hadn't really known Siobhan; and he still had no idea why she had married him.

If the truth be known, he shouldn't have proposed. He'd known that she'd manipulated him into it, but he'd been—or he thought he'd been— in love with the person that he'd thought she was. Six months of living with her had shown him that he'd made a mistake, but Dylan had been prepared to work on it.

His self-confidence had taken a hit, and he'd applied for—and thankfully been successful in winning—the job in Cornwall. He'd taken some time to travel around Europe before he'd started. The two years there had healed him; the divorce had been finalised quickly, and he'd moved on, immersing himself in his work.

There was no way he was going to let another woman manipulate him; he had a feeling that Odessa could be dangerous to his peace of mind.

***

Odessa

Odessa stepped out of the rainforest at the edge of the outdoor bar at the same time that Pippa walked in from a path that came down from the small hill. She swallowed, determined to be polite. Being with Dylan had been calming.

'Good morning, Pippa,' she said brightly.

She waited while Pippa walked across the lawn to join her, and Odessa saw her hesitation before she smiled back.

'You're up early. Your parents said you climbed the mountain to see the sun rise. It's spectacular, isn't it?'

'Pentecost Island is spectacular. And what you've done with the accommodation is beautiful.'

'Thank you. And welcome to our island. With the wedding and all that happened yesterday, I didn't get a chance to tell you how happy we are to have you here as a guest.'

Odessa hid a smile at the "we". Pippa was making it very clear that Rafe was hers, and that she was here as a guest and not a friend.

'Thank you, I'm looking forward to my time here. Would you mind if I have a quick private word to Rafe before we join the group?'

'Of course not. Why should I mind?' There was a defensiveness in Pippa's tone.

Odessa didn't reply. What could she say?

As they reached the restaurant, Rafe looked up and smiled, but his smile was for Pippa first.

Pippa left Odessa and walked across to the table where a large group of their friends were sitting. Odessa still hadn't worked out who was staff and who were friends. Uncertainty rippled through her and then she spotted her parents at the far end of the table. She headed over, but Rafe met her on the lawn when she was almost there.

'Good morning.' He reached down and brushed his lips across her cheek. 'Pippa said you wanted a word? Is everything okay?' His stare was intense. 'Are you okay?'

'I am. Your island is working its magic. I feel the best I have since . . . since the accident. I wanted to talk to you about an idea I have.'

'Of course.' Rafe led her over to the bar and pulled out one of the high stools. 'It's a bit quieter over here. I think that lot are still on a high from the wedding.' He smiled as they both looked over to the table where the laughter seemed to be nonstop. 'Then again it's like that here most of the time.' He gestured to the coffee bar. 'I'll get you a coffee. And what would you like to eat?'

She held up her hand. 'I've already eaten, thank you. Sit down, this won't take long.'

Chapter 23

Pippa

I tried not to let the little green monster niggle too much when Rafe and Odessa put their heads together and talked for a good half hour. They had known each other for a long time and they were friends. I had to remember that. The problem was I felt as though I was walking on eggshells whenever she was mentioned.

The same with Rafe. His voice was reserved when she came up in conversation. Maybe it would get easier when she'd been here a while.

And maybe it'll get worse, a little voice chirped in my head. Jenny and Bryant had gone back to their hut, and Renzo was waiting for Danny to reappear. He and Danny had come over in Renzo's motorboat, and he had looked around exasperated when Danny didn't come back.

'*Inaffidabile e pigro*,' Renzo muttered as he'd looked at his watch.

'Pardon?' I said.

He jumped to his feet. 'Please tell my *unreliable* and *lazy* little brother that he can get the launch back with Jiminy later. There's plenty for him to do here. He can start pegging out the building on the hill. I can't wait any longer.'

'Okay, have a good week, Renzo. And thanks for coming over on a Sunday. I'll see you when you get back.' I was thoughtful as I watched him stride down to the beach and head towards the jetty. I suspected that Danny had gone to see Sienna, and that worried me because she's looked upset when he'd had a partner with him at the wedding last night.

'Hey, girl, what are you looking so worried about the day after your wedding?' Tam had moved to the chair that Renzo had vacated.

I smiled at her. 'Absolutely nothing. Happy as.'

'So why the frown before?' Tam nodded towards the bar where Rafe and Odessa were still sitting close. 'Madam giving you sass too?'

'What do you mean too?' I burred up. Odessa could treat me however she liked, but she could treat my friends and the resort guests with respect.

'She has attitude,' Tam said folding her arms. 'Although it might have been because I interrupted a cosy brekky she was having with Dylan.'

'Where? Here? I thought she'd just surfaced.'

'No, over at the house.'

'She shouldn't have been there; it's not open for guests today.'

'I got the impression she was there with Dylan. He was cooking French toast for her.'

'Fair enough.' I shrugged. 'That's his call. And I suppose she's not technically a guest. She's Rafe's visitor. She's here to get better.'

Tam tipped her head to the side. 'You said yesterday she'd had a tragedy. Are we allowed to know what happened? Maybe I'll be a little bit more forgiving.'

'I suppose so. But let me check with Rafe first. I'd hate her to think I was gossiping about her.'

'She makes you uncomfortable, doesn't she, Pip?'

'A little, I guess, if I'm honest. It's a part of Rafe's life that I wasn't aware of, and it unsettles me a little bit. *She* unsettles me, but I've got to show some empathy.'

Tam reached over and gave me a quick hug.

'Well you know where to come if you need to talk. Now, I think a mimosa is on order to celebrate your first day of being married.' With a giggle she put her fingers up and clicked them as Nat headed for the bar.

'*Garçon, s'il vous plaît,*' she said in such an awful French accent, Phillipe rolled his eyes and Eliza giggled. 'Another round of mimosas for the girls, please. Oh and look here comes, Sienna, just in time.'

I turned to see Sienna walking up along the beach, and she looked happier. Maybe it was because Danny was walking beside her.

Maybe I needed to have a talk to her too.

But first I was going to relax and enjoy a pleasant Sunday. The first Sunday of my married life.

By the time I had a glass of champagne and orange juice in front of me and was chatting to Nell, Rafe was sitting beside me again and there was no sign of Odessa.

He put his arm around the back of my chair and I smiled up at him.

'Everything okay?' I asked.

'Yes, really good. Odessa is happy and I can see a change in her already. She's going to start work as soon as she can, and she had a suggestion, but I said I'd have to run it by you first.'

'What sort of work? Don't tell me she wants to be a waitress?'

'God, no. I can't see Odessa in a kitchen, can you?'

'To be honest? No.'

'It's all come from a talk she had with Hannah's grandmother about doing something worthwhile. Hannah was one of the friends who was killed in the accident. Odessa has always wanted to pursue a career in jewellery making, and she's asked if she could use a bench in the building at the back of the old house. She works with silver and she's going online to order all her supplies later today, and get them delivered here. She wants to talk to you about it when she comes back with her laptop later. Is that okay with you?' His voice was guarded.

'What, that I talk to her, or that she does it?'

'Both, I guess.'

'I can't see a problem. As long as it's away from the guests, and Dylan and Angus don't mind.'

'Thanks, love. I think having a focus is going to make a huge difference. She's quite excited about the idea.'

I shrugged. 'Whatever we can do to help.'

Chapter 24

Four days later

Dylan

Dylan wasn't sure how he felt about Odessa moving into the building. Pippa had come to see him on Sunday and had run Odessa's requests by him.

Requests.

He wasn't bothered by her working at a bench in the workshop; he barely spent any time in there, but he wasn't so sure about her moving into the spare bedroom at the back of the building.

He'd decided after breakfast on Sunday that he was way too interested in her, and that he'd be keeping his distance from now on. After all, she was a guest, and he was staff, he'd be working on the resort so there was really no need to see her.

'It's up to you, Dylan,' Pippa had said. 'But as Odessa pointed out, she's going to be on the island for a couple of months and staying there will free up one of the huts. I offered for her to stay with Rafe and I up at the house, but she said that wasn't fair to us.'

'That was very thoughtful of her. Pippa, I don't see any problem, apart from her having to share the bathroom with two blokes. Did you talk to Angus?'

'No need to.' Pippa's grin widened. 'The girls have all done a swap around. Cherry is taking one of the bigger bedrooms in the house—the one that Evie and Jed have been in— and Angus is going to share with her. Talk about an island of happy ever afters,' she said. 'Watch out you could be next.'

'No fear of that,' he said. 'I've tried that, and it didn't work for me.'

'I'm sorry to hear that,' Pippa said.

'Yep, married once. And that will do me for a lifetime. I'm here to make Pentecost Island one of the top tropical gardens in Queensland.'

'If that's your focus, I'm certainly not going to complain.'

'Look, I don't have a problem with her moving in. It'll give her a chance to get to know the girls better too. I'm sure Odessa and I won't see much of each other anyway. I'll be putting in some long hours over the summer.'

'Thanks, Dylan, I appreciate your co-operation. She'll spend the rest of the week in the hut, and then move over on Friday after her parents leave.'

##

It would have been a lot easier doing that week if Odessa had kept her distance. At least once each day, she would encounter him wherever he was working, and by the third day, when he changed his plans, so he was in a more isolated part of the forest, she still managed to 'stumble' upon him on one of her walks.

The problem was that Dylan enjoyed the daily visits and chats, and on the fourth day Odessa brought him a snack from the bar and a cold drink.

'I could get used to this,' he said as he sat beside her on one of the seats in the glade that Evie had created on the way up to the mountain.

'I hope you don't mind me seeking you out,' she said with a smile.

'No. I enjoy the company. How's your research going?' Odessa had told him that she was about to begin silversmithing in the workshop.

'Excellent. I've ordered the first of my supplies from Mackay, and they should come by express post any day.'

'That's great news.' Dylan put his drink down on the ground beside him and held her gaze. 'And how are you going? Are you feeling a bit more settled?'

She looked away from him, but she nodded. 'I am. It's amazing how the beauty of this place seeps into your soul. The only thing I'm a bit hesitant about is my parents leaving tomorrow. I know I've ordered those supplies, but I still wonder if I should go back with them.'

'I thought you were here for a while.'

'I am, but I'm a bit of a misfit on the island. The friendship group is so strong, I feel like I'm back at boarding school and not part of the "in" group.'

'I'm sure they don't mean to make you feel like that. They're all really nice women. I'd say it's because everything's back to normal and they're all busy.'

'Sienna's busy, but she still finds time to be pleasant to me. And as much as I enjoy spending time with Rafe, that's not fair on Pippa. I don't know why they didn't go away somewhere.'

Dylan changed the subject, because he had noticed that Odessa wasn't readily included, and he felt awkward discussing his employers with her. Maybe things would get better when she moved into the staff accommodation tomorrow.

'If there's any help you need in the workshop, just ask me.'

'Thank you for cleaning that space and setting up that light for me. Rafe took me in there the other day and he said that you'd done that. You've been very kind to me, Dylan, and I want you to know I really appreciate it.'

'Just being sociable,' he said.

'No, it's more than that. Even though I've only known you a matter of days, I consider you a friend. You're probably the most honest friend I've ever had. You don't want anything from me, and you care about how I feel.'

Odessa raised one hand and lifted her dark hair. Dylan found it hard to keep his eyes from her long graceful neck. Her skin had already picked up a light olive sheen and her cheeks glowed with colour.

'I like you very much,' she said shyly and looked away. 'If I'm a hassle or interfering with your work, let me know and I'll leave you in peace.'

Dylan reached for her hand and held it gently. 'I like you very much too, Odessa, and I enjoy your company. And I'm honoured to be classed as your friend.'

Her face lit up as she smiled back at him and squeezed his hand. 'And you make the best French toast ever.'

'Ah, wait until you taste my tacos,' he said.

Chapter 25

Odessa

Odessa had been fine when she went to the wharf to see her parents off on the morning boat on Friday. Determined not to cry—she was almost thirty years old, for God's sake—she'd held back the tears when Mummy had clung to her, but they'd spilled over when Dad had held her and said, 'You take care of yourself, chicken.' He hadn't called her that pet name for a long time.

Rafe and Pippa had come down to the boat to see them off, and they walked across to join Odessa at the end of the wharf once her parents were on the boat. Rafe slung an arm around each of their shoulders, and Odessa looked across at Pippa, but her smile was wide and looked genuine. Since she'd offered to vacate her hut and refused to go up and stay with them at the house, she'd sensed that Pippa now held a grudging respect for her.

The boat engines started, and the water churned at the back of the boat as Jiminy, the skipper, cast off the ropes.

'Holy hell,' he cried out.

Pippa stepped forward. 'What's the matter?'

'I had a delivery for one of your guests and I almost forgot. And your mail.' He threw the rope to Rafe and kept the engines idling as he disappeared below. After a moment he reappeared with two large boxes, and a mail satchel. 'Couriered up from Mackay early today. They just caught me before I headed out here. For an Odessa Walker.' He grinned at Odessa, knowing who she was from the wedding.

'Ooh, it's my silversmithing equipment.'

'Go you!' her father called as Jiminy passed the two boxes over to Rafe.

Odessa's smile was wide, and she was surprised when Pippa put an arm around her waist. 'I'm so pleased for you.'

'Thank you, Pippa. I'm pretty happy too.'

Pippa stood close to her as the boat pulled away and Odessa waved to her parents as the boat disappeared around the rocky point at the northern end of the bay.

'Come on. Let's get you set up in your workshop. Rafe, are you right with the boxes?' Pippa linked an arm through hers and a warm glow ran through Odessa, and the sadness at seeing her parents leave dissipated a little.

'Of course, I am.' He stacked the smaller box on top of the large one and followed them along the jetty.

'I know you're moving into the back building later, and we were hoping that you'd come and join us for dinner up at the house,' Pippa asked as they stepped onto the sand.

'I'd love to, thank you.' If Pippa could make an overture, the least Odessa could do was accept.

What a great day, Odessa thought. She was moving into her new room—although as Pippa had warned her, it was basic—her gear had arrived, and Pippa was being extra nice.

Rafe put the boxes on the bench that Dylan had cleared, and he and Pippa headed off to let her unpack.

'Come up at sunset. Champagne on the deck to celebrate your stay,' Pippa said as they left. 'Rafe's invited Dylan too, we haven't had him up for dinner yet.'

'Sounds good. I'll see you then.'

As much as she was tempted to start unpacking, Odessa knew she would get side-tracked. She had to go and pack up her gear and bring it down here. Even though she had a couple of hours before she had to vacate her room, the housemaids had come over with Jiminy, and it would be good for them if she moved now.

And it meant she'd have more time to unpack, and maybe start work.

Odessa hummed beneath her breath as she headed back to her hut.

*****

Dylan

Dylan spent the day working up on the hill above the old house with Danny Riccardo and his team. This week the builders had pegged out the site and had started the excavation for the foundations. He was up there today to plan the layout of the garden. Even though it was staff accommodation, Pippa had requested that the landscaping be in keeping with the rest of the island.

He was looking forward to having dinner up there tonight and running some ideas past Pippa. The morning boat had departed with Odessa's parents a couple of hours ago, and he wondered how she was feeling. He'd told her that he'd be up here today, and he kept an eye out hoping that she'd come up for morning tea.

'Smoko,' Danny called out to him as he walked past and headed down the hill. Dylan wondered what was going on there; Danny Riccardo spent a lot of time over at the day spa hut, "doing the last few jobs", he said every day.

The crew put their tools down, but Dylan decided to keep working in case Odessa came up a bit later.

He shook his head, not knowing where this "friendship" was going, or if he wanted it to go anywhere. He'd watched from the hill as Odessa and Pippa had walked ahead of Rafe who carried some boxes and he was excited for Odessa, knowing it was the equipment she'd been waiting for.

And today was the day that she was moving into his building.

Dylan went down to the staff kitchen at lunchtime and made himself a toasted sandwich. He had to fight the urge to go looking for Odessa. If she'd wanted his company, she would have come up the hill.

Or maybe it was because he was working with others.

Or maybe she was busy?

Dylan pushed the spade into the ground with unnecessary pressure.

Or maybe it was time he stopped thinking about her all day and all night. She needed space, and the last thing she needed to help her recovery was unwanted attention.

Chapter 26

Pippa

As we moved through spring, the south-easterly winds died off, and the weather came from the north. The daytime temperature was still comfortable, and the night temperature only got down to the low twenties. Stinger season was here, and I made sure that each guest was briefed about the necessity of wearing a stinger suit for swimming and snorkelling while they were on Pentecost Island. The last thing we wanted was a helicopter medivac.

'What are you looking so happy about?' Rafe asked as he came in from the garden carrying some fresh-cut herbs.

'That was Renzo on the phone. With some fabulous news. He met with his mate in Brisbane, the one with the pool company, and he's negotiated a good deal. The guy's had a couple of cancellations, and he thinks he can get our pool in by the end of November.'

'Fantastic.' Rafe walked over and kissed me. 'That will make a huge difference to the summer holiday bookings, I'd say.'

'I have to go and tell Eliza to see if we can do it without touching the overdraft and I'll have to meet with Dylan, and I'll have to—' I stopped talking as Rafe pulled me closer.

'Patience, my darling Phillipa. Does it have to be done right this instant? Or can you come and have a wine with me while I get my secret spaghetti sauce cooking?'

I grinned at this man who was teaching me very good habits. 'Yes, I can have a wine, and yes, you are right—as you always seem to be. Yes, I can do all that tomorrow.'

'And you know the best part of the time frame for the pool?'

'I do. It will keep me busy while you start your next book.'

'You do know me well. Now do you want to pour the wine while I chop the herbs?'

'For you, my gorgeous man, I can do that.'

By the time the spaghetti sauce was bubbling on the stove and Rafe and I had taken time out for a quick shower together, the sun was getting lower in the western sky, and it wasn't long before Dylan and Odessa would arrive.

I stood on the veranda and took a deep breath. Sometimes, my happiness frightened me. Warm hands slipped around my waist, and Rafe rested his chin on top of my head.

'Okay, babe?'

'Yes, very okay.' I reached down and put my hands over his. 'But I was just thinking how scary it is. I've had too many days that started with intense happiness and ended badly.'

'You still carry a lot of grief from losing your parents and not having any family, don't you, sweetheart?'

'I do. And I know that's why I'm afraid of embracing how I feel when I am happy.'

'I think we need to start our own family.'

I held my breath. 'What? What did you say?'

'I said I think we need to start our own family. I'm not getting any younger, and I'd like to have fun with our children while I'm still fit enough to give piggyback rides and read nursery rhymes.'

I laughed as happiness bubbled up. 'Oh my God, how long have we been married? Six days? And you want to start a family?'

'I do. I don't think we need to focus on it, or worry about it. We can just let nature take its course. What do you think?'

'I guess Tam and Gabe's bub would have a playmate if we did.'

'And we would have a family. A family of our own.' My husband of less than a week turned me around in his arms and lowered his head to kiss me. 'I love you, Pippa, and I can't think of anything I'd like more.'

'Not even a bestseller list?'

'Nope. Not even a bestseller list.'

Chapter 27

Dylan

The gods were looking after him this week, Dylan thought as he re-read the letter that had been waiting for him at the office when he'd stopped in on his way down the hill this afternoon. He was going troppo—too much tropical sun. Thinking about Odessa all the time and considering a relationship more than friendship after a week had been totally stupid.

The letter from Siobhan had been a much-needed wake-up call.

Dear Dylan. I hope you are well and enjoying your new job. I just wanted to let you know that we have a second son and all is well. Take care. Siobhan.

For God's sake, how many ex-wives—and one who had not even been a satisfactory wife for any time—would write to their ex-husband to tell them that they had had another baby to the guy who had been a better prospect as a husband?

His temper simmered and the last thing he wanted to do was have a social dinner with Rafe and Pippa—and Odessa. For a while, Dylan thought about coming up with an excuse, and then his better nature took hold.

That would be the wrong thing to do—

And he never did the wrong thing. Nothing in his life had changed, apart from him knowing that his ex now had two children. Thinking about Siobhan, his failed marriage, and the subsequent divorce always brought him down.

It was a timely warning to watch his emotions. He would forget about Siobhan and the new baby and take it as a wakeup call.

Dylan went back to his room, but there was no sign of Odessa. She must have gone up to the house already. He grabbed his towel and his toiletries bag and tapped carefully on the closed bathroom door.

There was no answer, and when he went in, he flicked the lock over, so he could take a shower without worrying about the door opening.

By the time he'd showered, had a second shave for the day, and put on a pair of dress shorts and a button-up shirt, Dylan was feeling marginally better. He pulled the door of his room closed behind him and headed for the outside door.

As he walked outside, a faint noise from the workshop caught his attention. He paused and listened as the low sounds turned into a full hammering.

Odessa must still be there. Reluctantly, he headed back inside and walked to the back of the building where the L-shaped workshop began. Odessa was sitting at the bench, the only light was the desk lamp he had placed there for her. A halo of light silhouetted her, and as he stood there, she lifted a piece of silver up to the light.

She twirled it slowly, and when she took a deep, shuddering breath, Dylan knew he had to let her know he was there.

'Odessa?' he said quietly.

She turned slowly, still holding the piece of silver. As she faced him, he could see the silver was shaped into a perfect H-shape.

'Hello, Dylan.' Her voice was thick, and tears were running down her face. He took a step back, knowing that he was intruding on a private moment.

'I'm just about to go up to Pippa and Rafe's. Are you still going up for dinner?'

Her eyes widened and she rubbed the back of her hand on her cheeks. 'I lost track of the time.'

'Would you like me to wait for you?'

When she shook her head, he was a little disappointed yet also relieved. 'Okay, I'll head on up, and let them know you'll be up soon.'

Dylan turned away, and he knew she'd forgotten he was there before he'd even reached the door.

***

Odessa

It was another hour before Odessa was satisfied with the piece she had created for Vivian. All the knowledge that she had learned in the silversmithing course came back to her as she sawed and filed, then soldered and buffed the shape.

Dylan had come in when she had first finished the soldering, but she had been so emotional when she saw the H, she had barely registered his presence.

He was a kind and gentle man, but she wasn't ready for a romance. She had a lot to sort out before she'd get to that. That was the sensible way to do things anyway.

After a quick wash and a change of clothes, she brushed her hair, and left it loose, before walking up the hill to Rafe's—and Pippa's—house.

The fragrant aroma of tomato and garlic reached her as she climbed the last steps. Rafe and Pippa, and Dylan were sitting outside watching the sunset.

As Odessa opened the gate, the last of the sun slipped below the horizon, sending a shimmering gold to touch the clouds above. It was one of the most beautiful sunsets she'd ever seen, and serenity filled her.

Dylan and Rafe both stood as she approached the table where the three of them were sitting. Rafe took her hand and kissed her cheek. 'Welcome to our home, Odessa.'

Pippa raised her glass and greeted her. 'Welcome.'

Dylan sat back down without speaking.

It was a strange night. Despite the fact that everyone seemed preoccupied, and conversation was desultory, Odessa felt at ease. Finishing the piece for Vivian in one afternoon and knowing that she could do it had given her a huge boost.

And a purpose.

The meal was delicious, and both she and Dylan covered yawns as Rafe brought coffee out.

'Sorry,' Odessa said. 'It's been a big day. I hope you don't mind but as soon as I finish my coffee, I'm going to go back down.'

'I'll walk down with you.' Dylan smiled for the first time that night. 'We're going to the same place.'

'That's fine,' Pippa said. 'I think we're all tired. tonight. The week has caught up with me, I know that.'

Rafe and Pippa both kissed Odessa goodnight as she and Dylan left, and Odessa felt as though she had been accepted . . . finally.

Epilogue

Odessa had done a lot of thinking this afternoon and if it suited Rafe and Pippa, she decided she would like to stay on the island for a longer time.

'Penny for your thoughts?' Dylan asked when they reached the jetty, and Odessa realised they had not spoken a word since they had said goodbye to Rafe and Pippa.

'I'm sorry. I was too quiet,' she said. 'That was rude of me.'

'In that case I was rude too as I was quiet too. We all seemed to be lost in our thoughts,' Dylan replied, and Odessa thought he sounded sad. He was right. No one had been themselves tonight. Pippa and Rafe had seemed to be in their own little world too.

'You have something on your mind?' she asked.

'Yeah, a couple of things.'

She stopped and took his hand. 'A problem shared and all that? If you want to talk, I'm a good listener.' She lightened her words with a chuckle. 'As long as you promise not to cry all over my shoulder.'

He smiled again. 'You've got enough on your plate without listening to my minor woes.'

'I'm feeling good, Dylan. It's all upwards from here for me now, so try me. You were a sounding board for me, so the least I can do is reciprocate.'

'Thank you.' Gentle hands touched her shoulders. 'I got a letter today from my ex-wife.'

'I didn't know you'd been married,' she said.

'My wife left me for my best mate. They've just had their second baby, and foolishly I let it bother me. And that was stupid. I wasn't unhappy for long when we got divorced, so I need to move on.'

'As long as you can talk about your feelings and understand them, that's a good thing. God, I'm sounding like my psychologist.

But you know what? I think I finally got there today. Making that piece of jewellery for Hannah's grandmother was a defining moment for me. I've decided I'd like to stay on Pentecost Island for at least six months. If it's okay with Pippa and Rafe, that is. I'm going to get a portfolio together, and I'm going to attempt a career as a silversmith.' She turned her face up to his and realised how close he was. A pleasant warmth ran down her back, and Odessa reached her hand up to touch Dylan's face. 'You said woes. As in more than one. What were the others?'

'There was only one other.' He cupped his palm over her hand and held it against his face.

'I'm going to be honest with you, Odessa. I've only known you for a week, but the attraction I feel for you is like nothing I've ever experienced before. I've fought it, and I decided I was going to avoid you. But you know what? I can't. I sat and watched you at Rafe and Pippa's tonight. And I loved watching you. I love being with you.'

'Well, I'm going to be here for a while, so maybe we could explore that more? How would that be?' As she spoke, she'd moved closer to him, and his breath fanned her face as he held her eyes with his.

'I think that would be a very good idea.' His lips were millimetres away from hers and Odessa closed them as he moved closer until their lips were touching. 'But we'll go slow. How does that sound?' His words vibrated against her lips.

'I think that sounds very suitable.'

All was quiet for a long time as Dylan held her close. His warm lips explored hers and his hands caressed her bare back.

Reluctantly, she pulled away as she heard a boat motor getting closer and louder.

They stood together in the dark, and there was just enough new moon to see the silhouette of a rubber tender as the vessel scraped on the shingly sand. A figure jumped out and ran up the beach as the boat left the beach and roared off into the night.

'That was strange,' Dylan said.

'It was, and you know what, I could have sworn that that was Sienna who ran up the beach.'

Dylan held her hand as they crossed the sand. As they approached the small glade at the top of the beach path, the hoarse sound of sobs reached them, and then faded. They paused and looked at each other as they caught a glimpse of a figure beneath the light of the veranda of the old house.

'It is Sienna,' Odessa said. 'I recognised the white jacket she wears in the spa.'

She stood on her toes and brushed her lips across Dylan's. 'You go back to your room, and I'll go and see what's wrong.'

'Try not to be too long. I'd like to talk some more.'

'I'll see you soon.' Odessa walked up the steps of the house as Dylan headed around the side. As she stepped inside, a light came on in the kitchen where Dylan had cooked her breakfast last weekend.

She moved quietly through the loungeroom and paused at the kitchen door. Odessa's eyes widened and a gasp escaped her lips.

Sienna was sitting at the table, her head in her hands as she cried soundlessly. Her white jacket was covered in blood.

SIENNA

PENTECOST ISLAND 8

Chapter 1

Pentecost Island - December

Sienna hadn't been back to Hamilton Island since she'd gone over for the girls' weekend with Evie and Tamsin a few months ago. They'd had such a good time over those three days, and she hadn't laughed so much in years. She hadn't had a lot to smile about before she'd come to the island, and forging new friendships with the women who worked there had lifted her spirits, She would be forever indebted to her best friend, Eliza, for suggesting her to Pippa for the day spa.

Sienna was very grateful to Pippa for giving her the chance to work on Pentecost Island, where the reputation of the "island of love" was quickly spreading. Pippa had giggled the other day when one of the guests had mentioned that—her boyfriend had proposed on their first night in one of the huts— and Pippa had immediately seized upon it and started work on an advertising slogan. Only married a short time, and with no honeymoon yet, Pippa was already back into her work, but Sienna firmly believed, it wasn't really work for her. For any of them really, it was such a good place to be. Whatever it was, Pippa, lived and breathed Ma Carmichael's Resort.

Everything about the island was fun, and the whole place seemed to run like clockwork with very little effort. Everyone who worked here seemed to love whatever their particular responsibility was. Nell and Tess in the office were always cheery, Tamsin, Cherry and Angus were always laughing in the kitchen, and when Eliza and Pippa held the planning meetings each week, there seemed to be more chat and joking than there was business discussed. Even Odessa had lightened up, and there was talk of her starting a small boutique next to the office down the track.

Sienna was determined to make *Hebe*, the day spa, a place

where guests—both men and women—would come to Pentecost Island especially for the treatments, and then book a longer holiday. Her training in Switzerland had given her an edge on the treatments and products that were available up here in the tropics, although she had heard of an exclusive island further north that ran courses. Sienna was determined to upskill more while she was here and make *Hebe* day spa even more exclusive.

So much had changed in the few months since that weekend away with the girls. Her best friend, Eliza, was settled with Phillipe—who Eliza said was the love of her life. Tamsin had met Gabe that weekend, and now they were a couple and expecting a baby. Evie's mysterious ex-husband had turned up on the island, and they had made up their differences and moved to the coast. Nell was with Nat, a guy from her past, and they were madly in love. it appeared Odessa, the latest arrival to their island, had hooked up with Dylan, the gardener.

And now Pippa and Rafe were married. It was hard to keep up with the changes, and if Sienna was honest, she sometimes felt lonely when she saw all the couples together and happy.

As she sat at the back of Jiminy's boat on this fine Sunday morning in early summer, she wondered what on earth she was doing going over to Hamilton Island to meet Danny. Was it because she was lonely and just jumping at the first man who had smiled at her and shown her some attention? She needed to be very careful; she had seen what had happened to Eliza when she had been smitten with Rocco. Sienna had also seen the unhappiness of her mother when she had been let down by the man she thought had loved her.

Go carefully, she told herself. Do not trust.

She would never be taken in by a man like her father. Wonderful on the outside, but cruel and hard when he showed his true colours.

The weather this weekend was perfect; too good for the guests to be inside, and now that Pippa had bought six small catamarans for the guests to sail in the bay, the spa appointments had dropped when it was a fine day. Not that it bothered Sienna; there was no way she could have kept that pace up without hiring another therapist. What bothered her was why she was jumping at Danny's suggestion that she come over for the day and spend it with him. Would she never learn?

Just for her day off, she told herself.

There was plenty she could be doing at the day spa, despite only having one appointment first thing this morning. She needed to practise the new treatment she had developed, her stock was running low and she should be back there placing an order, and—

She drew a deep breath as she stared out over the smooth silver Passage as Jiminy's launch took her to Hamilton Island—and to Danny Riccardo.

'Nothing fancy,' he'd said. 'We'll have a picnic at my favourite beach. You will love it, Sienna.'

Of course she'd agreed, even though she had been so disappointed with him at Pippa and Rafe's wedding. It still upset her when she thought about it. When she'd heard that Danny and Renzo had been invited to the wedding, Sienna had been excited. Over the weeks the Riccardo brothers had been working on the new buildings on Pentecost Island, Danny had taken every chance he could to come and talk to her. She had built foolish dreams in her head for the night of the wedding, but Danny had ignored her all night and she had been desperately disappointed. Since the wedding, he had been back to his normal attentive self, so Sienna had jumped at his suggestion, and organised for a boat ride to the island.

It had been like being back at high school when she'd had a crush on one of the older boys from the Catholic school beside the convent she attended in Lucerne before she'd been banished to boarding school. The same breathless anticipation, the same thudding of her heart that seemed to speed up whenever she saw him, and that wonder as she looked into his huge brown eyes, eyes that were framed by the longest eyelashes she'd ever seen. Danny was so good looking, yet he seemed totally unaware of his looks. The biggest shock, was that he seemed to like being with her.

With me, Sienna. She couldn't believe he was interested in her.

Trust. Go carefully, her inner voice warned her.

Yet, Sienna knew instinctively Danny was as interested in her as she was fascinated by him.

It had been like love at first sight for her and no matter how hard she tried, she couldn't put the feeling—or the temptation—

aside. The instant their eyes had met outside the spa hut the first time he'd come to work on her building, her breath had been stolen away. Their eyes had met and held, and she could even imagine the music that would have played if it had been a scene from a movie.

Violins and flowers would have surrounded them.

A smile tugged at her lips as Hamilton Island—and the date with Danny—approached.

As much as Sienna tried to tell herself it was dangerous, and only because Danny was so handsome, she wasn't able to stop that breathless feeling that was building inside her now. There was no harm in flirting, she just had to remind herself. It was a game, and some pleasant company, and there was no future to dream about.

No future. She didn't want a future with a man.

She had to go back to Switzerland one day, and from what Danny had told her, he was on the islands to stay. Even though his Italian accent was strong, he'd told her that despite quite a few trips back to Italy, he'd grown up in North Queensland and he loved working on the islands.

Renzo was always interrupting them, with a sharp word and a glare at Danny.

'I don't think your brother likes me,' Sienna said one day when Danny was installing a new cupboard in the spa foyer. Whenever he was there working she would find a reason to stay. She could have gone back to the house while he worked, but she loitered, talking to him and refolding towels that didn't need refolding.

They *always* talked. After only three weeks, she felt as though she knew everything there was to know about Danny Riccardo, and she had been open with him. She had hidden her lack of self-confidence, and was sure he thought of her as a woman of the world.

'Ah, don't you worry your pretty little head about my big brother. He pretends to be angry at me, because he knows I like to have fun when I work. He'—Danny threw his arms into the air, and his black curls fell around his face—'he thinks work is serious, I tell him, Renzo, you are *too* serious. We must laugh and enjoy what we do. It is not all about chasing the dollars. He is not like the happy brother I looked up to when I grew up. He has turned into a businessman, and I do not like it.'

'What will you do?' Sienna asked. 'If you leave, I mean.' Her face fell, it wouldn't be the same here without Danny calling in and seeing her every day. Mostly with a smile, but occasionally with a flower he picked from the garden on the way over. She knew there were months of building work ahead for them here, and she really hoped he would stay until it was completed.

'Oh, I will not be leaving.' His beautiful eyes widened and his mouth tipped into a huge smile as he reassured her. 'I will teach him how to be happy again. Don't worry, I am not going anywhere. Why would I leave a job when I can look at a beautiful young woman all day?'

Sienna's face had heated and she'd looked away from those eyes. She knew it was all light-hearted flirting and meant nothing, She had to learn not to take Danny seriously, but it was hard when he came to the day spa at every opportunity.

And that was why she'd jumped at the opportunity to see him on her day off.

Her early morning appointment had been finished by nine-thirty, and that had given Sienna enough time to catch the morning boat back to Hamilton Island with Jiminy. Instead of her usual silk trousers and top, she had worn a pretty dress beneath her white jacket to the appointment, and had left the jacket on when she had boarded the launch in case the wind was cool. Jiminy had dropped off the housemaids who came over to clean the huts. She would be ready to catch the four o'clock launch back when he returned to collect them and she would do her inventory then, she told herself sternly.

I will!

Chapter 2

Jiminy raised his eyebrows as he eased the boat into the marina on the northern side of Hamilton Island. For a moment, Sienna thought it was because Danny was sitting on the wharf waiting for them, looking casual as he swung his legs nonchalantly over the side of the wharf. His attention seemed to be focused on the large batfish breaking the surface of the water near the pylons.

But Jiminy whistled and pointed to a huge superyacht moored at the end of the row. 'If I'm not mistaken, I'd say that's Zac Montgomery's boat.'

'Who's that?' Sienna asked, her heart quivering when Danny pushed himself to his feet and sauntered along the wharf towards them.

'One of the bad boy billionaires of Hamilton Island,' Jiminy said, shaking his head. 'If you ever meet him and he looks your way, you run a mile, Sienna. He's not a good person, but he can put on a very gentlemanly face. But when he arrives, it's a big cash injection into the island economy, so he's welcomed with open arms. He always has an entourage on his boat, and they're always big spenders.' He chuckled and waved to Danny. 'Pippa needs to get him and his entourage over to Pentecost. Have you got any flyers for the day spa with you?'

Sienna patted her tote bag. 'Always.'

'Leave me half a dozen and I'll make sure they get to the Montgomery boat.'

'Thank you.' She nodded and as she dug in her bag for a wad of brochures, Jiminy called out to Danny.

'Hey, Dan.'

'Jiminy, how goes it?'

'If I have to work on a Sunday, at least this is a decent job to have,' the skipper replied.

Sienna passed the advertising material to Jiminy, and Danny held out his hand for her to hold when she stepped off the boat onto the wharf. When their hands met, the usual zing ran up her arm and took her breath away. She fought for normality in her voice as she smiled at him. 'Good morning.'

'Want a lift back over at four, Sienna?' Jiminy asked.

Before she could reply, Danny interrupted. 'It's okay. I'll run Sienna back to Pentecost before dark. We have a picnic planned.'

'Okie doke. See you both on the island through the week.'

'Thank you for the lift over, Jiminy,' Sienna said softly before they left the pen to walk along the wharf. She looked down and realised Danny was still holding her hand. Smiling, she left hers there; it felt right. 'Where are we going?'

'I have prepared a special picnic lunch for you, and I have already taken the basket and the drink cooler to the most romantic spot on Hamilton Island. It awaits you.'

Sienna giggled. 'So with all the romantic couples and honeymooners here on the island, I guess it's going to be busy.'

Danny shook his head. 'No, I can promise it will be only you and me.'

'You have me intrigued.' She lowered her lashes as his intense gaze snagged hers and a delicious shiver ran down her back. Her heart was just about jumping out of her chest, and her hands and legs felt shaky. She couldn't spend the rest of the day in this state. Maybe she shouldn't have come.

'It is nice to see you in a dress today.'

Sienna smoothed her hands nervously down the sides of her dress. 'I thought it would be cooler and I packed my swimming costume too.' As they walked into the sunshine, she reached for her floppy straw hat and put it on. The wind was brisk near the water, and she kept one hand on top of it to stop it from blowing off.

'Sienna?' They reached the entrance of the marina, and crowds were milling in the street ahead.

She lifted her head slowly and met his eyes. 'Yes.'

'I am sorry if I make you nervous. Tell me what I should do to make you relax with me. Is it because we are over here where there are many people?'

She hesitated before she replied. I'm sorry. I'm not very confident and I wondered why you wanted to spend the afternoon with me.'

'If only you knew how much I have been looking forward to today. It is all I have thought about all week.'

A flutter kicked in her chest and she looked up at him with a tentative smile.

'That's better,' he said.

Chapter 3

Excited anticipation of the day ahead kept the smile on Sienna's face. While they had walked through the busy shopping and restaurant area, Danny kept hold of her hand. They turned onto a narrow path off the crowded beach, stepping into the quiet and dim world of a lush green rainforest. Dappled shadows from the movement of the wind high in the trees created a lacy pattern on the path beneath their feet.

'Where are we going?' she asked as they left behind the happy noise from the beach.

Danny shook his head. 'You will see.'

'Just one clue?' she asked with a smile.

'It is a surprise.'

They continued through the forest and then came out beside the water again, stopping at rocks at the far end of the beach. To their left was a wide passage of water and another island. Unlike Hamilton Island, this island was high and mountainous, and there were no buildings to be seen; she hadn't noticed it from the marina.

'Is there another resort on that island?' she asked to fill the silence.

Danny shook his head again as he let go of her hand. 'No, that's Whitsunday Island. It's a national park. I'd love to take you there one day, it's very beautiful.' His glance was hesitant. 'That is, if you would like to go there with me.'

'Maybe another day when neither of us are working,' Sienna said shyly.

'I think a day off seems to be a rare event for us both at the moment.' Danny gestured to the track. 'This way now.'

'I don't mind. I love my job.' Sienna followed him onto the path. 'It's not like going to work, living on the island and doing what I love. What about you?'

'Renzo wanted me to do a job on Hayman Island today, but I insisted on a day off.' Danny's accent was stronger as he spoke quickly. '*Si,* I do love my work, but it can be very hard working for your older brother. He thinks he can boss me around.' He stopped again as the track forked and reached for her hand. 'This way. One day I will have my own business, I think.'

'You've been busy at Pentecost Island since I've been there.'

'We have, and there is a lot more work to be done yet. You might get bored with seeing me there every day.'

'No, I won't.' Sienna looked at him curiously. 'So it's not the Riccardo Brothers business?'

'It is, but not me. My two older brothers, Renzo and Dante are the brothers in the business name. Dante has gone back to live in Italy to help look after our mother. I've only worked with Renzo for two years. I am the youngest in our family. That is why Renzo thinks he can tell me what to do.'

'It must be difficult.'

Danny's voice was tight. 'You don't know the half of it.' After a moment, he chuckled. 'And you don't want to, so let's not give a thought to work for the rest of the day that is left to us.'

'You have a strong accent considering you grew up in Australia.'

'My family—and my extended family up at Ingham in the cane fields, still speak mostly Italian at home so my accent stayed.'

'Just one more question.' She tipped her head to the side and looked at him as they strolled along. It was good to hear about his background. 'What sort of work did you do before you worked in your brothers' business?'

Danny looked to the left where another track led down to the beach; Sienna wondered if they were going to the small beach she could see through the trees or keeping to the forest path. 'This way, almost to our beach,' he said. 'Before I came here, I travelled a lot, and I did a bit of this and a bit of that,' he said. 'A Jack of all trades, you could call it.'

Sienna didn't press him; she knew well what it was like to have secrets. Not one to talk about her past, she always preferred to keep it that way. Eliza knew some of her story, but it wasn't one that Sienna wanted to share—it was a past she wanted to forget— so if Danny preferred not to talk about his past, that was fine with her.

'What about you? he asked.

'I'm very boring. Always the same as I do now.'

'Never boring.' Danny rubbed his thumb over the back of her hand. They walked along side by side and the only sound was the crackle of the leaves beneath their feet.

Sienna smiled. They could have been miles from anywhere; the forest surrounded them, but the track was well-defined and was obviously leading somewhere.

'Are you going to tell me about this beach we are going to?' she asked. 'You said "our beach."'

Danny's smile was sweet. 'All I will tell you is, it is somewhere beautiful. Even more beautiful than your island.'

'I can't wait to see it.' She didn't mind if it took a long time to get there. Walking along holding Danny's hand filled Sienna with a contentment she hadn't felt for a long time. She had worked hard in the day spa in the months she'd been on Pentecost Island, not giving herself any time to dwell on the past. Some nights when she sat on the veranda by herself, looking at the water, she wondered if she had done the right thing leaving Europe and following Eliza to Australia. It was a different world here, and at times, she was able to forget her life in Switzerland. Last year, the months when Eliza was missing had added to her constant worries. That, and her other experience, had left its mark, and although the scars were not obvious to a casual observer, Sienna knew they ran deep. Being relaxed with a man, as she was with Danny, was very much a change for her.

She took a deep breath and let it out in a sigh. Being on Pentecost Island meant no one had high expectations of her, and even though no one was checking to see that she was immaculately presented every minute of the day, old habits were hard to shake.

She had to remember that there was no one here waiting to see her fail. No one waiting to criticise her every move.

That was why she loved being on the island with the girls. Pippa was the most incredible boss.

'All good?' Danny slowed his pace, and sounded worried. 'That was a big sigh. You are not sorry you came to see me today?'

'No, I was just thinking about the island, and how lucky I am. What a good boss I have. Pippa is amazing.'

'She is very organised and she knows exactly what she wants.'

'Eliza—we have been friends since school—wrote to me and told me about the island and how I should come and work here.'

'And you did.'

'I did, but I didn't expect it to be as good as she said it would be. She told me about this wonderful island where her life had been saved. I thought she was exaggerating.' Sienna bit her lip. She'd thought that Eliza had been overly impressed by Pentecost Island because of the dreadful life she'd had before she had escaped from her husband. Any new place would have been better than that life. Sienna would never forgive herself for not trying harder to talk Eliza out of marrying Rocco.

'You look very worried, Sienna. Don't be worried, we haven't got far to go. In one moment we will be back in civilisation. This is just a shortcut along the water to the bay beneath where I live. We can reach it by road but this is a much nicer way to come, especially from the marina through the forest.'

'Will I see your house?'

'No. You do not want to see that. Where we are going is much nicer. We will have a picnic lunch, and then we will swim and relax. Then we will have a wine to toast the sunset, and I shall take you back to your island in our boat.'

'Is that the boat that I have seen you come to work in?'

'No, that is the work boat with our tools and equipment. We—the family—have another boat that we use for pleasure.' His voice was eager, and Sienna glanced sideways at Danny as he hesitated, and then spoke again. 'Are you happy to stay on the beach and then go back in the boat? Would you have preferred to go to a restaurant?'

'I'm happy with whatever you choose. I think it sounds very nice. It is good to be away from the crowds.' She swallowed nervously. 'As long as it is a big boat.'

'It is. Not as big as Jiminy's, but it is a decent size to cross the Passage.'

'That is good to know.' Sienna gestured to the water. 'It is big water for little boats. I am used to my calm lake at home.'

Danny chuckled. 'We're almost there. I'll set your mind at

rest.'

Chapter 4

The light brightened as they approached the end of the path and ahead, framed by two huge mango trees, was a glimpse of sapphire blue water. In the middle of the vista a sleek white motor cruiser bobbed in the small waves. The lush canopy of leaves above thinned and sunlight lit the path.

'Almost to our beach. That is your taxi home, *bella.*'

Sienna wondered idly why Danny hadn't offered to come to the island to collect her, but she shrugged off the thought. As they got closer to the shore she drew in a short breath. 'Oh my goodness, I can see our island too. I didn't realise we were walking in that direction.' She turned to Danny. 'So your house is above here and you can see across the Passage to our island. I didn't think we could see Hamilton Island from our bay.'

'You can.' Danny stopped and put one hand on her shoulder and leaned down so that his cheek was close to hers. A citrus fragrance tickled her nostrils; she hadn't been this close to him before. Heat warmed her from her head to her toes as his smooth cheek pressed against hers. He lifted his arm and pointed across the water to Pentecost Island.

'Let your eyes follow where I am pointing to and keep your eye on the end of my finger as I move it downwards from the peak on your island.'

Sienna would have been happy to follow his finger for the whole day if it meant his cheek stayed against hers.

'If you look down the peak on this side, you should just be able to see a tree that is growing out of the cliff at a right angle. See it?' His warm breath puffed on her lips as he turned slightly towards her.

'I can.' Her voice was husky.

'Come down that ridge line, and can you see the tulip tree with the red flowers on the top?'

Sienna shook her head. 'You are teasing me. You can't see flowers from this far away.'

'No, I am not. If you stare hard enough, you can just see a faint brush of orange.'

Sienna stood back and shook her head as she looked up at him. A little warm butterfly beat its wings in her lower belly as his lips tilted in a huge smile.

'You are so teasing me!' she exclaimed.

Danny's eyes crinkled at the corners and his perfect teeth flashed white as he stared at her.

***

Sienna held Danny's gaze and the strangest feeling ran through him; it was more than desire—although there was a lot of that surging through him too—it was more a strong need to get to know this beautiful woman, to make her smile and take away the shadows from beneath her eyes. To protect her and keep her safe, and make her happy.

He shook himself mentally and looked past Sienna. He'd never felt like this in all of his twenty-nine years, but there was no point in following that line of thought until he'd sorted out the mess in his life. He knew he shouldn't have invited Sienna over today, but when she'd told him she had a rare day off, he hadn't been able to resist.

Renzo had lost his temper—as usual—and demanded to know why Danny couldn't work when he'd told him to go over to Hayman Island.

Danny had stood his ground. 'Because it's Sunday. And I am entitled to time off as per the agreement.'

That had set fuel to his brother's temper. 'We do not work to agreements. We work when there is work to be done. How do we expect our customers to come back to us when we say, "Ah, I cannot work. It is a Sunday?" Pah!'

'Perhaps I want to go to church.' Danny had kept a straight face 'Our mama would like that.'

'*Non dire cazzate!*' Renzo put his hands on his hips and stared at him. 'All right, then. You can have one day off but on one condition.'

'Oh?' Danny said, his temper about to match Renzo's 'And what would that be?'

'You do not go anywhere near Pentecost Island and that woman.'

Danny's tone was cold. 'And what woman would that be? Let me see, would it be Pippa, Eliza, Nell, Tamsin, Cherry, Odessa or Sienna? Oh, not to forget Tess, the new receptionist, and of course there are the housemaids and the kitchen hands. Should I not talk to any of them?'

'Don't be smart mouthed with me, Daniel. You know exactly who I mean.' His brother's voice was like a whip. 'I've seen you over there, mooning over that little Swiss girl. You forget your situation.'

'Oh no, I will never forget the situation you and Dante put me in. And one I will be out of very soon.'

'You have made a commitment. Remember that.'

'How could I forget?' Bitterness laced his voice as he turned to leave the office at the back of his brother's house.

'As you are having a day off, perhaps you could take Lucia into Airlie Beach for lunch. A change would be good for her. Maria said she has been unhappy.'

Danny had slammed the door behind him. His brother's suggestion did not deserve an answer.

'Danny?' Sienna's soft voice pulled him out of his thoughts. He looked down at pretty green eyes holding concern. 'Have I said something to upset you? You look angry.'

Regret flooded through him, and he opened his arms and pulled her close without giving himself time to think about what he was doing. 'Oh no, of course you haven't. I am so sorry. My mind was totally on something else.' As soon as Sienna rested her head on his shoulder, Danny knew he'd made a mistake.

A big mistake.

Her hair and skin held a beautiful fragrance, and he almost groaned as her hands tentatively slipped around his waist. They were standing in the path that led to the glade beneath his house, and he knew no one was there to see them, but he still felt guilty.

I should not feel guilty.

He had put Lucia and Maria on the ferry to the mainland an hour before Sienna had arrived, and they had decided to stay there for beauty treatments followed by dinner, planning to come back to Hamilton Island tomorrow. He'd had a horrible moment when Maria, his sister-in-law, had suggested that they should both go over to Pentecost Island and try *Hebe*, the new spa over there.

'I have heard very good things about it,' she'd said.

'Yes, it is very popular with the guests.' Danny had shaken his head in an effort to dissuade them. 'But the rooms are booked out for weeks, and we still have not finished the work over there. Wait a couple of months until the pool and the outdoor Jacuzzi are in. It will be a much better experience then.'

'That sounds as though it will be worth waiting for.' Maria smiled at him. 'We'll go to Airlie Beach for our pampering. Is that all right with you, Lucia?'

The short, plump woman's dark eyes glinted with malice as she stared at Danny, and then she eventually nodded. '*Si.*'

All the pampering in the world would not make a difference to that sour face, he'd thought uncharitably. *If you hate me so much, just do what I want and leave.*

Danny would have liked to have taken the motor cruiser over to Pentecost Island to collect Sienna, but he hadn't been prepared to risk it. Renzo could be very hard when he was crossed, despite the fact that he owed Danny big time for the sacrifice he had made for the family.

His brother had a short memory when it suited him.

Taking Sienna back to the island after dark would be safe enough. Renzo would be out playing cards with his mates, and the women wouldn't be back until tomorrow.

Danny jumped as a lorikeet squawked in the tree above them. Sienna's arms stayed around his back and he rested his head on top of hers. 'I swore to myself that we would have a day together today, that we would talk and swim and share a meal and watch the sunset, but I promised myself I would not touch you. We have not even reached the beach, and yet here I am holding you in my arms. And I know that you belong there. I'm sorry, Sienna.'

She moved away and lifted her head, her green eyes holding his. 'Why be sorry? I am holding you too.'

Danny let go and brushed off her question. 'You are, and it is very nice, but I think we both need to have a swim. What do you think?'

'It is very warm, and I would love to swim. Are you sure there are no stingers or anything in here?' she asked with a frown. 'Pippa makes everyone wear stinger suits over on the island. I don't have one.'

'No, it is safe here. Even if it wasn't, the wind is blowing from the south. It is the northerly that brings the dangerous jellyfish to the islands.'

'How can it be safe here?' Her aristocratic nose wrinkled as she frowned.

'Renzo hired some contractors who have done an excellent job of putting a net right across the entrance of our bay. It is so fine that no stingers can enter this protected bay.'

'We should do that at Pentecost Island. The guests tell me how much they hate having to wear those suits when they get in the water. I love to swim but I find it too confining in those suits.' Sienna's eyes were wide as she looked up at him and it was all Danny could do not to take her into his arms again.

'Pippa talked to us about that when she decided to put a pool in, and we explained that nets won't work there as the boats go into the wharf in your bay.'

Sienna pointed to their large white cruiser out beyond the buoys that held the net in place. 'But yours is there?'

'The nets are between the boat and the shore. We take a small tender out to get to the boat. It's kept in the boatshed over there.'

'Okay,' she said slowly. 'You have convinced me. A swim will be very welcome . . . and safe. I am getting used to all of the dangerous things in Australia.'

He turned to her. 'I hope you don't class me as one of those, Sienna.'

Her pretty lips tipped up in a smile, and he noticed how her eyes lit up when she smiled.

'No, I was talking about the snakes and spiders and the stingers, and the sharks and the crocodiles.'

He put his head back and laughed. 'Will it reassure you that I have lived in North Queensland for most of my life, and I'm yet to see any of them. In the wild, that is.'

Sienna put her hand on his arm, and her eyes were coquettish. Now she was flirting with him and he liked that.

'Now you are not being truthful with me. I've only been here a few weeks and I've even seen some spiders!' she said.

'I'm talking about real spiders. The man-eating size.'

'Man-eating?' Her eyes were dancing as she flirted with

him and Danny ignored the warmth of her hand on his arm. 'Not woman-eating?'

'Yes, the ones you see on the documentaries, they are as big as dinner plates. *And* yes, they are man- and woman-eating! I have never seen one of them. But yes, I've seen plenty of your everyday Incy Wincy spiders.'

Her laugh tinkled around him 'I have no idea what an Incy Wincy spider is, but I am guessing it is something very small like I have seen.'

Danny shook his head. 'You don't know your nursey rhymes. I have listened to my nephews and nieces recite that rhyme every time it rains.'

'Fair enough.' Her smile disappeared suddenly and her face closed. 'Where can I get changed into my swimming costume please?'

Chapter 5

Pippa

I balanced the small paring knife in my left hand and tried to hold the three mangos I'd just removed from the fridge in my right hand. The last mango was wet and slippery; juice had seeped from one overripe end, and it began to slip from my fingers. As I closed the fridge door with my elbow, I juggled and balanced, but the three large pieces of tropical fruit hit the tiled floor, closely followed by the knife.

'Bloody heck,' I muttered beneath my breath and quickly moved my bare foot as the knife narrowly missed my toes and bounced off the tiled floor. This cooking caper had not been a good idea. I should have asked Cherry and Angus to cook a meal and bring it up.

As I bent to retrieve the fruit—two intact and one mango splattered over the white tiles—the screen door to the veranda opened.

'Blooming hell,' I yelled as I stepped into the sticky mess.

'Hello, are you there, Pippa? Are you okay?'

'I'm in the kitchen. Come on in.'

I looked up as Eliza appeared in the kitchen doorway. 'You're early.'

'No, I'm not, we said eleven, didn't we?' Eliza's eyes widened. 'My God, Pippa! What are you doing?'

I turned and surveyed the usually clear granite worktops.

'You can barely see the gorgeous view out there today. My attention was immediately taken by that.' Eliza chuckled as she gestured to the mess on the counters and the floor.

'Rafe's coming home tonight and I decided to cook him a special welcome home dinner.'

'Hmm. I didn't think you cooked.'

'Hmm is right, and no, I don't very often. But so far I've made cold cucumber soup, even though it looks like mossy tank water. I did try to bake bread to go with it.' I pulled a face and gestured to the lump of glutinous dough on the sink and then held up my finger wrapped in a Band-Aid. 'This is from when I tried to butterfly a loin of pork to stuff with apricots. What a stupid thing to do, fancy trying to cut a slab of pork to look like a butterfly.'

Eliza began to laugh and I smiled with her. 'And that?' She pointed to the floor, where the mango juice was running along the grout between the tiles. 'I assume that is dessert.'

'Mango mousse. Rafe loves mangoes.' I shook my head and couldn't hold back my mirth. 'Stuff it. I think it's time for coffee.'

'How about I help you clean up the mess first, and then we'll have a coffee?'

'I won't say no to that.'

She laughed again as she reached down to pick up the mangoes I'd dropped. 'So what's for dinner?'

'I'll ditch the soup, take the pork down to Angus for him to fix it, and see if Cherry has time to whip up that mousse for me.' I shook my head. 'I should have known better. I hate cooking.'

'It's the thought that counts. I didn't realise Rafe was away. I haven't been off Phillipe's boat for a few days.'

'Relaxing?'

'No, working. I've been looking at ideas for the pool. Wait until you see what I've found.'

With Eliza loading the dishwasher, and me wiping the benchtops and washing the floor, it was not long before we were sitting out on the balcony with coffee. Eliza had brought cake up from the restaurant. 'Cherry wanted us to try it out. Salted caramel cake.'

'It's such a hard life, supervising a resort.' I sighed with pleasure as I took a bite and the moist cake melted in my mouth. 'Oh, yum. That is to die for.'

'So why the sudden domestic goddess cooking binge?' Eliza picked up her coffee and regarded me over the rim.

'Rafe's been in Brisbane at a book signing. He wanted me to go with him but I'm still hesitant about leaving the place. There's a few little bumps that we have to navigate and I like to keep an eye on things. And the staff.'

Eliza raised her eyebrows. 'Odessa?' She reached down to

the satchel that she'd brought in.

'Yes, even though she's not staff, I still worry about her. She's had a tough time but I think she's starting to go okay.'

'You're a control freak, Pippa. We're all responsible for our own happiness.'

'I know, but if I can make things a bit easier for the girls, I will.'

'You always have done, or ever since I met you anyway.'

'Oh, you didn't know me in the "before-Pentecost-Island-Pippa days." I'm a lot more patient and settled than I used to be. Aunty Vi leaving me the island was a life changer for me.'

Eliza smiled. 'And so has having a fabulous man like Rafe in your life.'

'I sure can't deny that,' I said. 'I think Dylan's been good for Odessa too. She's mellowed.'

'He has. She is more settled. She was telling me about the silverwork she's doing.'

'Her work is really good. I was thinking about opening a boutique when we renovate the old house. What do you think about that?'

'What sort of boutique?' Eliza asked.

'Maybe beach stuff. Locally sourced and exclusive, like hand printed sarongs and the like, And of course The jewellery created on our island.'

'Sounds like another forward step to me.'

I chuckled. 'I still can't believe it's only been a few months off two years since I got the letter from the solicitor saying I'd been left an island, and here we are now talking about building more huts, putting in a pool and opening a boutique. The restaurant is up and running, and look how many staff we've got now.'

Eliza shook her head. 'I never thought it would take off so much when I offered to come in as partner. It's been an incredible success. I think you really picked where there was a need.'

I shook my head. 'You know, I think it was more a fluke. Or being on the right place at the right time. It's our island that's half the attraction, it's such a beautiful place, and keeping it unspoiled and natural as an eco-resort, you wouldn't even know it was here. You could sail past and not even notice it.'

'I beg to disagree,' Eliza said. 'How many people were in

the bar last Saturday night? I couldn't believe it. We might even have to extend the restaurant and bar to keep up with the demand.'

'No,' I said. 'I think we'll keep it small and intimate like we started out.'

'I agree, I was just sounding you out, but one thing I do think we need to do is put the prices up.'

'I was thinking that too. The higher the tariff and food prices, the more exclusive it is, and that drives demand. It also means we can have special deals, and not lose money.'

'By Gawd, woman, we're a great team,' Eliza said in a strong Cockney accent.

'We sure are, but one of the things that's really attracting the girls' weekends is *Hebe*.' I watched Eliza carefully for her reaction. 'You know Sienna much better than I do. Do you think she'd be upset if I suggested getting a second therapist?'

'Normally I'd say she'd be fine, but I've been a bit worried about her over the past few weeks. She seems to have lost her spark.'

I leaned forward. 'I've noticed that too. I was worried she was working too hard; that's one of the reasons I thought about a second staff member there.'

'Any development on the Danny-Sienna romance front?'

I shook my head. 'Not that I've noticed. Although Sienna has gone over to Hamo for the day.'

'Maybe she's seeing him over there.'

'I doubt it. I think she was upset when he brought that woman to the wedding.'

'God, she was a sour cow. Phillipe and I sat with them for a while, and she spent most of the time glaring at any woman who came near the table. Lucia, her name was.'

'I tried to talk to her too, but I don't think her English is very good.' I dug in my pocket and reached for a tissue and dabbed at my face. The air was heavy with humidity and a line of towering white clouds rose in plumes above the horizon. The wet season was coming.

'Still no reason to be rude.' Eliza clicked the mouse on her laptop. 'Nell emailed me the forward bookings this morning. The good news is, even with the construction work happening we are booked out until the end of March. I was going to suggest having an Easter special, but I don't think there's any need.'

'I agree.'

Eliza turned the screen towards me and looked like the cat that got the cream. 'One more thing before we look at the finances. Look what I found.'

I stood and walked around the table to stand behind her chair so I could see the screen without the light reflecting on it.

'Oh my God, they're perfect. I love them. Where can we buy them?' I leaned forward and looked closely at the day beds around the infinity pool in the image. Tiled extensions held day beds at each corner of the pool and in the middle of the sides. Each bed had timber posts and privacy curtains.

'The good news is there is a supplier in Sydney. And I've called, and the lead time is only two weeks.'

'Fantastic. I'll see Renzo and Danny tomorrow and get them to talk to the pool people.'

'They're doing a great job. And they are so fast.' Eliza scrolled down. 'I thought these tables would look good in the area adjacent to the pool too.'

'Nice. And yes. I'm so pleased we got onto the Riccardos.'

The mention of the builders made me think of Danny . . . and Sienna. 'Do you think Sienna's okay?' I asked. It still surprised me that with my unhappy background I ended up as mother hen for the girls on the island.

'I've been wondering too,' Eliza said.

'She just doesn't seem happy.'

'And she spends most of her time off in the day spa too.' Eliza frowned. 'I know she loves living on the island, and the work in *Hebe*. But if you think about it, the rest of us have partners, and she's alone.'

'Do you think we need to matchmake? Give Danny a bit of a push?'

'I know she's keen on him.' The smile spread on Eliza's face. 'I think that's an excellent idea. I think the problem is she's too shy. And I'd say Danny doesn't know she's interested. She can come across as very proper and aloof, but I know the fun-loving person that's in there.'

'For someone as beautiful as she is, it surprises me how shy Sienna seems. She's always immaculately groomed and seems confident.'

'She does, but I don't think the confidence is there. I don't think she had a very happy childhood. I'm not breaking any confidence, because she's never talked about it, but I've always wondered.'

'Okay, that's our next task. Some careful and quiet matchmaking. Just you and me, I won't say anything to the others. Now, show me this spreadsheet, and then I'd better go down to the kitchen and see Angus and Cherry about Rafe's dinner.'

Chapter 6

Sienna

Not wanting to talk about nursery rhymes, children, or get into a discussion about why she didn't know the rhyme about the stupid small spider, Sienna waited for Danny to tell her where she could get changed.

He gestured to the path that led into the bush. 'If you follow that path, there is a small cabana at the base of the cliff. The door will be closed, but it is not locked. It is private and belongs to our family. My brothers built it before I moved here. You should also find some beach towels there.'

'Okay. I won't be long. Shall I get a towel for you too?' She turned and paused before she headed up the path. 'You are sure it will be private?'

He nodded. 'Yes, this is the only way to it. You can't get to it from the houses unless you come along the beach. No one will come along here, but in the small chance they do, I will ensure you are not disturbed. And yes please, to the towel.'

'I'll be quick.' Sienna put her head down and hurried along the path. As Danny had said, there was a small cabana there at the base of a rocky cliff. The small, brightly-coloured building took her straight back to her childhood holidays on *Lido di Venezia* when her parents had hired a beach hut on the long sandy beach.

Those were the days before *it* had happened, the days when they had been a happy family, and she and Max had played on the sand.

Max was perfect. He *had been* perfect. All her memories of those three years were happy. Every one that was imprinted on her mind. Her parents had been happy, and her life had been normal up until that day.

How could one day change so many lives?

Sienna pushed the door open and closed down her thoughts. It was going to be a happy day, and she would not ruin it by thinking of the past.

She changed quickly into her white one-piece swimsuit, and quickly twirled her hair up and secured it with a clip from her bag. Slipping her green sarong over her arm, she put her clothes and her sandals into her bag before selecting two beach towels from the shelf.

Danny was standing watching the motor cruiser bobbing gently in the small waves breaking with a splash at the edge of the bay near the rocks. Sienna caught her breath. While she had been getting changed, he had taken off his shirt and now wore only a pair of whiteboard shorts. Against the white fabric, his tanned, muscular legs looked even browner. He had a Mediterranean olive complexion. Letting her gaze run down the muscled and toned back, she finally forced herself to look away and put her bag down carefully on a rock. Her bare feet crunched in the shingly sand, and Danny swung around as she approached.

Heat filled her cheeks as his appreciative glance swept her from head to toe and settled on the folds of the ruched white swimsuit she'd bought the weekend she was on Hamo with the girls. She'd fallen in love with it the instant she had seen it in the exclusive boutique. The neckline plunged to the waist, but modesty was provided for, by the small gold buttons that ran down the front.

His voice was husky. 'You look like a Grecian goddess, Sienna.'

The heat intensified as he kept looking at her. The swimsuit had been horrendously expensive, but the look on Danny's face made every dollar spent worthwhile.

'Thank you.' She grinned at him and ran towards the water. 'Last one in is a rotten egg.'

A wide grin spread across Danny's face, and he took off after her as she ran for the water. They both reached the edge at exactly the same time and plunged into the warm water. Sienna swam out a few strokes and then dived down into the crystal clear depths. The sand was white, and shards of sunlight rippled through the water. Small fish darted along the bottom, and she held her breath as she struck out further. Eventually, she had to come up for a breath and was surprised to see that Danny had kept up with her and was treading water only a metre from where she surfaced.

'The water feels wonderful,' she said as she floated beside him.

'It does. I try to swim here every night after we get home from work.'

'In the dark?' She frowned.

'Yes, under the stars. You should try it, it's incredible in the moonlight.'

'I am, what is the English word? A squib?'

'You mean you're not very adventurous?'

'I do.'

'Yes, that is the word, but I don't believe it.'

'I used to be brave when I swam in our lake. Sometimes when I was young, I used to swim until that first snow of the winter, but I grew up and became sensible, and lost my courage.'

Danny swam over to her, and shook his head and flicked his hair back. His brown eyes held hers, and despite the warm water, a shiver ran down Sienna's back. The old Danny who had flirted with her before the wedding was back.

'I think you are adventurous to leave home and move to an Australian island.'

Sienna moved her legs in a bicycle motion to stay afloat. 'I left home a very long time ago.'

'Tell me about you growing up.'

She shook her head. 'That is very boring. It was much more fun when I left boarding school and moved out. I travelled across Europe with Eliza between doing my beauty courses. Then I got a job in London, and we stayed friends while she did her carpentry course—'

'Her what?' Danny's eyes were wide. 'She is a carpenter?'

Sienna nodded. 'A very good one. Did you know she built the first few huts on the island, before Pippa hired you and your brother?'

'No, I didn't. I thought she was one of the owners and lived on her yacht with Phillipe.'

'She is and she does.' Sienna smiled as Danny shook his head again.

'No wonder she pays close attention to what we are doing. I won't make such assumptions in future.'

'I'll race you out to the buoy,' Sienna called as she began

to swim.

'A rotten egg race again?' Danny said as he took off a few strokes behind her. Sienna smiled smugly as she beat him by three metres. He didn't know that she had been a champion swimmer.

They frolicked and played in the water like children for an hour until hunger called. In between swimming, diving, and watching the fish in the blue water, they talked and joked together.

As they waded through the shallows, Sienna pulled the clip from her hair and squeezed the water from her ponytail. She was relaxed in Danny's company and felt as though she had learned more about him in the past hour than she had in the two months since she had met him. The only problem was that her attraction had deepened in that hour, and she now found it hard to look away from him. Not only that, she was also aware of his eyes on her.

He was such a good-looking man, and his happy smile was hard to resist. She had laughed and smiled with him, until a fluid relaxation lightened her limbs so that she felt weightless in the water as she'd floated on her back beside him.

They walked up the beach together, and after Sienna had dried herself on the thick fluffy towel, she picked up her bag.

'I'll go and get dressed and make myself presentable.'

Danny's hand on her arm stopped her before she picked up her bag.

'There's no need to get dressed. Just put your sarong on and we'll sit under the trees and have some lunch. And then we'll have another swim later, so I can prove that I can win a race. I do not like being the rotten egg!'

'But—'

'But what?' Danny's arm slid around her waist, and the feel of his warm skin against hers chased away what she had been going to say. 'Um, I need—need to, I need to get tidy. I do not like looking—'

'Looking beautiful? Because you do.' His hands dropped away suddenly and he took a step back. 'Come over to the shade. I have a picnic that won't take long to serve. I'm starving.'

Sienna hesitated for a moment and bit her lip. Her hair was wet and in clumps, and her makeup had long gone, as she was sure the sun cream she had lathered on this morning had also. 'Okay, but I will just go and do my hair and put some more sunscreen on.'

She turned and hurried up the path, aware of Danny's eyes on her back. Her legs were shaky, and there was an exquisite longing tugging low in her belly. As well as combing her hair and at least putting some lipstick on, Sienna needed some time away from him to regain her equilibrium. A couple of times when they were close to each other in the water, she had been tempted to lean across and put her lips on his but had managed to resist.

Despite being wet and cool, she fanned her hand in front of her face as she walked to the cabana.

Pushing open the door, she put her bag down and looked in the small mirror that was above the wooden bench seat.

Her hair was damp, but her face had a pink glow, and her eyes were bright and clear. Reaching for her comb, she tugged it through the dampness, then twisted her hair back into a topknot and secured it with the clip.

Carefully she tied her sarong around her body and then reached for her lipstick. She opened it and looked at herself again in the mirror. Her lips were a rosy red from the exertion, and she looked down at the pale pink lipstick. With a determined nod, she replaced the cap and slipped it back into her makeup purse.

It was because her lips were already rosy, Sienna told herself firmly and had nothing to do with the thought that Danny might kiss her.

Nothing at all.

Humming beneath her breath, she picked up her bag and headed back to the beach.

Chapter 7

Danny

Danny grabbed the beach towel and wrapped it around his waist before he walked over to the tree where he'd left the cooler. Their time in the water had passed quickly and he was surprised to hear the horn of the two o'clock ferry as it left the marina.

By the time Sienna walked down the path, he had unpacked the gourmet sandwiches he'd bought at his favourite coffee shop this morning, had two glasses topped with ice sitting on a tray, and had unscrewed the cap off the bottle of wine he'd packed.

He reached for his shirt as she spread her towel beside the log where he'd set out their lunch. 'It's hot. Don't worry about a shirt for my benefit,' she said softly. 'I'm still in my swimsuit.'

'Are you sure you won't think I have bad manners?' he asked passing her a bottle of water from the cooler.

'Thank you, and of course not. We're on the beach on a holiday island, and we'll pretend we are on holiday, not just having a Sunday off.' Sienna sat on the towel and tipped the bottle up. It was hard not to stare at the elegant line of her neck. Her skin was flawless, even without the usual makeup she wore.

Danny forced his eyes away and held up the wine bottle. He had vowed that he would simply spend the day in Sienna's company, and not give in to his desire. 'Would you like a wine with your lunch?'

'We are both European, so I don't think I need to think about my answer, do I?' she said playfully. 'Will you have one?'

'Just one glass, as I will be driving the boat later when I take you back.'

The silence was pleasant as they ate the sandwiches that Danny had packed and sipped their wine.

'Would you like some fruit for dessert, madame?' His eyes crinkled at the edges as she looked into the cooler.

'We have peaches and grapes. What would you like?'

'A peach please.'

He handed a plump pink peach over and as their fingers brushed they both pulled away, and looked down. Danny kept his eyes on the grapes as he picked them off one by one.

He cleared his throat. 'So how long do you think you'll stay on the island?'

Sienna shrugged. 'As long as I can stay working here with my visa. I love my job, and I am very invested in *Hebe*. It will be very hard to leave.' Her tone held mirth. 'Maybe I'll have to find myself a local husband so I can stay.'

Danny jumped up and knocked the wine bottle over. 'Don't even think about that. It would be a very foolish move.'

'I wasn't meaning you,' she said and her cheeks coloured in a blush. A trickle of peach juice ran down from her lips to her chin as she turned away, and the half-eaten peach rolled along the towel.

Danny reached for her hand, but she pulled away as he tried to apologise. 'That was very rude of me, please don't take it like that. I know you didn't mean that.' He leaned over and picked up a paper serviette. 'Sienna, look at me.'

She turned slowly, and her eyes met his. Tears hovered on her lashes. A shaft of longing hit him so strong, it made his chest ache.

He cleared his throat. 'You have some peach juice on your chin.' He lifted the serviette and Sienna stood stiffly as he dabbed gently. 'Really, I didn't mean to upset you. Honestly, It's just that I know someone who is in that situation and it's not a wise thing to do.'

'I was being flippant,' she said, as she allowed him to wipe her face. 'I am never getting married.'

'A sensible idea,' he said. 'What would you like to do now?'

Chapter 8

Pippa

I stood on the wharf as Rafe's black speedboat appeared as a small dot between Hamo and our island. The sun had almost reached the horizon with its usual Whitsunday blaze of glory. The heavy orb hovered in an apricot sky shot with slivers of purple and gold. A few months ago we would have all been down here toasting the sunset and our futures, but life seemed to have been too busy lately. That once dreamed of future of a functioning resort was now a reality. I made a mental note to book everyone for next Friday night for sunset drinks down on the rocks; it was a habit we had let slip. Christmas was only a few weeks away too, and we hadn't planned anything social yet. We had a great team on the island and even the new arrivals were fast becoming friends. A Christmas party was called for; I'd close the restaurant for one night and the staff could be rewarded for their hard work.

Tam and Nell were so settled on the island they had recently approached Rafe and I to buy a portion of land each so they could build their own homes. Nell had told me—on the quiet—that she knew Nat had bought an engagement ring for a Christmas engagement. 'He thinks it's a surprise,' she'd chuckled when I was in the office with her the day Rafe left. 'But the silly man used our joint Visa card, and I saw it on the statement. I can't wait to see it, Pippa, I am so happy.'

I was surprised when Nell's eyes filled with tears. 'So what's wrong?' I put my arm around her shoulder.

Nell shook her head and put her hand over her mouth. 'Nothing. I'm just so happy, it overwhelms me at times. I had no idea that my life would turn out like this when I agreed to come to Pentecost Island with you.'

'It's sure beaten my wildest expectations,' I agreed. 'Okay, so when's our next wedding?'

Nell grinned widely. 'I haven't been proposed to yet.' She

pushed herself up from the desk chair and stood beside me. Her eyes filled with tears again as she held my shoulders. 'I'm so emotional these days, and I hope he proposes soon because I want to get married before June.'

'Oh?' I said. 'You don't want a winter wedding?'

Nell's grin was even wider as the first tear rolled down her cheek. 'No, I want to be married before I'm hugely pregnant.'

My high-pitched scream bounced off the walls as I grabbed Nell and danced around the room with her clinging to me. 'Oh my God, we're going to have two babies next year?'

'We are.'

'But only one wedding,' I said. As much as Gabe had tried to talk Tamsin into getting married before their baby was born in April, she stood firm. 'I don't have to have a piece of paper to make it formal. Our love is enough,' she'd told me.

'That's Tam and Gabe's call,' Nell said. 'I want to go the whole traditional route. The white wedding, the honeymoon, and a house.'

'And the good news I was holding in until Rafe was back, is that the subdivision of your blocks of land has been approved.'

This time Nell squealed.

'As long as you're sure you want to settle on the island,' I said wiping away my own happy tears.

'We are. All for one and one for all, remember.' Nell sat down and fanned herself with her hand.

'Are you well?' I asked. 'Have you been sick at all?'

'Yep, not like poor Tam. No morning sickness yet! Just tired and emotional.'

'When will you tell Tam?'

'Soon.'

Now, as I stood on the wharf watching Rafe come home to me, my happiness was complete. The three days he had been gone had dragged, and after years of sleeping alone I quickly discovered that I no longer enjoyed it. It was the first time we'd been apart since I'd moved up to his house.

Our house, he called it now.

Our house on *our* beautiful island.

His boat approached quickly and the white foam kicked up by the inboard motors fanned out across the Passage. My husband of two months stood at the wheel, his jet-black hair blowing in the wind. I lifted my phone and snapped a photo as he entered the bay. The black boat, the gorgeous man, the apricot sky and the silver water provided a perfect landscape shot. That was one to go on the wall in *our* house.

I reached down and threw the rope to Rafe as he cut the speed and the boat purred up to the wharf. He jumped out in one fluid movement, quickly tied off the rope and ran along to where I waited. I was in his arms and his lips were on mine within seconds.

Finally, after being thoroughly kissed, my husband lifted his head and smiled down at me with that intense blue-eyed stare I had missed. 'Next time I go away, you are coming with me, Pippa Rendell. No arguments allowed.'

I stood on my toes and brushed my lips against his. 'No argument given. I missed you so much. The days dragged.'

Rafe went back to the boat, collected his small suitcase and then linked his arm through mine as we walked up the steps to our home. 'I hope we don't have plans tonight, do we? I want you all to myself.'

I put on a sultry grin and fluttered my eyelashes. 'Oh, I do have plans for you.'

'You do?' His answering grin was wicked, and I couldn't get up that hill fast enough.

'I do,' I teased. 'I've planned a special dinner for you, and then I have lots of news for you.'

'Good news?' His dark eyebrows lifted in a question.

'All excellent news.'

'I have an idea,' he said. 'Even though I'm starving, we'll have a late dinner. Why don't we jump in the spa and then rest for a while? You can tell me all the news then.' He slipped his hand beneath my T-shirt and his hand crept upwards.

A shiver ran down my back and my legs almost went to jelly. 'I think that's an excellent idea, but I don't think I want a rest. And the news can wait.'

We reached the top of the steps and Rafe put his suitcase down as he lifted my T-shirt over my head, and I started on the buttons of his business shirt.

'Excellent,' he said. 'We obviously have the same idea.' The last of the sunset was blotted out as his head lowered to mine.

Dinner was *very* late.

Chapter 9

Danny

Danny was pleased that Sienna had kept hold of his hand as they walked back into the restaurant precinct. They'd decided to have a coffee in town and then Sienna wanted to call in at the beauty spa beneath the hotel on Catseye Beach to check out their products. He couldn't believe how immaculate she looked after five minutes getting changed in the cabana after lunch.

But he was simply content to be in her company. The mood was happy as they had coffee and shared a piece of cake.

Then they had planned another swim, and would watch the sunset together before he took her back across the Passage.

'Do you have anything planned tonight when you get back to Pentecost Island?' he asked as they came out of the coffee shop.

'Not really. Why do you ask?'

'I was thinking about going to the store while you checked out your opposition, and we could have a barbeque on the beach before I take you back.'

Sienna smiled and nodded. 'That would save me ferreting for something back at the house.'

'I wondered what you all did there. I thought you might eat in the restaurant every night.'

'Oh no, the food is too rich for me to eat there too often. And besides, since you and Renzo added those new huts, the restaurant is full each night. We—the staff—cook in the kitchen of the original house. Angus keeps the pantry and fridge stocked— meals are part of our salary package, thanks to Pippa—and most of us cook for ourselves. Sometimes we might take it in turns to cook for everyone and it's a good way to debrief after work. The best night is Monday when Cherry is off and she tries out her new creations on us.'

'Sounds like the perfect job.'

'It is,' she said as they reached the hotel.

'How long do you want to spend here?' Danny asked as they reached the hotel.

'Is an hour okay?'

'Perfect. It'll give me time to do some shopping. You eat steak?'

'I do.'

Once Sienna had entered the day spa, Danny called in at the general store, and when he'd shopped he took off up the hill behind the shops and headed for his house to collect some plates and barbeque tools. The last thing he wanted to do was take Sienna there.

He let himself in and put the shopping bag on the kitchen bench. Rolling his eyes, he tried to ignore the mess that surrounded him. The house was his brother Dante's house, and Danny had it rent free while his brother was in Italy. By the look of things—the health of their mother was not good—Dante would be away another year.

Until Lucia had arrived, Danny had kept the house neat and tidy, and had hired a cleaner once a week to do the floors and the bathroom. Despite the cleaner still coming once a week, the house was a pigsty. Lucia didn't put anything away, and when she cooked, she would go days without loading the dishwasher.

The one time he had raised it with her, her small black eyes had narrowed and she had shrugged. 'Not my job. You don't like, you fix.'

Danny pushed away the thought of her; he would not think of that problem today and let his bad mood ruin the perfect day with Sienna. Quickly loading a basket with plates, linen napkins, and the barbeque tools, he picked up the shopping bag holding the antipasto, meat and salad, and bread rolls, and then took the shortcut down the cliff to their beach. Quickly stowing the food in the cooler and snapping the lid back on, he turned to the path that would take him to the beach. With a frown he put a hand up to his eyes. The motor cruiser had been moved; it was now attached to the buoy at the southern end of the beach.

He stared for a while, but it appeared there was no one on board. If Renzo was on the boat and taking it out, Danny would have to get Sienna to the marina by four p.m. in time for her to catch a lift back to Pentecost Island with Jiminy.

Narrowing his eyes, he watched the cruiser, and pulled his phone out, hitting the speed dial for Renzo.

For a long while, he didn't think it was going to pick up, and then there was a click and a short, 'What?'

'I just wanted to check if you need me to get anything to take over to the island tomorrow.'

'No. I'm still working here. All good.' There were muffled voices in the background. Then Danny could have sworn he heard a giggle. A cold feeling consumed him; what if Lucia and Maria were over on Pentecost Island with Renzo? What if they'd changed their minds about where they were going?

'Are the girls over there with you?' he forced himself to ask.

'No, they're at Airlie Beach.'

Another muffled female voice in the background. Danny shrugged. It wasn't his concern who his brother talked to when he was working. Maybe Pippa had gone up to the building site to talk to him before he knocked off. He knew Renzo would be back on Hamo by six to go to his regular Sunday night poker game at the club.

At least he knew the boat was his for the night. Maybe one of Renzo's sons had taken it out for a quick spin while he and Sienna had been in town. He knew two of them had come home for the weekend. 'Okay. I'll see you in the morning.' He disconnected and made his way back to the hotel to wait for Sienna.

***

Sienna was smiling and carried a handful of brochures when she walked out of the day spa and into the foyer of the five star hotel. Danny was waiting for her and her heart kicked up a beat or two.

'Worth the visit?' He smiled down at her and she enjoyed the surge of excitement that ran through her.

'Oh, yes. I made some great contacts and I've found this course I'd like to go to.' She held up the brochure with a tropical vista across the front. 'Pippa's been talking about getting a second therapist. I'm not supposed to know but I have my sources.' She smiled. 'If she does, it will free me up to extend my skills at courses like this. And there was a girl there who's looking for more work.'

176

'Good stuff.' Danny held out his arm and she slipped her hand through the crook of his elbow. 'Ready to go back to the beach now?'

'I am.'

It wasn't long before they were on the beach and heading back into the water for a swim.

'I might have a serious swim this time, if you don't mind,' Sienna said.

'A serious swim?' He raised his eyebrows.

'Exercise.'

'Sure. Go for it.'

'You get your exercise at work every day. You look like you work out at the gym too.'

'No, I don't, no time. But you go swim and I'll float around like a lazy log.' He trailed his fingers down her bare arm.

A sweet ripple of desire clutched at Sienna's stomach, and she lifted her eyes to meet Danny's. In his eyes she saw the instant he decided to kiss her and she couldn't help herself, leaning forward to meet him halfway.

His lips were soft and cool against hers, and she closed her eyes, allowing herself a few seconds of doing what she wanted to do. That was something that didn't happen very often.

Danny groaned and his arms went around her as they stood in the warm shallows, and the pressure of his lips increased. Sienna opened her mouth to welcome him and the world disappeared as he slowly slid his lips back and forth across hers. The noise of water lapping around them, the gentle wind and the cries of the birds all disappeared as warmth suffused her. Despite the warmth, goose bumps ran up and down her back and arms, and an exquisite pleasure tugged at her lower belly.

Finally Danny pulled back and rested his forehead on hers. 'I'm sorry. I took a liberty I promised myself I wouldn't take. But, Sienna, I cannot get you from my thoughts. I love being with you.'

She decided to be honest. 'I am the same, Danny. And don't worry, I won't read too much into a simple kiss that has celebrated this beautiful day we have spent together.' Pulling away from his hold, her voice was brisk, even though her insides and legs were jelly. 'Now I am going to have a swim, while you lie in the water like your lazy log.'

'I'll start to get the barbeque ready while you have your exercise. I'll enjoy watching you.'

Sienna walked into the deeper water and set off on a brisk swim. She hadn't wanted Danny to see she was upset, even though she'd told him the truth. She had enjoyed his kiss, but that didn't mean she was going to get involved with him, even though he didn't seem keen to get involved anyway. He gave off mixed signals, and she didn't want to get hurt.

She wouldn't get hurt. Sienna knew very well not to give her trust—or love—to anyone.

Remember Max, she told herself. Once she reached the deeper water, she put her head down and focused her thoughts.

With each stroke, her mind yelled, 'Pull' as she relived the game that she had played with her little brother and the toy train he'd loved. To this day, she couldn't bear to see toys like that, and had avoided seeing her friends at home after they had children.

'Pull, 'enna, pull,' Max would squeal.

His baby laughter surrounded her as she churned through the water.

I loved him so much. His little voice churned through her head as she swam and she stroked harder and harder trying to clear the surging memories. Thoughts of dangerous creatures, sharks and stingers and crocodiles, were far from her mind. Now Danny was the only danger to her, and she had to do something about that.

Do something, do something, do something. The words blended together as she closed her eyes and swam harder and faster.

Sienna swam back and forth across the bay until she was exhausted and could barely lift her arms. As she tried to wade to the beach, she knew she had pushed herself too hard, and as her legs gave way she sank into the water. Lying back in the warm shallows she let her fingers brush against the tidal ridges in the sand, and smiled as tiny fish nibbled at her toes.

But she knew she had found the strength to resist Danny. She was strong, and she would not be tempted and she would not be hurt.

She would not put herself in that place again.

***

Danny packed up the last of the dishes and leftovers and

put them into the cooler bag, stowing the bag beneath the barbeque that he'd wheeled to the back of the cabana. On the way through the glade, he picked a frangipani flower. Sienna was standing near the edge of the water looking up at the stars, and he gently tucked it behind her ear.

'You are amazing,' he said looking down at his damp board shorts and crumpled T-shirt. He knew his hair would be a wild mass of tangled curls from the salt water.

'Amazing?' Her laugh was quiet. 'I don't think so.'

'You are, Sienna. We've been on the beach most of the day. We've been for a long walk, you've had a huge swim and sat on the sand and now look at you. You look like you've stepped from the pages of a beauty or fashion magazine. Your hair is perfect, your face is beautiful and your dress is unwrinkled. Your white jacket is spotless, and highlights your gorgeous hair.'

'I learned to be perfect at a very young age. But don't be fooled, Danny, it is only superficial. I am far from perfect within.'

He shook his head, and then was surprised by the bitterness in her voice; he hadn't heard that before. 'You are perfection.' Unable to help himself, despite his vow to himself that he would not touch her again, he held his arms open, and she stepped in and put her head on his shoulder. He lifted one hand and gently smoothed her hair. 'None of us are perfect. We all hide much of ourselves.' He lifted his head and looked down at her, her auburn hair glowing in the dim light of the new moon. 'Can we stay friends? Maybe until we can be more?'

Disappointment shot through him when she shook her head, but her words reassured him.

'Yes, we can stay friends, Danny, but we can never be more. If you knew the real me, trust me, you wouldn't want more.'

He spoke quietly. 'If you knew the real me, you would run a mile.'

Her head shook again, this time more vehemently. 'No, Danny. You are a good person, I know that, and I'm really sorry I have no more to offer you.'

His forehead rested against hers again, and he smoothed her hair with one hand. 'Don't say never. Let me get my life sorted and then be open to me. Will you agree to that?'

'I can't promise anything.' Tears filled her eyes as she

looked up at him. 'But I have had one of the best days of my life today, and I love being with you. If I could be different I would agree, but I can't.'

'Why? Can you tell me?' His hands caressed her shoulders and for a few seconds she was tempted to give in and admit that she could fall in love with him.

'It is a long story, but all you need to know is what you see is not the real me. I strive for perfection in my appearance and in my manner, and in my work, to cover the person that I am. The person who is never good enough. The person who is lacking in everything.'

He shook his head. 'I can't accept that. I see you for what you are, Sienna. You are a good and kind person. A person I would find it very easy to love if I was able to.'

Sienna smiled though her tears. 'We are a fine pair, aren't we? Do you want to share with me what makes you so unhappy?'

'No, I can't. But I am hoping that very soon the source of my unhappiness and my dilemma will be gone. And then, I promise you, I am going to do everything I can to win your heart.'

'Oh, Danny, that is a beautiful thing to say, but please don't. There is no heart there to win.'

'I will not give up, I promise you that.'

Sienna knew her smile was sad. 'And I will not give in because it will only lead to heartbreak.'

Before she could step back, Danny pulled her closer, and she couldn't resist. She felt safe and happy when he was holding her. He ran his hands down the back of her jacket but she could feel the heat of his touch through the thin fabric. Sienna sighed, reached up and ran her fingers through his wild curls. It was as though her body had a mind of its own, but no matter how hard she tried, it was impossible to move away from him.

She felt safe.

And cared for.

Sienna leaned into Danny; her lips were a breath away from his. He lowered his head, and she opened to him, her hands running down his strong shoulders and slipping naturally beneath his shirt. Danny groaned as she pressed her fingers into the warmth of his back. She welcomed his kiss as he deepened it, wanting, needing his mouth on hers.

'You are the most beautiful woman I have ever known,' he murmured against her mouth. 'You've bewitched me. You're in my blood.'

His voice was low and husky, and Sienna closed her eyes. A spark of mutual need passed between them as her heart pounded against his chest. She leaned against him for a moment and then lifted her head and smiled up at him as he lowered his mouth to hers again.

She was being very foolish, but her heart had taken over and was commanding her mind.

And her actions.

God help her, because she couldn't help herself.

Chapter 10

Sienna

Finally Danny lifted his head and stepped back. Sienna's chest was rising and falling, quickly, and she took a deep breath, unsure of what to say or do. Never in her life had she felt like that before. Being out of his arms filled her with a familiar emptiness.

Danny looked down at her as they both caught their breath. Sienna couldn't help smiling at him as he held her gaze. Finally he reached over and loosely linked his arms around her waist. 'It is good to see you happy, *bella*. It makes my heart sing that I can make you smile.'

'You make me feel. . . it is hard to find the right word,' she said softly. 'I guess it's because you make me feel good about myself. It's been a wonderful day. Thank you for bringing me to your beach. I will never forget today.'

Danny rested his forehead against hers and his breath was warm against her skin. 'Sometimes when I watch you when we are working, you look sad. When you smile, your expression lights up, but I do not see you smile very often. Tell me, is it because you would rather be at home in Lucerne? Are you homesick?'

She shook her head slowly, and lifted her head again. 'No. That is the last place I would want to be. It does not hold happy memories for me.'

'A broken heart? Or should I not ask?'

'Yes, a broken heart, but not from a man.'

'Would it help you to talk about it??

Tears welled in Sienna's eyes at the kindness in Danny's voice.

'I have never spoken of it. Not even to Eliza.'

His arms tightened around her. 'If it would help . . . '

'Let's sit on the sand for a while, And then you must take me home.'

The sand was still warm beneath their legs as they sat a

little way from the water's edge. Danny sat behind her, his arms around her. Sienna leaned back and rested her head on his shoulder. Taking another deep breath, she began to speak,

'When I was thirteen-years-old, my brother and I were swimming in the lake. He was only three, and he loved to be in the water. My mother was in her chair under the tree and watching him when I swam out into the lake. She checked on him and he was sitting up on the grass playing with his toy cars, and she read her book. She didn't see him run to the water. I think he was trying to come to me. When I swam back to the shore, he wasn't there. There had been no noise; he just went in over his head and drowned. Without a sound. We didn't find his little body for two days.' Her voice cracked.

'I'm sorry. That would have been unbearable for your family.' Danny's arms were comforting as they tightened around her.

'I've never told anyone about it, because I carried so much guilt. If I hadn't swum out—'

'Hush.' His lips were warm against her cheek, and she sighed.

'No, not yet. You will understand more about me, and why I will never marry. I want to tell you the rest. My father blamed me, and I could do nothing right from that day. I tried so hard to be perfect in everything I did, but my poor mama was in and out of hospital and my father, he sent me away to boarding school. That was where I met Eliza, and she was like a breath of fresh air to me. We had many holidays together, until the time came when I let her down too.'

Danny shook his head. 'You cannot blame yourself for things that happen. I am sure Eliza would agree.'

'I wasn't a good friend to her either. I should have tried harder to stop her making a mistake. A deadly mistake.'

Danny didn't ask what she was talking about. 'Sienna, I have only known you a short time, but I have seen how you are with people and I know you are a good person. That is very clear to me.'

'I try so hard, but I can never believe that I will make the right decisions. I shouldn't have accepted your invitation today, but I could not say no. I could not resist you. I am starting to care too much for you, and I will let you down too. I will not do that.'

Before she knew it, Danny's arms moved and she was lying against his chest. As she looked up at him, she could see that he was troubled and her heart sank.

'Sienna, you will not let me down, and I ask you to trust me. Trust me, until I can tell you my story. It is too soon, yet. There are others involved. Will you trust me?'

His dark eyes were intent on hers, and she nodded slowly.

'Yes, I will trust you.'

Danny's head lowered to hers, and this time his kiss held a promise as his lips took hers. She lifted her arms and put them around his neck, never wanting to leave him.

Eventually he pulled back and she caught her breath.

'I need to take you home before we both lose control, and cause too many problems for each other. I am not going to give up on you, Sienna. Can you accept that?'

She nodded, knowing that she couldn't bear to let him go. 'Yes,' she whispered.

'Just wait there and I'll get the tender out of the boatshed and take you over to the cruiser. It will only take us ten minutes to get to Pentecost Island once the motor warms up. It is very powerful and can go very fast.' Danny stood, pulled her to her feet, and kissed her again. 'We must go.' His voice was ragged. 'Or I cannot trust myself.'

'I trust you,' she said softly. Sienna crossed to the tree where the towels were spread and picked up her bag. She was very thankful they hadn't been lying here where it was more secluded when Danny had kissed her because she knew what could have easily happened.

She would not have been able to resist. Because Sienna knew she wanted Danny as much as he wanted her. The doors of the boatshed creaked open and then she heard a rough sliding noise followed by a splash as the tender hit the water. She hoped this vessel was bigger than the one on Evie's boat, because she wasn't sure about going out into the deep water in such a small boat.

Don't be silly, she told herself. It wasn't far to the buoys where the cruiser was moored; she'd swum almost to the buoys today. A motor started and then a light came on as Danny brought the small rubber boat up to the beach and jumped out.

'What about the towels under the tree?' she asked.

'I'll get them when I come back.'

'It's going to be a late night for you, and it's a work day tomorrow.'

'I'll be fine.' He held out his hand and helped her into the tender. 'Sit in the middle. No rogue waves will splash you there.'

Sienna did as he asked and sat straight and stiff on the wooden seat in the middle of the low boat, her bag clutched firmly in her lap. Danny climbed in and pushed the boat into the shallows with one foot before starting the motor again, and soon they were heading across the bay towards the large motor cruiser.

There was very little wind, and even though the sea was like a mill pond, Sienna's mouth was still dry with fear. She focused on her breathing and blocked her mind from the memories that tried to intrude. Memories she had summoned by being honest with Danny. She was fine when she was in the water and swimming, but the thought of falling from a boat and not having control had always frightened her.

He slowed the boat, turning it in a wide arc and then cut the engine when they were about fifty metres from the large boat. The small boat rocked in the wash as it crossed its own choppy wake.

'What's wrong?' she asked, clutching the side of the boat as panic clawed at her chest.

Danny's voice was low. 'I think someone might be squatting on the boat. I noticed it had been moved this afternoon, and now I'm sure I saw a light just go on and off in the cabin below decks.'

'What are you going to do?'

'I'm going to row the rest of the way, so they can't hear us approach, and then go onboard and check it out.' Danny reached over and gripped her hand, and his voice was low. 'I'll tie the tender to the back of the boat, but I want you to sit there quietly while I see if someone is there.'

Sienna nodded. She didn't think her legs would hold her anyway if she had to move. For the next five minutes the oars in the water were the only sound, and then a single bump as the tender hit the back of the boat.

'You stay here and keep quiet. I won't be long.'

'You be careful,' she whispered, her heart in her throat.

Danny tied the rope to the metal steps and went to swing himself up out of the boat. Sienna's hand went to her chest and she gasped as a sudden strong light flashed in their faces from the boat.

'You lying little shit,' a loud voice boomed from above them,

'Stay there, please Sienna,' Danny touched her shoulder briefly and pulled himself up the ladder.

'What are you doing here, Renzo?' His voice was like steel, and Sienna held her breath. 'You told me you were at work. Have you been on the boat all day?'

Renzo! It was Danny's brother. Sienna dropped her head into her hands. How guilty they must look skulking around and coming to the boat in the dark.

'What do you think you're doing?' Renzo's voice was slurred.

'I was going to use the cruiser to take a friend home, but it looks like you're otherwise occupied.' Sudden light bathed the whole deck of the large boat as another light came on and Sienna looked up to where the two brothers stood near the back of the boat. Renzo was bare-chested, and an unfamiliar blonde woman wearing only the bottom half of a bikini now stood on the top of the ladder peering down at Sienna. Her bare breasts jiggled as the boat rocked, and Sienna looked away, unsure of what was going on.

Renzo grabbed Danny's T-shirt and shook him. 'I told you to stay away from that Swiss girl, but you can't keep it in your pants, can you?'

'Look who's talking.' Danny's voice was full of disgust as he pulled away from his brother. 'What would your wife say about you entertaining your lady friend on the family boat?'

'About the same thing that *your* wife would say to you, little brother.'

Sienna gasped and her world spun.

His wife? Danny was married?

Harsh words were flung back and forth above her, and Sienna couldn't believe it when the woman started laughing.

'Bring your friend up here, Danny, and we'll all have a drink,' she said.

Sienna put her hands over her face. She had trusted Danny,

and she had told him her deepest secret, and all the time he had been pretending to being interested, simply so she would sleep with him. She had not long ago told him she trusted him.

Disgust flooded through her, and she felt dirty. Her father had been right.

All she wanted to do was run away from this awful, awful situation and hide, but she was trapped on a boat—a tiny boat—off an island. It was like something from a soap opera, but this was real.

Very real.

And she had no one to blame but herself.

Renzo's voice boomed again. 'Take the whore home and then go and wait for your wife.'

Danny charged at his brother, his fist raised and the woman screamed as the brothers' heads connected. Danny fell back against the side of the deck. Renzo lunged for him and threw a punch that connected with Danny's nose. Sienna widened her eyes as blood sprayed from his face. She felt so helpless sitting down here in this stupid little rubber boat, looking up at them.

If she knew how to start the motor, she would have untied the boat and headed to the shore. She looked down at the oars sitting on the floor of the rubber boat. As the idea came to her, she reached up to untie the boat and row to the shore. After all, she had swum that far today, and she knew how to row. Anger fuelled her.

As her fingers struggled with the knot the light from above was blocked as someone climbed down the ladder at the back of the boat. Sienna scurried back as far as she could without falling over the back of the boat, worried that Renzo had come to hurt her after he had assaulted his brother.

'What are you doing? Quickly move to the middle again.'

Not that that was any better.

It was Danny.

Danny who had a wife. Sienna fought the urge to be sick.

Oh, would she never learn?

Chapter 11

Sienna

Sienna stared straight ahead as Danny clambered into the boat. He stepped past her without a word and started the motor. He turned the boat in a wide arc, away from the boat and away from the shore towards the open water.

'Where are you taking me?' Her voice was quiet and shaky.

'I'm taking you back to the island.'

He stood above her at the back of the small boat, one hand on the tiller as he steered them, and the other holding his face.

'Which island? Back to Hamilton? Drop me at the beach and I will walk back and get a hotel room.'

He leaned forward so she could hear him over the motor. 'No. I'm taking you to your island. It will take a little longer than on the cruiser, but the water is calm and still and it's safe.'

Sienna blinked as something wet landed on her face. She looked down at her jacket and realised that the blood from Danny's nose had dripped onto her face and jacket.

Her fear about the trip across the wide waterway in this small boat was immediately replaced by concern. 'You're bleeding,' she said.

'I know.'

'You are not going to pass out and fall in the water, are you?'

'No, it's only a bleeding nose.'

It was hard to see in the dim light, but Sienna swivelled around looking for a rag or a towel to staunch the bleeding, but there was only a small bucket and a rope on the floor. Without hesitation, she shrugged her jacket off, rolled it into a wad, and passed it up to him.

'Thank you,' Danny's voice was muffled as he held it to his face.

She turned her back to him and squeezed her eyes closed as

they crossed the open water. Goose bumps ran up and down her arms and she wasn't sure if it was the cool wind or her fear that was bringing them.

'Please, let us get there safely,' she muttered under her breath as she thought of all the dangers that came with being out on the open water in this tiny boat. They had no lights and any ships or boats that were travelling out here wouldn't see them. There could be whales or sharks or crocodiles, all bigger than the boat, that could roll them over in an instant.

Sienna let all those fearful thoughts crowd her mind because she didn't want to think about what Renzo had said on the cruiser.

How fitting, she thought. Her final mistake would lead to her death by drowning. A fitting punishment in a way, and she wondered how her parents would cope again.

'I will replace your jacket.'

She jumped as Danny spoke and then he reached over and put the stained jacket on the seat beside her.

'No.' The one word was curt.

'Sienna, please listen to me. I will explain what you heard. What Renzo said.'

'No. Just answer one question. Do you have a wife?'

'I do, but—'

'But she doesn't understand you. I don't want to hear it.'

'No, that's—'

Sienna surprised herself as she raised her voice. 'I don't want to listen to you. I don't want to see you again, and I don't want to speak to you. You no longer exist in my world. Do you hear me?'

Danny stood straight and didn't speak again. It took twenty minutes before she could finally see the lights of Pentecost Island ahead. Danny slowed the boat to a crawl as they went across the top of the coral heads out from the jetty, and then he turned the tender to the island. A moment later, the aluminium base scraped onto the shingly sand and the tender came to a stop on the beach.

'Sienna—'

'No.' She picked up her jacket and then held her bag firmly with one hand and held the side of the boat with the other as she stepped over the low rubber side into the shallow water. She didn't care that her good leather sandals were in the water; she just wanted to get away from him.

'No. Just go. Leave me alone.'

'I want to make sure you are all right.'

'Just go.' Her voice was a screech, and she knew if she didn't get away quickly she would fall to her knees on the sand and cry. Putting the bloodstained jacket around her shoulders, she ran towards the path, pleased when she heard the motor start and the boat head back out across the bay.

Chapter 12

Sienna ran to the old house and was pleased it was in darkness. Through her tears, she could see no one was there. It was late, everyone would be in bed, ready for the start of the working week. Her legs were weak and shaking and about to give way, as she ran into the kitchen, flicking the light on before she sank into a chair at the table. Once she had composed herself, she would make a chamomile tea, and then go to bed.

And try not to think of the fool she had made of herself.

Composing herself proved impossible. Every time she managed to hold back a sob, Sienna thought of how Danny had kissed her this afternoon, and how she had been duped by a married man.

She was a stupid, stupid fool, and could do nothing right. Her father had told her that enough times, that she should have remembered. Being on the island with good people had lulled her into a false sense of confidence about herself and her decision-making. Giving into the attraction she had felt since that first day she had seen Danny had been so stupid. She should have known after Pippa's wedding something was not right, but he could be so persuasive. She had listened and believed those sweet words he had fed her this afternoon.

I am a stupid fool.

The age-old story of a woman falling for good looks and a silver tongue. A ragged sob tore through her and as she put her head in her hands the screen door opened behind her.

'My God. Sienna, sweetheart, what on earth has happened? You're bleeding.'

She lifted her head and turned around. Odessa stood in the doorway, her eyes wide, one hand over her mouth. As Sienna shook her head, she hurried across to her.

Sienna managed to put one hand up and speak, but her voice was thick. Mortification flooded through her as she realised her nose was running. 'No. I'm all right. It's not me. Someone else was bleeding and they used my jacket. I'm all right,' she repeated dully. 'Please just leave me. I was about to go to bed.'

'No. I most certainly will not. You look terrible and you can barely speak.' Odessa pulled out a chair and sat beside her. 'Are you sure you're not hurt?'

'Oh, I'm hurt all right.' Sienna managed to pull a grim smile. 'Not physically, but my heart is hurting. Honestly, I'll be all right.' What she couldn't stop was the sob that followed her words.

The words that were at odds with her thoughts. Sienna knew she wasn't all right. She couldn't stay here. The thought of seeing Danny again—and she would have to see him every day while he worked on the island—filled her with shame. She would leave tomorrow. She would get Jiminy to take her to Hamilton Island and she would hide there in a hotel room until she could get a flight home.

Odessa crouched beside her and put one arm along her shoulders. 'I'm not leaving you while you are crying. I'm not going anywhere until I'm sure you really are all right. I'm going to make us both a hot drink. What would you like?' Odessa stood and walked over to the gas stove. On her way, she took the box of tissues off the fridge and put it on the table beside Sienna.

'A chamomile tea, please. The tea bags are in the cupboard next to the fridge. In the green box.' Sienna sniffed and reached over for a tissue. She dabbed at her eyes and then wiped her face. With surprise she looked at the tissue that was stained pink. 'I'm sorry. I must look a fright.'

'Love, you still look perfect after crying your eyes out. Now that you've wiped the blood off your face, you've reassured me. Now, reassure me some more, and tell me what the hell happened. Your jacket is beyond repair.' Odessa turned the gas on and set the kettle on the flame.

Sienna took a breath. What did it matter if she told the truth to Odessa? It couldn't make things any worse than they already were.

'Is the person who's bled all over your jacket all right?'

Sienna shrugged. 'I think so.'

A few minutes later, Odessa poured the hot water onto the tea bags and came back to the table. She placed the mugs in the centre, and then when she was seated, she pulled the large mug across in front of Sienna. 'If you want to tell me what happened it will stay between you and me if that's what you'd prefer.'

'No, it's fine. I'll have to tell Pippa, and Eliza too.'

'Okay.'

Sienna sat straight. 'There was a fight and . . . and . . . Danny got punched in the nose and he had a nosebleed. I gave him my jacket to stop the bleeding. He was above me and some blood dropped down on me when he got back on the tender.'

'O . . . kay. Danny, as in Danny the builder here?'

'Yes.'

'So, is he okay? Was he assaulted?'

Sienna shook her head, and her hair fell forward. Her hands were shaking as she reached up to push it back. 'Not really. It was his brother who hit him.'

'Sounds like you've had a very dramatic night.' Odessa frowned as she reached for the other mug. 'Where did this all happen? Were you on one of the boats out past the bay?'

'On a boat, yes, but not here. We've been over on Hamilton Island all day,' Sienna said softly.

'My God!' Odessa's eyes widened. 'And you came all the way over the Passage on that tiny boat we saw? All the way from Hamo?'

Sienna nodded. 'Yes.'

'And Danny's gone back there now? With a bleeding head and an injury?'

'Yes.'

'I'm sorry, Sienna, but I think we need to call Pippa and Rafe right now. What if he passes out on the way back? It's not safe. Someone needs to make sure he gets back there safely.'

Weariness flowed through Sienna, but she knew Odessa was right. No matter what Danny had done, someone needed to make sure he was safe. That's all she needed. Another drowning on her conscience.

'Yes, call Pippa. Ask her to come down and then I can tell her I am leaving the island tomorrow.' She managed to get the words out before she burst into a fresh round of tears.

Chapter 13

Pippa

It was just before midnight when I heard my mobile ringing inside the house. Rafe and I looked at each other over the candlelit table on the balcony; we had spent a most enjoyable evening making up for the three days he'd been away, and we'd just sat down to an extremely late dinner.

'Stay there,' he said as it stopped ringing. 'I'll get it for you. I pushed my plate away and frowned. A call at this time of night was never good news.

Rafe handed me the phone as he came back outside. 'A missed call from Odessa.'

As he sat beside me, I returned the call and it picked up straight away.

'Odessa, it's me, Pip. What's wrong?'

'We have a bit of a situation here. I think you and Rafe need to come down.'

'Guest problem?'

'No. It's Sienna. She's okay, but we need to talk to you. We're at the house.'

'Okay, we're on our way.'

Rafe and I quicky changed from our PJs and hurried down to Aunty Vi's house. No matter how long I had lived on the island, and how much the old house changed, it was still Aunty Vi's house to me.

The lights glowed yellow at the back of the house and we hurried along the veranda and into the kitchen. Odessa and Sienna were sitting at the table, both holding a mug. Rafe stood back and let me take the lead.

'Okay, so what's the drama?' I said as I stood there looking at Sienna. I didn't like to say anything, but she looked dreadful. 'Is that blood on your dress?' I looked at the jacket on the back of her chair and my eyes widened, as did Rafe's as he followed my gaze.

We listened and when Odessa got to the part about being concerned about Danny getting back safely, Rafe nodded and held his hand out for my phone.

'His number's in your contacts, isn't it?'

I nodded and handed the phone over. Rafe headed out to the veranda, and as I pulled out a chair and sat beside Sienna, I could hear him talking.

'So what happened? Why did Danny bring you home in a tender? It seems a really dangerous thing to do.'

Sienna shook her head slowly and when she looked up at me, her eyes were vacant. 'Neither of us was thinking straight. Renzo had the boat, and after he hit Danny I had to get home.' She looked up as Rafe came back in.

'He's home safe.'

Odessa and I both jumped up to grab Sienna as her eyes rolled back and she slumped in the chair.

'Rafe, quick, can you lift her down onto the floor? In the recovery position.' Since the resort had started up, every one of us had done our emergency first aid training. I looked at Odessa. 'Do you think she's taken something?'

Rafe carefully laid Sienna on the floor, and Odessa grabbed a wad of tea towels from the shelf and put them beneath her head.

'No. I think she's had a shock. She's been coherent since I got here. Dylan and I were on the rocks and we saw her get out of the boat. She ran up here as though the hounds of hell were after her.'

Sienna's eyelids fluttered and she moaned softly and tried to sit up. 'What happened?'

I crouched down beside her. 'You fainted. Are you hurt anywhere?'

'No. I was just upset.'

We had a no drugs tolerance policy on the island, but I had to ask. 'Have you taken anything, Sienna?'

'No. I had a glass of wine this afternoon. Just one. I want to go and have a shower and go to bed.' Her voice was strained. 'I feel dirty.'

Rafe helped her to sit up and Odessa and I looked at each other. She gestured to the veranda and I nodded, before I followed her out.

She spoke softly. 'I only know what I told you about the fight and them coming back on the tender, but one thing Sienna did say was that she was leaving tomorrow. I think something's happened between her and Danny and she wants to get away.'

'Shit.' I shook my head. 'Sorry, that was unprofessional. You don't think he's assaulted her, do you?'

'No. I don't.' Odessa turned back to the kitchen. 'Do you want to talk to her now or in the morning?'

'Now, I think. I'll try and talk some sense into her. Where's she going to go?'

'Look, I'll just go and talk to Dylan. I'll stay in the house tonight and listen out for Sienna if you like.'

'Thank you, that'd be good. I appreciate it, Odessa.'

I stood outside the kitchen as she ran down the back steps and over to the building where she and Dylan each had a room. Although I did wonder if both the rooms were being used very often lately. Odessa and Dylan had struck up a close friendship. I knew Rafe was pleased about it; he thought highly of our new landscape gardener.

I wondered how to handle this at this time of the night.

Eliza would be the one who would know what to do, and who could talk sense to Sienna. They had been friends since boarding school. I was reluctant to call her at this time of night, and I wasn't sure whether they were even moored at the island or had gone for a sail today.

Tomorrow morning would be soon enough, but I was not letting Sienna off the island until Eliza arrived. I turned to go back into the kitchen wondering how much to say.

Sienna was sitting at the table again and I was pleased to see there was some colour back in her cheeks. Rafe was sitting beside her and I took the chair on the other side.

When she spoke, her voice was stronger. 'Pippa, I am really, really sorry for all this. I want to explain to you what has happened and why I have to leave.'

Rafe met my gaze across the table and raised his eyebrows.

'I can't stay here with Danny working on the island every day, and I know he has to stay because there is still so much building to be done.'

I leaned forward. 'Sienna. If Danny has touched you, or

hurt you in any way, he will not be working on the island anymore, so you don't have to worry.'

'Oh no, you can't do that. He's in enough trouble with his brother as it is. He didn't hurt me. I was stupid and trusting, and I just fell for the old lines.' She lifted her head and looked directly at me. 'I found out tonight that Danny has a wife.'

'Ah,' I said. 'Was that the short dark-haired woman with him at the wedding?'

'I guess it was. All I know is that he has a wife. Renzo abused him, and called him names before he punched him. Apparently *he* was on the boat with someone who was not *his* wife.' Sienna sighed and put her hand to her face. 'Danny asked him, "What would his *wife* say about him entertaining a lady on the family boat?" and then Renzo said, "About the same thing that *your* wife would say to you, little brother." And then they punched each other and there was blood everywhere.'

'You have had a big night,' I said.

'It's my own fault. I should never have gone out with Danny. If I had known he was married, I wouldn't have even spoken to him outside of work.'

'Are you sure it's right that he is married? It wasn't just Renzo talking?' I was trying to process everything my Riccardo builders had been up to. Talk about the lives of the rich and famous.

'Yes, he admitted to it when I asked him. I *have* to leave,' Sienna insisted. 'Immediately. I cannot stay with him working here every day. This island is too small. I would be very embarrassed with the mistake I made.'

I sat and looked at her for a long moment. 'No. You are *not* leaving. You have too much passion invested in *Hebe*, and we need you. I need you. You are one of us now, Sienna, and we look out for each other.' I stood and waited until she stood beside me. 'And don't blame yourself. You didn't make a mistake. Danny is the one who is in the wrong. He had no right chasing after you when he was married. Go to bed, and try to forget today. I will find a solution, I promise. Come up to the house when you wake in the morning, and we'll talk some more.'

Sienna's smile grew slowly, and I could tell she believed me. As soon as it was light I would ring Eliza.

And I would be talking to both the Riccardo brothers.

Chapter 14

Pippa

As it turned out, I didn't have to talk to the brothers; Sienna and Eliza came up with a solution, and then a call from Renzo Riccardo put the final touch on our plan. Sienna had called Eliza before I was even awake and I woke up to a text from Eliza, saying she and Phillipe would be in our bay by nine.

Rafe had gone down to talk to the Riccardos when they arrived at their usual time of eight a.m. and I waited with interest to see what information he came back with.

By ten a.m., he was still down there, but the immediate problem was solved; there were smiles all around, even if Sienna's was a little bit fragile.

'Are you sure?' she asked for about the fifth time as we carried a pot of fresh brewed coffee out to the balcony. It was another brilliant day, and I knew that was making everyone seem a little happier.

'I am sure. It's called professional development, and with you already finding a replacement for while you are away'—I had already rung the therapist on Hamilton Island Sienna had spoken to yesterday—'you can leave as soon as you can get into the course.'

Eliza chipped in. 'We've already rung, and there was a place in the course that starts next Monday. We've booked her in. Now all we have to do is get her out to the island.'

Sienna had brought the brochures up with them, and I picked one up.

'Esculanta Island, north of Port Douglas. I've never heard of it, but wow, it looks like a fabulous island. There's a flight direct from Cairns.'

'Philippe and I moored there on the way here,' Eliza said. 'You have no idea of the level of luxury. It is supposed to be the only seven-star island resort in the world.'

'Why have I never heard of it?' I said.

'Because they don't advertise. It has a different name on the map, and it's supposed to be a deserted island, but this resort was developed by a billionaire Englishman two years ago. It's a long way off the coast. It's where the international rich and famous go to be pampered.'

'When I saw the brochure yesterday, I had no idea it would be so expensive. Are you really sure, Pippa?' Sienna's eyes were wide but there were still shadows beneath her makeup.

'Yes. Eliza has offered to pay your way. I'll pay the wages for your replacement while you're gone.' I turned the brochure over and read the description aloud. 'The secluded island retreat is situated on idyllic sand-white beaches overlooking the dazzling blue waters of the Coral Sea. Bird of Paradise Spa has individual treatment villas. For couples, private suites are accessible via a secluded walkway over the water, allowing simultaneous treatments with spectacular views over the sea. The spa also offers vitality pools, steam rooms, saunas and Japanese water massage, with treatments inspired by age-old traditions that promote holistic rejuvenation.' I shook my head. 'I think we should have a girls' weekend in a few months.'

Eliza chuckled. 'We'd have to prise you away from your husband.'

An idea took form in my head. Rafe and I still hadn't had a honeymoon. As though I had conjured him up by simply thinking about him, my husband opened the side gate and came out onto the balcony. He caught my eye and nodded slightly to me, and I knew everything had gone well.

'Coffee smells good,' he said rubbing his hands together. 'I'll grab a mug and then tell you all the good news.' My lovely man squeezed Sienna's shoulder as he walked past her on his way inside. 'You can stop worrying, Sienna. Danny's not coming back to the island.'

He was soon back with a mug, and the plate of salted caramel cake that we hadn't got to last night before the frantic call had come from Odessa.

'Renzo looked a bit worse for wear—he's got a good shiner—but he was very subdued,' Rafe said after his coffee was poured. 'He said Danny has gone away to work on another big project, and he has another builder coming here to take his place.

Sienna, he particularly asked me to apologise to you for his behaviour last night, and to tell you he very much regrets that you had to witness the falling out with his brother.'

Sienna nodded and put her head down, but didn't speak.

'Sienna's going away for ten days to do a course later this week,' Eliza said.

'And then she's coming back to Pentecost Island to stay here,' I said with a smile.

An excellent solution all around,' Rafe said. He gestured to the cake on the table. 'Does anyone what to share the last piece with me?'

Sienna looked up and smiled. 'I think you deserve to have it all. Thank you, Rafe, and thank you, Pippa and Eliza for being so supportive. Her eyes were bright with tears. 'It's different for me. Apart from you, Eliza, I've never had support like this before. I've always had to stumble through and get myself out of trouble.'

Chapter 15

Danny

At six a.m. late on Thursday, Danny picked up his kitbag and his laptop and looked around the house he'd shared with Lucia for the past two and a half years. Although shared wasn't the right word for how they'd lived. He'd slept downstairs and used the kitchen when she was next door at Renzo and Maria's house. When she was home he'd walked down to a café or a hotel and have a meal. Danny would never forgive his brothers for putting him in that situation.

A situation that had just stuffed up any chance of telling Sienna he was in love with her. He had no right to, and now, he knew he would never see her again. His heart ached as he thought about it, and he tried to hold back the anger with his family. There was nothing to be gained by blame.

The floor of the living room was littered with shopping bags; dirty plates and coffee cups covered every flat surface. But he could ignore the mess; he was out of here for good. The mess had nothing to do with the way he was feeling; the last few days had been the worst of his entire life.

Renzo had sacked him from the company, and then twenty-four hours later—after he'd sobered up and thought about the situation—had reinstated him. Danny had told him to shove it, and had found himself another building job up the coast within a day.

Maria, his brother's wife, had packed her bags and taken Aldo—the only child who still lived on Hamo with them—and moved north to her sister's farm near Ingham. Danny had heard the argument from next door, Renzo had grovelled, but Maria's screams had filled the air.

'Last time you promised it had only happened once, and I forgave you. How long has this one been going on, *tuo marito traditore?* I am going to my sister's and I will not be back. You will hear from my lawyer. *Sei un sacco di feccia.*'

Danny put his pillow over his head as the argument next door continued well into the night. He didn't blame Maria one bit. She had put up with Renzo's infidelity for a long time, and he knew she'd forgiven him more than the one time she'd mentioned. She was right; his brother was a cheat and a scum bag. And the very reason that Danny swore he would never marry. Renzo's lack of commitment to his wife and family was a warning.

And Lucia . . . Danny shook his head; he couldn't stand to think about Lucia's intentions. A waste, a total bloody waste of almost three years.

And as for Sienna, his chest literally ached when he thought of never seeing her again. He now knew the meaning of heartbroken.

He pulled the door closed behind him for the last time. He would never come back to these islands; the memories were too sad.

##

The airport at Hamilton Island was crowded. School had ended for the year and locals were leaving the island to head to families around the country for Christmas. The December tourist influx had started and the noise and the bustle of the airport soothed Danny as he waited for his flight to Cairns to be called.

When he'd walked in, he'd caught a flash of auburn hair in the crowd milling around the check in counter and he'd looked away. He didn't want that surge of longing to hit him every time he spotted a woman with the same colour hair as Sienna.

An announcement that the arrival time of the incoming flight had been delayed by a few minutes came over the PA system. Danny looked over at the café; the crowd had thinned and he decided he had time to grab a sandwich and a coffee before it was time for him to board. He hoisted his laptop bag onto his shoulder and walked across to the café.

Five minutes later as he sat at a high table and drank his coffee, the jet taxied to the tarmac outside the building.

His new life was about to begin.

No wife. No family. No women.

***

Sienna's stomach churned as she sat beside Eliza in the business lounge at Hamilton Island airport. The flight had been delayed slightly and Eliza had gone to the bar to get them both a glass of champagne.

'It might be early, but it will help settle your nerves a bit, love. And I don't have to drive. Philippe is waiting at the marina and we're going to have dinner on Hamo,' Eliza said as she placed two icy glasses on the table between them. She settled in the comfy sofa chair, and leaned back. Sienna met her gaze as Eliza's brow creased.

'For the tenth time today, Liza, I am fine. Stop worrying about me. I feel much better. Just embarrassed at the performance I put on.'

Eliza pulled a face. 'I know you too well. Your face is perfect, your clothes are immaculate. Not a line, not a frown, not a wrinkle on your face or a shadow under your eyes but I can tell when you're nervous.' She pointed to Sienna's foot as it jigged on the floor beneath the table. 'Aha! See!'

Sienna rolled her eyes, but she smiled. 'For the *eleventh* time, I am fine. Danny has gone from the island, and he won't be back. Yes, I'm upset, but you know me, I'm strong, I'll get over it.'

'You are strong.' Eliza raised her eyebrows. 'I hope I can believe you.'

'You can. I'm looking forward to this course and learning new techniques. And I'm super excited about seeing this resort. Seven stars! I didn't know they gave more than five.'

'I don't think they do.' Eliza's tone held cynicism and her gaze stayed on Sienna.

It was so hard to stay upbeat and pretend to be happy when all Sienna wanted to do was curl up in a corner. But she knew if she did that, Eliza would worry about her the whole time she was gone.

'But to be honest, we only walked past the pool to go to the bar when we called in there, and it was pretty incredible. The male staff were all in white tuxedos.' Eliza put her hand over her mouth as she stifled a giggle.

Sienna couldn't help smiling. 'What's so funny about that? I think it sounds very Gatsbyish.'

Eliza's giggle turned into a snort. 'Even the pooper scooper men wore tuxedos and the shiniest black shoes I've ever seen.'

Sienna's giggle followed naturally. 'Pooper scooper men! What on earth are they?'

Eliza was shaking with laughter now. 'Oh my God. Wait until you see it. Behind the huge swimming pool, there's this spectacular water feature. A huge lake with an artificial waterfall cascading down a manmade cliff. It's really beautiful, but it has ducks paddling around on it, and what do ducks do?'

This time Sienna snorted as she remembered the trip she and Eliza had taken to Scotland when they'd finished school. They had spent the afternoon at a whisky distillery, watching the ducks in a pond in the garden as they floated around with their little bums sticking up in the air. She and Eliza had lost it; laughing until they cried. The more the other patrons looked at them, confused by what they were laughing at, the harder they laughed. The next morning they decided it was more the whisky than the ducks that had brought them undone. They each had the headache to prove it.

'Paddle with their heads down?'

Eliza snorted again. 'That too. God, I'd forgotten about that trip. We had the best time, didn't we? No, they poo and the resort at Esculanta Island have men in white tuxedos whose sole job is to scoop up the duck poo into little purpose-built poo collectors.'

'I can't wait to see it all. Maybe we'd better suggest that to Pippa for when the new pool goes in.'

'No, not that, but I do have some ideas for the pool.' Eliza's smile was wide. 'I am going to suggest we hire a pool boy who is built.'

'Built?'

'Built, as in a pleasure to look at. I want you to back me when I broach it to Pippa. You just check out the action around the pool at Esculanta. Phillipe almost had to drag me away. He reckoned I was salivating.' Eliza smiled. 'The pool boys wear the bottom half of a tuxedo only, and they come around with silver trays carrying hot towels to refresh the sunbakers. With silver tongs to hand them over.'

'No wonder Phillipe dragged you away. Okay, I'll check it out. This place sounds as good as it looked on the brochure.'

They both listened as the first call was made for the flight to board.

'Hurry up and drink your bubbles.' Eliza reached over and

held Sienna's arm. 'Now, despite your broken heart, I want you to promise me you'll try to forget you ever met Danny Riccardo and have the best time while you're there.'

Sienna leaned forward and hugged Eliza. 'Thank you, *meine liebe Freundin.* You are the best friend a girl could ask for.'

Eliza hugged her back. 'And you remember that the rest of the girls on Pentecost care about you too. We're all worried about you.'

'All good. When I get back, I'll practise on you all. A pampering session.'

'Sounds good to me. Now have you got everything? Your bag? Your boarding pass?'

'Yes, Mama.'

They stood and quickly finished off their drinks, and headed out to the boarding gate. As she moved away from Eliza with a wave, Sienna looked up at the jet and she could have sworn it was Danny ducking his head to enter the front door of the plane.

She shook her head as she handed over her pass to the steward at the door. She was seeing him everywhere. That had to stop.

'Have a good trip, madam.'

'Thank you.' Sienna looked ahead as she strode towards the plane. That was the last time she would let herself think about Danny Riccardo.

Ever.

Chapter 16

Sienna- Esculanta Island

Being in the second row of the large jet, Sienna was first to disembark at Cairns airport. She glanced at her fine gold watch, conscious of the time; the slight delay on the departure on the flight from Hamilton Island made the time between the two flights a bit tight. At least she didn't have to worry about going to the baggage carousel to get her suitcase. She'd been assured as she'd boarded that her luggage would be sent across to the small airline that flew out to the island.

Excitement fizzed in her chest as she made her way to the lounge at the end of the building where her flight would board in fifteen minutes. The same as Hamilton Island, the airport was crowded with tourists in brightly-coloured clothes and looking relaxed and happy. For the first time since Sunday night, she let go of some of the sadness and tension that had held her in its unrelenting grip since Renzo and Danny had fought on the motor cruiser. She was going to do her best to put it aside and focus on this course. She had flown in early as she had decided to have a short luxury holiday for the weekend before she moved to the other side of the island where the course was being held. It was costing a fortune, but Sienna told herself she deserved it. Even though he had let her down in the worst possible way, telling Danny her story had been cathartic. This was the first step in her healing.

Somehow.

Pippa had smiled when Sienna had told her she was going to have a beauty treatment on the island while she was a guest. She had walked down to the wharf where Eliza and Phillipe had picked her up for the trip across to Hamilton Island.

'Sort of like a mystery shopper,' she'd said. 'You make sure you enjoy your time there, Sienna. You've been working very hard. Don't worry about *Hebe* while you're away. I was impressed with Jenny from Hamo when I spoke to her. Her light-hearted manner will entertain the guests, although I have a feeling she was putting it on a bit with all those jokes and funny sayings. She seems a bit of a character, but I did warm to her. She'll fit in well. If you're happy with her work, we might put her on as a second therapist and add another treatment room in the next couple of months.

At least Danny wouldn't be there to build it, Sienna thought.

Pippa's eyes had been kind and sympathetic as she'd looked at Sienna. 'That is if you've really decided to stay? You know we don't want to lose you? You're one of us now.'

'Yes, I've committed to you, and I love being on the island. And I love working with all of you. I've never had so many friends before. I'm here to stay for as long as I can.'

Sienna settled in a seat beside the window as she waited for her flight. When she turned her phone on, it buzzed with an incoming message.

Probably Eliza checking on her again.

Sienna's smile faded as she read the message from her father in Lucerne: **Your mother has been unwell but she is recovered now.**

The only messages she ever had from her father were sent with the sole intention of making her feel guilty, but she had long stopped letting them worry her.

Mostly anyway.

This message was having a swipe at her for being overseas.

Sienna's fingers flew over the phone as she sent a brief reply. **I am pleased Mama has recovered.**

She was determined not to let her father's communication bother her, so she focused on watching the planes take off and land. Gradually, her breathing returned to normal, and her hands relaxed in her lap. It was only a matter of minutes before a small plane with blue and gold writing on the side landed.

A *very* small seaplane.

Her excitement was replaced with nerves as she watched only four passengers duck their heads as they came out the low door of the plane. They were smiling and laughing, so the flight couldn't be that bad, she told herself firmly.

She'd had the choice between a fifteen-minute flight or a

two-hour launch trip from Port Douglas, and the logistics of simply transferring flights was the easier option. It had been an easy choice, but now that she saw the tiny seaplane, her stomach plummeted.

The pilot exited the plane and walked across to the terminal; a tall man in a white shirt with gold epaulettes, he carried himself with a smile and confidence.

Maybe it wouldn't be so bad, she thought. It was a popular island, and no planes had crashed into the sea yet. When the flight was called, she stood, and then, with a young couple and another single woman, Sienna made her way to the desk at the door, her boarding pass in hand. The pilot was standing beside the steward at the gate and he smiled at each of them as they made their way to the gate.

'Good afternoon,' he said to Sienna with a wide smile. 'It is a pleasure to have you on our flight, madam.'

She nodded and followed the three other passengers across the tarmac to the small seaplane. The pilot caught up with her as she reached the steps. He held the metal frame steady as the couple, followed by the other woman, and then Sienna climbed into the plane after them. She had to duck her head, and it was only the fact that the door closed behind her, and the steps were wheeled away, that kept her on the plane and hurriedly sitting in one of the six empty seats.

When she was seated, she realised that she'd sat next to the other woman who appeared to be travelling alone.

Once she was buckled into her seatbelt, her sweaty hands slipping on the clasp, Sienna leaned back and closed her eyes.

Fifteen minutes, that's all she had to endure, she thought, wishing she was back in her hut on Pentecost Island.

'You know the worst of these small planes?' a shaky voice whispered beside her.

Sienna opened her eyes and for the first time took notice of the young woman she was sitting beside.

She shook her head. 'No, what is?'

'The fact that you can see through the windscreen in front of the pilot and watch him flying the plane. I swore I would never do this again after the last time.'

'The last time?' Sienna looked at the woman with the

strong Irish accent who was probably close to her age.

'Yes, I was flying to a lodge in Canada in a plane just like this and when the pilot let go of the steering wheel, I screamed at him and asked what in the name of Mary and Joseph he thought he was doing.' The woman giggled. 'I really lost it. I asked him who was flying the effing plane.'

Sienna smiled, already enjoying her company. 'And what did he say?'

'He turned around and grinned at me, and waggled both his hands and said. "Mr Autopilot". He asked me out for a drink when we landed, and I spent a few weeks in Alaska with him. And now here I am again. Another small plane flying itself. I should have taken the launch.' She held her hand out. 'Hi, I'm Isla.'

'I'm Sienna.' She shook Isla's hand. 'And I was just thinking the same thing.'

'Let's close our eyes and pretend we're on a bus,' Isla said, doing just that. 'We can talk with our eyes shut.' She giggled again. 'My five brothers tell me I can talk underwater too. If you get sick of me talking, just tell me to button it. I'm used to it.'

Sienna smiled again, put her head back, and closed her eyes, but before she could reply, the microphone crackled, and the pilot began the safety briefing. Once she knew where the life jacket was and heard that they wouldn't be going high enough to need oxygen masks in an emergency, Sienna relaxed a little more.

As soon as their pilot stopped talking, Isla filled the silence. 'How long are you on the island for? You are obviously going for a holiday. You look very elegant.'

Sienna opened her eyes and looked down at her silk trousers and loose tunic top. 'This is pretty much what I wear all the time. Just in different colours. Easy to pack when I'm travelling.'

'Well, you look lovely. I always wear jeans and shorts, but I did pack a couple of dresses for the island. Are you German?' she asked. 'I'm trying to pick your accent.'

'Swiss,' Sienna replied. 'We speak Swiss German in Lucerne.'

'Lucerne! I was there last year,' Isla exclaimed. 'I had my photo taken on that gorgeous bridge with all the flower baskets.'

'The *Kapellbrücke?* The Chapel bridge.'

'Yes, that was it. Remind me to show you the photos on my phone when we land. I met up with this gorgeous Italian guy in Cologne and we travelled to Switzerland together in his old Kombi van. He was the best-looking guy I've ever met.'

Sienna froze when Isla mentioned her Italian companion. That was the last thing she wanted to hear about.

Sienna's lack of response went unnoticed as Isla kept talking. 'I'm going over to the island to do a course there,' she said, opening her eyes again as the plane began to taxi down the tarmac. Isla shook her head. 'It still beats me how a plane can take off from a tarmac and then land on the bloody water.'

'What do you mean the water. I saw it was a seaplane but isn't there an airport on the island?'

'No, we come down in the harbour and then go into the marina. I read up my brochures.'

'Oh dear.' Sienna's mouth dried and she fanned herself with the boarding pass she was still clutching. 'I should have got the launch out instead of the plane.'

'I may still get it back, depending on how boyo here handles the water landing.' Isla gestured to the captain. She narrowed her eyes as Sienna watched her. 'Although he is quite cute, don't you think?

'Sssh. He'll hear you.'

'That's fine, lovey. Then he knows I'm interested.'

Sienna couldn't help smiling. Isla was like a breath of fresh air. 'Okay, so tell me what sort of course you're going to do,' she asked. She wasn't sure if the beauty course was the only one, or if there was a training centre at the resort for different trades.

'Promise not to laugh?'

Sienna nodded, wondering what was coming.

'I mightn't look like one, but I'm a beauty therapist.' Isla's accent got broader the faster she spoke and Sienna had to concentrate to understand the words delivered in the Irish brogue.

'Excellent,' Sienna said. 'So am I. Doing the course too, that is.'

'Oh, how cool is that, darlin'! We can hang together. Although I must admit I did splurge. I'm having three days at the resort before the course starts. My dear Da sent me money for my birthday so he was sure I could eat for the next three months, but I figured I'd eat well enough at the resort to last me. Once I've tried out the cocktail bar and the restaurants, I want to check out the day spa.'

The giggle bubbled in Sienna's chest, and she couldn't help laughing as she held up her hand for a high five. 'Me too! The holiday for me as well and I'm planning the "mystery shopper" thing too.'

'Oh, that's even better.' Isla looked out the window and her eyes widened. 'Wow, look we've already taken off and we're over the water.'

'I have a feeling this is going to be a good weekend.' Sienna calmed and the ache in her heart lessened a tiny bit more. 'Now, Isla, tell me where are you from?'

By the time they landed with barely a splash, taxied across the water and disembarked, and were met by a welcome guide in the luxurious arrivals lounge, Sienna knew Isla's entire life history. Listening to her talk—and yes, it was true, she could talk underwater, but she was fun—had made the trip go in an instant. Before they knew it, the pilot was announcing they had arrived on Esculanta Island.

The captain—who *was* very good looking—held Sienna's hand a little longer than he needed to as he helped her down the stairs. 'You are a very beautiful woman, *bella.'*

She stiffened when he called her *bella*, nodded briskly and pulled her hand away. Her heels clicked on the concrete as she crossed to the air conditioned arrivals room, and the welcome guide held the door open for her.

'Welcome to Esculanta Island, madame.'

Sienna smiled and waited for Isla to come in, but when she looked through the large window overlooking the marina, she could see her new friend, head to head with the captain. From a distance his dark hair and broad shoulders reminded her of Danny, and the ache in her chest came back with a vengeance.

Maybe she'd keep her distance from Isla; the last thing she wanted to do was spend time in a bar chatting to men who were on the prowl.

Yes, she nodded to herself. Quiet time alone, to get ready for her course. That was what she needed and what she would do.

Sienna turned to the welcome guide and asked to be shown

Annie Seaton

to her room.

Chapter 17

Danny - Port Douglas

Danny sat on the bed in the small bedroom at the Air BnB at Port Douglas checking his phone for messages. He had caught the bus from Cairns up to Port Douglas where the launch departed for Esculanta Island. Even though he knew Sienna was unlikely to contact him, he still held a slim hope. Pippa had his number and if Sienna wanted it, she could soon get it. He'd booked the room here for two nights because he didn't start in his new job until the day after tomorrow and then he was booked to go on the launch out to the island. Today was the day he'd set aside to talk to a lawyer and get himself out of the complicated mess that his two brothers had got him into. Dante and Renzo owed him.

He'd made an appointment with a divorce lawyer in Port Douglas; he'd been grateful to get in at short notice. It was time to disassociate himself from Lucia once and for all.

God, he'd been so bloody naïve. And the promise of the money from his brothers had blinded him to the long-term ramifications of what they'd wanted.

And the impact of what he had done by marrying a stranger—or a bloody fourth cousin ten times removed or whatever she was. All because Lucia Berretta had wanted to live in Australia, and his family owed her family from some feud decades back.

He had been the fall guy. The whole arrangement had been made before he'd even been asked.

No—not *asked*—before he'd been *told* what was happening and the telling had been sweetened with a significant cash deposit.

If he'd laid eyes on the sour woman before it was a done deal, he would have run for the hills. It didn't matter to Danny that she wasn't a particularly attractive woman; it was her sour face, her nasty attitude and her bitter tongue that he'd discovered after the town hall wedding in Castellina. And her absolute pleasure in making his life miserable when they were in the same place.

He'd never figured her out. Lucia had got what she wanted. Maybe it was genetic memory, the thought. A continuation of the family feud fifty years later.

Danny stared at his phone. No messages, no calls. He grabbed his clothes out of his bag and headed for the shower; it was almost time to leave for his ten o'clock appointment.

##

'It really is a difficult situation you are in, Mr Riccardo.' Mr James, the lawyer sat back and tapped his pencil on the desk. 'Even though I know as you say it was all organised for you by your family, you must take responsibility for going ahead with the wedding. You are the one who made the vows and signed the marriage certificate.'

Danny nodded. 'I know. And I very much regret that I agreed to the plan. Without going through all of the legalities one by one, can you just tell me the bottom line.'

'Very well.' The lawyer turned on his computer and didn't talk for a few moments as he read the screen and clicked the mouse.

'As you married in Italy, it potentially makes the situation even more problematic. The process can be long and expensive. Your wife—'

Danny shook his head. 'Please don't call her that. She has never been my wife.'

Mr James raised his eyebrows. 'Very well. This Italian woman has married you, an Australian citizen. I understand she would have applied for a temporary partner visa, once you travelled back to Australia.'

He stared at Danny as he nodded and held the lawyer's gaze steadily. 'This is where the sticking point is, and creates potential legal action for you. If you cannot prove a genuine relationship, and you are found guilty of arranging a marriage to obtain permanent residence for your spouse, the maximum penalty is a fine up to $210,000 and ten years imprisonment.'

Danny's jaw dropped, and his stomach churned.

'What?'

'However, let us assume that the relationship was genuine and you are merely wanting to divorce.' He looked at Danny as though encouraging him to agree.

'Yes, let's go down that track. It was genuine at the time,' he said, swallowing the unpalatable lie. 'Lucia no longer wants to be married to me, or wants residency or citizenship'—he didn't repeat the harsh words she had thrown at him the other night—'she has decided to go back to Italy.' He looked at his watch. 'In fact she would be on the flight now.'

'Have you lived in Australia for the past twelve months?'

Danny nodded. 'I have.'

'Well, then, we can file for divorce without too much trouble.'

Danny's step was lighter as he headed along the beach at Port Douglas. A huge load had been lifted from him in that one simple meeting. Mr James had warned that the divorce would be a long process if Lucia did decide to contest it, but Danny couldn't see why she'd do that. One of the things she'd thrown at him was that she had a real man waiting for her back in Castellina. He had kept his cool and not demanded to know why she'd been here for the past two years trying to get citizenship, if that was the case.

After the formalities were completed, and the paperwork signed, he and Mr James had chatted about the tourist town and the local lawyer told him about the huge prawns that would come in on the trawlers late morning.

The older man looked at Danny. 'This is off the record now. I sense there is more that you're not telling me, but I've had an idea. Were either of you forced into the marriage under duress?

Danny's voice was bitter. 'I suppose you could call it duress, if I was told by my two older brothers that I was getting married to a woman I'd never met and that the ceremony was taking place the next day.'

'Excellent,' Mr James said.

'We've never shared a bed, if that helps.' Danny added.

'Non-consummation is an old law that no longer exists,' the lawyer said. 'However, I think we may have a solution. It's called declaration of nullity. Do you think your brothers would be willing to make an affidavit of what happened.'

'I'll make sure of it,' Danny said.

'In that case I'll apply to the Family Court on your behalf. However the bad news is it will cost you thirteen hundred and twenty dollars.'

'Mr James, that is the best news I've heard in a very long time.'

By way of a quiet celebration Danny collected two fresh bread rolls from the baker in the main street, a kilo of prawns, some seafood sauce in a small plastic container and a bottle of Coke and headed for the beach. He couldn't help thinking how it would have been perfect if Sienna had been beside him, but he quickly closed down that line of thought.

He would enjoy his own company for the next two days before he started his four week trial at Esculanta Island. If the work suited him, he would stay there for the six months contract they'd offered him.

And then he would decide where to go.

All he knew was he was not going back to Pentecost Island to work with his lowlife brother.

His family no longer existed for him. He hadn't even told them where he was going.

Chapter 18

Sienna

A mix of hunger and curiosity chased Sienna from her room a few hours after she'd arrived. She'd unpacked and pressed all of her clothes with the travel iron she carried—she'd never trusted the irons in hotel rooms with her silk garments—and hung her clothes in the huge wardrobe. Her room was huge, and looked over the pool to the sea beyond. The view through the entire glass wall at the end of the living room was framed by lush palm trees, and the best thing was the three-rung stainless steel ladder that led from her balcony straight into the hexagonal swimming pool. Once she'd unpacked, she had slipped on her costume and gone for a quick swim.

Quick for her, anyway, as she did twenty laps of the pool. Taking a quick shower, she dried off, blew dry her hair into her usual bob and slipped on a turquoise green pair of silk pants with a loose white top.

She clutched the map of the resort that had been on the coffee table in the living room and followed the directions to the day spa with the intention of making an appointment. As she made her way along outside corridors with marble flooring, she didn't pass one other person, and she couldn't help the comparison that sprang to mind.

While this might be a seven-star resort, and the fittings and furnishing were of the highest quality, it seemed soulless and didn't have the warm atmosphere that permeated Pentecost Island. Maybe it was simply because she felt at home there and had the support network of the girls who all looked out for each other.

'Boo!'

Sienna jumped and clutched her chest as Isla appeared from behind a marble column.

'I wondered where you'd got to. I was going to go and ask reception for your room number, but they all seem so stuck up here

I didn't think they'd give it to me. I knew we'd run into each other somewhere. What have you been doing? Have you checked out the whole place? Isn't it amazing?' The Irish girl didn't draw breath as she continued to pepper Sienna with questions.

Finally Sienna put up her hand and grinned at her. 'How can I tell you what I've been doing if I can't get a word in?'

'I told you to tell me to button it if I got carried away, and I haven't spoken to a soul for two whole hours!' Isla chuckled. 'So I decided to go to the day spa and check it out. My God, did you see the prices in the compendium? I don't think I'll be having more than the basic treatment.'

'Okay to answer your question. I unpacked, and I had a swim. Then I decided to explore. It is very quiet here, I agree.' Sienna flicked a cheeky glance at Isla. 'I thought you might have still been with Mr Autopilot.'

'Nah, he was just a flirt. But you should have seen him checking you out when you walked away. You could have scored there if you'd wanted to. He wasn't interested in me.'

Sienna shook her head. 'No, thank you. I don't want to score with anyone. I'm here to research, have a rest, and then work on the course.'

'Just as well, because I checked out the talent around the bar at the far end of the pool on my first walk around. They're all over sixty, fat and hairy, and wearing gold chains.' Sienna grinned and Isla pulled a face. 'Unless you're looking for a sugar Daddy, the field is way too old, I suppose their wives are all shopping in the boutiques or having a beauty treatment.'

Sienna shook her head and put her arm through Isla's. 'Come on, let's go explore.'

It was impossible to be offended by Isla; she was full of fun and harmless, but her next words did put Sienna on edge.

'But never fear, if there is talent to be found, I will find it, and I did! Over the hill, there is a construction site where they are building another accommodation wing near the rainforest, and oh, be still my beating heart, there were some buff builders there. I'd say we'll get to meet them when we're staying in the accommodation where the course is being held. That's the staff end of the island, so let's soak up this luxury while we're here!'

Sienna tensed. The last thing she wanted to look at was a

buff builder and be reminded of Danny Riccardo. She stared over the balcony above the Bird of Paradise day spa and didn't speak.

'Look, I'm sorry, I do prattle on, but if you'd rather me leave you in peace, all you have to do is say the word, and I'll go.' Isla looked crestfallen and Sienna felt guilty for being aloof.

'No, of course not.' She let go of Isla's arm and smoothed her hands over her long pants. 'I'm just used to being quiet. I've always been that way.'

'Let me guess. Only child?'

'Yes.' Sienna swallowed and nodded. 'And boarding school.'

'Lucky you. I went to the village school in Dingle. That's where I learned to be loud. If you wanted to be heard so you could learn anything, you had to be.' Isla giggled. 'The poor teacher, can you imagine a class full of me? And then I went home to a little house filled with my five brothers, my parents and one set of grandparents. And the poor dears can't understand why I want to travel the world. "Why didn't you marry Tommy McEvoy when he asked you?" my mother said to me when they saw me off at the airport.'

'Your family sounds wonderful, 'Sienna said softly. 'And I'm so envious of your confidence.'

'They're not half bad. I miss them, you know. Paulie, Johnnie, Archie, Barrie and Frankie are all older than me, and only two of them are married. Me poor old Da was upset when Mum called me Isla. Broke the "ie" tradition. He wanted Mary!'

Sienna waited for her to draw breath, but it didn't happen.

'But hey, I'm envious of your elegance, and the way you look. I'd give anything to look like you do. You are so calm and serene. Maybe we can teach each other a few tricks.'

'Sounds like a plan. Now let's go and check out this day spa.'

##

The three days spent as guests at the resort before their course began flew by. Sienna and Isla tried out a couple of the basic treatments in the day spa and were both very impressed.

'Lots to learn, haven't we?' Isla said as they compared notes after the treatments.

They went shopping in the boutiques and Isla bought the

220

basics of a new wardrobe with Sienna's help. But most of all they laughed as Isla taught Sienna the rudimentary facts about being self-confident.

On Saturday night, they chose the Italian restaurant for dinner. The tables were set with red checked tablecloths, and wine bottles with candles in the middle of the table. Dean Martin was crooning *It's Amore* as they were seated by a waiter with a fake Italian accent.

Isla rolled her eyes and grinned. 'I rest my case.'

'What?'

'It's all in the perception. The props.'

Sienna wasn't sure what her new friend meant, so Isla set an exercise for Sienna. As they sipped their wine Sienna's task was to look at each person in the restaurant, and tell Isla the background that she perceived they were from.

The more they drank, the sillier the conversation became, but Isla proved her point and Sienna took it on board.

'See, we each look at the people in here, and we both see something different, but none of it matters. What is important is what that person thinks of themself, and sweetie, that's what you have to work on.'

Sienna picked up the fine crystal glass and looked over her wine at Isla. 'So, tell me, how did you get your self-confidence? Was it something you had to work on?'

Isla shook her head. 'Lovey, the family I grew up in made me the way I am. There were ten of us in a tiny house, and we had to be loud and brash to be heard. Dinner around our table wasn't a posh affair.' Isla gestured with her fork at a couple on the other side of the restaurant. The woman was wearing a bronze silk dress, and the man a dinner suit. 'Now look at that pair. They're sitting there looking very confident and if I'm correct, they think they are better than many of the other guests in the restaurant. But—she leaned forward and whispered—'why? What makes them better than everyone else? What makes them better than us?'

Sienna shook her head slowly. 'Nothing.'

'Exactly! Now, what you have to do is tell yourself that that self-confidence that you give out in bucket loads is true and not just a front you hide behind. You think you can do that, woman?'

Sienna sat straight in her chair. 'I'll give it my best shot.'

As she said the words she knew she could do it, and she would do it.

'One more thing, you have to shed, before you pass the Isla O'Sullivan self-confidence course. And it's the hard one. You have to think deeply, and then you have to acknowledge who has done that damage to you. And then the fun begins when we deal with them.'

'But what if we're nowhere near them?' Sienna protested, thinking of her father in that huge draughty house on the lake in Switzerland.

Isla leaned forward and tapped her nose. 'But lovey, I'm Irish and I can show you the magic, and we can do it from here.'

Sienna burst out laughing and Isla put one hand on her chest. 'Now, it's hurting me you are. How can a girl help her friend if she laughs at her?' Isla leaned forward and lowered her voice. 'You have to tell me who did this number on you, and then we deal with it. A couple of candles, a lock of hair, and we burn some notes and you'll be as right as rain, Sienna Marino!'

Sienna leaned back. One thing Isla had taught her was to take herself less seriously. They were quiet as the fake Italian waiter placed two steaming bowls of spaghetti marinara in front of them.

Isla ploughed straight in as Sienna unfolded her napkin and laid it on her lap. She picked up the silver fork, as Isla sucked a piece of spaghetti in.

Finally Sienna shook her head. 'It's no use. No matter. It's no use, I can't do it.'

'Okay, I'll lance the wound for you myself. Figuratively speaking, that is. Who was the person who did this to you? The person who made you believe that you're not good enough?'

'It was my father,' Sienna mumbled. 'But I can't blame him. It was as much my fault as his.'

'Ah, that's a bit harder than a past love who broke your heart.'

Sienna looked down. 'There was one of them too. Not long ago.'

'We've got our work cut out, girlfriend, but we've got ten days to work on you.' Isla leaned forward and her gaze was intense. 'If you put your trust in me, I guarantee you that the

Sienna who leaves this island will be a different—and stronger—person than the one she is now. So, do you trust me?'

Sienna nodded slowly. 'Strangely, Isla O' Sullivan, I do.'

Chapter 19

Danny

Danny was up bright and early on Sunday morning to travel to Esculanta Island. The Air BnB was within walking distance of the marina, and he'd already checked out the launch that would take him out to the island. Surprisingly, his mood was upbeat— he'd had a good break at Port Douglas and had got his head in order and he was looking forward to starting afresh. It was time to put the past behind him and move on. There was one thing he'd like to do, but knew it was impossible.

He would have liked to have known that Sienna was all right. He would never forget the shock on her face when he'd climbed back into the boat, his nose dripping with blood.

It hadn't been the injury that had shocked her; he knew it had been Renzo's loud comment about him having a wife. All he could hope for was that Sienna's friends on the island would rally around her; he'd seen them in action, and they were a tight support group. He was going to have to try hard to get over his feelings for her. He was going to steer clear of women for a long time. But he would have liked to have spoken to her one more time and told her his story.

It was time to focus on his new job; Danny had no doubt he had the skills listed by the recruitment service when he had applied, and once he had provided evidence of his trade qualification to the project manager on the island, he should be clear to start work tomorrow.

Locking the door behind him and dropping the key into the return box, he headed for the marina to catch the launch to the island.

To save time on arrival at the worksite, the construction company had a temporary counter on the wharf on the mainland. Danny was early and was first at the desk.

'Daniel Riccardo, carpenter,' he answered when asked for his name and the position he was filling.

The man at the desk ran his finger down a list and checked Danny's name off. 'You have a copy of your tickets with you?'

Danny nodded and slipped them from his wallet.

Another four ticks on the list.

'Excellent, thank you.' His name was crossed off and the guy handed him a name tag, and an envelope. 'You're in the staff accommodation on the eastern side of the island. Please read this and sign your agreement.' He slid a single page across the desk.

Danny widened his eyes as he read the conditions of employment. No visiting the resort, no drinking at the bar or eating at the restaurant, and no fraternising with the guests. He had no problem with it, but it was not what he'd expected. He signed the paper. 'I was expecting a construction site. I didn't know the resort was already open,' he commented as he passed the form back over.

'Does that create a problem for you?' the guy asked. Danny looked at his name tag. 'No, Jim. No problem. I wasn't aware there would be guests there, that's all. I didn't know it was already open.'

'It's totally separate,' Jim replied. 'You'll be working on the new hotel wing in the centre of the island. The existing resort is on the western side, and the staff and builders' accommodation, and the training centre is on the east. It's quite a large island, and the guests are discouraged from going beyond the resort fence.'

'Fair enough.'

'In your envelope, you'll find the details of your accommodation and the arrangements for meals and leisure activities on the island. He nodded to Danny. 'You can board the launch now. I think you'll be pleasantly surprised.'

As Danny move away towards the boat, he noticed a queue had formed behind him. To his dismay, there was a large group of women standing at the back and they were looking his way and obviously talking about him. He put his head down and headed onboard, choosing a corner seat at the back. He rolled his jacket up and put it between his head and the window. It was almost a three hour trip out to the island; he'd sleep rather than get caught up in conversations.

He was pleased when a guy took the seat beside him, gave

him a brief nod and immediately opened his laptop. The group of women went upstairs to the open deck, chattering and giggling as they went.

God, he was getting cynical for a bloke his age.

***

Sienna had been woken at seven-thirty by the phone beside her bed. She and Isla had had a late night last night—after dinner, they had watched a show and then gone to the small cinema behind the restaurant to watch the latest Liam Hemsworth movie.

Isla had chuckled. 'One of my reasons for coming to Australia. How about you?'

Sienna had shaken her head. 'No. I'm here to work. No time for that sort of thing.'

'Well, you won't have been disappointed because there's not been one decent man to look at over the weekend.'

'I haven't been looking.

'I noticed,' Isla had said drily. 'We're going to work on that too.'

Now Sienna rolled over and reached for the phone. 'Hello?'

'Ms Marino? It's Andie from reception here. You are checking out this morning and we have no travel arrangements in the system for you. Were you taking the seaplane back to the mainland or the launch? I need to generate a ticket for you.'

'Ah.' Sienna hesitated as she tried to wake up and gather her thoughts. 'I'm not going back today. I'm moving across to the training centre for a course.'

'I wasn't aware of that. Just one moment.' Silence and then the clicking of a keyboard. 'My apologies, Ms Marino. I see that you and Ms O'Sullivan are both moving over to the training centre.' There was a crisp tone in the voice now, almost as though they were in trouble. Sienna sat up and pushed her hair back with one hand as she leaned on the silk pillowcase. 'There are regulations about moving between sites.' Definitely a frosty tone now. 'You can both have a late checkout and then if you come down to reception at eleven a.m., we will transport you over so that you arrive at the same time as the launch with the other course attendees.'

Sienna went to speak, but the call disconnected; she pulled a face, and reception wouldn't be getting a good score on the evaluation form. Course attendees were obviously second-class citizens from the resort staff's point of view. She snuggled back down in the bed. If she had a late checkout, she would make the most of it with a lie-in. She had a feeling the next ten days would be very busy.

Busy was good. Busy would help her get into the right headspace before she went back to Pentecost Island.

A head space and a location where Danny wouldn't be anymore.

Sienna turned her head into the pillow and, for the first time in two days, gave in to tears.

Chapter 20

Sienna

Isla was waiting at reception when Sienna stepped out of the lift. Her new friend was wearing one of the new outfits she'd bought with Sienna's help.

'Morning, lovey.' Her shrill voice filled the foyer and heads turned as Sienna crossed the marble floor.

'You look lovely, Isla,' she said and meant it. Isla had pulled her loose curls back and subdued them in a French roll.

'I did until you walked across.' Her grin was cheeky. 'My elegance fades in your shadow.'

'As my self-confidence does in yours.' Sienna nudged her. 'Did you get the frosty call from Andie?'

'I did,' Isla said mournfully, but loudly. 'No longer are we guests to be pampered.'

The receptionist looked over at them and raised her eyebrows. 'Your luggage has been taken out, and your transport will be here shortly if you would like to wait on the seat outside.'

Sienna glanced back at the rude woman as they headed to the doors. 'She wouldn't last five minutes on Pentecost Island. One of Pippa's rules is perfect and appropriate behaviour with the guests at all times.'

'We are no longer guests. But I do like the sound of your island and your Pippa.'

'We were tested a couple of months back with a new arrival who rubbed everyone up the wrong way, but Odessa turned out to be a good person. We never know what baggage people carry, do we?'

'No, we don't.'

Sienna glanced at Isla. Her tone had held a rare note of bitterness.

'Any jobs coming up on your island?'

Sienna looked at her as she wondered,

No, it wasn't the right time to say anything. She'd only known Isla for three days and as much as she enjoyed her company, she'd have to see what sort of therapist she was before she mentioned any jobs that might be coming up.

'You'll be the first to know,' she replied. 'You'd love the island and the girls. It's a pretty special place.'

'You never know, I might come for a holiday. Depends if I get a job out of this course. I have heard that therapists who have completed Madame Eleve's course are in high demand.'

'Fingers crossed,' Sienna said. 'Look, here comes our chariot. She stifled a giggle as a buggy the same as those on Hamo came around the corner.

'And here was I thinking we'd have a limousine,' Isla said with a chuckle.

The ride across to the other side of the island took them along a winding road with an overhanging canopy of rainforest trees. Brightly coloured birds jumped from branch to branch above them, squawking as the buggy disturbed them. Like the rest of the island, the road was clear of leaves and bird droppings and Sienna smothered a smile, remembering Eliza's pooper scooper story.

It had been true; she and Isla had checked it out. They'd also checked out the bare-chested waiters around the pool and the hot towels that were hand-delivered for their comfort.

'We had a good holiday, didn't we?' she said with a smile as they approached the end of the road.

'I did, and by the look of you, you did too. You look much more relaxed than you did when you got on the plane.'

The buggy driver turned around to speak to them. 'I'll drop you off where you register your arrival, but I'll take your bags to your rooms. Might be a bit of a wait, girls, it's a large group, plus there's new workmen coming over for the week on this morning's launch. There's a coffee shop there, so I'd suggest making that your first stop.'

'Thank you.' Isla patted his shoulder as they left the buggy. 'I'll be recommending you for a staff recognition award. It's a pleasure to have someone friendly.'

With a smile and a wave, he headed off to a building at the end of a circular drive.

'That must be our accommodation. It doesn't look too bad.' Sienna stared at the four-storey building ahead. Each room appeared to have a balcony that overlooked the sea, and the gardens were colourful and well looked after.

'I guess they have to keep it looking on a par with the rest of the place in case any guests wander over here. There's the coffee shop. Looks like we're first to arrive.'

As they crossed the paved area to the small coffee shop, Sienna spotted a large boat coming across the small bay. 'Look, there's the launch now. Let's get a coffee and see where we have to register.'

'Over there, Sienna.' Isla pointed to a separate building next to the coffee shop. 'It says. Madame Eleve course attendees register here. And there's a spare table right near it. You grab the table, I'll get our coffees.'

'Espresso, double shot, please,' Sienna said as she moved across to the table. She sat down and watched the launch as it headed for the wharf.

It was very different from Jiminy's boat, which made the run to Pentecost Island. This was a two-deck boat with an open seating area on the upper deck and a cabin.

Sienna was surprised to see how many passengers were on the launch. There was a large group of women sitting in the open air on the top deck. As she watched the boat manoeuvre in, it was obvious that the bottom deck was full too. There were faces at each window. As the boat got closer, her breath caught, and she put her hand to her mouth.

'I got us a piece of carrot cake to share too,' Isla said as she sat down. The girl in there's a sweetie. She's bringing it out. Real cups too.' Her eyes narrowed as she looked at Sienna. 'You okay? You're a bit pale.'

Sienna looked back at the launch, but there was no one at the window where she could have sworn she'd seen Danny.

She nodded. 'I'm okay. Just losing the plot.'

'Join me, girlfriend. I lost it years ago.'

Sienna kept her attention on the boat as the coffee and cake was brought out to them.

'This is Sienna,' Isla said.

'Hi, welcome to the best side of the island. I'm Frannie.'

'Hi, Frannie.' Sienna glanced at her briefly with a quick smile, keeping her attention on the passengers as they disembarked. Isla chattered away, and as the last group came off the boat, Sienna let out the breath she'd been holding. It had been her imagination.

Frannie went back inside and Sienna pulled her coffee over to her.

'Go you halvies in the cake?' Isla asked, spoon poised.

'No, thanks, I'm not hungry.'

'You okay, lovey? You looked like you'd seen a ghost before.'

Sienna flopped back into the chair. 'I thought I almost had for a moment. I mean, not a ghost, just someone I don't want to see.'

'That wouldn't be the cause of the broken heart you mentioned the other night?'

She nodded. 'Yes, it's still pretty raw. Only happened a few days before I came up here. I'm still a bit fragile.'

'Tell Aunty Isla all about it. I always wanted to be one of those agony aunts that people wrote to in the women's mags.'

'No, there's no need. It's all over and it was my imagination. I was seeing things.'

Isla picked up her coffee and looked over Sienna's shoulder. 'Seeing things or not, there's some definite talent heading this way. Check them out. I think they're coming into the coffee shop.'

Sienna pulled a face. 'I'll drink my coffee while you check them out.'

'I've always been a sucker for a man in a suit. Always looks like he has a bit of class, but then you shouldn't stereotype and make assumptions, should you?'

Sienna half switched off, as Isla continued her constant talking. She didn't often seem to expect an answer. She looked down at her coffee, and then picked up her spoon to stir the chocolate in.

'Now the one with the curly black hair with him looks like that pretend Italian waiter we had the other night. They're coming this way.'

Sienna's neck prickled and she sat still, staring into her cup as a shadow passed the table. Finally looking up, she saw the back of a man in a suit as he went into the coffee shop. She looked back at Isla, who was staring past her shoulder.

Sienna held her breath as a shadow crossed the table and then stopped. She looked down at a pair of work boots. Work boots she had seen before.

Her eyes travelled slowly up a fine set of tanned, muscular legs.

Legs that she recognised.

She held her breath as she lifted her gaze and her vision blurred as her heart began to thump erratically. She stared into a beautiful face.

A face that was imprinted on her heart.

'Sienna?' Danny was staring at her with his mouth open.

Isla stood and came around to Sienna's side of the table. Her eyes held concern. 'Time we were heading, lovey. There's quite a queue over at the registration office now.'

Sienna moved her eyes from Danny's face and looked down at the table.

'Isla, you finish your cake and coffee. I'm sure they'll wait for us to register. I have a conversation to have.' She was very proud of her firm voice. 'It'll only take a few minutes.'

Sienna glanced over at the launch wondering how long it was before it left. With Danny Riccardo on it.

The look of hopeful expectation on his face fuelled her growing anger even more.

'Danny, walk with me, please. We need to talk.'

Chapter 21

Danny

When Danny had seen the woman with the auburn hair sitting at the coffee table, his heart had kicked, and then he'd chastised himself for seeing Sienna everywhere he went.

How long was this going to last?

She was sitting beside a slim girl with dark hair who was staring at him.

'A word of warning, Dan.' Eric, the guy he'd sat next to on the trip over—the architect who designed the new wing—leaned over and dropped his voice. 'Don't get involved with any of the course participants while they're on the island. There's been a few guys losing their jobs over it. The construction firm are pretty hard taskmasters and expectations are a bit over the top.

'No fear of that from me,' he said.

'Good to meet you. I hope it works out for you.' Eric nodded, and hurried across to the coffee shop and disappeared inside.

As Danny got closer to the table, his heart kicked up even more when he saw the graceful neck above the white silk shirt. He knew that skin and that neck and that hair.

It was Sienna.

His first thought was that she'd found out he was coming to the island and had organised to meet him.

Hope surged through him, until she lifted her eyes and her icy glare raked him. Twin spots of red coloured her usually fair cheeks, and her eyes glittered.

Then he remembered that no one knew he was coming here, so there was no way she could have known.

'Danny, walk with me please. We need to talk.'

She stood and her chair scraped on the pavers. 'Now.'

The girl standing beside her looked worried. 'I'll wait for you here, Sienna.'

'No, you go and join the queue, Isla. I won't be long.'

The course.

The penny dropped. This was the course Sienna had found out about last Sunday when they were on Hamo. The course with the tropical resort on the front of the brochure. Danny bit back the groan that threatened to spill out.

What were the chances of that? Out of all of the jobs he'd considered, how the hell did he end up applying for and getting one on the very island where her course was being held? And what were the chances of her being here the same day he arrived?

Sienna's low heels clicked on the road beneath their feet as she led him towards a road that seemed to lead to a rainforest. As they reached the corner, he could see it was a wide paved road overhung with a canopy of trees.

'This is far enough,' she said. 'No one can hear us here.'

'So?' He put his hands on his hip, and his laptop case swung around.

'So?' Her voice was vicious. 'Is that all you have to say?'

'At this stage, yes, until I hear what you want to talk to me about.'

'What I want to talk to you about?' Her chest was heaving as her voice got louder. 'I'll tell you what I want to talk to you about! What sort of ego do you have to follow me here? Who told you? Did Pippa tell your sleazeball brother I was on Esculanta Island?'

'I—'

'How dare you, Danny? Isn't it enough that you're married? What does your poor wife have to say about you chasing after me? I cannot believe you are here. I want you to get on that launch and go away and leave me in peace. I never want to see you again.'

As she spoke, the launch's hooter boomed, and the engines' roar reached them as it pulled away from the wharf.

'Looks like it's too late.' He couldn't help himself, but Danny was starting to get angry.

'You planned all this, didn't you?'

'Yeah, sure I did. I made sure that you were sitting in that seat so you could see me as soon as I got off the boat. Wake up to yourself, Sienna, and stop being so selfish and one-eyed. You wouldn't let me explain myself to you the other night. It's about time you got out of your fantasy world and listened.'

'Fantasy world? How dare you!'

Before he saw it coming, Sienna had lifted her hand and slapped his face. But his reflexes were fast, and he caught her hand in his on the way down. His cheek was stinging where her hand had landed but he ignored it.

'I'll tell you how I dare to. I left my job on Pentecost Island, so you didn't have to see me. I told my brother to shove his job, and I left my home. I was overjoyed when the woman my family arranged for me to marry went back to Italy. I was ecstatic when I filed for divorce. But you didn't care enough to wait and listen and hear any of that, did you? You thought the worst of me and gave me no chance. So, you know what? I don't care what you think of me now. I don't want to have anything to do with you. I've started a new life, and you have no place in it. I have a four-week contract here and I'm going to give it a go. I had no idea that you were here. If I had, I would have gone in the other direction, as far as I could and very fast. You showed me no respect, and you gave me no trust, so you can now do whatever it is you're here to do, but don't you come near me. Is that clear?'

'Very. Now let go of me.'

He dropped her hand.

She turned on her heel and walked away, leaving him standing in the shadow of a huge mango tree. His heart was thumping, and his head was pounding.

And God help him, he couldn't help watching her as she strode away.

She even did that bloody elegantly.

But it was the yearning that filled him that pissed Danny off more than anything.

Chapter 22

Sienna

By the time she had settled into the shared room with Isla, Sienna had achieved a measure of calm. She couldn't believe she'd slapped Danny's face; she had no idea where that had come from. Her temperament had always been calm, no matter how much her father had goaded her. The incident today had been the culmination of her rage; she'd become so angry she hadn't even realised she'd slapped him until he'd grabbed her hand.

Embarrassment sat uncomfortably in her stomach the whole time they'd registered for the course, and then sat through an introductory talk before she and Isla had been given their room keys. The rest of the day was theirs to read some course materials and explore their side of the island. They had access to small catamarans and kayaks and a long stretch of beach that was for staff only.

Sienna was conscious of Danny being close by; she'd seen the workers go into a room in the same building for what she assumed was their orientation. All she wanted was to be somewhere else. Somewhere she could climb into bed and pull the sheets over her head, and forget what Danny had said.

She'd made assumptions about him, and she'd judged him without knowing the facts. Worse than that, he'd listened to her secrets, he had been kind and he hadn't judged her. She had not given him the same courtesy, without knowing the facts.

Tears pricked at her eyes as Sienna listened to a boring woman drone on about what the course would cover for the next ten days. Her interest level was zero. She was beginning to doubt that she had the staying power to be here and do the course, and then she remembered the huge amount that Eliza had paid so she could, and she knew she had to do it. Isla must have sensed her turmoil because she was unusually quiet, and at one stage, when

Sienna teared up, she reached over and squeezed her hand.

When the woman—Madame Eleve by all accounts—finally stopped talking about herself and how wonderful this course was because she'd created it, Sienna was ready to go to her room and crash.

She must have looked wrecked, because when they stood, Isla took her elbow and guided her outside.

'It's very regimented, isn't it,' she whispered. 'Nothing like I was expecting. In fact, the whole island is a bit—I don't know, almost like something out of a horror movie.'

Sienna managed to pull herself out of her funk. 'It's going to be okay. It's had all those excellent reviews.'

'Hmm. We'll see. Now did you hear what she said? We're to go to our rooms and rest and read, and then come back in two hours for dinner. Are you okay with that? You have to eat, you know, lovey.

Sienna smiled as Isla looked at her with concern. 'You're a good friend, Isla. And yes, I know. I won't be a coward. I'll come to dinner. Even though I know Danny will be there. It's the dining area for everyone on this side of the island.'

'Well, chin up, lovey. Come and make yourself even more beautiful, and we'll go slay them!'

Sienna almost managed a laugh, but she couldn't hold back her smile.

***

Danny

Danny had thought it was impossible to feel any worse than he had when he had taken Sienna back to the island after Renzo had spilled the beans on him being married, but after the tirade he'd unleashed on Sienna in the forest this afternoon, he felt dreadful. Guilt and regret vied for the top spot, and he sat in the orientation session, completely unaware of what was going on around him.

Luckily the guy beside him nodded to him as the speaker turned the microphone off. 'Coming for a beer, mate? I think we need one after that.'

'Sounds good. I switched off. What did I miss?'

The guy laughed and held out his hand. 'I'm Brad. Don't worry. I picked up the good stuff. Where the bar and the restaurant are. The staff ones, that is. Stick with me, and I'll show you the way.'

The bar beside the open dining area was large and already half filled with men and women. Danny had a furtive look around, and once he was sure that a certain redhead wasn't in the room, he let himself relax. He and Brad sat at a large table by themselves and chatted about their first impressions of the island.

'I'm a bit disappointed, to be honest,' Danny said.

Maybe it was because he was used to Pentecost and the vibe there, but so far, he wasn't impressed. He'd had it good on Pentecost Island. Not just because Sienna was there to talk to, but he'd also enjoyed working with the rest of the staff; the atmosphere was always happy.

If he was honest, even he and Renzo worked well together.

With a sigh, he looked up as he caught the flash of red he'd been waiting for. No, it wasn't fair to call the gorgeous colour red.

Sienna and her friend were standing in the doorway. He felt the instant her eyes settled on him and looked down at his beer. She could decide whether to go or stay. It didn't matter to him.

Oh yes, it does, a little voice pounded at him.

Okay, so it did. He'd like to sit and talk to her and ignore the past week.

Danny didn't resent the way Sienna had spoken to him. Hell, he could understand exactly where she was coming from. He could even forgive her for slapping him. Finding out he was married after he had kissed her like he had last Sunday must have been a shock to her.

There had been times over the past three years when he'd woken up in a cold sweat—Lucia in the next room she had never ventured from—when he'd not been able to believe he was married. It remained a shock to him almost three years later.

So, he couldn't blame Sienna for her reaction. The sad part was that he really liked her, and that day together on Hamo had shown him that it could be much more.

So much more. He really cared for her. He'd loved talking to her and spending time with her. Even watching her potter around her day spa had given him pleasure. Folding towels and arranging the flowers, he had been a sucker for anything she did.

He refused to let himself think of that afternoon on Hamo

when they could have very easily become a lot more than friends.

He'd blown it now, and he just had to get on with the four weeks on the island and let her get on with her life.

It was too late.

'Another beer, mate?' he asked Brad.

Chapter 23

Pippa

Sienna had only been gone for four days when it became very obvious to me that her replacement was not going to make it. Jen had whined almost nonstop since she'd come to the island, and I was over it.

The hut was too far from everyone else.

There were too many bookings in the day.

The old house was not suitable accommodation. Her list of complaints was never-ending.

On the fifth morning, she was on the island, and my phone rang for the third time; Rafe looked at me with sympathy in his eyes.

'You're going to send her back to Hamo, aren't you, sweetheart?'

'Am I that obvious?' I let out a satisfied sigh as my husband put his arms around me.

'Only to someone who loves you,' he said.

'Sure makes me appreciate the excellent staff we have here.'

The sky was dark with grey clouds, and a brisk wind was blowing from the north. It had rained on and off for the past few days, and I was frustrated that it was holding up the work on our new pool. Renzo had talked to the designer, the plans had gone to council, and we'd managed to get them fast-tracked, but I had no control over the weather.

It hadn't been a good week. Nat and Nate had gone down to Brisbane to look at a new reservation system we were thinking of installing. Yesterday's meat delivery for the restaurant had gone astray and Angus had to change the menu at short notice. The whining beautician had been the last straw.

Half an hour later, I walked back up the hill and a tiny spurt of jealousy went through me as I spotted Odessa sitting outside with Rafe. I knew I had nothing to worry about, but she still held a place in his heart from before I had known him.

I pushed it away.

'Hey, Odessa. I haven't seen you for a few days.'

Her smile was natural and warm, and I realised how unfair I was being. I'd had my friends from before Rafe, and I shouldn't worry about his. I should know to be secure in his love, but sometimes my past baggage made itself known.

My husband reached up and took my hand as I stopped behind his chair.

'Ready for a coffee, love?' he asked.

'I am.'

'I'll get you one. And Odessa bought cake from Cherry.'

'Hummingbird cake,' Odessa said.

'Oh, yum, that has just improved my day,' I said.

'That's good,' Odessa said with a nervous smile. I was surprised; I hadn't seen her less than composed before.

'Why good?' I asked.

She swallowed and moistened her lips with the tip of her tongue. 'I wanted to ask your opinion on something.'

I tipped my head to the side. Even after almost two years, I still didn't have a complete handle on being the boss. It didn't come naturally, and this week had made me wonder if I really wanted to be in charge of a resort that was growing faster than we'd ever imagined.

'Fire away.'

'Well'—she toyed with the fringe on the edge of her skirt—'when I went over to Hamo the other day, I got talking to a couple of the designers in the jewellery outlets. I just happened to have a few of my pieces with me, and I was surprised that they thought they were good.'

I smiled. 'I'm not surprised at all. You're very talented.'

'You really think so, you're not just saying that?'

'I do.'

'Okay.' She took a deep breath. 'How would you feel about me having an exhibition here? Just a small function in the restaurant, and then I'd leave some of my work on display there. Of course, I'd pay for the catering and any costs that came from it, and I'd give you a percentage of any sales I made. I'd much rather have it here where it's familiar than over on Hamo.' She put her hands on the table and stopped fidgeting. 'Take a while to think about it, talk it over with Rafe. There's no rush.'

As I looked at her, Rafe came out with the coffee and three slices of cake on a plate.

'I don't have to think.'

Odessa's face fell. 'Oh, it doesn't matter. Don't worry, it was just an idea.'

I leaned forward and put my hand on hers. 'Odessa, I think it's a great idea. Just the sort of thing we need here to put us on the map.' My advertising brain kicked in. 'We could advertise in the national papers, and social media. When do you want to have it?'

I was surprised when Odessa jumped up and did a happy dance. 'Oh my God, you want to do it!'

Rafe trailed his fingers along my shoulder as he walked past, and I took that as approval.

'Let's talk dates,' I said. 'And then I can draft some ads.'

##

A couple of hours later, Odessa had gone back down to the house, and Rafe and I were sitting together in the swing chair, watching the water. I leaned back against him and closed my eyes.

'You've finally accepted Odessa,' he said softly, brushing his lips over my forehead.

'She's lovely. And she's really settled in on the island.'

'I'm pleased,' was all he said.

'It's been a tough week. I'll be pleased when Sienna comes back. I really hope she does.'

'You think she mightn't?'

I finally gave voice to what had been bugging me all day. 'I was talking to Renzo at the pool site this morning, and he told me where Danny's gone. He's not supposed to know, but the foreman of the company knew Renzo and rang him when he saw Danny's surname.'

'And?'

'He's working on Esculanta Island.'

'Oh dear. That could be interesting,' Rafe said. 'Do you think you should call her?'

'Probably too late. They'll be there by now.'

Rafe settled me comfortably against him. 'You know what?

It might not be a bad thing, throwing them together like that away from everything they know. They obviously had a spark going.'

'So you think I should just let it run its natural course?' I asked.

Rafe's arms went around me. 'I do, sweetheart. You have to learn you can't fix everything yourself.'

Chapter 24

Sienna

It hadn't taken long for Sienna's anger to morph into guilt, and then the resultant plummet of her new self-confidence followed soon after.

Isla sat next to her at the long dining table. They had come in late and the only seats left had been at a table for two right next to where Danny was sitting at a large table with five other men.

Sienna had taken a bowl of salad from the buffet and was twirling her fork in it. She'd sat at the side of the table so her back was to Danny and then worried that he would be looking at her.

Isla leaned forward over the bowl of pasta and whispered. 'Relax, sweetie. He's not even looking this way. He's talking to the others at the table.'

'Thank you, you're a mind reader.'

'I am, and I'm going to play agony aunt here. You, my dear have ten huge days of work ahead of you, and I want to see you eat properly and sleep well. Or you are going to fall in a heap. You told me your boss paid for this. Do you want to let her down?'

Sienna shook her head. 'No, I don't want to. I won't let Pippa and Eliza down.'

'So what do you have to do?'

'I'm going to eat my dinner.' She looked across at Isla and put on as much of a smile as she could muster. 'Even if it chokes me.'

'And then we will have pudding,' Isla said.

'Pudding? What's that?' Sienna frowned. 'What are you going to make me do?'

Isla burst out laughing, and heads turned. 'I guess you call it *torte* or something. A sweet after our dinner. And I saw a big pot of rice pudding over there. Not the sort of thing we were offered in the seven-star resort, was it?'

'I'll look forward to trying it,' Sienna said softly. 'I've never had rice pudding, and, yes, the food was awful at the resort. I can't wait to tell Pippa. If that was seven star our island is ten!'

Isla laughed again. 'That's a girl. Good to see some life coming back into you.' I was worried you were going to bail on me.'

'No. I'm staying. Even if Danny is staying too.'

'What did you say to him this afternoon? He looked shattered when he came back.'

Sienna shook her head and lowered her voice even more. 'I said some pretty horrible things. I think I'm going to have to apologise. I was out of line, but the shock of seeing him here made me see red. I thought he'd followed me here, but he didn't know I was here.'

'Are you sure? Is he being honest?'

She nodded. 'I believe him. He was as shocked to see me as I was to see him.'

'This might sound silly, but what are the chances of you both turning up here, unknown to each other, at the same time.'

'I'd say about one in a million.' It was all Sienna could do, not to turn around and look at the man they were talking about.

'I'm a great believer in fate, lovey. Do you think fate has stepped in here?'

'What do you mean?' Sienna sighed as there was movement beside their table and Danny walked past with three other men, but he didn't even look her way. 'He's still angry with me.'

'And that's part of it. I have some very strong ideas about how we end up with our soulmates,' Isla said, her expression more serious than Sienna had seen up until now. 'I know I'm looking too hard, because I want to be part of a couple, and I always make the wrong choices. But never have I met the person who I knew I was destined to be with. So, when we've moved on, I've never cared very much. And I've gone looking again.'

'You're saying Danny is my soul mate?' Sienna propped her chin in her hand on the table.

'Has there been really strong emotion between you? I don't want to get too personal, but even the anger between you today is a sign of a connection. It wouldn't have been there without there being a connection.' Isla jumped to her feet. 'Stay there while I get our pudding, and when I come back I want you to tell me every emotion you've shared with that man.' She turned as she went to walk to the *bain maries*. 'And to make it even stranger, if you're not a believer, we were destined to meet so I could help you on your path.'

Sienna sat there with her mouth open as Isla walked away. She looked down at her salad bowl, surprised to see it empty.

Closing her eyes, she thought back over the past few months that she'd been on the island.

***

Danny was restless. The guys he'd sat with at dinner had invited him back to the bar, but he'd excused himself saying he was going to have an early night. He couldn't bear the thought that Sienna might be there, and he couldn't go near her, couldn't talk to her, couldn't touch her.

Not because she was angry at him, but because it wasn't the right thing to do. He went back to his room—pleased that they all had single rooms—and changed out of his work clothes and boots. Putting on a pair of boardshorts and a T-shirt, he decided to walk along the beach. The weather had turned, but despite the wind and the scudding grey clouds, it was still warm. There was a compendium in his room, and according to the rules, swimming was not permitted at the beach. There was a small staff pool behind the bar for exercise, and a gym adjacent to the conference room where they'd met this afternoon.

He pulled the door shut behind him and turned his face to the sky, letting the first few drops of rain hit his face. It was cool and refreshing, and made him feel slightly better. When Sienna had calmed down, he intended to seek her out and apologise. As he stepped onto the narrow sandy beach, he could see a light a few hundred metres away. According to the rule book—and there seemed to be a lot of rules on the island, that was as far as staff could go.

The rain was light as he walked and by the time he reached the end of the beach and turned around the sky had cleared. As he got closer to the accommodation buildings, he could see a lone figure sitting on the seat where the path went down to the beach. His heart kicked as hope took hold of him, but he told himself it wouldn't be Sienna. There were thirty other women on this island, and she wouldn't be sitting out here alone.

Or would she?

No, she would be in the bar talking to her new friend.

Danny put his head down stepped from the beach onto the path, and kept walking. The bar was lit up, and he could hear music coming from the building.

'Danny.'

The soft voice stopped him in his tracks.

'Can we talk, please?'

He put his hands in his pockets and walked over to the bench seat where Sienna was sitting. She sat up straight as he approached and the wind caught her hair. She reached up and pushed it back, and a whiff of her fragrance reached him.

Danny took a deep breath and struggled to think of the right words. He wanted to talk to her, too, but he didn't want to frighten her or hurt her any more than he already had.

Without saying a word, he sat at the other end of the seat, taking his hands from his pockets. He leaned back, taking another deep breath.

They sat there quietly as the wind gusted in from the sea.

Finally, Danny found the courage to speak. 'We can. I just want to say how sorry I am for what I said this afternoon. I was cruel, and I didn't mean one word of it.'

Sienna moved along the seat so she was closer to him, and Danny almost groaned.

'I am sorry too. What I said was unforgivable, and I hope you can forget everything I said. And I hope you can forgive me for not trusting you. I knew you were a good person, and I should have let you tell me your story. Especially after I dumped all my baggage on you.'

Danny looked down, unable to believe what he was hearing and unable to believe that Sienna had moved closer and had reached for his hand. She laced her fingers through his.

'Why?' he said. 'What changed your mind?'

'Advice from a very wise woman. Advice that I should have known instinctively. Even though we began as friends, Danny, I think it became very clear to both of us that there was something there. You held back because of your situation, and I held back because I don't know—or I didn't know— how to trust. Can we start again?'

'As friends?' he asked carefully.

'I believe the right people come into our lives when they're meant to. Up until you, it was a friendship level, the girls who've helped me. Eliza and Pippa, and now my new and very wise friend Isla, have made me see the truth.'

'Up until me?' he said carefully reaching for her other hand.

'I care about you, Danny, and if all you want is friendship, I can accept that. I know you're not in a position for more than that.'

Danny couldn't put into words the joy that was coursing through him. Finally, he stood and pulled Sienna to her feet. 'I am now, and I'm finding it very hard to speak. Can I show you what I need to say?'

Sienna stepped into his arms.

***

The words that she had ready for Isla when she had come back with their rice pudding ran through Sienna's mind as Danny held her close. She whispered the words as he held her. 'Friendship, caring, laughter, hope, inspiration, joy, amusement, serenity, and maybe even love.'

Danny put his cheek against hers as she whispered. She could feel his smile against her skin. His fingers smoothed her hair as he held her close. For the first time in her life, she knew she was safe and happy. Reaching up with one hand, she brushed his face with trembling fingers. 'You're a good man, Danny.'

'What were those words about?' he asked.

'All of the emotions we've shared so far.'

'You are a beautiful woman,' he said. 'How could I not feel those emotions when I'm with you.?'

Sienna looked up and saw her own need mirrored in those dark brown eyes. She lifted her face and touched her lips to his. Danny's hold tightened, but he lifted his head away from her kiss.

'Wait. I haven't told you the best news yet. In about a week, I will no longer be married, and the record will say I have never been married.'

She widened her eyes and his smile grew. 'Thanks to a kind

old lawyer, and a declaration of nullity, the record will show I've never been married. It's a long story but not one I want to tell you tonight. Tonight is for kissing you, my Sienna.'

Chapter 25

Pippa - Ten days later

Sienna had stayed away for an extra week after her course finished but she promised that she was coming back. None of us knew what had happened, but Rafe looked smug when I told him how happy she'd sounded when she'd called.

'Told you they would work it out,' he said.

'You're jumping to conclusions,' I said as I rolled over and put my head on his chest. We had slept in, and it was time we were up. I had a big day ahead, but I always found it hard to leave Rafe in bed.

'I'll make a bet with you that she and Danny have sorted it out.' Rafe ran his fingers down my spine and I decided I definitely was getting out of bed.

'What makes you so sure?'

'Because I write stories and I like a happy ending,' he said, making me smile.

'How about a happy ending now?' I said cheekily as my fingers started a journey down his chest.

##

An hour later, I was running around trying to get ready for an interview I'd forgotten I had at the house at a quarter past ten. Eliza had insisted that I interview this guy for the lifeguard position at the pool. Apparently, she and Phillipe had met him and decided he would be perfect for the position. Renzo's guys had already done the excavation for the pool, and the logistics of getting an excavator over, and then to the location on the point where the pool was to be located had been a stressful exercise.

The guy, Zachary Johnson, was coming over with Jiminy on the ten o'clock launch.

Tonight was the staff Christmas party, and we'd closed the restaurant. Angus had called a couple of casual chefs in to cater as well as doing a buffet dinner at the old house for the guests.

'I'm going now, Rafe.' I called, grabbing a piece of toast, and my coffee. 'I'll be back for lunch.'

Rafe came out of the study. 'I'll walk down with you. I want to talk to Tess about a reservation for a couple of friends who emailed me overnight.'

I laughed as we headed to the gate. 'More Odessas?'

He bumped me with his hip and my coffee spilled. 'Behave, wife. But no. One is enough.'

'Oh quick, the launch is coming into the bay. 'As we hurried down the hill, I scoffed my toast, drained my coffee and then passed the empty mug to Rafe as I wiped my mouth, and brushed the crumbs off my shirt.

As we reached the steps at the bottom of the hill, Jiminy was tying off the rope.

I was surprised to see how many people were on the boat, and then exclaimed as I realised Sienna was stepping onto the wharf. 'Look, Sienna's home.'

Rafe followed me as I walked quickly along to meet her. My smile widened as I noticed the man behind her. 'And Danny's back!'

'Looks like I won the bet,' Rafe said as he leaned down to brush his lips over my cheek.

'I didn't agree to a bet.'

'Piker,' he said, and then he stopped walking. 'Blimey, who's that guy?'

I followed his gaze to the boat and spotted the guy talking to Jiminy. He had to be one of the tallest men I had ever seen, and as Eliza had described, he was "built," not to mention extremely good-looking.

'That, my dear, is most probably our new lifeguard.'

I opened my arms to hug Sienna as she and Danny reached the end of the wharf. 'Well, don't you two look happy and relaxed,' I said.

Sienna's cheeks were pink, and she smiled at me and then up at Danny. 'We are.'

Epilogue

Tess

The first staff Christmas party on Pentecost Island was in full swing. Tess had finished up at the office, insisting that Nell knock off first to go and get ready for the party. Nell had finished the check ins while Tess ran the reports in the back office.

Once she'd finished, she checked that the guests on the veranda were being looked after by the casual restaurant staff over from Hamo. Jiminy was coming back at midnight to take them back across the Passage, with the staff who'd come over for the function.

Tess hurried to her room, had a quick wash, changed her clothes, and put on some lipstick. She hadn't eaten since lunchtime and the aroma of the curries the casual staff had put on made her stomach grumble. Pulling her door shut behind her, she made her way down the steps towards the restaurant. The music was loud and had a great beat, half a dozen couples were already on the dance floor, and as she walked along the path, she was sure it was Rafe she saw dip Pippa almost to the floor in a fancy move. Sienna and Danny were cheek to cheek dancing slowly, despite the disco beat. The tables were full of happy people speaking loudly to be heard over the music. Pippa had even brought the housemaids and kitchen hands over for the party.

It was going to be a great night and Tess was looking forward to letting her hair down for the first time in a couple of years. She loved working on Pentecost Island, and it had given her a chance to consider her options and what she was going to do with her life. Cherry had suggested her to Pippa, and when the job had turned into a traineeship, Tess had been ecstatic. Working on the island was the first step in a new career.

She hurried along the path and when she was almost to the bar, someone stepped from the rainforest and blocked her way.

'Tess,' an all too familiar voice said.

Her eyes widened and her hand went to her mouth. 'What the hell are you doing here?'

'I need you to keep a secret.'

Tess

Pentecost Island 9

Prologue

Tess

Tess closed the desk drawer beneath the reception counter and locked it. She looked at the key in her hand, thinking locking the drawer was probably overkill in the office at Ma Carmichael's resort on Pentecost Island, but events in her former working life had led to a huge lack of trust. Taking the key through to the back office behind reception, she hung it on the hook behind the filing cabinet.

Tess was in a place where she knew she was safe. Looking around the office, she smiled. She loved working here and knew she had found the right solution for her life. Her healing had begun, and her confidence had returned; Tess knew she was respected by the rest of the staff—male and female. She was treated kindly, and, best of all, she had forged new friendships with women who liked her for who she was and not what she had or what she could do for them. She would be forever grateful to Cherry for recommending her for the office position on Pentecost Island after they had met up again on Hamilton Island. They had clicked as they had worked together in the bar and when they moved into a shared apartment, Cherry was an easy roommate.

Working as a casual housemaid on Pentecost Island before she started work in the office had been okay—it was a job, and on an isolated island—but when the part-time office work job had turned into a traineeship, Tess had been ecstatic. Working on the island was the first step in a new career. With Nell being pregnant, there was a chance she would be promoted while her boss was on maternity leave.

Tess had finished the day's work in the office and offered to stay for lock-up so Nell could get ready for the staff Christmas party. Nell finished the check-ins and headed off while Tess ran the reports in the back office.

The fileserver whirred in the background; being Saturday, it was a weekly backup as well, and the run would take a bit longer. Tess glanced at her watch; she had time for a quick call home while she waited for the reports to back up to the cloud and the file server that Nell's partner Nat had installed a couple of weeks ago. She pulled out her mobile and pressed the speed dial for home. They would have had dinner by now and Mum would be in the kitchen cleaning up while Dad watched the news and the boys went to the pub.

Home was as predictable as sunrise and sunset, as was the time it took for Mum to pick up the call.

'Hi, Mum.'

'Hello, love. I was going to call you later. We haven't talked for a couple of weeks.'

'Sorry, it's been really hectic here. And I've started my online course, and that keeps me busy at night.'

'Are you good? Are you eating properly?'

Tess smiled. 'Yes, I am. I love living on the island, and the new job's fantastic. And I've put a bit of weight on too. The food here is too good.'

'I'm just pleased that you're not working in those rough hotels anymore. I didn't sleep the whole year you lived on the Gold Coast. Isn't it about time you came home?'

Tess rolled her eyes. Just like the predictability of a day in her family home, her mother's conversation would go down the same track it always did. She waited for the "Are you getting eight hours of sleep every night?" question but was surprised when Mum hesitated and cleared her throat.

'Theresa? I wasn't going to tell you this, but your father told me I had to.'

'What, Mum? Are you all right? You're not sick, are you?'

Her mother's laugh boomed over the phone. 'Gawd, no, love. I'm as fit as a mallee bull.' She hesitated again, and Tess waited.

'So what do you have to tell me?'

'That . . . that man has been looking for you. He rang here twice asking to speak to you and then he turned up. Dad had to get the boys to the door to convince him he wasn't welcome.'

'You didn't tell him where I am, did you?' Tess's skin started to crawl and she fought the urge to scratch. She'd done enough of that in the middle of the worst time two years ago.

'No. I'm not silly, love. I recognised his voice. It's a lovely voice, deep and quite sexy, isn't it?'

'Mum!'

'Sorry . . . but he did take me in the first time I met him, but now I know how he treated you, I'll give him what for if he shows his snooty rich nose back here. If you'd been charged, I reckon your Dad and the boys would have gone after him. It was all his doing.'

'So no one said I'm in Queensland, did they?'

Her mother cackled. 'No, but the boys were ready for him. Ted let slip that you were in Exmouth in Western Australia. They put on a good show. When he did that, Dad clipped his ear and told him he was a dickhead. Hopefully, the tosser's gone off on a wild goose chase now.'

'How long ago was this?' Tess's scalp *was* crawling now.

'Oh, about six weeks ago. I wasn't going to tell you, but Dad's been onto me every time I hang up the phone from you. Just so you watch your back, he said.'

'Thanks. Mum and say thanks to Dad for me. Tell him this place is almost like Fort Knox, and being in reservations, I get to see the guests' names before they arrive. If *he* turned up, I'd scarper.'

'Good. You might come home.'

Tess sighed. 'No, Mum, but I'd have to hide again. I'm over it. I feel safe here. You should come here for a holiday.'

Her mother's laugh boomed over the phone, and Tess felt slightly better. Her family had her back, that was for sure.

'Ha, can you see your father on a beach and me in a bikini?'

This time Tess couldn't stop the smile tugging at her lips. 'I can, Mum.'

'One more thing. Have you told anyone there what happened? So they know to watch your back too?'

'God, no. I'm making a totally fresh start. I'm happy, and I'm well. And I'm safe here. That's all you need to worry about.'

'Maybe you should tell one person. That Cherry girl was a good friend to you on the Gold Coast.'

'No, Mum. There's no need. Listen, I have to go now. We have the staff Christmas party tonight. Say hello to Dad and the boys for me.'

'I will, and you look after yourself, love. The chooks miss you too. They haven't laid anywhere near as well since you left.'

Tess could always depend on Mum to bring a smile to her face, although this smile was brief. The call had shaken her, but forewarned was forearmed. She'd covered her tracks really well when she'd left her job in Sydney; even the media hadn't found her on the Gold Coast. She'd been big news in Sydney for a couple of weeks, and when she'd disappeared, they'd left her in peace as someone else had made the news. Tess lifted one hand to her head and ruffled her short-cropped hair.

I will not scratch!

Trying to forget Mum's words, she convinced herself she was all right.

I am.

She was safe here, but no, she wasn't going to tell anyone her past history. She hadn't been charged, and she'd left the city, and it was no-one's business.

As Tess closed the office door—and locked it—the music from the restaurant drifted across through the glade. It lifted her spirits; there was no point being down. What was in the past would stay there. What upset her the most was despite what he'd done, she still missed him and dreamed about him some nights.

The disco beat pulsed through the forest; Pippa was obviously in charge of the music selection The girls had been teasing Pippa—her boss and owner of the resort—about her music tastes the other day when they'd gathered for sunset drinks on the beach to welcome Sienna, the day spa therapist, back from her time away at a course on another island further north.

Tess's foot began to tap and before she reached the end of the veranda she was dancing, singing along with the music as the song changed to *I Will Survive.* That had become her theme song over the past two years.

Before she reached the turn leading to the side veranda, she stopped dancing, stood straight and put on her professional face. She looked down at her uniform and debated whether to get changed. Yes, she would; tonight she'd let her hair down, have a few drinks and enjoy herself. Every night her eyes scanned the booking sheets for the following day, reassuring herself that she would not be found.

At least it was better here than when she'd been doing bar and hospitality work on the Gold Coast. Every night there, her eyes roamed over the bar patrons, terrified she would see a familiar face.

But the people she'd worked with in Sydney wouldn't be frequenting cheap bars on the Gold Coast; they had more upmarket tastes. Her hair was now short and blonde; her long dark hair had been chopped off the day after she arrived at Coolangatta. She'd worried about the three new piercings in her ears, but Pippa hadn't cared.

'Looks fine to me,' her boss had said with a grin when Tess checked. 'As long as you do your work well, and fit in with the rest of us, I don't care what colour hair you have, or how many earrings you wear. We're pretty laidback here.'

Tess grinned as she walked along the veranda. Blonde hair, pierced ears and blue contact lenses. Her parents wouldn't even recognise her She could just imagine what they would say if they ever saw her new look. Dad would be unbearable.

She shook her head. It was a new look, but it would be a *temporary* one. Another couple of years, when she was convinced all was well, she'd grow her hair back. She missed long hair brushing on her shoulders.

Before Tess headed to her room, she checked that the guests at the temporary restaurant on the veranda were being looked after by the casual restaurant staff over from Hamo. Jiminy was coming at midnight to take them back across the Passage with the rest of the staff who'd come over for the staff function.

'Sounds like a good Christmas party,' an older gentleman sitting with his wife said as Tess paused to speak to them. 'We used to disco dance when we were young, didn't we, love?'

His wife laughed. 'I danced, Reg. I recall you propping up the bar. You hated dancing!'

Tess smiled at them and went into the kitchen. 'All good in here, guys?' she asked.

'Yep,' Greg, the temporary chef replied. 'Mains are done and cleared, dessert's about to go out.'

'Great, thanks. Pippa said to make sure you all come over for a drink before Jiminy arrives later. And thanks for stepping in. It meant that all the staff here could have a night off.'

'What about you? You're working,' he said moving a bit too close for her comfort.

'Me? I'm going to the party now.'

'Save me a seat, I'll have a drink with you.'

Tess flashed him a non-committal smile, and hurried out of the kitchen and down the back steps.

Her time for romance was done. Casual or long term. Her experience in Sydney had put paid to any dreams of marriage, kids, the white picket fence, and the lemon tree in the backyard. To have that, you had to have trust, and Tess had not one skerrick of that left in her.

Burned once, never again.

This traineeship on Pentecost Island was a new start for her; the beginning of a new career and she was going to give it one hundred percent.

Hurrying to her room, and keeping an eye out for anyone loitering, Tess had a quick wash, changed her clothes, and put on some lipstick. She hadn't eaten since lunchtime and the aroma of the curries the casual staff had put on for the guests had made her stomach grumble. Pulling her door shut behind her, she made her way along the back lawn to the glade.

The first staff Christmas party on Pentecost Island was in full swing.

The music was louder and had that great beat, and through the trees she could see half a dozen couples on the dance floor. As she walked along the path, she was sure it was Rafe who dipped Pippa almost to the floor in a fancy move. Sienna and Danny were cheek to cheek dancing slowly, despite the disco beat. The tables were full of happy people speaking loudly over the music. Pippa had brought the housemaids and kitchenhands over from Hamo for the party.

It was going to be a great night and Tess was looking forward to letting her hair down for the first time in a couple of years. Well, maybe not her hair, but she'd let her guard down and relax.

And by God, she needed that. The past two years of bar work—where she had met Cherry on the Gold Coast and then followed her to Hamilton Island—had been hard work and so different to what she was used to, but Tess had needed that sort of job to recover. It might not have been exactly what she was qualified for—an honours degree in economics wasn't exactly a prerequisite for bar work. When she'd been knocked back for the first jobs she'd applied for, Tess had soon learned not to mention her qualifications or where she'd previously worked. After the early sceptical receptions she'd received, she'd soon learned to mention only the waitressing and bar work she'd done when she was at uni.

But as hard as it was, the work on the Gold Coast and Hamilton Island had been for a reason and had eventually brought her to Pentecost Island.

She hurried through the glade and was almost to the bar when someone stepped from the rainforest and blocked her way.

'Theresa.'

Tess put her hand to her throat as her past came rushing back to her with that one simple word. Her name whispered in that deep voice, the voice that had once sent pleasant shivers down her back. Now, sheer terror caused the shiver that made her whole body shake. Her ears buzzed, and Tess stepped back as fear consumed her.

She struggled to speak. 'What the hell are you doing here?'

'I'll tell you, but first, I need you to keep a secret. Please don't tell anyone who I am.'

Her nemesis stepped closer to her, and Tess shrunk away, fighting the faintness that threatened to consume her.

Chapter 1

Two years earlier - Sydney

Theresa Anderson took a deep breath, pushed her umbrella up, and stepped onto George Street. An autumn southerly buster had come barrelling in from the Antarctic just before five o'clock and the gutters in the city were already running like creeks that reminded her more of home than the city.

She stepped onto the wet pavement and shivered as a strong gust of icy wind turned her umbrella inside out and rendered it useless.

That'd be right. A rotten end to a rotten day. Pulling a face as she muttered a curse, Theresa shoved the cheap umbrella into the nearest bin, put her head down and headed for Wynyard Station. She wasn't looking forward to the long train trip out to Brentwood tonight; her clothes were drenched already, and the air conditioning on the train was always too cold. The last thing she needed was a head cold.

With a sigh, she strode out. As much as it would be more convenient to live closer to the city, Theresa simply couldn't afford it.

Not being able to stay in the office and work back really peed her off. Even though she was the first assistant to the executive officer on the trading floor, she hadn't reached a senior enough level to be allowed to stay in the office after five. It was a ridiculous policy. If she was allowed to, she could have waited until the rain had eased, finished the international transaction she was working on and taken the late train home. As she'd worked through the afternoon, Theresa had lost track of the time, and when the five o'clock bell had rung, she'd been in the middle of a complex foreign transfer.

'Shit,' she'd muttered. If she logged off now, she'd have to start again on Monday.

'What's up, Reeza?' Boyd Drummond, the trader opposite her—and son of the CEO of the bank—looked at her around his computer screen.

'I didn't realise the time and I have to leave this Swiss Bank transaction.'

'Don't worry; stay logged in, and I'll finish it off for you. Is that the Zurich one?'

'It is.'

'Okay, you get going, and I'll sort it.' Boyd stood, and not for the first time, Theresa repressed the revulsion that his cold eyes always sent running through her. She was also aware of the admiration in his eyes, and the way he would stand closer than necessary to her in the small alcove where they always seemed to arrive at the same time.

It made her very uncomfortable.

Theresa was focused on making her way up to a senior position, and there was no way she would compromise that by going out with anyone in the bank. Or responding to Brad's frequent flirting, even if he was the CEO's son. Any promotion she got, she would earn by exemplary work.

'Thanks, appreciate your offer, Brad, but it's okay. It can wait until Monday.' Reeza forced herself to smile at him, but not so much that he took it as a come-on. She reached down and grabbed her bag, slipped on the high heels that she'd kicked off beneath her desk after the last coffee break, and headed for the lift that would take her from the top of the skyscraper near the harbour, and down to George Street.

Being a Friday evening the crowd from the bars would usually spill out onto the street, but because of the rain, the patrons were crammed at tables beneath the awnings. And that meant that most of her walk to the station was in the drenching, cold rain. Within minutes, her black corporate suit was sodden, her shoes were ruined, and her hair was plastered to the sides of her cheeks. Theresa's foul temper worsened, as she tottered along on her four inch heels and stepped into a deep puddle where the gutter had overflowed into a dip on the footpath.

'Bloody hell.' She stopped, pulled her shoes off, tucked

them beneath her arm and walked along in wet stockinged feet. Those shoes had been her one splurge this year—she hadn't been able to resist them—and she might as well put them in the bin with the umbrella now.

As she reached Jamison Street, she turned up the steep hill, grateful for the overhanging roof of the hotel that kept the rain off. The regular concierge smiled as she passed and she looked down, a glimmer of a smile breaking through her bad mood.

'Evening, Theresa.'

'Evening, John. Have a good weekend.'

'You too.' His grin was wider than usual.

I must look a right sight, she thought.

Five minutes later, Theresa was through the station, her Opal card safely back in her purse and settled into a seat in the middle carriage.

She pulled her phone out.

Pick me up at Brentwood Station at 7.15 pls, she texted home.

Sorry no can do. Picking, came straight back from Ted. **You'll have to leg it, sis.**

Mum? she sent back.

Out, was the reply.

Raining? she asked.

'No, just the bloody wind. Peaches are falling at the rate of knots. Dad has the shits.

Just what she needed. A walk home and a cranky father on arrival. With a bit of luck, he'd go to the pub after they finished picking. Tess put her head back on the damp cushion of the high-backed seat and closed her eyes, letting the movement of the train soothe her as it pulled out of the station right on time.

She'd worry about how to get to the farm when she got off the train. Maybe it was time to consider moving closer to the city. Maybe a share house in the inner western suburbs would be affordable.

Maybe.

##

Two hours later, Theresa's suit had dried a little from the air conditioning on the train, but it had been an unpleasant trip; she'd shivered most of the way. She'd changed trains at

Campbelltown to get the Intercity train to Brentwood and now, after another half an hour, the train finally approached her station. She slipped her still-wet shoes back on and made her way to the automatic door. The train was almost full as commuters made their way to Melbourne for the weekend.

She peered through the glass door as the train approached the station. At least the rain had only been coastal; the trees were swaying in the strong southerly wind as they entered the small township. That's why Dad and the boys would be out-picking. With a wind like this, the last of the peach crop would be at risk.

Theresa stepped off the train and crossed her fingers there would be a taxi at the rank. But of course, in line with the rest of the day, the street was empty, and there was no sign of a taxi.

Maybe Mum was in town at a meeting, she thought. She could find her car, using the spare key that was in a magnetised container under the back mudguard, and then come back later and pick Mum up. Pulling out her phone, she pressed the speed dial for Mum, thinking how ridiculous it was that a woman of twenty-nine years of age was ringing her mother to try and get home.

Home to the family farm where she'd grown up and had never left. When her friends had moved into the city to go to uni, Theresa had opted to stay at home and work on the family stone fruit orchard. Money had always been tight in the seasonal industry that was so dependent on the weather each summer.

Three years later, she decided that she was going to go to uni and do the study she had always wanted to pursue. The train commute to uni three days a week was the price she'd paid for wanting to save as she studied for her economics degree.

Dad had stared at her as though she had two heads when she'd announced she was going to uni on the night of her twenty-first birthday. 'Why the hell would you do that? There's plenty of work for you in the orchard.'

'No. I want to have a career,' she'd said.

He'd shaken his head. 'We can't afford it.'

'It won't cost you anything, Dad. I'll live at home, and I'll work in the shed on the days I don't have lectures.'

'Whatever.' His attitude hadn't improved over the six years it had taken her to complete her degree, and her honours years. She had worked in the shed and in the orchard and held down two part-time jobs in town Even landing a job at one of the biggest trading banks in the country when she'd graduated hadn't impressed her father. Nor did the fact that she had a huge HECS debt to pay back for her university course.

No wonder her desire to get away to the city and live there was so strong. There was a whole world out there for Theresa to see, and she now had a job that had kickstarted her career in finance and gave her the salary she needed to be a part of that world.

A world where she wasn't standing in a packing shed grading peaches and apricots, or out in the hot summer sun pruning trees.

But Theresa was not a risktaker, and she was frugal and sensible with her spending and saving. As soon as she'd paid off her HECS debt, she would move to the city. She figured it would take another three months, and then she could maybe consider it. Excitement rippled through her.

And then her life would begin in the city.

The *inner* city where one day she'd have a swanky apartment with white carpet, her *own* huge television for watching what she wanted when she wanted and not have to fight with her brothers for the remote or use her phone to watch Netflix. She would have an all-white bathroom with a heart-shaped spa bath, and a state of the art kitchen with a coffee machine.

Dream on, girl, she told herself as she waited for her mother to pick up the call, but there was no answer.

With a sigh, she called Ted, her oldest brother. He answered straight away.

'Can you pick me up in town when you finish picking please?' she asked. 'There's no taxis around.

'We'll be a couple of hours yet.'

'Where's Mum?'

'At a meeting in Thirlmere.'

'Okay. I'll grab some dinner at the Federal and wait for you there.'

'Hang on.'

She could hear Ted talking to someone and rolled her eyes when he came back and told her what was happening.

'Dad said he'll pick you up in an hour.'

Great, just what she needed. Another lecture on how selfish she was.

'Thank you. I'll be in the bistro.'

Theresa disconnected the call, and as she set off for the hotel two kilometres away, the sky opened and it began to bucket down.

Maybe Dad was right. Maybe she was a fool.

Chapter 2

Zac Montgomery turned off the Hume Highway onto the narrow country road. Anticipation built as his black BMW purred along, leading him towards the small town of Brentwood. This weekend he was going to find his new home in the country. The windscreen wipers swished back and forward rhythmically and Zac yawned. An accident on the M5 had held him up for an hour, and another big day at the bank had taken its toll. Dinner, a whisky and bed were looking very attractive. The weather forecast for the weekend ahead wasn't boding well for an outdoor auction, and a tinge of disappointment dampened his anticipation slightly. He'd been looking forward to trudging over the grassy hills, checking the property out before the auction. They'd have to move the auction to the office. He was determined to look the place over first. The auction wasn't until early afternoon; hopefully, the rain would ease overnight. It would be a pain if this heavy rain didn't let up.

The railway station flashed by on his right, and Zac peered ahead, looking for the turnoff to the main part of town where the hotels were located. Flicking on his GPS, he keyed in the hotel and the route came up. He'd grab a pub meal before he checked into the motel, which he knew was simply a room with basic facilities. He could have stayed at the country resort on the other side of town, but figured there was no point as he intended being out and about all weekend.

Zac frowned as the headlights picked up a dark shape ahead. He slowed the car as he approached a person walking on the left-hand side of the bitumen road. As he got closer, he could see the high heels and knee-length skirt of a woman tramping along in the rain. He almost felt guilty sitting in the warm and dry interior of his BMW. As he drew level with her, he slowed the car to a crawl and pressed the button to take down the electric window on the passenger side.

'Would you like a lift into town? I'm heading there now,' he called out.

She lifted her head, and he stared as the familiar voice came through the window.

'Mr Montgomery?'

'Reeza? Is that you?'

As she nodded, he stared at the wide-eyed, pale face stuck with damp strands of hair. It was Theresa Anderson, the senior assistant to the executive officer on the international trading floor. She looked like a waif rather than the best-looking, most sophisticated woman on the trading floor. Zac had noticed her the first day she'd started work there a couple of years ago, and over the time, he had been very impressed with her dedication to her work. As far as he knew, she never socialised with the staff and never attended the Friday night drinks at Jacksons down the road from the bank. That hadn't stopped him looking for her on the nights he'd gone there with the crowd, but she'd never been there.

He had eventually assumed that she had a partner she was keen to get home to, and the glimmer of jealousy had surprised him. After that he'd found himself going to that floor more than he'd really needed to, but she had always been professional and not engaged in social chat when he'd tried to start a conversation. Her hands were ring free, not that that meant anything these days.

And not that he'd been looking.

'Quick, jump in. I'll give you a lift.'

'It's okay. It's not far now. I'm too wet to get into your lovely car. I'll ruin the seat.'

Zac drove a short distance past her, pulled to the side of the road and turned the motor off before he got out.

He walked around the back of the car to where Theresa was standing, took her arm and guided her to the passenger door before she had time to object. 'Don't be silly. Jump in. The leather seats will dry.'

'Are you sure?'

'Of course I am, now hurry up and hop in because I'm getting soaked out here too.'

She quickly climbed into the front seat and Zac shut the door before hurrying around to his side. Once back in the car, he flicked the interior light on and gestured to the glove box.

'There's a box of tissues in there if you'd like to wipe yourself down a bit. You look miserably wet and cold.'

She opened the glove box and soon there was a small pile of sodden tissues on the floor next to her handbag after she'd dabbed at her hair and face. 'Thank you. I feel a bit more civilised now.'

'I'm assuming you caught a train out here? I passed a railway station a way back. Are you here for the weekend too?' He smiled at her as the thought struck him. 'You're not going to the auction, are you?'

She shook her head. 'No. I don't know about any auction.'

'Ah, that's good then, I'd hate to have to bid against you.' He tried to make her relax with his light-hearted tone. 'Sorry, I'm not sure what to call you. I know your name is Theresa, but I've heard you referred to as Reeza more than that. What shall I call you?'

Even though the light in the car was dim, he noticed her cheeks turn pink.

'Reeza is fine, Mr Montgomery.'

'Zac, please. It's the weekend. There's no need to be formal.'

'What's this auction?' she asked.

'I'm really keen on having a place in the country, and this property ticks all the boxes, so I drove out from the city. If I'd known you were coming this way I could have given you a lift.'

Reeza nodded shyly and gestured outside. 'It's quite pretty out here. When it's not bucketing down, that is. The rain wasn't forecast this far west.'

Zac chuckled. 'If we made as many mistakes with our trading as the weather forecasters do, we'd all be out of a job.'

'I tend to look at the sky and make my own judgement,' she said with a gentle smile. 'Although I did misjudge badly tonight.'

'Why were you walking from the railway station? You weren't getting picked up?'

'Someone from home usually picks me up, but they were madly picking tonight to beat the wind. My dad is picking me up in town in an hour.'

Someone from home? My dad, he wondered. That didn't sound like a partner. And if her dad was picking her up, home must be with family. She must have come out for the weekend.

'You come home on the weekends?'

'No, I live out here.'

Zac stared at her. Even with her makeup washed off, apart from some of that eyelash black stuff under her eyes, Reeza was still a very beautiful woman. 'You mean you do that two-hour commute each way every day?' he said, turning his attention back to the car.

'I do. It's good downtime.' This time she chuckled. 'Except when it decides to rain, my shoes are sodden, and there's no one waiting for me at the station.'

'So you were walking until you got picked up. Do you live in town?'

'No, out of town. On fifty acres. My family has a stone fruit orchard.'

Zac started the engine, and the cosy warmth of the heater surrounded them. Neither of them spoke for a couple of moments as the headlights pierced the darkness ahead. His perception of Theresa Anderson had been way off. She wasn't going home to a partner; she'd been commuting all those months. His interest quickened.

'The turn-off to town is about five hundred metres ahead. On the left.' Reeza broke the silence. 'Just drop me anywhere in the main street.' She reached down and picked up her bag from the floor. 'Thank you very much for the lift.'

Zac hesitated. 'You said you had an hour to wait. Would you have dinner with me? I was going to have a quick meal at a pub. Being a local you might be able to steer me in the right direction.'

'The Federal is the best and quickest meal.'

'Is that a yes to the invitation?' He glanced across at her with a smile.

Chapter 3

For the life of her, Reeza couldn't understand why she'd agreed to have dinner with Zac Montgomery, one of the big bosses from the bank. It had been such a surprise when he'd asked, she hadn't been able to come up with a quick or suitable reason why she couldn't, and anyway, she guessed she had to eat. She couldn't very well show him the Federal Hotel and then sit at a table by herself. Zac was way up the ladder past her, and the word in the bank was that one day he'd take over the top position. He'd always made her nervous when he came to their floor, because he was such a good looking guy, and he had presence. He'd tried to be friendly but she'd put her head down and worked harder whenever he'd come to the floor.

Reeza was used to her father and brothers in their navy blue King Gee work clothes. Zac Montgomery was always beautifully groomed and wore the best suits. His skin was tanned, his hair was jet black, and he had dark blue eyes that a girl could lose herself in. When she'd finally got hold of the remote to the TV last week, she'd binge watched *Poldark*, and as soon as he'd had made his entrance, he had reminded her of Zac Montgomery. A touch of arrogance, and *bucketloads* of sex appeal.

Nervous tingles scurried around inside her as he held the door of the Federal Hotel bistro open for her.

Zac Montgomery having dinner with Reeza Anderson!

She wondered if her wet skirt was sticking to her behind, and how damp her white shirt was beneath her jacket. There was no way she was taking it off, despite the pretty lacy underwear that was another of her weaknesses.

The bistro was busy and several locals waved to her, looking curious as Zac led her across to a vacant table near the window.

'That's good, I'll be able to watch for my lift,' she said. He was very polite and went to take her jacket off, but she shook her head. 'Thanks. I'll just slip to the restroom and try to do something with my wet hair.'

'It looks busy here and I know you've only got an hour before your lift, so I'll order while you've gone. What would you like to eat?'

Heat ran into her cheeks this time, and Reeza felt about fifteen again as she stumbled over a coherent response. 'Ah, no . . . um . . . it's okay. Ah, maybe just a salad. Yes, a salad, thanks. A Caesar salad.' Reeza dug in her bag for her purse, but Zac held up his hand and that sexy smile took her breath away.

'We'll sort it later.'

'Thanks. I won't be long.' She turned and looked around when she reached the door of the bistro.

Zac had put his car keys on the table to claim it, and had joined the long queue at the counter. He was taller, better dressed, and *way* better looking than any other man in the room.

Than any other man in the state.

Reeza groaned as she opened the door to the restroom. Heat rushed through her again.

Why was she here with him? What the hell were they going to talk about?

Her mortification was complete when she stood in front of the mirror above the basin. Her hair hung in rats' tails and her mascara had run and was now stuck in clumps below her eyes. Turning to the full length mirror beside the door, she was relieved to see her clothes didn't look too bad. A bit of mud was splashed up the back of her pantihose but she scrubbed that off with her hand before digging into her handbag for her hairbrush.

She grinned at her reflection as she dipped her head beneath the hand dryer and fluffed out her hair before brushing it and securing it in the clip. A dab with a wet tissue to remove the mascara spots, and a quick flick of red lipstick and she looked almost the same as she had when she had left for the office this morning.

Almost.

Certainly not up there with Mr Zac Montgomery.

With straight shoulders and her chin lifted high, she tried to look confident as she slipped her handbag over her shoulder. Reeza pulled a face at her reflection; it didn't work. She looked just as nervous as she felt. It was stupid; this was her town and her home turf, and she'd been having dinner at the Federal Hotel for as long as she could remember. She wasn't at work, and she should be able to consider Zac Montgomery as an acquaintance and not one of the big bosses from work.

A very good looking boss from work.

She swallowed and headed back out to the table. The bistro was even busier, and the local band had started up in the covered beer garden. Children ran around between the tables and she finally relaxed, smothering a grin as she wondered if the family pub atmosphere would turn a city slicker off country life. Maybe it wasn't the bucolic setting that he was imagining. He might think twice about a move out here; Brentwood living was very different to the country life that the glossy magazines and weekend supplements painted of the country west of the city.

Then again, Reeza had never moved in that set. Maybe they went to the swanky restaurants like the one out at the resort. There probably was a whole life out here that she'd never experienced.

Zac stood as she approached the table and she waved at him to sit down.

'I wasn't sure what you'd like to drink, so I bought a glass of white wine and a soft drink to cover all bases.'

'Thank you. A wine will hit the spot. It's been a very long day.' She glanced at the beer sitting on the table in front of him.

'It has.' Zac leaned back in his chair and looked at her, and she returned his gaze steadily, and decided to take the initiative. Picking up her wine and sipping it, Reeza kept her eyes on his. They were as deep a blue as she'd noticed from a distance over the trading floor, and surrounded by thick dark lashes that were the same colour as his almost jet black hair. 'So a house in the country?' she asked trying to sound interested and sophisticated.

'That's the plan.'

'And I guess it's not for commuting to the city from.'

He lifted his beer and took a sip. 'Who knows? Maybe one day not too far away.'

Reeza nodded. 'Sounds like early retirement.'

'Retirement! I'm not that old.'

He looked most affronted, and she smiled. 'I didn't say you were old. Who knows ? You could be planning to start a horse stud, or plant peach trees.' She picked up her wine and took another sip. 'Although I wouldn't recommend the peaches.'

'I've always wanted to live in the country. I grew up in Sydney. Went to uni there, and I've worked there for fifteen years. I can see myself as a gentleman farmer.'

From the tone of his voice, Reeza knew he was teasing her. She chuckled. 'And here am I. I've lived here all my life and it's my dream to live in the city. Right smack bang in the middle where I can see the harbour if I want to and listen to the traffic instead of cows and chooks, and walk to any restaurant. You might think I'm silly, but I've already chosen the colours and the fittings for the day in about twenty years when I can afford my luxury apartment.'

'Nothing like having a plan.' This time Zac smiled and she thought how much younger he looked. 'So you're going to commute until then. That's a lot of train rides.'

She pulled a face and nodded. 'Yep.'

'Next time you're in the city for the weekend let me know.'

She looked at him curiously but he didn't elaborate. 'So tell me about the local area, Reeza. You must know it well.'

'Too well.'

'Have you travelled much?'

She shook her head. 'No. I've been pretty boring. School, uni work. I'm embarrassed to say I've never been out of New South Wales.'

His eyes widened and Reeza found it hard to look away. For the first time she noticed the unusual dark flecks in the blue of his eyes.

'Never?'

Embarrassment flooded her.

Why the hell did I say that?

Pulling herself up straight Reeza looked around, trying to think of another subject apart from how boring her life was. She was no good at this social stuff, especially with someone who was way above her level, professionally and socially.

She was surprised when Zac leaned over and took her hand. 'There's no need to feel as though you're less of a person because you haven't travelled. Let me tell you about my Mum. You'd love her; she is one of the most interesting, well-informed people you'd ever meet. She didn't go to university, and she's never been out of Australia. She still lives in the same house my parents bought at

Balgowlah Heights when she married my father. She grew up in a house around the corner from there and always says why would she go anywhere else?'

'What does she do?' Reeza's interest had been piqued.

'She writes poetry.'

'She sounds interesting. What about your Dad?'

'I don't have a father anymore.' Zac's voice was controlled, and his smile disappeared.

'I'm—' Reeza was saved by the loud vibration of the buzzer on the table. She jumped up. 'I'll get the meals. You stay there.'

Before he could answer she'd picked up the buzzer and shot off to the bistro. She glanced at her watch on her way. Forty-five minutes until pick up if Dad was on time. She hoped he'd be running late tonight.

'Hi Reeza. Night out on the town?' Helen, the waitress on the cash register at the bistro smiled at her. They'd gone to school together, and Helen was one of the few who'd stayed local. Reeza had worked in the bistro as a kitchen hand in her first two years at uni, and then graduated to bar work.

'No. Just a late one. Dad's picking me up in in a while.'

'That's a shame. I was checking out the sex on legs you're sitting with. Not a bad looker, love. He looks like that guy in *Poldark*. Where did you find him?'

'He does, doesn't he?' Reeza laughed. 'He's one of my bosses and he gave me a lift in the rain, and then took pity on me and offered me dinner. Which reminds me. How much is the Caesar Salad these days?'

'Twenty-four dollars.' Helen handed over the salad, and a plate holding a huge steak. She winked. 'And here I was thinking he was building up his energy for a big night, and what a lucky girl you were.'

Reeza smiled and shook her head. 'No such luck in my life.' She turned, heated from head to toe as she bumped into Zac who was standing close enough to have heard the entire conversation. A smile played around his mouth and she looked away as he reached for the two plates. 'You get the cutlery, Reeza. I'll take these to the table.'

'Sorry, 'Helen mouthed.

'Shoot me now,' Reza whispered back. She collected two cutlery bags and followed Zac back to the tables. After she'd placed the cutlery on the table, she reached down and pulled out her purse.

'Twenty-four dollars,' she said, pushing the right money across towards him. 'For the salad. I'll get us another drink. My shout. What would you like?' She knew she was babbling but she was worried that he'd overheard Helen's comments.

And her reply!

Zac put his hand over hers and pushed it, and the money back to her side of the table. Reeza's mouth dried and she looked down at her hand; it had zinged with an electric shock when he'd touched her fingers.

His eyes were intent on hers when she looked up. 'You don't have to pay me for your dinner, Reeza. I asked you to join me. I've got a favour to ask and that will pay me back anything you think you owe me.'

'A favour?' she said slowly.

'I'd really appreciate if you could spend some time with me tomorrow and show me around the district. That is, unless you have other plans.'

'Um. No. I don't have plans.'

'Excellent. Would you prefer I met you in town or can I pick you up? I'd be interested to see an orchard.'

'If you'd really like to see an orchard you could pick me up.'

Reeza Anderson, what the hell are you doing? She wished she could pull the words right back into the mouth they'd come from.

'We live at Stony Park Orchard. About ten kilometres out on the Thirlmere Road. The orchard name is on the gate. You can't miss it.'

'Good. Say ten?' He tipped his head to the side and his eyes were dancing.

'Ten is fine.'

'Now we'd better eat up. We'll need to build up our energy for our day tomorrow.'

Reeza almost choked on the wine she had just sipped.

Chapter 4

Pentecost Island - Pippa

The music was still thumping, and I shook my head as Rafe tried to pull me up from my chair and take me out to the dance floor again.

'I'm too hot. Go and dance with Cherry. Angus has gone to check on the food. He can't help himself.'

My husband leaned down and kissed me and gave me a sweet smile before he held his hand out to Cherry, and soon they were jiving on the dance floor. Rafe could dance, and he'd confessed to me one day before our wedding that he'd attended weekly dance lessons right through his teens.

He was damn good. I sat there for a minute, fanning myself as I let my eyes wander over him. I'd thought he looked like a pirate the first time I'd ever seen him, and tonight he wore one of his long-sleeved white silk shirts with the V-neck and the loose ties open at the front.

No shorts and T-shirts for my elegant man. Love for Rafe surged in my chest—so strong it frightened me. I just hoped that I could live up to his expectations and be the wife he needed.

I left our table and walked across to where Tamsin and Nell were deep in conversation. I smiled as I looked at the two plates laden with food in front of them. 'Private conversation or can anyone join in?'

'Sit down, Pip. We were talking about you,' Tamsin said

I sat down and looked at them both. 'What did I do?'

They stared at each other and grinned. 'It's not what you've done,' Nell said.

'Although we hope you have been.' Tamsin's voice was as dry as ever.

Nell chuckled. 'Didn't you notice Rafe and Pippa were late *again*?'

'Have been what?' I said, pretending not to know that I

knew exactly what they were talking about.

Nell was the first to break. 'We were wondering how long it'll be before you're pregnant.'

'Or maybe you are already?' Tam's grin was cheeky. 'You've got a real glow about you lately.' She tapped the side of her nose. 'I notice things like that these days.'

'I sure do have a glow. It's called happy.'

Tam and Nell high-fived each other.

'And before your pregnant imaginations run away with you, it's called happiness from full bookings, the staff accommodation being almost finished, the excavator has finished digging the hole for the pool, the concreters are coming and—'

'And?' Nell and Tamsin both leaned forward.

'And my two best friends are going to make me a surrogate aunty twice in the next few months. Sorry gals, I'm not ready yet. Too much is happening here. And I'd like to have some time with my man before I start the nappy and bottle brigade.'

There was no way I was going to let on that Rafe had announced to me six days after our wedding that he was ready to start a family. Even though I'd told him I was happy, I'd worried about it nonstop ever since. So much it was keeping me awake at night.

Rafe had noticed I was preoccupied, but I had blamed Ma Carmichael's and the hectic work schedule as we expanded so quickly.

He'd looked at me for a while, and then agreed. 'You work too hard.'

'Not for much longer.' I said. 'The major stuff is underway. And then we can have our honeymoon.'

But he was not easily distracted. 'And our first baby. I'm not getting any younger,' he'd said, 'and I'd like to have fun with our children while I'm still fit enough to give piggyback rides and read nursery rhymes.'

'First?' I'd managed to joke. 'How many do you plan on having?'

He'd grinned and swooped a kiss on my neck. 'At least five.'

I vaguely recall that I had managed a smile and then headed off on the pretext of seeing the Riccardos. I'd taken myself for a long walk to the other side of the island, knowing I should tell him how I was feeling.

But I was too scared to tell him. I didn't want Rafe to stop loving me. I would rather lose everything if it meant Rafe would still love me.

The problem was I didn't know whether I could be a mother. I mean, I'm sure there was no physical reason that I couldn't, I'd never had any problems in the female department, regular as clockwork since the first summer I'd moved here to live with Aunty Vi.

That first time I'd got my period was such a shock I'd taken myself to bed on the side veranda for the day; I hadn't had a mother to tell me about female things and periods. After a couple of hours Aunty Vi had turned up with a hot water bottle.

'Put that on your tummy, Phillipa. It will ease the cramps and don't worry, they only last for the first day.'

'The first day,' I'd squawked. 'How many days does this go for?'

'Three or four if you're lucky, seven or eight if you're not.'

'God, I want to die,' I'd said dramatically, flinging myself back on the pillow, one hand over my face.

Aunty Vi had stood over me. 'Don't you ever let me hear you say that again.' She looked down at me for a moment, before brushing the hair back from my forehead, and then she'd turned on her heel and left me alone.

I'd lain back on my bed and looked at the horizontal slats on the old fashioned pull down wooden blinds. One of these horrid things every month from now—I was almost twelve—until I was ancient, about fifty or more. That was almost forty multiplied by twelve months every year. I counted the slats until my eyes blurred and I fell asleep.

I can still remember that day as though it was yesterday. The blinds had gone when we moved back to the island and had been replaced by those horrid thick pull down plastic blinds that kept the weather out. They also kept the view out, so they'd been taken down very quickly when Nell and Tam and I moved into the house.

I'd read the leaflet Aunty Vi gave me. It must have come with the sanitary pads because I couldn't imagine that she would have had it lying around.

But then, Aunty Vi was always full of surprises, and had been well prepared when I'd arrived there when I was eleven. She'd done a good job of getting me through my teens; I'd survived them anyway, and I became a master at hiding the scars that I carried.

Nell and Tam always said I had abandonment issues, but it went a lot deeper than that. Rafe had brought me to a good place, but I'd never told him about the bad times before my mum had taken her own life.

And that was the crux of my problem.

I didn't know if I was capable of being a *good* mother. What if I carried the same problems as my mother had? That same weakness? What if childbirth set me on that same path?

The chances of that happening were pretty good. I had never even told the counsellor my deepest fear.

'Earth to Pippa,' Tam's chuckle interrupted my brooding, and I forced a smile on my face, but they both knew me too well. 'Okay, spill, girlfriend. Why the worried face?'

'What were you thinking about then?' Nell asked softly.

This time I worked really hard at the smile. 'You really want to know?

Two nods and intent stares met my gaze.

'I was thinking about the first time I got my period and how Aunty Vi dealt with me.' I chuckled, and this time, it was half genuine. 'God, I was a drama queen back then.'

Tam nudged me. 'Back then? You still are!'

'Thanks, I love you too. Be careful if you plan on asking me to babysit. I'll teach your children as many bad habits as I can.' I leaned back in the chair. 'Now, are you two going to eat all that food or are you going to share.'

The music and happy voices surrounded me and I managed to smile as I let go of my dark thoughts for a moment.

I had a deeper worry.

Chapter 5

As Reeza stood in front of her open wardrobe in her underwear the following morning she wondered what on earth she'd done accepting an invitation to spend the day showing Zac Montgomery the local district. Not only that, she'd also given him her address to pick her up. The rain must have soaked into her head last night and given her a brain fade.

When she'd seen her father pull up outside the Federal Hotel as she'd been finishing off her salad, she'd jumped up and said a quick goodbye to Zac before Dad could come into the pub.

'See you in the morning,' Zac had said with that sexy smile as she'd fled. What a stupid thing she'd agreed to. His reputation at the bank was that of a lady killer, and she wondered why on earth he'd asked her to come with him tomorrow, although, to be honest, there'd been no sign of a lady killer—apart from the blue eyes and the sexy smile— he had been very polite and reserved over dinner. Plus it *had* been kind of him to offer her a lift in the rain. He could have sailed straight past her last night.

Today was probably because he wanted directions to get around. Um, no, he would have a Sat Nav, she told herself.

Maybe he thought she'd know of other properties for sale. Anyway, Zac insisted that he was very interested in the one up for auction out near the Oaks. Shite, he was picking her up in fifteen minutes, and she still hadn't decided what to wear.

She stood at the open door of her old wooden wardrobe and stared at the selection. Three black and two navy-blue suits that she rotated for work, and six white shirts. At the far end were three dresses she'd had for years. Two of them had been bought for friends' weddings, and the other was the dress she'd worn to her twenty-first birthday party. Buying clothes meant she paid less of her uni debt and added time to when she could move to the city. For the first time Teresa regretted her lack of clothes.

On the shelf above the hanging space were shorts and T-shirts she wore in the orchard, and one good pair of jeans.

So the choice was the jeans and a white shirt from work, or the twenty-first party dress.

She stood there tapping one finger on her lips, aware that the minutes were scooting by.

Okay, it was warm enough for a dress. The rain had cleared overnight, and the southerly had dropped. Reeza grabbed the blue and white floral dress from the hanger and slipped it over her underwear. She knew she had a pair of matching sandals somewhere. Scrabbling around in the bottom of her wardrobe gave no success, and another five minutes passed before she finally found the blue and white shoes, covered in mould, in a box in the laundry.

It took a few minutes to wipe the mould off with a damp rag, and she threw the shoes into the clothes dryer for five minutes. The banging of the shoes in the drum thumped through the house as she hurried to the bathroom to do something with her face and hair.

'Shite, shite, shite,' Reeza muttered three minutes before ten. Hopefully, Zac would be late. She raced into the bathroom she shared with her brothers and groaned when she opened the drawer. Someone had tidied it; her hairbrush and clips had all disappeared. Even the one she'd put on the side of the sink last night wasn't there anymore.

As she pulled open the other drawers, Reeza groaned as she saw two boxes of condoms. One day she would have her own apartment and not have to share with her brothers.

Gawd, if she even needed condoms—not that there was any chance of that—she'd know where to look now. But a hair clip? Not a blasted one in sight.

When she had her own unit, everything would be in its place, and she'd have time to get ready in a leisurely manner.

And have nice things at her fingertips, where she put them, and where no one interfered with them.

As she slammed the drawer shut, the front doorbell rang. Grabbing a comb from the shelf, she ran it through her hair, fluffed it up and left it loose.

No time.

Grabbing her lipstick off the hallstand, she hurried towards the front door. At least there was no one else home. Her parents and both her brothers had headed out straight after breakfast. Dad had glared at her when he'd told her she was pruning the back half of the house paddock this morning, and she'd shaken her head.

'Sorry, I have plans,' she said.

Lyle had added his glare and his mouth to the disapproval around the table.

'Jeez, Reez, that makes more work for Ted and I.'

Ted, God love him, flashed her a sympathetic look. He was her favourite brother. Lyle was just like Dad.

'Well, I'm sorry, but I do have a life outside the orchard,' she said crossly. 'And I have been at work all week.'

'That's your choice,' Dad muttered.

Reeza had rolled her eyes, and Mum called out as she went down the hall. 'Can you do the chooks for me this morning, please, love? I have to go into town again. It's my morning on the CWA stall, and with the two auctions on, there'll be a crowd in town for morning tea.'

Feeding the chooks and collecting six dozen eggs had made Reeza even later, and by the time she came back to the house, she'd needed another shower, and her hair got wet again.

Maybe it would be worth the extra expense to move out now; she thought as she hurried to the front door. Life at the bank was a breeze compared to a weekend at home.

Opening the front door, she pulled it hard because it always stuck, but someone had obviously greased the lock, and the door almost knocked her off her feet before slamming into the wall with a loud bang that echoed down the hall.

Heat ran into her cheeks as she looked into Zac Montgomery's amused eyes.

'I'm delighted by your enthusiasm to see me,' he said with a cheeky grin.

God, now he even sounded like Ross Poldark.

'Someone oiled the catch,' she said in her defence, trying not to stare at the gorgeous man standing on the doorstep.

'And I thought it was me.' He gestured to the car parked in the circular drive. 'Your chariot awaits, madame.'

'I just have to get my bag. Oh, and my shoes. Have a wander around and look at Mum's roses. They're her pride and joy.'

Before he had a chance to agree or disagree, Reeza ran to collect her shoes from the clothes dryer and find her bag that she hadn't seen anywhere this morning,

Damn. The sole on each shoe had come away, and it was sticky beneath her feet. With a grimace, she pulled both shoes on. She'd just have to ignore the stickiness all day.

Not a good start.

She'd left her handbag in the living room last night, and of course Mum had put it away somewhere when she'd tidied up this morning.

Their mother drove them all crazy with her tidiness. The only problem was she would get side-tracked and put things in the strangest places. It was another five minutes before Reeza found her handbag in the pantry next to the spare egg cartons. Grabbing a handful of tissues from the top of the fridge, she shoved them in her bag, checked her purse was in there, and ran for the front door, grabbing her lipstick off the hallstand on the way past. She still hadn't put any on.

Zac was waiting by his car.

'Sorry,' she said. 'You wouldn't believe my life here. I change universes when I get off the train every day, I'm sure.'

'No problem. Don't stress. We have plenty of time. I thought a coffee in town first?'

'That would be good.' Zac held the door open for her, and she looked up at him. 'At least I'm dry today.'

'And looking very lovely, might I say,' he said. 'I'm used to the corporate Ms Anderson with the pulled back hair and the black suit.'

Reeza smiled. 'You're looking very casual too, Mr Montgomery. I'm used to the navy blue suit and the ties, and the artfully styled hair.'

Shite. Did I actually say that?

'That's my work look. This is the real me,' he said. 'Sometimes I wonder why I ever went into the business world.'

Reeza settled into the car as he walked around the front and settled into the driver's seat. She'd always found Mr Mont—Zac— friendly and polite in the office, but this was a new lighter side she was seeing today.

And she liked it.

She liked him. Boyish and relaxed.

Letting out a breath, Reeza decided she could relax too. It was Saturday. The sun was shining, they were away from the bank, and she had no one to impress.

'It's a great day. Would it mess with your hair if I put the top down?' Zac asked.

'Not at all, I should have a hair band in here somewhere.' She dug in her bag and was in luck for the first time this morning. She pulled out a blue scrunchie to match her dress and her hair was restrained in seconds. 'I'd love it. It's on my bucket list to ride in a sports car with the top down.

'I'm impressed,' he said. 'No fuss, no bother with your hair.'

'That's the me I would like to be,' she said with a rueful smile. 'But living at home does not lend itself to being organised.'

'I know what you mean. I'm embarrassed to admit to it, but would you believe I'm living back in the family home where I grew up?'

'Really?' Her smile widened. 'I don't feel so old-fashioned when I hear that.'

Zac pressed a button and when the soft top had slid down silently, he started the engine. 'It's not old-fashioned. It's the new way. So many thirty somethings still live at home with their parents these days.' He chuckled. 'I invited Mum to come with me last night, but she was horrified.'

'Horrified?' Reeza stretched her legs out in the generous space in the front of the car. 'Why horrified?'

'Horrified that a man of my age was asking his mother to go with him. I get the regular "when are you going to get married and give me grandchildren?" talk. But it's getting a bit too frequent for comfort now. So I'm looking for my own place.'

'How old are you?' She slid a sideways glance at him, wondering if that was the right thing to ask.

'I'll be thirty-seven next birthday.'

'Never married?' she asked, feeling very game.

'No. Went close once, but I managed to escape.'

Reeza chuckled because it seemed to be the response he wanted.

Zac turned the sports car to the right onto the main road,

and she crossed her fingers hoping that Dad and the boys wouldn't be in the front paddock near the road.

No such luck. As the sports car gathered speed, she spotted Dad up a ladder in the front of the orchard, and Lyle and Ted at the fence taking a break. Lyle pointed to the car and Ted turned around, and then both her brothers' eyes widened when they saw her sitting in the front seat.

'I'll cop some teasing about that tonight,' she said, pulling a face. 'Honestly, it's like being fifteen-years-old still. Sorry, you don't want to hear my woes.' Embarrassment flooded through her as Reeza realised how gauche she must seem. If Zac had been with one of the women she'd seen with him in the social pages—yes, she had taken note—they'd probably be talking about overseas trips, or skiing in Aspen, or the state of the stock market.

A light bulb came on in her head.

I can do that.

'Did you see the All Ordinaries was up this morning?' she said turning to him.

He looked at her curiously. 'No.'

'Oh.'

'I'd rather hear about your family, and your life out here. Is that all they do? I mean is the farm a working farm? Not a hobby for your family?' Zac changed back a gear as they zoomed up the last hill before town.

'Yes. It's a working farm and I'm the black sheep of the family because I went to uni and got a real job. Dad would much rather have me at home in the packing shed all day.'

'If you had done that, it would have been a loss for the bank. You're very good at your job, Reeza.'

Oh wow.

She looked away at the peach trees flashing past so he didn't see the smile that lifted her lips. 'Thank you. I do enjoy it,' she said quietly. 'Now enough about me. Tell me what we're doing today and where this property is.'

Chapter 6

Zac stilled as attraction slammed into him. Reeza had put her head back and laughed when the tiny teacup almost slipped from his fingers, but he caught it before any tea spilled. She'd relaxed after a half hour of sitting in the garden at the back of a quaint coffee shop that she'd insisted was the best in town.

'What?' He grinned. 'A man is allowed to love his cup of tea.'

'I know, but it was seeing you trying to put your finger through that handle that tickled me. Look, this is how you do it.' Her fingers brushed his as she reached across and took his teacup, holding the fine gold handle between her thumb and two fingers. 'See?'

He nodded gravely. 'You obviously have more experience than me in the art of tea drinking. I usually have mine in a mug.'

'Philistine,' she said. Reeza's smile was wide and her eyes were dancing.

After she'd put his cup back on the saucer, Zac reached over and took her fingers before she could pull away. Her pretty green eyes met his. 'It's good to see you finally relax. You have a lovely smile.'

'Thank you. I'm feeling good. It's Saturday, the sun is shining, and we have a fun day ahead. I've never been to an auction before. And you know what the best thing of all is?'

'Me?' He quirked an eyebrow and tried to look hopeful, but it didn't work because she chuckled again.

Reeza put her other hand to her chest. 'I'm sorry. I'm acting like a fourteen-year-old. I'll be serious now.' She composed her face into an expression more like the one she wore at work, and two tiny frown lines appeared on her forehead, but her eyes still held his.

Zac realised her hand was still in his, but she seemed comfortable. 'No. I much prefer the giggling Reeza. And if I'm not the best thing of all, what is? Or should I ask who is?'

She leaned forward and spoke quietly. 'The best thing is you got me out of pruning peach trees.'

Zac let go of her hand and focused on lifting the tiny cup. 'You still work in the orchard too?'

She nodded glumly. 'Yep, it's a family concern, and the family is expected to pitch in. I can't complain because my brothers work a seven day week.'

'Still, you must find it hard after a week at the bank, and that huge commute every day.'

Reeza dropped her eyes from his. 'I guess I feel guilty and I'm trying to make up to Dad for going to uni and getting a job in town..'

'Your steel trap mind would be a whiz with the financial records of the orchard.' Zac had seen a lot of her work at the bank and she was one very smart economist.

She shook her head. 'No, that's his domain. I just get to do the outside work with the boys. But enough about me. I've got the day off, and I'm going to make the most of it, so tell me about this property, and why you would want to move here from the city.' She tipped her head to the side as though it was hard to believe that he was really interested in moving out to the country.

Zac marshalled his thoughts and looked past her. Her eyes were distracting him every time he looked at her. They were an unusual shade of green with flecks of gold and fringed by dark eyelashes that he was pretty sure were natural. Her skin was flawless and as far as he could tell she wasn't wearing makeup. 'I want to have something of my own, with lots of space around me, where I can relax and be away from the crowds in the city. To start with it'll just be for weekends, but when I leave the bank, it will be my home.'

Her eyes met his again, and that strange jolt ran along his nerve endings. 'By yourself?'

He nodded. 'Yes, at this stage. I'm happy in my own company, and there's no one in my life that I want to live with. 'He lowered his voice and smiled. 'But if you ever meet my mother, please don't repeat that.'

He frowned as her voice rose and she looked over his shoulder.

'Oh, no.' Her eyes widened and she picked her cup up and

then put her head down. 'Brace yourself,' she whispered.

Before Zac could turn around, a firm hand settled on his shoulder.

'Well, well, hello there. Aren't you a dark horse, Theresa Anderson? When were you going to tell us you've got yourself a man? No wonder you wouldn't help Dad today.'

Zac looked up into eyes that were the same colour as Reeza's. Before he could speak, she replied to the woman he assumed was her mother. Apart from the eyes there was absolutely no other resemblance. Even though it wasn't raining, for some reason this buxom, ruddy-cheeked woman was wearing a yellow raincoat, and a rain hat inside.

'Mum, please. This is Mr Montgomery, my *boss* from work. I'm helping him with a business transaction this weekend. Mr Montgomery, this is my mother, Heather.'

'Oh.' The word was laced with disappointment. 'So it's work, is it?'

Zac put the teacup down and held his hand out. 'How do you do, Mrs Anderson. It's a pleasure to meet you. I'm sorry I took your daughter away from her work at the orchard, but I needed assistance today, and I couldn't expect her to come all the way into town.'

Her mother nodded, and lifted her hand. 'That's a shame, but at least if you get home early enough, Reez, you can still help Dad and the boys.'

Zac frowned wondering what the "that's a shame" referred to.

'I'll see,' Reeza replied.

'Did you do the chooks?'

She nodded and her expression was bland. 'Yes, there were six dozen eggs.'

'Good,' her mother said briskly, and nodded at Zac. 'Try not to keep her out too long, will you, mate?'

'Mum?' Reeza frowned at her mother. 'Why are you wearing a raincoat and that crazy hat?

Her mother's laugh was rich and warm. 'While the girls were manning the cake stall, I cleaned out the fridge in the CWA rooms. I didn't want to get my good dress dirty.'

Reeza's eyes lit up. 'Um, and the hat?'

'Oh, my stars! It fell out of my pocket when I was in the fridge, and I put it on so I wouldn't lose it. I forgot I had it on. How embarrassing. You'll think I'm a complete country yokel, Mr Montgomery.' Her ruddy cheeks deepened to a burnished red. Taking the hat off and stuffing it into her pocket, her eyes met Zac's and she grinned. 'Please don't judge my sweet daughter by her silly mum, will you? We're nothing alike.' She turned and went to the counter, and Zac and Reeza sat there without speaking until she'd collected her takeaway coffee and strode from the shop.

Reeza's head was down and her shoulders were shaking. Her hand was clenched on top of the table and Zac put his on top of it. And he thought he had problems with his mother telling him what to do.

'God, I'm sorry if I made things really hard for you. You should have—'

He stopped as Reeza lifted her head and he looked into a pair of dancing eyes and a wicked grin. '"Try not to keep me out too long, mate?" I've a good mind to stay out in the sticks the whole weekend. And did I feed the chooks! Of course I fed the bloody chooks. I do every morning. Honestly, if I didn't laugh, I'd—' She chuckled again.

'I thought you were crying,' he said quietly.

'God no. Laughing's the only way you can survive in our household. Otherwise I'd be as crazy as my mad family. They're okay. Mum's a sweetheart. She always has a cause and is running around looking after someone in need.' Reeza picked up her cup and sipped. 'But you know what? I am, you know.'

'You are what?'

'Like Mum. The Reeza you see at the bank is on her best behaviour. I'm afraid I inherited Mum's habit of telling it how it is. I've learned to control my tongue in the hallowed halls of the bank.'

'I can deal with that. I admire honesty. I just have one request.'

Her eyes met his again and those blasted nerves skittered around. 'What would that be?'

'No yellow rain hats.'

'I think I can do that for today.' Her smile was sweet. 'Although I could have done with one last night.'

Zac leaned forward. 'Have I created an inconvenience for the whole family by asking you out today?' He hadn't been able to resist her. And he had taken a while to get to sleep last night as he couldn't get Reeza out of his mind. While her local knowledge was handy, it was the thought of spending the day in her company that had prompted his invitation at dinner last night.

'No, you haven't. I'm a big girl now. I don't have to ask permission, even if Dad doesn't like it. Come on, let's get out of here before Mum's curiosity gets the better of her and she comes back.'

Zac jumped up and waited as Reeza stood and lifted her bag off the spare chair.

'Welcome to the country,' she said. 'My country. I think it's a bit different to your genteel expectations.'

Chapter 7

The day in the sticks—as Reeza had called it after Mum's country bumpkin performance—went way too fast. She enjoyed watching the auction, even though Zac didn't bid because he said the property wasn't as good as he'd thought it would be.

The crowd bidding was all out of the city. There wasn't one local face; even the real estate agent was from Sydney. When the auctioneer's hammer came down at 2.4 million dollars, Reeza stood there staring at Zac, her mouth open in disbelief.

'Who on earth would pay that for a scrappy bit of land and a house that needs a motza spent on it? And the orchard needs chopping out.'

'You'd be surprised.'

'Stunned is a better word.' As they walked back to the car, she turned to Zac. 'I can't believe anyone would pay that sort of money for any house and land.'

He looked at her curiously. 'With the transactions you handle every day, you must realise how much is spent on real estate internationally. The local market is the same.'

'I guess. It makes me think I'll never be able to afford the apartment I'm saving for.' As they reached the car, she paused. 'Anyway, it's been a lovely day. Thank you for asking me. I've had fun.'

'It's not over yet,' Zac said as he opened the passenger door.

'Aren't you driving back to the city now?'

'No, I booked the motel for another night. I'm going to have a bit more of a look around. I was hoping you'd come with me this afternoon and . . .' Reeza waited as he hesitated.

'And?'

'And have dinner with me tonight.'

'At the pub again?'

'No. I'd like to check out the restaurant at that country resort we passed.' Zac reached for her hand. 'Please? I'll be lonely by myself.'

'This is the man who told me he doesn't mind being by himself. Yes, I'll have dinner with you, but do you know how exxie it is?'

'Exxie?'

'Expensive.'

'Ah. Not an economic term I'm familiar with.' He grinned down at her, and that warm feeling that had tugged at her all day came rushing back.

'Well, you need to broaden your vocabulary,' she said. 'And if you want to go there for dinner, I'd say you'll have to book.'

'Is that a yes?'

Reeza hesitated, as the contents of her wardrobe filled her thoughts. 'Do you think it would be pretty posh? I mean, what should I wear?'

Zac shook his head. 'Something like you're wearing now will be fine. I'm not dressing up. I wear a suit all week. I'll just change my shirt. If you want to get changed, I can drop you home and pick you up later.'

Reeza weighed up the choices. Her oldest bridesmaid dress was a red sheath, and not too dressy. Formal would have been good; she adored the other dress. Go as she was, or go home and change into the red one and risk Zac encountering Mum again, or even worse, Dad.

'Okay, I'll get changed at home later, if you're happy to wait for me.'

He held her eyes with his. 'Of course I, am. Ah, will your mother be there?'

'Probably.' Reeza laughed as she got into the car. 'Why? Are you scared of her?

She couldn't stop laughing when Zac nodded. 'I think so.'

Chapter 8

Zac looked out over the orchard as he sat on the side veranda of Reeza's family home. He'd been relieved when they'd pulled up and there'd been no one else there.

'Looks like the pruning all got done,' she said. 'Dad and the boys will be down at the pub having a bet.'

She'd led him through the old farmhouse to the kitchen and made him a coffee, and then settled him on the veranda while she changed for dinner.

A table was booked at the Country Pines Resort for six-thirty. When he'd made the booking, Zac had raised his eyebrows when he'd been told that the dress was formal.

'Just one moment, please.' He'd put his hand over the phone. 'You were right; it is formal. Is that a problem?'

Reeza shook her head. 'No. I've got something suitable at home.'

He'd booked early for six-thirty in the bar and seven to be seated for dinner. Zac was starving, they'd only had a light lunch before they'd gone to the auction and then gone for a long drive around the district for a few hours, and didn't pass one coffee shop the whole time.

He sat outside sipping a coffee—instant—and looked out over the orchard. Daylight saving hadn't ended yet, and the sun was hovering over the horizon now. It was a pretty sight, the orchards back lit by the golden sun. Even though the farmhouse here was old, the land was prime. The fruit trees that hadn't been pruned looked lush and healthy. There were a couple of boxes of peaches and apricots on a table near where he was sitting, and he'd never seen such plump, healthy fruit in the supermarket.

If he could find land like this, he'd retire and become a gentleman farmer, He'd done well in the fifteen years he'd worked for the international bank, and his investments were solid.

There was also the inheritance from his father that he refused to touch, much to Mum's displeasure.

'I don't understand you, Zac. Tell me honestly. You don't enjoy working at the bank anymore, do you?'

'Not really.'

'You have no commitments, no one to tie you down. You should be off travelling and experiencing life. I worry about you, darling. Promise me, you'll think about it.'

'Okay,' he'd said. 'I promise to think about it.'

And he had. Here he was looking at land, and planning his exit from the bank. Zac stood and put the mug on the table and wandered over to the railing. He smiled, a dozen chickens were picking around the grass, and the low moo of a cow drifted up the valley. There was no sound of traffic, no voices.

Just blissful quiet. He could get used to this very quickly. The toxic atmosphere in the bank had been pissing him off lately, and he was unimpressed with the new CEO. Getting a call at home at eleven p.m. and having to find files and print and bind them, and then deliver them to the CEO's house at Double Bay in time for a nine a.m. meeting was becoming a too frequent occurrence. He was smart enough to know that it was Drummond trying to exert his authority.

'Confidential, Montgomery,' he would say. 'I can't trust those figures with anyone else.'

It made Zac feel like a glorified secretary rather than the head of the trading floor. Some of the deals and meetings over the past three months had made him feel uncomfortable. There was an execution mentality if analysts didn't deliver. They had lost a lot of staff in the short time since Drummond had taken over, and he knew he wasn't going to be far behind.

But Zac would go by choice. When he was ready.

'I'm ready.' A soft voice interrupted his brooding and echoed his thoughts.

His breath caught in his throat as he swung around, and his heart began to thud. Reeza stood there looking like . . . looking like something he'd never seen before. Her blue and silver dress clung to her body like a second skin. It was low cut in a straight line and the sleeves began at the top of her arms, leaving both shoulders bare.

Finally, he managed to speak. 'Wow.'

Her face coloured pink and she frowned. 'Is it a bit

overdone?'

'No, it's perfect.'

'And my shoes don't match.' She held out one foot to show him the same blue shoes he'd noticed her wearing today.

'Trust me.' He walked over and stood beside her and was enveloped in a sweet floral fragrance. 'No one is going to be looking at your shoes. You look amazing.'

Her cheeks were even pinker. 'Thank you. I was a bridesmaid a few years ago, and I haven't worn it since.'

'I feel sorry for the bride. Nothing could match that dress.'

'There were six of us, but Natalie looked stunning.'

'Let's go.' Zac reached for her hand and was pleased when she didn't hesitate to curl her hand in is. 'I've got a couple of quick stops to make on our way.'

Chapter 9

Zac was quiet as they drove back through town and Reeza wondered if he'd regretted asking her for dinner. He put the indicator on and turned into the car park of the local motel.

'First stop. I'll be quick. Just wait there.'

While she was waiting, she slipped her shoes off and scrubbed at the soles with a tissue, but all it did was stick bits of tissue to the shoe beneath her feet. The stickiness had been driving her crazy all day. Last time she'd ever put shoes in the clothes dryer. She could have worn her high black work shoes, but she was sure they weren't going to recover from the drenching they got last night. At least in the restaurant, she could hopefully slip the sticky sandals off under the table.

The door of Zac's motel room closed behind him and Reeza quickly slipped her shoes back on as he walked over to the car. She smiled when he got into the car.

'Wow,' she said. 'Nice suit.'

He pulled a face as he started the car. 'It's not, you know. It's the one I wore to work yesterday and was still wearing when I encountered the waif in the rain last night.'

'Looks as good as new to me, and you know, you didn't have to pick me up.'

Zac's voice was low and sent a shiver down her spine. 'I am very pleased I did.

The shiver was replaced by warmth that went from her toes to her head. 'Anyway,' she said casually, 'we both look the part, so let's go and try this posh restaurant. I'm starving!'

'Me too.' His eyes lingered on her face before he turned the car towards the road.

##

An hour later, they'd had a couple of predinner drinks in the bar of the poshest place that Reeza had ever been in, and the maître 'd came to escort them to their table.

She kept her voice low. 'I had no idea there was anything

like this near Brentwood. It's way out of my usual scene.' She moved closer so Zac could hear her low words and was surprised at his reply when he leaned closer.

'It's way out of my usual scene too.'

'I thought you'd be out most weekends.'

'I am, but nothing to compare to this.' His breath brushed her cheek as she leaned closer. 'I spend a lot of time on the harbour. I love being on the water.'

Once they were settled at their table by the window, the maître 'd filled their water glasses and directed their attention to the menus that were at the side of each setting. 'I shall return with the wine list, sir. There doesn't appear to be one on your table. I am very sorry.'

Zac waved a casual hand. 'No worries.'

Reeza looked through the panoramic window at the rolling hills dotted with sheep. The early evening set a rosy glow on the trees and ethereal light hit the top of the hill in shafts of gold. 'And you want to move to the bush? When it looks like this it really is appealing. It's not how it is you know, in drought and storm, and isolation from all the facilities in the city,'

He pulled a face. 'I want to move to the country.'

'Uh uh.' Reeza shook her head. 'It's the bush. I haven't been there, but I've seen the photos. You're not in the Cotswolds here.'

Zac held her gaze intently. 'You're right you know. Maybe I'm following a dream I really don't want.'

'Especially if you love the water. The best we can offer is the water storage reservoir at the back of the Oaks.' She tipped her head to the side and held those blue eyes with hers. 'If you could do anything you wanted, and money and time and people didn't matter, what would you do?'

'That's easy. I'd have a big luxury boat and travel around the world.'

'Sounds pretty good to me.' Reeza chuckled and earned a glimmer of a smile from the maître 'd as he glided to the table and handed the wine list to Zac.

'Is this table suitable for sir's requirements?'

Zac nodded. 'It is excellent, thank you, Raoul.' He read the name off the badge pinned to the man's white shirt.

Raoul reached for the white linen napkin in the circular crystal holder in front of Reeza and placed it carefully on her lap before he did the same for Zac. 'If you choose the degustation menu, sir, the wine is included with the meal.'

'Thank you, we'll have a look.' Zac held up his hand as Raoul went to move away. 'Raoul, may I ask you if there is a taxi service from here to town?'

The man frowned and shook his head. 'No, sir. Are you not an in-house guest?'

'No. We drove out from town.'

He shook his head mournfully as though someone had died in his restaurant. 'Well then, sir, the only thing I can suggest if you would like to have wine tonight is that you book a room. I believe there is a vacancy.'

'Thank you. If you could leave the menus and the wine list, and give us ten minutes that would be excellent.'

Reeza opened her menu and her eyes went straight to the prices. She'd intended having the cheapest meal, but she frowned; there were no prices listed.

Zac looked over the top of his menu as she closed hers and laid it on the table. 'Problem?' he asked.

Reeza shook her head. 'It's in French.'

'My favourite food,' he said with a smile. 'All those garlic cream sauces. To die for.' He put his menu down and leaned forward. 'I do fancy the look of the degustation option, and there is a different wine with each of the courses. Seems a shame to miss out on it, just because there's no taxi service. Please don't take this the wrong way, but what do you think if I book a suite. A *two* bedroom suite.'

Reeza decided to play this in a sophisticated manner, although her legs had gone to jelly when Zac mentioned booking a room. 'I think that sounds like a sensible idea. The only other alternative would be to get someone from home to come out and pick us up.' She shook her head. 'But it's too far, and I'd never hear the end of it.' She stifled a giggle. 'And I can't see you in Dad's work ute.'

'Oh no, don't do that. If there's no suite, we'll have a simple meal, share a bottle of wine and an early night. But we will come back out here when we can try the degustation menu.

Apparently they only offer it once a month.'

Excitement zinged along Reeza's nerves. It sounded like he wanted to see her again. She looked up as Raoul appeared beside Zac.

'Ah, Raoul. We would like to have the degustation menu, but before we decide, could you please check the availability of a suite for the evening.'

'Certainly, sir.'

Reeza sat there biting her lip, recalling the balance of her working account and wondering how much this was going to cost. Because there was no way she was going to let Zac pay for dinner and the accommodation. She could afford it, but she'd have to transfer some funds across with her phone.

There was also no way she was going to end the night early and go back to a house where the TV would be blaring, and smart comments would be made about her dress, and her having a date. Her face heated as he stared at her intently.

'You look worried. If you'd like to have the simple menu and an early night, just say it. I won't mind at all. We can come back next month.'

'I'm happy to stay. I'd like to stay. We're all dolled up and sitting in a beautiful restaurant. And you saw how hard it is to get a taxi around here. I very much doubt that the one local taxi would drive out this far.' She swallowed and her cheeks warmed as she held his eyes and spoke honestly. 'I did like hearing you say we could come back another time.'

Zac reached over and took her hand. 'I've enjoyed spending time with you, Reeza. I've really enjoyed today, and I'd like to do it again.'

'Me too,' she said shyly. 'But what about work? It will cause talk. You know the problem with favouritism and all that. Seeing the boss is not a good idea.' Her face flamed as he frowned and she wondered if she'd said too much. Maybe he'd only wanted company to go out, not "seeing", but Zac's next words filled her with relief.

'What we do on the weekends and at night has nothing to do with the bank. I want to get to know you, and I hope you feel the same way. I find your honesty refreshing, Reeza.'

Raoul came back to the table and handed Zac a bill fold.

'You are in luck, sir. We can accommodate you.'

'Thank you, Raoul.'

'If you could note your details in the folder, and slip your credit card in, I'll get it organised for you over at reception.'

Zac did as requested and sat back. 'Would you like me to read the menu to you?'

Reeza was excited but still trying to look as though she did this on a regular basis. She didn't get out much, and she was going to savour every minute of the night and the new experience.

Oh shite! she thought. If she was going to go out with him again, she'd have to go clothes shopping. And shoe shopping. In one day, Zac had seen two of the three dresses in her wardrobe, and he was very familiar with the corporate suits and white shirts she wore to work each day.

Reeza blinked as she realised he was staring at her again, but this time a smile tipped his lips. 'Sorry, I was miles away,' she said,

The main lights had dimmed as the restaurant had filled up, and Raoul lit the two long tapers on their table.

'You have the most expressive face, Reeza. It's not going to stand you in good stead if you want to be promoted to a trading role.'

She grinned at him. 'Okay, let's see how good you are. Tell me what I was thinking.'

'You were wondering if you made the right choice. You were thinking how hungry you are, and how tempting the menu is, not to mention the attentive partner you have tonight.' His thumb rubbed the skin on the back of her hand. 'I hope you weren't worrying if you've made the right choice or not.'

'Shall I tell you how far off the mark you are?'

'Am I?' He pulled a mock pout. 'You were thinking of ringing your dad to pick us up so you could get away from your boring boss.'

'I was thinking about shoes.'

'Shoes?' She was getting used to that sexy grin.

'Uh huh.' She nodded. 'Yes, shoes.'

Chapter 10

Reeza leaned back in her chair and pushed her dessert plate away. Zac grinned at her as he had been all night, and she had relaxed in his company as each of the nine courses had been served.

'My God,' she said. 'I don't think I'll need to eat until next weekend. I thought a degustation menu was supposed to be small portions!'

Zac picked up the course list that Raoul had placed on the table when they indicated that they would choose the degustation option. As he read, his deep voice sent a warm shiver down Reeza's spine.

'Degustation at our fine restaurant is a slow appreciative tasting of our local produce food, focusing on the senses, high culinary art and good company. We hope you will enjoy sampling the *small* portions of all of our chef's signature dishes.'

'I certainly enjoyed every mouthful. But they weren't small.'

Zac leaned over and touched the corner of her lips with his thumb. 'You missed a little bit of apricot mousse.'

'Oh, how embarrassing. You can't take me anywhere.' Reeza picked up her napkin and dabbed at her mouth.

'I enjoyed watching you eat. It's good to see a woman with an appetite.' He dropped his eyes back to the menu. 'Look. There's your orchard. Peaches and apricots supplied by our local Stony Park Orchard.'

'Wow. I didn't know that.' Reeza pulled a face. 'But then again, I don't have much to do with the business. Dad pretty much wiped me when I told him I was going to uni. They weren't impressed with my choice of career.'

'I'm pleased you made that choice. I wouldn't have met you if you hadn't.'

She looked up as Raoul hovered at the side of their table and held up a bottle of liqueur. 'The final drink on the menu tonight is our peach brandy. May I tempt you both? Just a taste.'

Reeza blinked. She'd been feeling warm and fuzzy since the small glass of red they'd sampled with the local lamb, and she knew that had a lot to do with how much she'd relaxed. Holding up her glass, she nodded. 'Just a taste, thank you, Raoul.'

The maître 'de smiled and half-filled the small liqueur glass. 'Sip it slowly, madam. It's quite potent.'

Zac held her eyes as she picked up the glass and sipped. The liqueur fizzed on her tongue and warmed her throat on the way down.

His smile was lazy as she blinked. 'Good?'

'Excellent,' she said, but her tongue felt thick and it was hard to pronounce the word. 'But I think one sip will do me.'

Zac sipped his peach brandy slowly until the glass was empty. 'Thank you for your company. I haven't enjoyed a meal as much for a long time. Are you right to leave?'

Reeza was feeling mellow and the nervousness that had gripped her earlier about sharing a suite with Zac had disappeared.

'I am.'

'I was going to suggest a walk around the grounds to walk off some of that food. Or would you prefer to go straight to bed?'

Heat zinged through Reeza's blood. It had been a long time since she had spent a night with man. Not since she and Jai, a fellow student, had gone out for a while in third year uni. She wasn't sure what Zac's expectations were, so she would tread carefully.

'A walk is a good idea,' she said softly.

Zac stood and came around behind her and took her hand as she rose. As they walked to the door he paused at the counter. 'Please charge the meals to my room, Raoul. Thank you for a fine evening.'

'Thank you, Raoul.' Reeza echoed. The night had been a whole new experience for her, and she'd felt very well looked after. Growing up on a farm where every dollar was watched, and then being a uni student, had meant any nights out had been at pubs and bistros. She turned to Zac as they reached the main door of the building. 'And thank you, Zac, for suggesting coming here. It was amazing.' She hesitated and bit her lips wondering how to bring up sharing the bill. 'Um, I would be much more comfortable splitting the bill when we check out tomorrow.'

He shook his head immediately. 'No, this was my idea, and I invited you out.'

'But the room, the cost—' she said.

'Reeza, please.' He held her hand as they walked down the steps to the circular drive that was edged by a rose garden. The smell of the blossoms filled the night air. 'I insist, and I can afford it, if that bothers you.'

'Okay, well I insist that you let me take you to a place I love in Oxford Street one night, and that will be my shout.'

'Okay, we'll see.' Zac tucked her hand into the crook of his arm and they stepped off the drive and followed a path through the gardens. 'Are you warm enough?'

'Yes, I'm still glowing from all that food and wine,' she said with a chuckle.

They were quiet as they walked through the magnificent gardens. The late summer blooms were almost done but the smell of lavender and roses surrounded them as they trod on the petals littering the path. As they turned to come back around to the building, Zac let go of her hand and turned to face her. His hands were warm on each side of her waist as he lowered his head, and a thrill of anticipation sent a flutter though her lower belly. Reeza closed her eyes as his lips gently brushed hers in a butterfly kiss. Her hands crept up and she slipped her arms around his neck, and Zac's lips were warm on hers as he deepened the kiss.

After a while, he lifted his head and rested his forehead against hers. 'I'm not going to rush you, Reeza. I couldn't help kissing you.' His lips slid slowly across her cheek and he feathered kisses at the side of her mouth. 'I'll be honest. I haven't felt like this before.'

Reeza lowered her hands and stepped back as her nerves jolted in response to his kiss. 'You're not rushing me, Zac.' She lifted her head and held his gaze. 'I feel the same way.'

'Shall we go to our room?' He pulled her close as his head lowered to hers again.

'I think that would be a very good idea,' Reeza said, her voice husky.

Chapter 11

'I don't care if he's the king of England, I don't like the man.' Dad sat at the kitchen table and glowered at her over the bacon and eggs that Mum had put in front of him. 'He's not our type.'

Reeza's temper grew as she stood in the kitchen at six o'clock on a Thursday three weeks later.

'And,' Dad ignored her question and picked up his fork, jabbing it in the air at her. 'Who does he think he is, keeping you away from home every weekend? From bloody Thursday night? It's not even the weekend. You're not going to stay in the city this weekend. I want you to come home, you're needed here.'

'No,' Reeza said.

Mum shook her head at her behind Dad's back, but Reeza had had enough.

'Dad. I am twenty-nine years old, I have a career, I earn my own keep, and *you* have no say in what I do on my weekends, or who I see. I'll be home on Sunday afternoon. Zac said he will drive me home.'

'Like I said before, he's not our type.'

And just what is our type, Dad? Someone who goes to the pub, and drinks too much and then has a bet on the horses?'

'No, someone who works a real job, someone who doesn't make money out of other people.'

'So you think that's what I do?'

Yes,' he said tersely. 'A bloody economics degree. I thought it was ridiculous when you enrolled, but I let you do it.'

'You let me do it? I paid my own way, and I have a huge bloody HECS debt, *and* I worked on the farm the whole four years I was studying. What more do you want from me?'

'I want you to give up working in the city, hanging about with ponces that aren't our type, and come home and work in the orchard.'

Reeza picked up the overnight bag she'd packed for the

weekend; she was staying at Zac's place in the city tonight, and taking him to her favourite Thai restaurant in Surry Hills for dinner after work.

Her voice was hard and cold. 'I'll see you on Sunday afternoon, and I'd appreciate it if you could be civil to Zac when he brings me home. His mother has invited me to their house and I'm looking forward to meeting her.'

Her father always had to have the last word. 'Christ, and he's a Mummy's boy to boot. How old is he? Still lives with his mother? Jeez, now I've heard it all.'

'No, he hasn't—' Reeza cut her words off. There was no point arguing or explaining herself to Dad. She leaned over and kissed her mother on the cheek. 'I'll see you on Sunday, Mum. Don't work too hard on the weekend, will you? Ted said he'd drive me to the train station this morning. I'll take my stuff out to the garage.'

'He should make you bloody walk,' her father muttered as he shovelled bacon into his mouth.

Reeza rolled her eyes and headed outside. It really was past time she looked at renting a place in the city.

***

Late that afternoon Zac was about to leave his office and meet Reeza in the foyer when the CEO stepped through the door. 'Montgomery, I want you to clear your calendar for the day tomorrow. We've got a serious problem, and we need to spend all day going through transactions and interviewing staff.'

'What sort of problem?'

Gregor Drummond, the CEO, waved a dismissive hand. 'I'll fill you in tomorrow. Just clear your calendar. And be here early—a seven a.m. start.'

Zac nodded at Drummond's back as he left the room. The atmosphere in the bank had changed since Drummond had taken over, and Zac was considering his options. The more he had to do with the new CEO, the more he was considering moving on. It was time for a change. He had been planning to take Reeza out for an early breakfast on the harbour and drive her to the office in the morning, but those plans were cactus now.

Zac was preoccupied as he headed down the elevator. Being surrounded by suits and serious faces depressed him. As he stepped out into the foyer, he looked over towards the bank of elevators that went down to the basement car park.

His heart lifted as his gaze settled on Reeza. She was sitting on the seat where he'd told her to wait. She'd changed from her dark business suit and her bright pink dress cheered him.

She stood as he walked over and his heartbeat crept up. He'd worked with Reeza for almost two years, and he'd always found her to be sweet, but after spending the past three weekends with her, he found it hard to stop thinking about her day and night. He'd tried to stay away from the trading floor, but every opportunity that came up, he was out there, mooning around like an adolescent and not a thirty-seven-year-old man. Today, he'd made a conscious effort not to go to her floor, and then she'd been in his head all day because he'd missed seeing her. Three nights this week, he'd called her when she'd been on the train home to Brentwood, and they'd talked for an hour.

Not about work, or their day, but about all sorts of other things. It had only been three weeks since he'd driven past her that rainy night but he knew her well. The first night they'd spent together—in one room—at the Country Pines Resort, there had been little talking done. Zac had done a double take when he'd seen the charge on his credit card, but spending that night with Reeza had been worth every cent.

The last two weekends she'd stayed in Sydney in his apartment.

He hoped that Reeza was going to be a permanent part of his future. The love word hadn't been mentioned, but he knew he'd fallen head over heels.

He'd made a call today about a night at the Hydro Majestic in the Blue Mountains, and he was going to ask her tonight to come away with him next weekend.

'Hello, Mr Montgomery,' she said softly as he reached her.

'Good afternoon, Ms Anderson. You are looking very lovely.'

'Thank you, I went shopping in my lunch hour.'

'Don't tell me you wore colour on the trading floor? That would have stirred the old codgers up.'

'Ssh. Someone will hear you,' she said looking around.

'There's no one here. But it wouldn't hurt to stir them up a bit.'

'You don't enjoy working here very much, do you?' she said as they stepped into the empty elevator.

'You're getting to know me well. I'm a bit over the place at the moment. I'm thinking about moving on.'

'Not too far away, I hope?' Disappointment flooded through Reeza as she looked up at him.

Zac put his hands on her shoulders and lowered his lips to hers. The elevator dinged as they reached the basement and he stepped away. 'Don't you worry about that. I won't be going far. And to be honest, it'll make things easier if we don't work at the same place. Come on, let's go. This isn't the right place for this conversation.'

Half an hour later they were sitting at a bench in the Thai restaurant overlooking Oxford Street, waiting for their meals.

'Are you still thinking of buying a property out Brentwood way?' Reeza asked.

Zac linked his fingers with hers as they looked out over the busy street. 'To be honest, I'm not sure now. I think wanting to move out of the city was a bit of a knee-jerk reaction to being unsettled at the bank. So maybe not.'

'That's good because I've decided to move into town. I had another argument with Dad this morning, and I figured it's time to leave home. I think I've got enough saved for a deposit on an apartment.' She looked at him and smiled; Zac's head was close to hers. 'There's a lot of attraction to being in the city all of a sudden.'

'I'm pleased to hear that.'

They moved apart as the waitress stood behind them and reached over with two steaming bowls of laksa.

As they waited for their meals to cool, Reeza looked at Zac curiously. 'No specifics, but why are you unhappy working at the bank? I've always had the impression you loved the place and were pretty much wedded to your job.' He hesitated and she put up her hand. 'No, that was out of line. You're my boss, and I have no right to ask you that.'

Zac reached over and took her hand. 'You know I'd like to be more than a boss to you, Reeza, so you have a right to know what makes me happy. We've come a long way from a working relationship in three weeks.' He let out a long sigh, and she frowned. 'The management ethos has changed a lot over the past year. It probably hasn't filtered down to the trading floor, but the direction of the new strategic plan doesn't sit comfortably with me. I guess dreaming about buying a farm and leaving the bank was an escape. It might sound like bragging, but I've made an obscene amount of money in the fifteen years I've worked there. I could afford to retire now, but really, what would I do? How would I fill my days?'

Reeza nodded. 'I know what you mean. You dream of what you think you want out of a career, and then you find that it's other things in life that you really want, but if you want to get those things, you have to keep up with the career to earn enough money to get what you want out of life.'

'So you're not happy at the bank either, by the sound of that.'

'I am, but like you, there has been a change in the atmosphere. I hope it'll go back to what it used to be eventually. Bosses come and go, and management practice changes. I love the work I do, and it might sound as though I'm bragging too, but I'm very good at it. I've made a lot of money for the bank in the last six months. It's good to be appreciated and recognised; it's not something that happens anywhere else in my life. But it's a job where I will achieve my dream. I want to make enough money to get what I want out of life.'

'And your goal is to get your dream apartment like you told me that night at the Country Pines.'

Reeza smiled. 'I think my dream is more about having my own space than anything luxurious. Although luxury would be nice. What about you, Zac? If you could do exactly what you wanted, would you really go cruising?'

He shook his head as she looked across at him. His eyes were dancing and a surge of attraction hit her squarely in her lower belly. As it had regularly over the last three weeks. 'Do you think that's a foolish dream?'

'No dreams are foolish. They are a part of us.' She couldn't help reaching out and touching his arm. Skin to skin contact eased that desire a little bit. At least it did until Zac ran his fingers up and down the inside of her wrist, and the desire surged back. Getting to know him as a person over the past few weeks, rather than as the aloof boss, had stirred something deep in her. 'So tell me more about your dream.'

'I love being on the water. I'd love to be more adventurous. I'd like to challenge myself. Go places where there is little in the way of civilisation. The west coast. The Kimberleys.'

'It's a big dream. And an adventure to boot.'

'What about you? Are you a boat person?' he asked as he stopped stroking her arm and picked up his spoon. 'Could I tempt you to come with me?'

'Really?' Reeza picked up her spoon. 'Now you have to promise not to laugh.'

'Okay.'

'Growing up on the orchard meant very few trips into town, and even fewer holidays when I was growing up. The sum total of my boating experience is the small punt that we had down on our back dam when we were kids.'

'Sounds like I will have to take you out on the harbour.'

'You have a boat already?'

'Just a small one, but it's fed my dream for the past ten years.'

'Sounds like it might be the time to follow that dream.'

'Could be,' he said.

Chapter 12

Zac found it hard to leave Tess at five a.m. the next morning. He'd set the alarm on low volume, but she'd still woken up when he did.

'Stay there,' he said as she went to climb out of his bed. 'You've got another couple of hours before you have to get up.'

'No, I'll have a cuppa with you.' She swung her long legs over the side of the bed and reached for the T-shirt that had barely covered her thighs last night.

Zac groaned and pulled her close. 'Do you know how hard it is not to climb back into bed with you? The last thing I want to do is go to the office and have a day closeted with Bulldog.'

'Bulldog? That's what you call the CEO?'

Zac nodded and looked a bit embarrassed. 'That was very unprofessional. Forget I said that.'

'Forgotten already.' Reeza nodded and then reached up to kiss him. 'We have all weekend ahead of us.'

'I wasn't disappointed when Mum decided to go to Newcastle to the art gallery. She'll be back for lunch tomorrow.'

'I'm looking forward to meeting her.' She stepped back and let him go. 'Now go and have a shower and I'll put the coffee on.'

'Are you right to get to George Street from here? Grab a cab.'

'No, that's a waste of money. The bus will get me there.'

'Okay, if you're happy with that.' Zac shrugged and looked after Reeza as she went into the kitchen. He had never had to take public transport. His respect for her grew each day. He'd grown up in an affluent family, and they had had a good income. When his father had walked out on them when Zac was ten, his mother had a high income and there'd been no hardship. It had been a natural progression for him to follow that path, but more and more lately, he'd been dissatisfied with his life.

Reeza was very different to him, extremely conscious of what she spent, and she'd told him how she had almost paid her

HECS debt off, and had saved enough for a deposit on an apartment. She'd only been at the bank for two years and he was amazed by how much she'd managed to save in such a short time. He wondered if she knew how much of a deposit she'd need in the city. Sometimes, her naivete surprised him, but it was refreshing and one of the things he was beginning to love about her.

Zac had fallen, and fallen hard. Even though it had been less than a month, he was going to ask her to move in with him when they went to the Blue Mountains. It could be a trial run, and it would save her that long commute in and out of town each day. And she wouldn't have to worry about looking for an apartment. He imagined she wouldn't be able to afford anything within a twenty-kilometre—or more—radius of the inner city.

Fifteen minutes later, Zac had showered, shaved and dressed in one of the corporate suits he was beginning to hate.

'What's that sad face all about?' Reeza asked as she passed him a coffee. Her hair was tousled, and her cheeks flushed pink, and Zac thought he'd never seen a more beautiful sight.

'I'd much rather be doing something with you than spending the day in a monkey suit in Gregor Drummond's office.'

'I wondered why you had to go in so early.' She looked at him curiously. 'What's happening?'

Zac shook his head. 'Who knows? He's got a bee in his bonnet about something. I'm going in early at his direction, but I'm not working back. It's Friday night, and we're going somewhere special for dinner.'

'Are we?' A sexy smile tilted her lips. 'I was thinking we could stay in and have an early night before your mother comes home tomorrow.' Her dark brown eyes were full of mischief. 'You'll be tired after all your meetings, and we'll probably need a big sleep-in in the morning too. Did I tell you how comfortable your bed is?'

'Is that the only attraction here, witch? My soft bed?' Zac pulled her close and kissed her. 'You are a temptress, madame, but I think that's an excellent idea. I'll meet you in the basement at five-fifteen and we'll pick up something for dinner on the way back here.'

'I'll look forward to it.' Her breasts were soft against his chest as she pressed closer to him and looped her arms around his neck. 'You have a good day, and I'll see you this afternoon.' She stood on her toes, and her lips were warm against his.

'Okay. Time to go.' Finally, he pulled away and couldn't help himself. He would ask her tonight, not next weekend. 'I have something to ask you at dinner.'

'What?' Her smile was cheeky.

'You'll have to wait.'

'Oh, that's mean. Now I'll wonder what it is all day. Will I like it?'

'I hope so.' Zac ran his finger down Reeza's nose to her lips. 'Have a good day.' He whistled happily as he pulled the door shut behind him and headed to the garage beside the house. It was going to be an excellent weekend.

***

Reeza's day went downhill from the minute she crossed the road outside Zac's mother's house and saw the bus she'd hoped to catch heading away from her through the traffic lights. She glanced at her watch; it was half an hour until the next bus was due, and it would be after nine before she reached the bank. Despite being two floors above her, she knew the CEO kept an eagle eye on each level and the arrival and departure times of each employee. Sitting opposite Brad Drummond—who took advantage of being the boss's son and had extra-long lunch breaks—Reeza had no doubt that if she was late, her lateness would be noted and passed on to his father. She hated the lack of trust in the organisation; they were responsible adults and knew what was required without being checked on as though they were still at school. The atmosphere had become toxic since Drummond had taken over, but still she had been surprised to hear Zac criticise him.

The new culture at the office was the main reason that she and Zac were keeping their—their what?—under wraps.

Relationship? Romance? Fling? Anyway, whatever it was, they were keeping it private. Even though they had agreed to keep things the same at work, Zac hadn't seemed worried about taking her out in the city. The word would filter back one day, and she knew it wouldn't go down well with the CEO.

Not that there was a policy about it, but there were strict expectations about confidentiality. After Drummond had taken over as CEO, one of the women on her floor had transferred to another bank, because both she and her husband worked for the bank. Crazy, Reeza had thought. That would be more of a conflict of interest.

She knew that she was more uncomfortable than Zac was, but he'd agreed to keep things at a low profile.

It was all right for him; he'd had the promotions and had reached a high level in the bank, even though he did seem discontented there. Reeza didn't want to put her position in jeopardy at the beginning of her career, and just when her work was getting noticed.

She stepped to the edge of the footpath and hailed the vacant taxi cruising down Peronne Avenue. There'd been a pile of incoming transactions on her desk when she'd left last night, and it would be good to get in early and get them cleared.

The traffic was heavy as they crossed the Spit Bridge, but it lightened as they approached the city.

To Reeza's surprise, Brad Drummond was sitting at her desk when she walked onto the trading floor twenty minutes before nine. He was the only one in the room and was looking through the papers in her in-tray.

'What are you doing, Brad?' Reeza asked as she hurried across to her desk. It was an unwritten law on the floor that a banker's desk was private.

He jumped, and when he turned around, his eyes were narrowed. 'Morning, Theresa.'

'What are you looking for?' she persisted.

'I was after a red pen.'

'I don't have one.'

He kept sitting there looking up at her, a smug look on his face. 'You're early. Stayed in town, did you?'

'Early enough to catch you going through my files. Red pen, be buggered,' she said. Reeza was angry. 'I don't believe a word you're saying. Do it again and I'll report you, Brad.'

He rolled her chair back and laughed. 'Will you just? And who are you going to report me to? Zaccy boy?'

'What?' Her breath caught as unease grabbed her. She could feel the heat rising up her neck as he stood and looked down at her. He was an unattractive man, and he took no pride in cleanliness; his clothes smelled stale and there was a definite whiff of body odour emanating from him.

'You and Zachary were very cosy together at *Lom Sam* last night. Don't you worry, sweetheart, sleeping with Zac's not going to get you a promotion. Or out of trouble.' He put a hand to his mouth and chuckled. 'Oops, not yet. You're a woman, and my father won't have a female trader in his bank.'

Reeza was lost for words as a myriad of emotions gripped her. She knew that Brad was just mouthing off. Drummond was savvy enough to know that a rumour like that would put his position as CEO at risk.

'You talk garbage, Bradley. It's not *his* bank and I don't imagine the board would be impressed to hear a sexist statement like that. And whatever I do in my own time is my business and none of yours.'

Her voice was calm and controlled as she pushed past him. She froze when Brad grabbed her arm. 'You think you're pretty fucking special, don't you?' Reeza stared at him, horrified, as spit flew from his mouth and just missed her face. 'You can be as cocky as you like now, Theresa, but let's see what the day brings.'

She sat at her desk, ignoring him, but her hands shook as she put her handbag in the drawer. As he went back to his own desk, Brad laughed and a shiver ran down her back. Turning her computer on, she logged in and reached for the transactions awaiting her attention. With a frown, she flicked through them; she thought there'd been more than that. Maybe she'd been wrong, but she wondered what Brad had been doing with them.

Three hours later Reeza finally looked up as Brad stood and disappeared for his usual lunch break. She had not spoken to him, or looked at him since she'd started work. Leaning back, she stretched her arms and looked around. The floor was quiet today; there was a strange atmosphere in the office.

She opened the desk drawer and took her purse from her handbag, and made her way to the elevator. Zac was occasionally down near the sandwich shop on the floor below reception when she went down at lunchtime, but she didn't hold out much hope today; he'd said it was an all-day meeting. Knowing Drummond, they'd have a fully catered lunch.

Reeza purchased an egg salad roll and a takeaway coffee and headed back to the floor. She'd stay close to her desk; she didn't want Brad going through her files again. From today, she'd be more careful of what she left in her tray overnight. For a moment, she wondered about raising it with Zac and then realised that was the very thing she didn't want to do. She wasn't going to take advantage of their relationship.

Two of the guys from her floor were in the small kitchen that doubled as a lunchroom. Reeza sat at the table with them, but apart from a brief nod her way as they each looked up from their phones, there was no conversation, which was unusual.

Worry nagged at her; she wondered if Brad had been mouthing off about seeing her out with Zac last night. With a sigh, she pushed away her bread roll and reached for her coffee. Her appetite had gone.

Finally, Steven, the guy opposite her, looked up from his phone and spoke quietly. 'I noticed you've had your head down all morning, Theresa. Just a heads up, you're likely to be called into the boss's office after lunch. We've both been grilled this morning and it wasn't pleasant.'

Paul looked up and nodded. 'No, it wasn't.'

'Grilled about what? And whose office? Zac Montgomery's?'

Paul pulled a face. 'No, the big boss, Drummond. It was so unpleasant I wished I'd asked for a support person or the union guy to come in with me.'

'What's it all about?' she asked with a frown.

Paul and Steven exchanged a glance. 'Better off to let you go in cold,' Steven said. 'Just be careful what you say, though. Drummond won't be left looking bad. There's been a dud transaction, and he won't take the fall for it. Just answer what he asks, and don't be tempted to say anything else.'

'About anybody,' Paul added.

'No one,' Steven said with a nod.

Reeza knew exactly who they were talking about.

Brad Drummond.

'Thanks, guys.' She stood and put the last half of her lunch in the bin. 'I'll get back to work. Hopefully I won't get called in.'

'Hope you don't,' Steven said. 'I'm pleased it's the weekend. It's been a shit of a day.'

Reeza went back to her desk, and even though she had

plenty of work to keep her occupied, the afternoon dragged. Every time the door opened, she expected to be called in, and her stomach was tight with tension.

The worst of it was that she knew if she got called in, that Zac would be in there too, and she would have to be very careful with her reactions, and her responses.

Brad didn't come back from lunch, and that worried her too. She'd stood up to him, and she'd seen the nastiness in his expression. She didn't trust him. With a sigh, she tried to focus on her work. The next time she looked at the clock on her computer, it was five minutes before five, and relief flooded through her. She'd obviously missed out on a grilling and could start to look forward to the weekend.

Probably because she was too junior to have any initiatives that could be questioned. Her level of work was a bit like a glorified clerk, although she had spotted some opportunities that had been acted upon a couple of months ago.

As the bell went, indicating local trading was over, Reeza took her handbag from the drawer and stood. As she shut down the computer, the door opened and Drummond's executive assistant came in and walked over to her.

'Mr Drummond would like to see you, Ms Anderson.'

She glanced up at the clock on the wall. 'Now?' She was supposed to be meeting Zac in fifteen minutes in the basement car park.

He nodded. 'Yes, now.'

She went to put her bag away, but he shook his head. 'Bring your bag with you. You'll be leaving after the meeting. Do you have any other personal effects in the office?'

Reeza frowned, not understanding what he meant. 'Personal effects?'

'Anything that belongs to you.'

'No, I don't.'

'Very well. Come with me, please.'

The air in the corridor was cold and smelled sterile. Reeza found it difficult to walk after him to the elevator. Her knees were shaking, and her legs were like jelly, and her heels clicked loudly on the tiled floor as she followed him into the elevator. The silence was fraught with tension, and Reeza's stomach clenched.

'I need to use the bathroom before I see Mr Drummond please,' she said politely.

'Very well, but I'll take your handbag.' The assistant escorted her to the entrance to the ladies' room and then held his hand out for her bag.

'I beg your pardon? Why do you have to hold my bag?' She stared at him, confused by his instruction.

'For security.'

'Why?'

He looked at her as though she was being difficult. 'So you can't remove anything from your bag.'

Reeza held her tongue and passed her bag over and went into the ladies. On the way to the cubicle, she caught sight of herself in the mirror.

Gone was the happy, glowing face that had looked back at her from the ensuite mirror in Zac's bedroom this morning. In its place was a pale wide-eyed face that showed her lack of confidence; a dreadful feeling of foreboding gripped her. Brad's words kept going around in her head. *You can be as cocky as you like now, Theresa, but let's see what the day brings.* The fact that he hadn't come back to the floor also worried her. It had been a very strange day.

Reeza came out of the toilet cubicle, washed her face and hands, and then pinched her cheeks; she looked slightly better as she went back into the corridor.

'This way, please, Ms Anderson.'

Reeza swallowed as she followed him into the inner sanctum where she had never been before.

Chapter 13

Zac sat straight and held his breath as the door opened. Reeza stepped in and looked first at Drummond and then at him. It was impossible to read her expression.

It was almost impossible to hide his anger and disgust. She had played him for the utter fool he was. As Drummond had laid out each piece of evidence against Reeza, Zac had examined them with intense focus. To the best of his knowledge, the CEO didn't know that they'd been seeing each other.

Christ, he'd been going to ask her to move in with him. And she was going to meet his mother tomorrow.

An absolute fool. Theresa Anderson had played him to perfection. He lifted his head and stared at her when she sat down. They were sitting informally on three soft chairs around a low table.

Her face was pale and her green eyes shimmered. Reeza knew she'd been caught out. She widened her eyes and raised her eyebrows as she lifted her eyes to meet his.

Zac looked away, and the next time he looked at her, her face was white.

Guilty as sin. Had she known he was going to Brentwood that night and timed her walk in the rain so he'd pick her up? Or was that stretching it? The rest of the evidence was there and it made him sick to the stomach. All the guff about saving for an apartment. Christ, she had more in her investment portfolio than he did.

'Thank you for meeting with us, Ms Anderson,' Drummond said evenly.

Zac looked at her again, and she inclined her head. It was hard to believe this was the pink-faced woman who had been in his bed last night. If he'd been asked to describe a guilty person, he could describe Reeza's face.

'I don't understand what this is about,' she replied. 'Or why you need to talk to me.' Her voice was quiet, but still familiar enough to wrench Zac's heart.

'There has been a serious breach in the security of our foreign transactions and it has cost the bank a considerable amount of money. There have been breakdowns in internal controls. We have some questions for you. I'll hand over to Mr Montgomery as your direct supervisor.'

'I hope you will answer my question honestly, and with as much information as you can, Ms Anderson. Any information that you withhold will go against you.' Zac kept his voice formal.

Her bottom lip trembled, and all he could think about was how soft her lips had felt beneath his. He reached for the folder on the table in front of them. The knowledge that he had been duped—both personally and professionally—came rushing back, and his tone was curt and hard when he spoke.

'On Friday the fifteenth of last month, you completed a transaction in Swiss dollars that breached bank protocol. Can you please explain the nature of that transaction to us?'

Her voice was surprisingly even as she lifted her eyes to hold his. '*Mr* Montgomery, since the fifteenth of last month I would have handled hundreds of transactions and many in Swiss dollars, none of which have breached protocol. If you would like me to explain a particular one, you will have to be more specific.'

Zac removed the printout of the transaction that Reeza had pocketed a neat seven hundred thousand dollars from, and handed it to her. She didn't need to know yet, that the deposit into her account was now on record. Her fingers brushed his as she took the paper, and he cursed himself for being every kind of fool under the sun as the nerves in his arm kicked from her brief touch.

He sat back and folded his arms as he watched her read it. Slowly the little remaining colour leached from her lips.

'This is not my work.'

'I beg to differ,' he said. 'The keystrokes have been audited as being directly from both your log in and from the computer in your office.' He glanced down at the copy of the transaction that he had retained. 'At five twenty-seven on the fifteenth of March.'

Her face cleared and he didn't like the smile that crossed her face.

'You do realise, Ms Anderson, that this will result in the termination of your employment,' Drummond's voice filled the silence.

'I don't think it will, Mr Drummond.' Her voice was clear and true, and Zac shook his head. 'I can prove it wasn't me.'

Reeza went to speak, and then she looked at Zac and closed her mouth. Confusion crossed her face, and she dropped her gaze to her hands as though she was considering something. She sat like that for a full five minutes until the CEO cleared his throat. When she lifted her head, her eyes were sad, and Zac found it hard to stay strong.

'If you check with security records, you will see that I have never stayed past five o'clock. Her voice strengthened. 'The fact that I couldn't stay back had bothered me, but on this occasion, it appears that I will be vindicated because of that stupid rule.'

The CEO leaned forward. 'Mr Montgomery?'

Zac pulled out the next piece of paper that recorded her departure from the trading floor at five forty on that afternoon. Until he'd seen that security record, he'd doubted her guilt, but when he'd examined the data for the third time and listened to the evidence of the other traders on the floor, he knew he'd been trying to find excuses because he didn't want to believe Reeza was guilty.

Theresa Anderson was not the woman he had thought she was. The woman he had kidded himself into believing he had fallen in love with.

'Ms Anderson, there is a detective in the foyer waiting to take you to the police station to be charged. There is a security guard outside who will take you down to meet him.'

Even knowing her guilt, when Reeza began to stand and then fell back into the chair, all Zac wanted to do was hold her and protect her.

Not caring what Drummond thought, Zac leaned forward and put his head in his hands as Reeza sobbed.

'I didn't do anything wrong.'

Chapter 14

Pentecost Island

'Theresa.' When Zac's deep voice came from the forest behind her, Tess put her hand to her throat. Her legs began to shake uncontrollably and she grabbed for the tree that was beside her.

'What the hell are you doing here?' Her voice shook so much she wasn't sure if her words were clear enough to be understood. She let go of the tree and wrapped her arms across her chest. Despite the hot, humid night, her blood was chilled, and goosebumps rose on her skin as she shivered.

'I need you to keep a secret.' Zac walked towards her and she took a step back.

'What? Are you for real? What the bloody hell are you doing here? Can't you leave me alone? You've already ruined my life. Why are you hounding me? How much more damage can you do? Just go away!'

'I need to talk to you, Reeza. I have to talk to you.'

She twisted around so quickly that she saw stars. 'Don't you dare call me that. My name is Tess.'

His voice was quiet. 'It suits you. So does the hair.' Zac leaned forward, so close she could feel his breath on her skin. For one awful moment, she thought he was going to touch her. The worst thing was, for all the hatred that had consumed her over the past two years, Tess knew Zac's touch would bring her undone. 'And the blue eyes,' he said. 'If I hadn't tracked you down and verified it was you, I would never have recognised you.'

'Why? What have you tracked me down for? Are you going to call the police? The media? I can just see the headline. Woman on the run found in tropical paradise.'

'No, listen to me.'

'No, you listen to me. Leave me alone! Just leave me in peace to get on with my life. Haven't you done enough damage already?'

'I need to talk you to you, Ree—'

'Why?' Her voice shook as the futility of it all overwhelmed her.

The waste.

Her university study.

The hard work she'd done for two years.

Reinventing herself, finding safety on the island, a new career and now having Zac turn up with no warning and—

'Wait a minute,' she said. 'How did you get here? Did you book in under a false name? And what do you mean, verified it was me?'

As she stood there staring at him, voices reached them as someone walked from the bar through the glade.

'Quickly. Please listen to me. I'm known as Monty these days. Rafe knows me and he knows why I'm here. You can let people know we knew each other in the past but don't mention the bank. Please . . . Tess . . please. Trust me. I'll explain everything later.'

Trust him!

Not a snowball's chance in hell of that. Reeza trusted no one these days. As she stared at Zac, wondering what the hell he was up to and what she should do, Pippa and Rafe walked into the glade.

'There you are, Tess. We were coming to see what was holding you up. The party's in full swing.'

'I was running the weekly backup, and then I went to get changed. And then'—she flicked a glance to Zac—'then on the way here I bumped into . . . Monty.'

The relief on his face was clear and Zac smiled at Tess before he turned to Rafe. 'I was walking over from the pool area, and I literally bumped into Tess. Neither of us could believe it.'

Pippa turned to Rafe. 'Are you going to introduce us?'

'Sorry, love, I forgot you hadn't met Monty. Monty, this is my wife, Phillipa, known to all as Pippa. Pippa knows about you, and what a great job you'll do.'

Tess looked from one to the other wondering what job Zac—Monty—was going to do on the island. As far as she knew it wasn't the place for an investment banker. He wasn't a guest; she racked her brains as she ran the guest list through her head. There had been no Monty anything on it.

As Zac held his hand out and shook Pippa's hand, Tess took the opportunity to study him. He'd changed in the past two years, as she had. His hair was longer and curled onto his neck, his skin held a deeper tan, but most of all—and strangely—he'd grown. He had obviously been working out because his muscles were much more defined and his shoulders seemed broader. When he had been her boss, he had been good looking but in an urbane sort of way. Back then, he had been fit—lithe and taut—now he was big and had a sort of roughness that had been polished out of him before.

'Good to meet, you, Pippa. I've heard a lot about you from Rafe.'

'Have you?' Pippa said. 'Welcome aboard. It's good to have you here. I'm sorry I wasn't at your interview. It was a manic day.'

Tess's head turned from left to right as she followed the conversation. An interview? Even though she hadn't met him, Pippa obviously knew why he was there.

Zac had a job here? That was the last thing that Tess would have guessed in a million years.

'So, let's head back to the party,' Pippa said with a smile. 'A great opportunity for you to meet the rest of the staff. I'll leave Tess to introduce you around.'

Great, she thought. Just great. She could barely function now that Zac had stunned her with his arrival on the island. She knew nothing about him now, or why he was here, looking so buff and tanned, and she was going to introduce him to everyone?

Fear ate away at her. She didn't want to leave here, but if he was going to open his mouth and say who she was, she would be gone tomorrow.

Maybe she could develop a migraine in the next two minutes. Before she could open her mouth, Pippa and Rafe headed back to the bar, and Zac took her hand and tucked it into the crook of his arm.

He leaned down and whispered. 'I'll explain everything later.'

Tess jerked her arm away. 'Too bloody right you will. And

then you'll leave.'

Chapter 15

Sydney -Two years earlier

Reeza had no memory of riding down to the foyer in the elevator with the security guard accompanying her. She blinked as he led her out into the foyer. She wasn't sure where they were supposed to be going.

'Will you be all right, Ms Anderson?' Ken, the security guy she'd greeted every morning for two years looked at her with concern. He knew she wasn't a thief and a criminal. Why did he have to take her to a detective, and then what was going to happen? Surely no one really believed she was a criminal.

'This way.' His phone rang as he touched her elbow gently and steered her to the right. 'Excuse me, a moment. He turned away from her; he obviously trusted her. Reeza blinked, wondering if she was asleep and in the middle of a bad dream.

'Yes, sir. No problem. Yes, I will.'

As he disconnected there was a bright flash. Reeza turned wide-eyed, and another flash went off.

'That's her,' a man in a suit stood beside the photographer. 'Miss Anderson,' he called out as he came closer.

Ken grabbed her arm. 'Come into my room, love, and I'll get rid of the newspaper vultures.'

Reeza shook her head. 'Why are they here? Who called them?'

'I don't know.' He opened the door to his small room off the foyer, and when Reeza was inside, he closed it. 'I'll be back in a minute.'

There was a plastic chair next to the desk, and she sat on it and put her bag on the floor. Shaking her head, she rubbed her hand over her eyes, trying to make sense of what had happened. The CEO had accused her of fraud, and she'd had no chance to defend herself. As for Zac, his behaviour made her feel sick to the stomach.

After a few minutes, the door opened. 'The coast's clear. I've put the skids under them. You can go.'

'Go where? To the police station?'

'Oh, sorry, Ms Anderson. Those bloody journalists distracted me. Mr Drummond rang down. I'm to allow you to leave. The charges have been dropped.'

'So I still have a job?'

He stared at her for a moment and then shook his head. 'I'm sorry. No. I'm really sorry, love. I'm sure you've noticed things aren't good here. This isn't the first time I've had to tell a staff member this. If you enter the building the police will be called.'

Reeza nodded. 'Thank you for being kind to me. I'll go now. I'll leave. I'll . . .um. . . guess I'll go home.'

By home, she meant home to Brentwood. She couldn't face Zac at the moment, not after he'd sat there and let her face those ridiculous accusations. She'd wait until he rang—if he rang—and see what he had to say. As far as spending this weekend with him, all desire to do that had gone.

In fact, Reeza was finding it hard to think. 'Thank you, Ken.' She smiled at him and was surprised to see that everything was hazy, through a blur of tears. She had lost her job.

Hitching her handbag over her shoulder, she walked out the main bank doors for the last time. It was a crisp autumn evening. The muted roar of traffic from the Cahill Expressway filled the air, punctuated by blaring horns and the roar of a bus as it accelerated past the building. As she tried to focus on which way to go, a movement and another flash on the footpath caught her attention.

'Theresa.' She turned slowly and stared at the man in the crumpled grey suit. 'A word, love?'

She frowned. 'A word?'

'Tell us what happened in there. Have you been charged? What did you do? What have you done with the money? Almost a million, they said.'

Horror filled her as she realised it was the journalist again. As she stared at him, her mouth open and tears rolling down her cheeks, a man with a large camera on his shoulder stepped between them. She turned and ran, ran as fast as she could, weaving through back streets, up and down steep streets until she had no idea where she was. Finally all was quiet, and she stopped to catch her breath and looked around. An old hotel sat on the corner opposite her and when she turned and saw the pylons of the Harbour Bridge above her, Reeza realised she had come under the Expressway and was on the other side of The Rocks.

A long way from any train station, but she'd probably missed the last train south anyway. As she contemplated what to do—she could always go back to Zac's house—her phone buzzed in her handbag.

She reached in and pulled it out and the screen lit up; it was Mum.

'Mum?' she said quietly.

'No, it's not your mother. She's hysterical in the kitchen,' Dad roared. 'What the bloody hell is going on, Theresa? What have you done?'

'Done? I've done nothing. Why, what's wrong with Mum?'

'There's a bloody helicopter in the paddock. Journalists crawling all over the place, waiting for you to get home, and you're plastered all over the six o'clock TV news. What the fuck have you done, girl?'

Reeza gasped. In all of her twenty-nine years, she had never once heard Dad use the F word. 'I haven't done anything wrong.'

'They said you were at the police station, being charged. Why would they say that?' His voice had quietened a fraction.

'Because they're lying. It was all a mistake. I'm trying to find a way home.'

'Don't you dare come home. I thought you were going to the precious boyfriend's mother's place for the weekend. Or are the media there too?'

Reeza sighed. 'I don't know.'

'Where are you?'

'I'm lost.'

Finally a bit of concern in Dad's voice. 'Are you safe where you are?'

'I think so.'

'Good. I'll put your mother on.'

Reeza waited for a full minute before her mother took the phone.

'Theresa, Dad said you're lost. Where are you?'

'In the city. Dad said you were hysterical, There's no need to be, Mum.'

'I wasn't bloody hysterical. I was yelling at him because he got his shotgun out, and he was going to fire it over the heads of the journalists. I was simply yelling at him to stop.'

'Oh, God. And did he?' Reeza put her hand to her head.

'Yes, he did. But they're all camped out there waiting for you to come home. Bloody dozens of them. Cameras and all. We told them you weren't coming home. Where's Zac, Theresa? And how did you get lost?'

'Long story, Mum.' Reeza bit her lip as she decided what to do. It was hard to think straight. 'Can you do me a really, really big favour?'

'What do you want me to do?'

'Can you go into my room and pack me a bag with some clean undies, and my shorts and T-shirts, dresses, and my toiletries and meet me in town.'

'What? Tonight?'

'No tomorrow, will do.'

'All right. I'll get one of the boys to drive me in.' Mum lowered her voice. 'What's Zac's mother's address.'

'I won't be there. I'll meet you at Central Station.'

'Why?'

'I'm going to go away for a while.' Reeza's lip quivered. 'I lost my job today, Mum. They sacked me and I did nothing wrong.'

'Oh, Theresa. I'm sorry, love. But you don't have to go away. You can come home and work in the orchard.'

'No.' Reeza stared up at the bridge. The coloured lights were on, and the flash of headlights and taillights illuminated the pylons in a myriad of blues, reds and whites as commuters made their way home. 'I'm leaving. I'll see you tomorrow. I'll wait in the coffee shop on Eddy Street after nine. The one under the back of the station.'

'All right, if that's what you think is the right thing for you. You always have been the strongest of our three. You take care tonight, and get yourself unlost.'

Reeza chuckled, but her breath caught and it turned into a

sob. 'I am "unlost", Mum. I know where I am now, and I've found somewhere to stay tonight.' She stared over as the Vacancy sign lit up outside the Lord Nelson Hotel. 'Goodnight, Mum.'

She opened her phone, pulled the SIM card out, and broke it in half. There was no way the media could track her.

Chapter 16

Pippa - Pentecost Island

I sat beside Rafe on a stool at the bar and reached for my glass. The soda water bubbles tickled my nose as I lifted it to sip slowly. Nat had looked at me curiously when I had asked for soda water in a champagne glass. If Nell said anything about it later, I'd say I'd had enough wine.

I actually hadn't had any. To my horror, I had missed two periods, but I hadn't told a soul. Not even Rafe. And that added to my guilt.

Rafe turned back to face me when Dylan left the bar and got Odessa up for a dance.

'He's a good guy,' Rafe said. 'He was asking about the gardens around the pool, and I told him it was a party and no work talk allowed.'

'He is. He and Odessa are looking very lovey-dovey.'

'I've never seen her so happy, in all the time I've known her. She's really excited about the store opening in Vi's house once the staff move up the hill. Have you seen some of the silver pieces she's made?'

'I have and she's really good.' I reached over and put my hand on my husband's arm. 'And Rafe, I really like her. After a rocky start, she's settled in here well. She came up and had a coffee with me a couple of days ago when she brought some of jewellery up to show me.'

'I'm pleased you've become friends.'

'Speaking of which,'—I moved closer and lowered my voice—'tell me about this Monty. I thought you said his name was Zac when he was going to be interviewed.'

I'd been watching Monty and Tess since they'd walked to the bar with us. Monty had stopped at a table at the edge of the restaurant away from everyone, but I'd seen Tess shake her head and he'd followed her to a table where Sienna and Danny, and Eliza and Phillipe were sitting. Tess's body language was off, and she was pale.

I knew I was like a mother hen to my friends. Some people saw them as our staff—Eliza, Tam and Nell were part owners of Ma Carmichael's, but I considered all of the staff as friends. I cared about them, and I wanted to make sure they were happy. There'd been some difficult situations since Tam and Nell and I had moved to the island, but everything had settled, the staff all seemed happy, and the building and development were ahead of schedule. We had created a unique establishment here and it was going to be better than we had ever dared dream.

Rafe looked at me, and then turned away.

'Rafe? That's your guilty look. What aren't you telling me?'

He put his arm around my shoulder and chuckled. 'You know me too well, Mrs Rendell.'

'I do. What are you up to?'

'Remember the day Sienna and Danny came back from Esculanta Island and you were going to interview him?'

'Yes, I do, and then there was an emergency up at the building site, and you interviewed him for me and gave him the job.' I narrowed my eyes. 'Zachary Johnson, you said his name was that day. Is Monty a nickname?'

'Sort of.'

'Rafe, what are you up to? You said he was perfect for the job. And I trust you. What's going on?'

'He is perfect, and he's a great guy. Now, Pip, this is for your ears only. He uses Johnson, his mother's name, because he hates people knowing who he is.'

'Who is he? A movie star or something? He could be, he's easy enough on the eye.'

Rafe cleared his throat. 'Um, have you heard me talk about my mate, Zac Montgomery?'

'Ah, yes,' I said slowly, as the light began to dawn. 'Zac Montgomery with the massive boat, you've been friends with for a couple of years. The one I've never met because he's been cruising around the Australian coast.'

'Yes, that's the one.'

'Can't be. Jiminy told me once they call him the bad boy billionaire of Hamo. He doesn't like him.'

'He's just jealous of his boat.'

'He is not!' I burred up. 'Rafe. What's going on? Why do we have a millionaire playboy as our pool lifeguard and why is he here before the pool is finished?'

'Zac is a good man, and has been a good friend to me. He has a problem, and I knew we could help. And it was all in the timing. Don't worry, we're not paying him. He wants to be known as Monty so no one realises he's the guy who owns *Myr*, the big cruiser in the marina over there.'

I slid out from beneath his arm and wagged a finger at him. 'You'll have a problem if you don't tell me what's going on.' I winced as a muscle seemed to pull in my stomach.

'Well, I—' He stopped as I doubled over and put my hand on my stomach. 'What's wrong?' His eyes were wide as he reached for my hand. 'Are you okay?'

The sudden pain had eased, and I shook my head. 'I'm okay, now—' Another sudden pain gripped me and I felt the warm dampness between my thighs. It wasn't the usual monthly pain. This was a lot worse. 'Quick, we need to go back to the house.'

I was embarrassed, but luckily I had on a dark dress, and we managed to leave without drawing any attention to ourselves.

I doubled over again when we reached the stairs at the base of the cliff, and Rafe's eyes were filled with concern as he lifted me into his arms and carried me up the hill to our home.

'Hush, sweetheart, it's okay,' he whispered as I began to cry.

Chapter 17

Zac couldn't keep his eyes off Reeza as she chatted to the others at the table. Once she'd introduced him as Monty, the conversation had been casual, as he'd been welcomed, and then she'd pretty much ignored him.

But he knew those nervous gestures.

Tess, he corrected himself, not Reeza. She looked so different, but still the same. The blonde short hair suited her. It accentuated her high cheekbones and made her eyes look bigger. The one thing he couldn't get used to was the blue eyes. He'd spent a lot of time looking into those pretty green eyes that he knew were now behind coloured lens.

God, what he'd done to her, and what it had done to her life. His stomach churned as he thought about it, and as he wondered what was the best way to get her to listen to him.

Zac had been looking for Reeza for a long time, and he knew now that her family had sent him on a wild goose chase to Western Australia.

Not that he could blame them. They had been protecting her. What the media had done to Theresa Anderson was almost criminal, considering she had been innocent of any wrongdoing.

What had amazed him was how quickly she had managed to disappear into thin air. In a few hours. She'd left her bag at his mother's house—it had been on his boat for the past two years—and as far as he could discover she had never gone home that night.

'Monty? Monty?' The name was said more loudly the second time, and then Zac realised he was being addressed.

'Sorry, Eliza. I was miles away. What did you say?'

'I shouldn't talk about this tonight, but I just wanted to check if you could meet with Pippa and me tomorrow at the pool site. We have a couple of questions about the pool shape from a safety point of view. I wouldn't ask but the form workers had a couple of questions about putting in the day bed platforms on each side. We were lucky Renzo's concreting workers were free, and if we sort this tomorrow, the concrete will be poured before Christmas.'

'Sure.' Zac was aware of Tess's close scrutiny. Her eyes had narrowed when Eliza had asked him about the pool. 'Just give me a time and I'll be there.'

'Have you started work already or are you just over for tonight?' Eliza asked.

'I'm going back with Jiminy tonight, but I'll come back over tomorrow. I came for the Christmas party, but I feel like a bit of a fraud.'

'A fraud? Do you? Why's that?' Tess asked loudly.

He held her blue gaze as he answered. 'Because it seems strange to be at a staff Christmas party before I've even started work.'

'It's a good casual way to settle in. Once you're here working you'll be surprised how busy the days are on the island,' Eliza said with a smile. 'How long have you been living on Hamilton island?'

'Oh, I come and go,' he said. 'I've just come back from Ningaloo in the west. I was looking for a friend who was supposed to be over there.' When Tess's cheeks coloured, he knew that she was aware of the bum steer her brothers had given him. Good, maybe she'd realise how determined he had been to find her, and maybe she'd wonder why.

He'd searched for her nonstop over the past two years, and he had vowed that he would not give up until he found her. He knew what she'd done for him, and he wanted her to know that.

Zac knew her well, and he knew to tread softly. But he was going to talk to Tess tonight, because he was worried she would take off now that he'd found her.

'When do you start work, *Monty?*' Tess stared at him. There was a hardness in her gaze that had never been there before.

'We don't have a date yet. Rafe said he would let me know. But I will come over tomorrow.' He held her gaze and neither looked away until Eliza spoke.

The completion of the pool won't be far off.' Eliza looked at them curiously. The undercurrent between them must be obvious. 'The concrete has to cure for four weeks and Dylan's organised for the landscaping to be done in that time. The bar will be built before the pool is filled, so there's going to be plenty for you to do. Anyway, enough work. Who'd like another drink?' Eliza jumped up and grabbed Philippe's hand. 'And a dance, please, my love.'

'Tess?' He waited until Sienna and Danny got up to dance too.

She looked at him and raised her eyebrows, and again Zac was struck by her new confidence. 'Yes?'

'Come for a walk with me? I want to talk to you.'

'I don't want to talk to you, though, so that's a no.'

'Tess—'

'No, *Zac*. You listen to me. I don't owe you anything. I don't have to talk to you, and I don't want to listen to you.'

He ran his hand through his hair, frustrated. Short of kidnapping her, Tess wasn't going to let him explain. His voice was low and he tried to keep it level. 'Do you know how many months I've spent looking for you? Do you know how worried I am that you'll disappear again before I can talk to you.'

'That's all very nice to hear, but I'm not going anywhere. You've chased me from one career, and I've developed a lot of self-preservation skills since then, so I'm not going anywhere. That being said, I really can't see the need for you to stay and wait around to "talk" to me. So if that's your only reason for taking on a job on Pentecost Island—which I find ridiculous—you might as well leave now and not come back.' She sat back and folded her arms, her eyes challenging him. 'What sort of job is it, anyway? Are you providing financial advice to the guests as they lie around the pool?' The sarcasm in her voice stung, but he bit his tongue.

Zac had spent so much time and energy trying to find her, that snarky comment really pissed him off. But despite the anger that gripped him, he couldn't stop looking at her. He'd thought she was beautiful before—inside and out—but with her chin in the air and her eyes wide as she stared him down, he thought she'd never looked so vital, and full of life, her eyes snapping at him.

'You *have* matured, Tess. And no, I'll not be giving financial advice. Like you, I've reinvented myself. What happened to you was a wakeup call for me. It made me realise what's important in life.'

'I'm not interested in any of that, Zac. I only have one

question for you.' She leaned forward and keep her voice low. They were still alone at the table, but she obviously didn't want their argument to be overheard.

He looked past her and was dismayed to see the two couples at the table across from them all paying close interest, obviously intrigued by their interaction. Zac leaned closer to her, and took her hand, speaking quickly. 'The group at the table behind you are very interested in what we're doing, so I'd suggest that we both chill a bit, unless you want to be the centre of attention. Smile at me, be nice and I'll answer anything you want to know.'

As he watched, Tess relaxed, her shoulders loosened, and her chin lowered. He kept smiling at her and flicked a quick glance to the other table as one of the two couples got up to dance.

'Okay, it's cool now,' he said.

But as the couple walked past the table the woman paused and spoke to Tess, after flicking a curious glance at Zac. 'Thanks again for giving me an early mark, Tess. I appreciated it. We'—she patted her stomach—'even had a quick nap.'

Tess was on her best behaviour now. She smiled across at Zac. 'Zac, have you met Nell and Nat?'

He stood, reached over and shook the guy's hand. 'No. I haven't. Nice to meet you, Monty's the nickname.'

'Welcome,' Nell said, but Nat looked at him curiously. 'I think we've met before, Monty? Haven't we?'

Zac shook his head. 'I don't think so.'

Nat frowned. 'I think I've seen you around on Hamo.'

'That's probably it.'

Nat took Nell's hand and they headed to the dance floor.

Zac sat down and turned back to Tess. Her smile had gone and she looked past him over his shoulder. 'Your question?'

'How did you find me?'

Chapter 18

Pippa

Tonight was the first time I'd ever seen Rafe cry, and he broke my heart. He was trying to comfort *me*, and I was the one who did most of the comforting, although I did cry with him.

'I thought I was pregnant, but I hadn't been to the doctor. I was going to tell you this week and then go over to Hamo to the doctor. I've had no symptoms at all. I've been Googling but I don't—didn't—have any of the things they said I probably would.' Tears pricked at my eyes again as I realised I could probably stop looking for any changes in my body.

We were lying together on our bed. I'd had to talk Rafe out of putting me in the boat and going straight over to the medical centre on Hamilton Island. The cramps had eased, and the shock of knowing I had been pregnant, and had now miscarried had exhausted me.

He lay on his side, his hand smoothing my hair gently. His eyes were sad, but I could still see the love there as he soothed me. Guilt hit me in the chest and I swallowed.

'I'm going to tell you the truth, Rafe,' I whispered. 'We promised each other we would be honest, didn't we? But I wasn't.'

'We did.' His hand stilled. 'It's okay, love. Just lie there and rest.'

'No. I want to tell you, so you know. I was scared. More than bloody scared. I was terrified because I didn't know if I wanted to be pregnant, and I knew how much you wanted us to have a baby quickly. I didn't know how to tell you that. And when I missed my monthlies, I didn't want to get your hopes up, but more than anything, if I told you, it would make it real and I didn't know how I felt about that. But now I feel guilty because I didn't tell you how I felt. I'm sorry. I've let you down.' I started to cry again.

'No, Pip.'

He made a strangled sound and lifted his hand, but I put my mine on his.

'Hear me out. I was worried I would be like my mother, and that I wouldn't love our child, like she never loved me.' I found my tissue and dabbed at my eyes and blew my nose. 'She loved my dad, and she didn't have enough love to go around. Aunty Vi told me that wasn't normal, and that my mum had other issues too. Issues that I was too young to see. And then I worried that I had those issues too. I was so worried; my head was a mess, and I wasn't game to tell you I thought I was pregnant, and I would have to come to terms with how I felt.' My voice shook again. 'And I didn't know how I felt, apart from being bloody scared. It was the worst I'd ever felt in my life. Even worse than when my dad died.'

'Babe, I want what you want. And if you don't want to have children, that's the way it will be. As long as I've got you in my life, that's all I need.'

I shook my head from side to side. 'No. Losing this little one, even though he or she would have only been a couple of months old—no bigger than a jelly bean I read the other day—has broken my heart and made me realise that I *can* do this. That baby was part of us. He or she was us. A physical person that we created out of our love. I *can* do this. I *want* to do it. If I struggle, you'll be there by my side. You are the one constant in my life. The one person I can trust. That's how much I love you, Rafe.' My voice thickened and more tears rolled down my cheeks.

Rafe rolled over and held me close. His cheek was wet against mine. 'There is nothing more in my life than you. I love you, Phillipa.'

'I wondered if he somehow knew that I had doubts and that's why he didn't want to stay,' I sobbed.

'Oh sweetheart, don't blame yourself.' His voice broke.

I buried my face in his neck and cried with the man I loved with my heart and soul.

Chapter 19

Tess rose before sunrise the next morning and climbed the hill so she could watch the sun rise over the ocean. Over the past few months, she'd loved standing on the hill above the resort and watching the dawn lighten the sky. The sky would be dark when she sat on her favourite rock, and then it would lighten and that gorgeous apricot colour would creep up from the sea, until the sky turned gold and red and pink. Watching the sunrise had always soothed her but she'd let the habit slip lately as she got busier with her job in the office.

She needed its calming influence today. Seeing Zac last night had rocked Tess's world. Sitting beside him, and looking at him as he spoke to the others had been hard. The attraction that she had felt for him two years ago hadn't lessened one bit—even though she knew he was not to be trusted. Her body had betrayed her, and all she could think of was how his skin had felt beneath her fingertips, his lips on hers, his breath tickling her ear as he talked to her. Her body had forgotten the confusion, the sadness and the bewilderment, and the unbearable betrayal when she'd realised Zac had believed the worst of her.

She had been young—even though she was only two years older now than when she'd fallen in love with him, when she had spent one glorious month hoping he was her future—Tess felt about twenty years older now.

In maturity and common sense anyway. It had been a very quick way to learn self-confidence, and to be self-reliant.

Dad had been right all along; she should have listened to him. Zac Montgomery was way out of her league. He'd come from a different world to her; he had different standards and values. It was about the dollar. It had been a good wake up call for Theresa Anderson.

A goat bleated up the hill and brought her back to the

present. She was on the first shift in the office this morning, and as soon as the sun had cleared the horizon, she'd jog back down the hill, have a quick shower, and grab some breakfast.

At least she didn't have to worry about running into Zac this morning because he'd said he was going back to Hamo last night with Jiminy. After talking to Eliza, she'd made her excuses and left the party.

She'd run through the forest, remembering the night she'd run through The Rocks and got lost.

Mum had cried when they'd said goodbye at Central Station the next morning and even Ted had hugged her.

It had been two years since she'd seen them. Zac could shoulder the blame for the loss of her family too.

The first launch wasn't over until ten so Tess knew she had some respite. With a bit of luck, they wouldn't cross paths. She'd stay in the office between the launch and the next day. If he did appear in the office, she'd go in the back room and Nell could deal with him.

With a yawn, Tess lifted her face to the first warm rays of the sun. Any sleep she'd managed to snatch had been broken by dreams of Zac holding her. She took a deep breath and held it, letting the serenity fill her before she headed back down to the old house. There were some decisions to make.

As her former boss, Tess was concerned that Zac would share her past job history with Pippa and that her position—her traineeship—would be compromised. While she kept that in her mind, and how he had immediately thought she had done the wrong thing and not given her a chance to defend herself, she was able to stay strong and push away the attraction that he damn well still held for her.

How the hell had he found her?

Loose stones slipped beneath her shoes as Tess turned and made her way down the hill. She would be strong, because she would not give up her job. If Zac raised anything with Pippa, she would pull out the one ace she had up her sleeve. The one that she had not spoken of two years ago, because she had foolishly tried to protect Zac.

He hadn't even sought her out. She had been tried and found guilty by the CEO, but worst of all, Zac had believed that she had done the wrong thing.

With a determined grunt. Tess picked up her pace and as soon as the hill levelled out, she began to jog, forcing herself to go faster, and enjoying the pain it caused. While ever she was dealing with that, she would not think about the past and Zac Montgomery.

I can do it.

By the time she reached the site of the new pool, Tess was a lather of perspiration, and her breath was ragged.

***

It had been well after midnight when Zac got back to his boat in the marina; he'd lingered talking to Jiminy, not wanting any of the staff who'd travelled back to Hamo to see him go to his vessel at the middle wharf. Once he was in the master suite he found it impossible to sleep. Spending the night in Tess's company had brought back the great times they had spent together two years ago, and the strong feelings that he'd held for her.

The love that he still felt for her.

Those feelings had never left him and had fed his determination to find her. It had been a long and hard road, and her family had been impossible. He knew when Reeza's brothers had told him she was in Western Australia that they'd been lying, but he wasn't prepared to risk it, just in case she was there. He admired them for respecting her privacy even though it had made his job of finding her bloody nigh impossible.

He would never forget the moment when he'd spotted the photo on the noticeboard in the staff quarters on his boat. Even with her short blonde hair, he'd recognised Reeza straight away. The relief had been overwhelming, but a photo was only the start. When he'd asked about it he'd discovered it had been taken about three months ago in a bar on Hamilton Island.

The last time he'd been at Hamo. He shook his head as he realised she'd been there on the same island, and he hadn't known.

The problem was that when he'd seen the photo they'd been moored off Exmouth in Western Australia. The staff and crew had been surprised when he'd told them they were going straight back to the east coast. They'd only been in this incredible location for a week; it had taken three weeks to cruise around the Top End and reach Exmouth.

'Now?' Marty, his captain—and the one who'd pinned the

photo on the board—had screwed his face up. 'You want to go back to the east coast now? We've only just got here, Zac.'

'Yes, humour me, please, Marty.' Zac gripped the photo in his hand and stared down at it. 'Now tell me the name of the bar where this was taken? And when?'

The photo was of his skipper with his arm around a dark-haired woman, but all Zac was interested in was the woman behind the bar. She was looking at the camera.

It was *Reeza.* Working in a bar, for fuck's sake.

He knew it was her. He was as sure of that as he was that the sun would set over the sea this afternoon. He had been looking for her for almost two years hounding her family, and following false leads.

Whoever would have guessed that she would appear in the background of a random photo pinned up on the staff announcement board of his cruiser?

Marty took the photo from his hand and frowned. 'It was taken in the Bristolian Bar a couple of months ago, the week you flew back to Sydney when *Myr* was being serviced at Hamo.'

Zac had rolled his eyes and groaned. He'd left the boat and the crew at Hamilton Island to fly back and beg Reeza's family one last time, and that's when they'd told him she was in the west. He'd come back and they'd headed west two weeks later. She'd been on the island the whole time.

'Cindy was looking for a job on the boats, and we agreed to meet at the bar that night. I know it was two months ago, because she had to be back in Cairns to go back to work at the end of September.'

'Okay. And can you tell me anything about the girl behind the bar? The one in the photo.' Zac had taken the photo back from Marty and stared at him.

'I'm sorry, mate. I never even noticed her. What's the big deal?'

'The big deal is we're going back to Hamilton Island. Now. Tell the crew to pull up anchor and get moving.'

'Ah, boss? Some of them are onshore at Exmouth.'

'Well, get them back to the boat as quickly as you can and then we're going. Thank you.'

The two weeks it took to cruise back to the east coast were

the longest of Zac's life. They needed to plot the route so they reached ports to refuel in the daylight and his frustration had built as they'd had to spend a night in Broome, Darwin, Cooktown, and Townsville. He'd thought about flying back, but told himself it had been two years, and he would wait, and think about his approach.

If indeed she was still there.

He knew Marty, his captain, thought he was mad, and maybe he had been. But now he was back in the Whitsundays, he'd tracked Reeza down from the bar to Pentecost Island and discovered she now called herself Tess. Then his first stroke of good luck arrived; his mate, Rafe lived on Pentecost Island and his wife ran the resort. He'd talked to Rafe—they'd been friends since they'd met when Zac had first come to the islands. He'd told him the whole story and asked him to keep it to himself, and Rafe had come up with the idea of a job on the island.

Zac gave up trying to sleep and went up to the deck. *Myr*, his forty metre yacht, had been his escape after he had walked out of the bank, the week after Reeza had been accused of theft. It had taken three months to have the luxury yacht delivered, and he'd lived on board ever since. If it hadn't been for his lack of success finding Reeza, he could have settled into his new life. The life of his dreams. But the worry of what had happened to her had refused to leave him.

Zac had discovered the truth within hours; it hadn't taken much. Reeza had been set up, and he was determined to find her and make amends. And support her. But to his dismay, she had disappeared that night, and had proved impossible to find.

Myr had been the realisation of his dream, to live on the water. But that dream had turned to dust, and when he hadn't been able to find Reeza, he'd taken little pleasure from the new life he'd tried to live. His search had become an obsession and Zac knew he couldn't go on like that forever. The trip to Exmouth was going to be his last attempt.

He lay back and looked at the night sky. The velvet background was black and dotted with millions of stars. The only sound was the slap of the water on the hull, and he tried to focus on what he'd do.

He had one shot with Reeza. *Tess,* he reminded himself. And he would not stuff up.

The warm breeze played on his face and Zac closed his eyes and drifted off to sleep as the stars moved across the sky.

Chapter 20

When Tess heard voices from behind the huts where the formwork for the pool was being built, she decided to have a look at the pool area. Eliza and Pippa were excited about the development, and by all accounts, the infinity pool was going to be pretty spectacular. Tess hadn't been to the site since the hole was dug last week.

The view from the pool site looked out over an expanse of the Passage where there were no other islands to impede the view. Just endless clear blue water and sky. The pool design had platforms holding eight day beds. The view was framed by two well-established palm trees on the edge of the shore. Apparently, Eliza had sourced some timber-framed day beds, which would give privacy options to guests as they visited the pool. Their plan was to have a bar at the island edge of the pool, and to make it another activity hub along with the main bar and restaurant.

Tess sighed; she really wanted Zac—or Monty, or whoever he was these days— to be gone. She loved her job and her life on Pentecost Island, and she didn't want to have to start over. But if he made it too hard, she would go. No matter how attracted to him she still was, she would never forgive Zac for not supporting her on that dreadful day.

Tess turned along the garden-edged path that led to the pool area. Even though she knew Zac was coming here to meet with Pippa and Eliza today, it was too early for him to have arrived yet and Jiminy wouldn't arrive with the day's passengers for another three hours yet. She lifted her arm and wiped the perspiration from her face as she stepped out of the rainforest. Even though it was just after six, the heat was building. She followed the voices and when she stepped past the last hut on the waterfront, she drew a quick breath.

He'd lied. Zac hadn't left the island last night at all. He was standing on the beach below the pool talking to Danny Riccardo.

Why was she not surprised? Whatever he did he couldn't

be trusted, and he hadn't changed. He had to call the shots. She'd fallen for it once, but she'd learned a lot since then. She had been a naive young woman who'd fallen for a sophisticated man with a smooth spiel. The events that had led to the end of her career had hurt, but the way Zac had used her had hurt a hundred times more. Tess stepped back slowly into the glade so they wouldn't see her, but she was too late.

'Morning, Tess,' Zac called cheerily and Danny echoed the greeting.

'I saw you up on the hill as Renzo and I came into the bay,' Danny said. 'You're keen to jog at this time of the year.'

'Gets the blood pumping,' Tess said as she walked over to them, but was careful to keep her eyes on Danny, and not look at Zac.

'I didn't know you jogged, Tess,' Zac said.

'Why would you?' she said sharply and Danny looked at her curiously.

Zac shrugged and there was silence for a moment.

'Did you stay the night on the island after all, *Monty*?' she couldn't resist asking.

'No, I came over on my boat half an hour ago. Danny told me last night before I left with Jiminy that he'd be here early, so I decided to come over early too,' he said.

Tess widened her eyes, but was determined not to comment. *His boat?* He'd achieved his dream and had a boat?

'I haven't had a chance to see Pippa and Eliza yet, but Renzo managed to double the formwork crew today and we're set.' Danny laughed. 'Sometimes it helps to be Italian.'

'Why's that?' Tess asked.

'Half of our cousins are concreters,' Danny said with a grin.

'Do you want me to let Pippa and Eliza know you're looking for them when I get to the office? I start work at seven.'

'That's early enough, thanks. The guys won't be here until nine-thirty. They were driving down from Ingham last night.' Danny nodded. 'If you could get a message to Eliza, that'd be great. Pippa's not here. We passed Rafe's boat heading to Hamo on the way over, and Pippa and Rafe were both on it.'

Tess frowned. 'That's early.'

'Yeah, I wondered myself where they were going.' Danny said. 'Anyway, if Eliza's here that's fine.' He turned to Zac. 'I've got to go up the hill and help Renzo at the new staff apartments for an hour or so. Have a look around, and see what you reckon. It'll be good to have another opinion. See you later, Tess.'

Tess froze as she realised she was going to be left alone with Zac. She turned away. 'I have to go and get ready for work.'

'Tess, wait. Please. We need to talk. And this is a perfect opportunity. There's no one around, and we can be frank.' She looked down as he touched her arm, but Zac must have thought better of it and he lifted his hand straight away.

She put her hands on her hips. 'I can be frank all right. I don't want to talk to you, I don't want you on the island, and I have no idea what you're doing here.'

'I'm here because I have a job, and the bonus is I get to see you. I'd like to make amends, Tess, and spend some time with you and get to know you all over again.'

'Make amends? That's a joke.' She stared at Zac, and for the first time Tess noticed the shadows beneath his eyes.

'I'm serious. But we need to talk.'

'We're just going around in circles here, Zac. The sooner you realise I don't want to talk to you the better. I don't want to be in your company.' Tess had no idea what skills Zac could bring to the island. 'What sort of job are you doing? There's not much of a demand for investment bankers here.'

'I don't do that anymore,' he said quietly.

'So what are you doing here?'

'I'm here to see you.'

'You've wasted your time.' She shook her head slowly as she stared at him, 'And you have a boat too?'

'I do.'

'What sort of boat?'

'The boat I came over on is a small runabout but it's big enough to get me from Hamilton Island to here, or to the mainland.' He stared at her, and she found it hard to look away. 'It's moored at the jetty if you want to see it.'

'No. I'm not interested. I was just curious.' She tipped her head to the side and held his blue-eyed gaze, ignoring the ripple that tugged at her. 'So you left the bank and followed your dream?'

***

Zac had been surprised, but very pleased, when Tess walked out of the glade when he was talking to Danny. And happy. It was the first time he'd seen her in running clothes and he was surprised at how fit and toned she was. Over the past two years, she'd changed in many ways; she had matured and her self-confidence was obvious. Her skin had more colour and she looked healthy.

But the change in her had not lessened the strong attraction he felt; it was still there as strong as ever.

The problem was that Tess was looking at him as though he was something that had crawled from beneath a rock. But her comment about following his dream encouraged him; maybe she wasn't as resistant to him as he'd thought. Maybe it was a front she was putting up.

Whatever it was, Zac knew to tread carefully.

'I did follow my dream,' he said. 'I just have one more thing to do and I will be very content with my life.'

She didn't ask what that was, but she stood there sizing him up. When Zac had left the bank, he'd embraced a more physical life. He'd joined a gym and a swimming club, and built his fitness and taken on a variety of outdoor activities. The only thing he couldn't understand was why it had taken him so long to realise how his quality of life had been lacking those fifteen years he'd worked at the bank.

'You look well, anyway. I have to go to work now.' Tess turned away and Zac went to speak, and ask her to see him after work, but something told him not to push.

'Have a good day.' Turning away and not watching Tess walk away was hard, but Zac was beginning to realise how carefully he was going to have to approach this. He'd been naive, kidding himself that all he had to do was find Tess, apologise, and all would be right. He'd focused on the search and on finding her, and not given any thought to the fact that she wouldn't be receptive.

'You're a fool,' he told himself. Zac knew he needed help; Rafe knew the situation and was a level-headed guy. He'd head up to the house when they got back to the island and use him as a sounding board.

And maybe Pippa too.

Maybe she knew the new Tess, and that approach might work.

The last thing Zac wanted was to have Tess disappear again.

Chapter 21

'Damn it.' Tess shook her hand and put it up to her mouth. She'd shut the filing cabinet too hard and jammed her thumb.

'Coffee time?' Nell asked looking at her over the top of her glasses. Nell had been humming and singing and smiling all morning, the direct opposite of Tess's grumpy mood.

'Sure is. I didn't sleep too well.' Tess smoothed her hands down her black shorts. 'Would you like a herbal tea?' Nell had given up coffee while she was pregnant.

'That'd be good, thanks. There's some peppermint teabags in the kitchen. Now that all the checkouts are done, we've got an hour before Jiminy arrives with the next lot. You and I are going to go out to the veranda and have a chat.'

Tess's stomach clenched; she jerked her head up and stared at Nell. Had Zac already told them about her past? 'Why, have I done something wrong?' Once she would have waited to be told, but these days with her new confidence, she was on the front foot and she challenged.

'God, no. Don't be silly. I want to talk to you because I'm worried about you. You've been like a cat on a hot tin roof all morning.'

Sweet relief loosened Tess's limbs and she flopped into the desk chair. 'Sorry, I'm a bit touchy this morning. I thought I must have been a bit short with one of the guests or something.'

Or something. That the girls on the island had found out that she supposedly stole almost a million dollars two years ago. Tess had never found out what the upshot of it all had been. One minute she was going to be arrested, then the charges were dropped, the media came baying for her blood, and she took off.

And not one call from Zac.

Total silence. No contact. He'd believed the worst of her, and had never even realised what she had done to save his skin. She could have blurted out that that he had been with him on that Friday night when she allegedly had been in the bank stealing money, but she had thought of Zac and his position. A lot of good that had done.

And now it appeared he'd left the bank, and had a boat.

And he'd turned up at the same island where she was beginning to find her happiness.

Why was he here? It seemed Zac had known she was already here, and she had no idea how that had happened. He'd been waiting for her in the glade to come from the office.

Tess frowned. Was there someone on the island she couldn't trust? There was something not quite right with that scenario.

Nell's laugh pulled her out of her thoughts. 'No, quite the opposite. I was wishing I had your patience when you were dealing with that grumpy old bloke who checked out last. The one who wouldn't let his wife say a word. Every time she went to speak he would make that awful clicking noise in his throat.'

'Mr Gray? He reminded me of my dad. He was easy enough to deal with, but I did feel sorry for his wife.' Tess laughed too. 'Poor lady was too soft. My mum developed a thick skin over the years. She's louder than Dad is now. I'll go and get that cuppa. Do you want some morning tea with it? Cherry brought up some lemon drizzle cake.'

'I shouldn't, but yes, please. If I'm going to look fat at my wedding'—she shot a cheeky glance at Tess—'I want it to be all baby, not too much fat from cake.'

'Wedding? What wedding?'

'Our wedding beside the pool as soon as it's finished.' Nell held her hand out and Tess felt mean. She'd been so damn cranky she hadn't even noticed the diamond ring on Nell's left hand all morning. 'You're the first to know. Officially, anyway. Pippa and Tamsin knew it was going to happen, but Nat surprised me.'

Tears stung Tess's eyes. 'Really? When did this happen?'

'Last night after the party. I knew Nat had the ring and I thought he was going to wait for Christmas to ask me, but he took me down to the beach and popped the question last night.'

Tess jumped up and hugged Nell. 'That is such good news. You've improved my mood!'

'Can I ask why it needed improving?' Nell asked quietly.

'Just some past worries resurfaced. But I'm fine. I'll get

through it.'

'If you ever need a shoulder . . .'

'Thanks, Nell. I'm all good. But I appreciate it. One of the things I love about being on Pentecost is the warm friendship I've been offered.'

'We're a pretty special place.' Nell stretched and rubbed her back. 'Now go and get our drinks and I'll finish up here and we'll sit on the veranda. There's about sixteen new guests coming in on the morning boat, I think.'

'Yes, seven couples and two singles,' Tess confirmed as she headed out the door 'And they're all here for the week. Which will save a bit of checking in and out. I like it when they all arrive at the same time.'

'Me too.'

Ten minutes later, Tess carried a tray out to the veranda where Nell was sitting gazing over the bay. The sky was a deep cloudless blue and the water was barely ruffled by the slight breeze that blew from the north. The azure water was dotted with white sails as yachts tried to catch the very occasional puff of wind.

'Sometimes I pinch myself to believe I really live here. It looks smooth out on the water today,' Nell commented as she reached for the cup of tea on the tray. 'Have you had a chance to go out for a sail since you've been up here?'

'No, I haven't. I worked long hours on Hamo when I was there, and now I'm happy to chill here on Pentecost when I'm not working.'

'Where did you live before you came to the islands, Tess?' Nell's voice was casual, but Tess knew she was digging. But it wasn't curiosity for gossip. She knew Nell was concerned.

'On our family orchard west of Sydney.'

'Nice. We'll have to organise a trip to Whitehaven Beach for you.'

'One day,' Tess said. 'There's so much to do here. But I have plenty of time.'

'When the staff accommodation is built and the pool area is done, there'll be a bit of a break.'

Tess raised her eyebrows. 'You really think so?'

'Probably not, knowing Pippa,' Nell said. 'And I think Eliza is her clone. They'll have some other project on the go. They are both full of ideas.'

'And energy.' Tess lifted one of the cake plates from the tray and handed it to Nell. 'I only cut two small pieces. I'm so excited to hear there's a wedding coming up. There's always something happening here.'

'There is, but it's been a quiet morning apart from checkouts. I've been waiting for Eliza and Pippa to come into the office, but there's been no sign of them.'

'Pippa and Rafe went to Hamo early, and Eliza's over at the pool site with Danny. Apparently, the pool is going to be finished a lot earlier than they thought.' Tess sat opposite Nell.

Nell put her tea down and clapped her hands. 'Really? That's fantastic. We might even get a February wedding, and I won't be too huge.'

'When's the baby due?' Tess asked as she reached for her slice of cake.

'Ours at the end of June and Tamsin in mid-April. The babies will have a playmate.'

'Lots of excitement coming up. A wedding and two babies.'

'And our new houses are starting to be built as soon as the pool and staff accommodation are done. With the birth, a new baby and a move to our home, I'm hoping that you'll be able to take over the office while I take a few months off.'

'Really? Oh yes, that would be—' Tess cut her words off.

'That would be?' Nell looked at her curiously.

'I *think* that will be fine,' Tess said quietly.

'You're not going to run away with that gorgeous Monty and leave us, are you?'

Tess's face heated. 'Oh, God no.'

That's the last thing she'd do.

She lifted her head and held Nell's gaze. 'Thank you. I would be pleased to look after the office while you are off. I'll stay here as long as there's a job for me. Thank you for having faith in me.' Tess took a deep breath. 'You don't know how much that trust means to me.'

She would not let Zac chase her away. This was her place. Whatever his secret was, when she agreed to talk to him, she would keep, and he could keep quiet about their past.

'Are you sure you don't want to talk about what's bothering you, hun?' Nell asked.

'Thanks, Nell. That's lovely of you, but it involves someone else, and I agreed not to discuss it.'

Secrets! What was he on about?

'Fair enough. But I assume it's our new lifeguard?' Nell put her hand up. 'I won't ask anymore. I picked up on the tension last night. Just know if you ever need an ear, I'm happy to listen.'

Tess's eyes widened and she couldn't help the grin that was tugging at her lips. 'Did you say lifeguard?'

Nell nodded. 'Apparently Monty is our pool lifeguard, and new barman. For the pool bar and the restaurant bar. It was organised pretty quickly. I still don't have any employment stuff or tax forms through. Remind me to ask Pippa about them.'

'That will be *interesting*.' Tess stood and picked up the tray. 'And that's all I'm going to say. Being a lifeguard is interesting, I mean.' As she looked out over the water, Rafe's boat motored into the bay. 'Look here's Rafe and Pippa now.'

'Are you okay here? I'd like to go over and meet them at the wharf.' Nell waggled her left hand. 'After I show them this, I'll chase up those forms for Monty.'

'Don't rush, we've still got a while before Jiminy arrives with the check ins.'

Chapter 22

Pippa

Rafe had one arm around my shoulder and held me close as he kept his other hand on the helm. He steered the motorboat into the jetty in his usual careful way and I glanced at the small runabout that was tied up to the other side.

'I wonder who that belongs to.'

'Zac,' Rafe said as the boat slid in alongside the jetty. When I went to step onto the wharf to help with the ropes as I always did, he shook his head and grabbed my hand. 'No, you stay right there. Here comes Zac now. He can do it. You're going to take it easy for a couple of days.'

'Nell's coming through the glade too. Rafe?' I looked up at his shadowed eyes, and my heart broke all over again. I had to be strong in front of Nell. She would guess something was wrong. I was about to put on the best act of my life. 'I don't want to tell anyone about the miscarriage. Okay? I don't want to upset Nell and Tam.'

'Okay, if anyone asks, I took you over for breakfast.'

'Thank you. Also is it Zac or Monty? I'm confused.'

'I'll tell you the story when we get up to the house. Probably Monty's best for now because that's what he's asked to be known as.'

My appointment at the medical centre had been quick. The doctor had confirmed the miscarriage and booked me into the hospital on the mainland for a D&C next week. She had been lovely and told me how common miscarriage was and not to be too concerned.

'When you're pregnant again, the anxiety and sometimes mixed emotions you feel about the pregnancy are completely normal. Don't be frightened by your feelings, Phillipa. And also, it's really important that you try not to be hard on yourself. Some women feel guilty that they may have let their partner down, that's not the case. There's usually a reason for miscarriage. Come and see me in a couple of weeks, okay?'

I'd nodded, holding back my tears, and went back to Rafe in the waiting room.

I swallowed as Nell walked across the sand. Tam's pregnancy was very obvious already, but Nell only had a tiny bump so far; if you didn't know she was pregnant, you'd never notice.

'Morning, Pip. Hi, Rafe. Where have you two been off to so early?'

'Breakfast,' I said with a smile. 'Rafe offered to spoil me before the day began.'

Nell laughed. 'Pippa Rendell, your husband spoils you twenty-four seven.'

I managed to look nonchalant, and wave a lazy hand. 'And so he should. I'm worth it.'

'Hi Monty.' I turned as Rafe's friend walked along the wharf and stood behind Nell.

'Sorry to interrupt, but can I come up to the house and see you both sometime this morning?'

'Sure,' I said. 'Come up now.' It would give me an out with Nell before I gave into the tears I could feel building again. 'Nell, did you need me for something?' I asked as Rafe threw the line to Monty to secure us to the jetty.

Nell smiled and shook her head before she lifted her hand. 'No, nothing important.' Her smile was incandescent, and I waited for her to finish. 'Just wanted to tell you Nat asked me to marry him and we're engaged, and to ask you if we can get married by the pool in February.'

My mouth dropped and I moved to the swim platform at the back of the boat to step off. Normally I would have climbed over the side but I was feeling a bit fragile. My throat clogged as I walked to Nell and when I reached her, I burst into tears. I grabbed her in a big hug as the tears ran down my face. 'Oh, Nellie, that is wonderful.'

Eventually I stepped back, unsurprised to see tears in Nell's eyes. I cleared my throat. 'Did you say February?'

She nodded and wiped her eyes. 'If we can book a wedding in.'

I linked my arm through hers. 'Do you want to come up for

a cuppa?'

'Later. I have to get back to the office now. Tess'll need a hand with the check ins. We've got a few in today. A big changeover.'

I swallowed. 'I think this calls for drinks at sunset. Just you and me and Tam. Is that okay?'

'Sure is. All for one drinks, hey? Just the three of us.'

'Yes, just the three of us,' I said, my voice husky.

Nell smiled through her tears. 'Sound good to me. I'll go over to the restaurant and tell Tam at lunchtime. And before I forget, Danny wants to see you and Eliza as soon as you can get over there.'

Normal life had returned, and I had to get used to it. My universe had shifted, but Rafe was still the centre of it. I was really happy for Nell, but my smile was sad as I walked across to Rafe.

He put his arm around me. 'Okay, love?'

'I'm okay.'

Chapter 23

Tess

Check-in time was hectic, like it always was. The new arrivals were keen to get to their huts and explore the island, and Tess and Nell were keen to process them quickly. They handed out the brochures that Pippa had produced about the Red Wall walk—with a warning about the feral goats—and took bookings for the restaurant sittings tonight.

Just after one, Tess sat back with a sigh of relief. 'I think we're done, Nell.'

'I've never had so many questions asked,' Nell said. 'They were a curious lot. Especially that rock climbing group.'

'Mine all booked into the day spa. That took ages,' Tess said. 'Sienna is going to be really busy for the next few days. Did I hear there's another therapist coming to work on the island?'

'Yes. Pippa's interviewing an Irish girl Sienna met at her course, but not until next week. And there's no room in the house for more staff, so I guess if she's suitable, she won't start until the staff accommodation is ready.'

'So she won't be here to help with these bookings.' Tess closed the check-in program on her screen, and asked casually. 'Is that why Monty isn't staying on the island?'

Nell stood and stretched, and giggled when her stomach rumbled. 'Probably. Although we have so many staff coming over on Jiminy's launch these days, I think he's going to increase to two trips each way every day soon.' Nell covered her mouth as she yawned. 'Do you want to have your lunch break first?'

'No, you go first. I've got a few things to finish up here,' Tess said. Plus she had no desire to go for her usual midday walk and risk bumping into Zac.

'Thanks. I'll be back in an hour. Do you want me to order you some lunch from the restaurant while I'm down there?'

'No, I'm fine thanks. I'll just make a sandwich in the kitchen here.'

Nell nodded and was gone quickly. Tess sat back and

stretched her arms above her head, feeling the best she had since last night when she'd bumped into Zac. The busy morning had put things in perspective for her. As much as she still had feelings for Zac she could put her head down and do her work, and keep to herself. At night, she had study to do, and didn't have to socialise with the staff group and risk seeing him. Not that that was likely to happen because he apparently was living over on Hamo.

The only thing that worried her was why he was there. She knew he was here because she was—and his insistence that they had to talk—confirmed that.

But why?

If it was about what happened at the bank, Tess knew she wasn't strong enough to deal with that.

Not yet. The experience and the very brief run in with the media had traumatised her, along with the knowledge that Zac hadn't even bothered to contact her.

If he was here to try and resurrect a relationship, she knew she definitely wasn't strong enough for that. It made her angry that she was still so attracted to him.

She'd put her head down, avoid the pool when he was at work, and ignore him if he came on her radar, and get on with her life. Hopefully he'd take the hint and go back to wherever he came from.

And she would forget about how incredibly sexy he looked these days with his longer hair and buff body. For an almost forty-year-old guy, he was hot.

Tess walked out to the veranda and stared at the water. Strangely, she had found being near the sea was soothing. Growing up on the orchard had meant very little time by the ocean, and she hadn't experienced that way of relaxing before. When she'd commented to Tamsin one night how the water calmed her, Tam had tipped her head to the side and observed her carefully.

'Cancerian?'

Tess had nodded. 'Yes, I was a June baby.'

'Water is your element. I'll do your astrological chart for you one night.'

Tess had smiled. 'I don't think I believe in all that stuff.'

'Oh, girlfriend, trust me. You'll be very surprised. Pippa was the most sceptical of all when I did hers, and you ask her how it all turned out. You watch, I guarantee she'll be pregnant by the end of this year.'

'Okay, I'll get you to do it one night. Could be fun.'

'An eye-opener too.' Tam had smiled and looked at her curiously. 'It might pull up some things you don't like.'

Tess had grinned. 'If it does I can pull up my big girl panties and move on.'

But that was before Zac Montgomery had turned up on the island. Until she knew why he was here, she wasn't going to settle. Tess leaned down and put her elbows on the railing and propped her chin in her hands. From here she could just see the wharf at the base of the hill where Rafe's black boat was moored. There was an unfamiliar small runabout toed up on the other side. She guessed that was Zac's boat. A long way from the dream cruiser he'd talked about.

She wondered why he'd left the bank.

Maybe she would have that talk with him, and find out what his secret was. He'd never said what he'd meant when he'd said, "I need you to keep a secret." But she'd guessed it was about him going by the name of Monty. But Tess had no idea why he would have changed his name.

With a shrug, she went back to the office and sat down. If she refused to listen to him and whatever he wanted to say, she would be on tenterhooks waiting.

She wouldn't seek him out, but next time she saw him, she'd agree to listen. Then, not only could she make a plan of action, but with any luck, he'd jump in his little runabout, go back to Hamilton Island—which was still too close for her peace of mind—and leave her alone,

By the time Nell came back to relieve her for her lunch, Tess had decided there was no point in putting off *the talk* any longer.

Chapter 24

Zac

Zac sat out on the balcony at Pippa and Rafe's house overlooking the wharf. He'd agreed to tell Pippa why he was on the island when Rafe had asked if he would share his story. Pippa was a lovely person, and she listened sympathetically.

'Would you like a woman's point of view?' she'd asked before she'd left them at the house to go down and meet with Eliza.

'I would.' He nodded. 'Please.'

'From what I saw in the brief time I saw you both together last night, it's obvious that Tess is not immune to you.'

'That's one way to put it,' Zac said sadly. 'She hates me for what happened. And I don't blame her.'

'My advice? You've found her, and she knows you want to talk to her.'

'That's right.'

'I'd give her some space. We don't need you here for about two weeks. Go back to Hamo, and as hard as it might be, chill. She knows you're around, and she'll eventually be curious to hear what you've got to say. I admire her; she's obviously a strong person. We had no idea she'd been through that trauma. She never mentioned a word.'

'Perhaps I shouldn't have told you,' Zac said. 'I'm hopeless at handling stuff like this.'

'Don't worry,' Pippa said. 'Rafe and I won't tell a soul. And if you would prefer that Tess doesn't know that we know, I'll forget you've told me anything this morning.'

'Thank you. You've given me some hope.'

Pippa reached for Rafe's hand as Zac watched. 'Do you love her?' she asked.

He nodded. 'I do. Not being able to find her almost did my head in.'

'So if that's how you feel, you never give up. Give it two

weeks and come looking for her again, and I guarantee she'll listen. Now I have to get down to the pool and see what's happening.'

Rafe jumped up. 'Are you okay to walk down there.'

Zac saw the warning look that Pippa threw at Rafe. 'Of course, I am. It's not that hot. I won't be long.'

Rafe had stared after her as she'd left and Zac noted that he didn't relax until she was down the hill and out of sight.

'Thanks for the ear, mate,' he said to Rafe as they stood at the top of the steps. 'I'll do what Pippa suggests. If you need me, you know where my boat's moored.'

'And you still want it kept quiet that you're Zac Montgomery and that *Myr* is yours?'

Zac nodded. 'Yes, please. Until I get Tess to listen to me, anyway.'

'Rightio,' Rafe said. He held his hand out and shook Zac's hand. 'Good luck. Keep me in the loop and let us know when you're coming back over.'

'I will. And can I ask you one thing?'

'Of course.'

'If it looks like Tess is going to do a runner, let me know. Now that I've found her, I don't want to have to start at the beginning again.'

'Not a problem. We've got a good vantage point of who comes and goes from up here.'

'Thanks, Rafe. I appreciate it.'

'Mate, I went through the same with Pippa when she first moved here. I knew she was the one for me, but it took a night up a tree to convince her. When you and Tess get sorted, I'll tell you the story.'

'I'll hold you to that. I'll go back to my boat now.'

'That reminds me,' Rafe said as they walked to the gate together. 'Why *Myr*? She's new, isn't she, and you named her?'

Zac nodded. '*Myr*? My Reeza. That's what Tess's name was before she disappeared.'

Chapter 25
Tess - four weeks later.

Christmas had been and gone on Pentecost Island and January had flown by. The Riccardo team had worked and had only taken Christmas Day and Boxing Day off. The pool had been finished and was waiting for the concrete to cure before it was filled. The bar building was taking shape and the day beds had been constructed on the edge of the pool.

Tess was at a loss. Work had been frantic, but she still had time at night to worry and to wonder. The resort had been at full capacity over the Christmas period and the bookings were coming in constantly. Nell and Nat's wedding was only two weeks away, and preparations were in full swing. Nell was ging to take a week off and fly to Brisbane with Tamsin and Pippa to buy their wedding clothes, and Pippa had put Tess in charge of the office.

Her confidence had had a huge boost from that, and the week had been so busy learning more about the office, she'd crashed into bed at night and not had time to think about Zac, although she had dreamed about him every night.

Since she had decided to listen to him, he'd disappeared. There's been no sign of him on the island, and she'd worried that he'd left.

It was strange. For the past two years Zac Montgomery had been the bad person in her thoughts, and she had let that consume her. But the Zac who had tried to speak to her a month ago was the same Zac she had fallen in love with two years ago and not the monster in her dreams.

A couple of days before the girls headed to Brisbane, Pippa came down to the office to take Tess through some things she wanted done. Tess had forced a casual note into her voice as she took the opportunity that presented itself.

'The pay run is automatic,' Pippa had said. 'Just get Angus to confirm the hours of the kitchen hands, and enter them where Nell showed you, and then everything from the pay slip emails to the bank deposit is automated. Eliza will check the house maid hours and confirm them with you.'

Tess swallowed. 'What about the lifeguard. Are his hours the same?'

'Monty? We decided to put off his starting date until the pool is filled. He was happy to wait until then.' Pippa lifted her head from the printout she was checking and smiled. 'If he comes over before we get back, just get him to let you know the hours he works. I'll make you his supervisor and Dylan's. Good experience for you. You can keep it on after we come back from Brisbane, because Nell will take a couple of weeks off around the wedding, and then she'll be off having the bub.' She looked at Tess curiously. 'Are you happy with that? Can you handle it?'

Tess swallowed and nodded, even though her heart sank. 'Ah yes, like you say. Good experience,' she said briskly. 'Yes, I can handle that.'

'Excellent. The staff quarters are just waiting for the carpet to be laid the day before we get back, and then you can all move up there. And that means Isla, the new beauty therapist will start work, and we'll convert the bedrooms off the eastern veranda into Odessa's boutique. It might get a bit noisy in here when Danny and Renzo are knocking walls out. And when the store is done, they're going to make a start on Tam and Gabe's, and Nell and Nate's houses.'

'Wow,' Tess said. 'Never a dull moment here.'

'So you'll be right while we're gone?' Pippa put the files in the desk drawer.

'I will. I'm looking forward to the extra responsibility.'

'Excellent.' Pippa stood and crossed to the door. 'Now there's only one more thing.'

Tess looked up from the keyboard. 'Yes?'

'I want you to take tomorrow off, and go over to Hamo. You're going to be working hard, and it'll be a day for *you*.'

'Oh. I don't need that,' Tess protested.

Pippa's smile was crafty. 'I have an ulterior motive. I'd like some more brochures dropped over there, and I know Jiminy's busy. I've printed them out. If you go over with him in the morning, and drop them off to the places on the list I've put with them, that would be a great help. And then shout yourself a rest day. Get your hair cut or shop, whatever you need to do. You deserve it, Tess. You've worked hard for us over the past three months, and I want you to know it's appreciated.'

Heat filled Tess's cheeks and she blinked away the moisture that filled her eyes.

'Thank you. That's a lovely thing to say.' She pulled a face. 'I've never been thanked in the workplace before. You know you'll never get rid of me now.'

'I'm pleased to hear that. Okay, I'll see you before we leave on Friday. Have a good day tomorrow.'

'Thank you, I will.'

***

Zac

'Thank you. I owe you one, mate.' Zac disconnected the call and stared out from the top deck of his boat. The four weeks that had passed since he'd been on Pentecost Island had dragged, but Rafe's constant reassurance that Tess was still there had helped him to stay patient. Next week, he would go over and start work there, and he'd been looking forward to it. Rafe's call had filled him with excitement, and he knew that tomorrow would be the day that he would mend bridges and start again with Tess—or it could be the day that he gave up forever. It all depended on if she listened to him, and if she trusted him.

With a deep sigh, he walked down to the galley to throw a meal together. He'd given the crew ten days off, in preparation for the coming weeks when he'd be working on Pentecost Island.

At least he hoped he would. Everything hinged on speaking to Tess tomorrow, and the reception she gave him. He stood at the galley window as his thoughts took him back to that day two years ago.

Chapter 26

Zac – two years ago

Zac sat shell-shocked as Ken, the security guard, escorted Reeza out to the corridor. Gregor Drummond stood and crossed to the bar in the alcove at the side of the CEO's office.

'An excellent outcome,' Drummond said. 'I thought it might take a lot longer to get to the bottom of that transaction, but the evidence was all there. She did it. I have no doubt.'

Zac leaned forward and stared at the floor as Drummond put a crystal tumbler of whisky in front of him. Something was niggling at him, and he couldn't put his finger in it. The evidence was all there, but his heart and mind were telling him it couldn't be true.

Not his Reeza. No way.

When Drummond first laid out the evidence for him that Reeza had fraudulently changed the transaction and deposited seven hundred thousand dollars into her account, he was speechless. Disbelief rocked him, and he refused to believe it until the CEO had gone step-by-step through the transaction. He had even produced a time-stamped photo of Reeza at her desk at five thirty on the afternoon in question.

Zac frowned as he reached for the glass of scotch and took a hefty swig. Why would they have done that? It was the first he'd ever heard of time-stamped photos of workers at their desks. It was just a little bit too convenient. He leaned back in the high-backed chair as Drummond sat opposite him.

'So, that's all behind us now. I'm playing golf this weekend, what are your plans, Montgomery? Would you like to join us?'

My plans? I was going to ask Reeza to move in with me, Zac thought. Before he could say he was busy on the weekend—the last thing he wanted to do was spend it in the CEO's company—the door hidden in the alcove behind him opened and someone walked into the back of the office. Zac was hidden from view but the frown on Drummond's face caught his attention.

The CEO put his hand up as a glass clinked in the bar.

'So the bitch took the fall?' a voice said. 'The journos and cameras are swarming downstairs.'

Zac jumped to his feet and stared at Bradley Drummond, the CEO's son. 'What did you say?' Zac strode across the room to him.

'Bradley, keep your mouth shut. Don't say another word.' The CEO jumped from his chair, but his son sneered at Zac.

'I said, did the bitch take the fall?'

'That's a strange way to phrase it.' He turned to Drummond. 'How appropriate is it for your son, a minor trader, to know what's going on?'

'How appropriate is it for you to be screwing a minor trader?' Bradley shouted back at him.

As Zac stared at them both, he realised what he'd been trying to remember. 'You're lying. You've framed her, haven't you?' He pointed at Drummond. 'Pick up that phone and tell the police the charges have been dropped. Put it on speakerphone so I can hear you. Now, you bastard!'

Drummond's hand shook as he did as Zac directed.

Once Zac was sure the detective in the foyer had been told the charges against Reeza had been dropped, he raced for the door.

'I'll be back to deal with this in a while. I strongly suggest you don't leave the building.'

He slammed the door behind him and stabbed his finger at the elevator button, hoping and praying that Reeza was still in the foyer with Ken.

Chapter 27

Reeza

The wind blew through Reeza's hair as she stood at the front of Jiminy's launch. She'd taken notice of Pippa's suggestion and had made a hair appointment this afternoon. Not for a cut, but for a colour. It was time to lose the blonde and go back to her natural brunette and grow her hair back. Now that Zac had found her, there was no point in trying to hide behind a different look.

As well as having a haircut, she had decided to seek Zac out while she was on Hamo and listen to what he had to say to her. She'd spent a lot of time thinking about it over the past four weeks and knew if she had it out with him, she could move on once and for all. At the end of the year when she was due holidays, she'd go back home and visit her parents and the boys.

She'd casually asked Pippa, as she'd left yesterday, if she knew where Monty lived on Hamilton Island.

'Rafe said he lives near the marina.' Pippa's smile was strange. 'Do you know where the new menu file is?'

It wasn't long before they approached the marina at Hamilton. Tess walked to the wheelhouse, as they turned into the channel. 'Jiminy, do you know a guy called Monty who lives near the marina?' she asked.

'Um.' Another strange look. 'Monty?'

'That's his nickname. His real name is Zac Montgomery.'

'Yeah. Yes, I do. Why do you ask?'

'I want to catch up with him today. He's an old . . . acquaintance.'

Jiminy pointed to the other side of the marina. 'Yeah, he lives on his boat over there.'

'On his boat? That's not very big.' Tess frowned.

'I wouldn't say no to living on it,' Jiminy said as he brought the launch alongside the wharf. 'Just walk to the end and turn left and you can't miss it.'

'Okay. Thanks. I'll see you at four. Is that when you go over?'

'Yep, four o'clock. You take care today.'

Tess frowned. That was a strange thing to say. 'I will. See you later.' She hoisted her bag over her shoulder and was first off the launch. She'd go down to where Jiminy pointed and try to see Zac first and then the day would be hers.

Her attention was caught by a child squealing as a man pointed to a large batfish that had come right to the edge of the wharf. She watched them feed it bread for a while and looked up as she walked along the concourse.

Her breath caught as she saw the tall man in denim shorts and a black T-shirt waiting where the wharf joined the path. Composing herself, Tess ignored the thudding of her heart and walked casually over to him. 'Hello, Zac. I was coming to look for you. Jiminy said you live on your boat down there.' She waved in the direction that Jiminy had told her.

'Yes. Yes. I do.' He nodded tersely. 'Let's go and have a coffee somewhere.' His words were clipped and he seemed ill at ease.

Tess's heart sank. Maybe he didn't want to talk to her anymore. Just when she had herself all geared up for it. 'It's okay. If you have something else to do, it's fine. I have all day. Or it doesn't matter. We don't have to talk if you don't want to anymore.'

He took her arm and his fingers were warm against her skin. 'Tess, I have been standing here waiting for you to arrive for almost an hour. I'm not letting you out of my sight until you hear what I have to say.'

She stared up at him. 'How did you know I was coming?'

'Rafe called me.'

'Why would he do that?'

'I'll be honest with you. And I want you to know that every word I tell you today is the honest truth. Rafe and Pippa know our story.'

'Our story?' Her voice came out in a squeak. 'What story?'

'What you need to hear.'

'Do I want to hear this "story"?'

'I sincerely hope so.' He let go of her arm and ran his hand through his hair. 'Okay, honesty all around. We'll start with honesty straight up. We'll have coffee on the boat and then you can scream and yell at me if you want to.'

'Okay. But only a quick coffee. I have things to do here.' Tess was cautious. They would be too close in the confines of that small boat.

'Okay. *Myr* is down here.'

'*Myr*?' she said looking up at him. If she didn't know better, he looked even bigger and more muscled than he had a month ago.

Zac's gaze was intense as it pinned hers. 'When I got my dream boat, I called her *Myr*. My Reeza.'

Her heart set up a slow and steady beat as she looked at him. 'Why would you do that?'

'Because of the way I felt about you. That Friday night when everything went to shit, I was going to ask you to move in with me.'

Tess widened her eyes. '"Went to shit?" I suppose that's one way of saying you accused me of fraud.'

Zac lifted both his hands. 'Wait. Let's just wait until we can sit down and I'll start at the beginning.'

Tess nodded and didn't speak as she followed him along the concourse. They might as well have been kilometres apart. The tension was palpable as she kept her distance. She clutched her bag to her chest as she followed him.

At the last wharf, Zac turned to the left, and Tess stared at the only boat rocking in the gentle swell.

'Bloody hell,' she whispered as she read *Myr* on the side of the luxury cruiser. 'You got your dream. I thought we were going to the boat you had at Rafe's wharf.'

'I got half my dream,' he said quietly. 'But not the most important part.'

The water lapping against the hull of the huge white luxury cruiser was a deep aquamarine, even in the small finger wharves of the Hamilton Island Marina. Dwarfing all of the other boats along the boardwalks, the white boat sat there enticing tourists who milled around, looking up and admiring the vessel. Finally, the dark weight that had filled Tess over the past two years began to lift, and she, too, looked up at the massive power cruiser, and anticipation filled her with hope. Zac wouldn't have brought her here unless he had something good to tell her. If he still believed she was guilty he wouldn't have chased her to the Whitsunday Islands.

He led her to the back of the boat and they stepped onto the timber swimming platform. 'Welcome,' he said.

Her voice shook as she answered. 'It's good to be here . . . I think.'

'Have faith in me, Reeza, please.'

Tears stung at her eyes when he called her Reeza. She cleared her throat and nodded. Words failed her. Fear and anticipation mixed together as she followed Zac up a set of polished timber steps. Her eyes widened as she took in the luxury boat. 'You did it, you really did it,' she whispered. 'You left the bank?'

'After what they did to you, I couldn't stay.' Again he raised his hand. 'Wait until we sit down. Let me start at the beginning.'

Tess was torn. After two years of blaming Zac and hating him in her mind—but never in her heart and dreams—she was wondering what had really happened. She was beginning to doubt her perception of the events of that day.

No words were spoken as they stepped onto the top deck. Tess shook her head. A timber bar divided the main living area from a formal dining area. A table setting for two was laid out on the huge glass topped table. Elegant glasses caught the morning sunlight that streamed in through the large windows. Plush white leather sofas formed a square around a circular glass table at the end of the spacious room with some colourful throw rugs over the soft sofas.

Finally Tess breathed the words. 'Oh my God, this is stunning.'

Zac took her hand and led her to the white leather sofa. 'Sit down. Do you want a coffee?'

Tess shook her head. 'No, thank you. I want you to talk to me. Tell me what you need to say.'

With a sigh, Zac sat opposite her on the second double sofa. 'I want you to listen and no comments, reactions or questions until I finish. Okay?'

Tess nodded, overwhelmed by her surroundings. 'Okay.'

She listened as Zac took her through the events of that afternoon. The audit trail of her login, the time-stamped photograph, the supposed proof that she had transferred the money to her account.

'I knew it was wrong,' he said quietly, 'but it wasn't until bloody Bradley Drummond came in gloating that I realised what I was trying to remember.'

'What was that?' she asked, her eyes glued to his.

'It was the fifteenth of the month. The night that I picked you up at Brentwood, when you got off the train and were caught in the rain. They alleged they had a time stamped video of you at your desk at five thirty-seven. It was fraudulent because I knew you were on the train at that time, because I picked you up at Brentwood.'

Tess nodded. 'That was the night that Bradley Drummond offered to complete a Swiss transaction for me. My big mistake.'

'I knew it wasn't you as soon as they accused you. Drummond didn't show me the evidence until you were about to be called in. I didn't get a chance to think and the date didn't register.'

Tess shook her head from side to side as she stared at him. 'Why?'

'Let me finish. If you hate me for this, so be it, but I want you to know every thought I had when he showed me that "evidence". I doubted you for a minute, Reeza. I thought you had made sure I bumped into you that night to somehow use me, and then I thought of you, the woman I had fallen in love with, and how sweet and innocent and honest you were, and how I knew you wouldn't have done that. But I did doubt you for a moment.'

'There was evidence, Zac,' Tess said quietly as emotion tumbled through her.

'They set you up. It was Bradley Drummond, his father knew that. He came in gloating and didn't see me there. I challenged them and they crumbled. I made him call the foyer and tell Ken to tell the police to drop the charges and then I ran out looking for you, but when I got summoned to the police station I tried to call you but your phone didn't connect?'

Tess fought the happiness and relief that was stealing over her. 'You believed in me?'

'Of course I did. But I couldn't find you. Where did you go?'

'I was on a train to Brisbane the next morning. Mum met me at Central. I was so upset because I thought you believed them.'

'When you didn't answer your phone I called your home and they wouldn't tell me.'

'I was so scared of the media tracking me. I took the SIM card out of my mobile and put it in the rubbish bin on the train. I bought a new one when I got to Brisbane.'

Zac hesitated; he sat back on the sofa and looked at her and his expression almost broke her heart. 'I've searched for you for almost two years. I wasn't going to give up.'

'You believed in me. You believed in me all that time.' Tess swallowed, and then she stood and crossed to where Zac sat. 'That's going to take some getting used to.'

He stood and opened his arms. 'Sweetheart. I vowed not to stop until I found you.'

She stepped towards him and as Zac's arms held her close, the past two years faded to nothing. Reeza had come home to the place she wanted to be.

Epilogue

Pippa - February 14

A crowd had gathered around our new pool on Pentecost Island on Valentine's Day. The water glinted in the morning sunlight, and the weather gods had put on a spectacular day for us. The expanse of water out to the horizon was the usual sapphire blue. As always lately, the huts were booked to capacity and the guests stood on the other side of the pool. Rafe and I had decided to have it filled last night so that it was a surprise for everyone when they arrived for our official "first splash" at nine a.m. That way everyone could be there before they started work for the day.

Evie and Jed were on the island. Evie had come back to help Dylan with the final landscaping, and they had done a superb job. Full-grown tropical shrubs in bloom edged the paths and surrounded the bar.

I smiled as my gaze swept over the group waiting for our new lifeguard to do the honours. At the girls' sunset drinks on the beach last Friday night, I had asked for a vote on who should do the first dive into the pool at our opening.

Tess blushed as Zac received the winning vote, with Rafe and Philippe tied for a close second.

I had been so happy the day before I flew to Brisbane two weeks earlier with Nell and Tamsin when Zac had brought Tess back over to the island.

Rafe and I had been on our balcony and he'd smiled when he drew my attention to the couple who had come in by tender to our wharf.

I looked down as Zac took Tess into his arms and kissed her thoroughly, and then my gaze had lifted to the white cruiser moored outside the bay.

A soft sigh had escaped my lips. 'Another happy couple on our island.'

Zac and Tess had been inseparable ever since, and Zac's boat was now a permanent feature outside our bay. To our surprise once he'd sorted things with Tess, Zac had asked if he could stay on and do the lifeguard and bar job.

Now he and Rafe stood in the middle of the narrow walkway between the pool and the waters of the Whitsunday Passage. Tess and Cherry held the bright pink ribbon that went along the length of the path. Rafe was doing the official opening and cutting the ribbon, and then Zac—looking very tanned and muscular—was diving into the pool.

Happiness filled me as I looked around at the staff.

My *friends.*

Tam and Gabe, Nell and Nat, Eliza, Evie and Jed, Angus, Odessa and Dylan, Sienna and Danny stood together. Renzo Riccardo and his wife had come across for the opening too.

Our island was almost complete.

I had recovered physically and emotionally from my recent miscarriage, and was looking forward to being pregnant again soon. I had faith that it would happen and I had managed to shed my doubts with Rafe's love and support.

We were all looking forward to Nell and Nat's wedding in two weeks, and I know Sienna was excited about the arrival of Isla who was due on Jiminy's launch this morning.

Rafe held the microphone up and I shivered as my husband's deep voice with the gorgeous accent filled the air. I smiled; he was good with the written word, but Rafe hated speaking in public, so his speech was short and sweet.

'It gives me great pleasure to declare Ma Carmichael's pool open. Zac, over to you.'

I glanced at Tess as Zac stepped up onto the short springboard. The love on her face was clear to see, and it brought a smile to my lips.

Zac walked to the end of the board and stood on his toes. He looked up and lifted a hand to his lips and blew a kiss to Tess. My smile widened as a collective sigh came from the girls. He was a fine looking man.

As Zac executed a perfect dive into the pool, a cheer went up and champagne corks popped. Rafe had insisted that it wasn't too early to celebrate the pool opening with mimosas. Dylan and Angus were soon walking around with trays.

A hooter sounded and I looked across to the east of the bay.

Jiminy's launch was early.

I frowned as a tall girl with dark hair climbed onto the top of Jiminy's wheelhouse and waved madly.

'Sienna,' I called. 'Isla's arrived.'

Isla

Pentecost Island 10

Prologue

Pippa

'We're ready to go, girls,' I said as I opened the gate to the new pool area on Pentecost Island. Tamsin and Nell, my two best friends in the whole world—after my husband, of course—followed me onto the new lawn. Our island was being tagged on social media as the island of love, so Valentine's Day morning was an appropriate day to open our new infinity pool.

'Oh, my freakin' God, the pool has water in it,' Tam squealed.

'Of course it does,' I said with a smile. 'Did you think Zac was going to jump into an empty pool?'

Rafe and I had decided to have the pool filled late yesterday afternoon so that it was a surprise for the staff when they walked across to the infinity pool by the water's edge behind the huts this morning.

'Look at those incredible day beds.' Nell clapped her hands in almost childish delight. 'I want to have a holiday here.'

'You live here, Nelly,' Tam said with a grin.

'I know, but what a place to have a holiday!'

I reached out and linked my arms through my friends' arms. 'We've done good, gals. We've *all* done good.' I sent a quick thank-you up to my Aunty Vi who'd left me the island last year, and now we'd planned and almost completed what was becoming a high-demand resort. Bookings were at full capacity, and we were booked ahead for months, even though it was the low tourist season in North Queensland. My only worry was the weather, but our new facilities had been built to cyclone standard. The original house—my great-aunt Vi's dwelling—had survived cyclones, Ada and Debbie, in the past, so I was confident we could ride the next one out when it came, as we knew it would.

A crowd had gathered around the new pool. I was pretty sure every guest in the resort had turned up for the opening. The water glinted in the morning sunlight; the weather gods had put on a spectacular day for us. The expanse of the Whitsunday Passage towards the mainland was the usual sapphire blue, dotted with white sails as bareboat yachts enjoyed the paradise that the Whitsunday Islands offered. Being a part of a business that provided a holiday destination to those who needed a recharge was very satisfying. Just looking at that body of water created calm in the most troubled soul.

I knew that very well.

Sitting on the balcony in our house up on the hill, looking out over the Passage over the past few weeks had contributed to my healing. I had healed fast physically, but the emotional toll from losing our baby was hard to deal with.

The morning was hot and humid and many of the guests were already in their swimming costumes, keen to have a dip as soon as the pool was officially open. Especially those who would be departing on the late morning launch. Our official "first splash" was at nine a.m. before the sun was too hot, although we had provided lots of shade around the perimeter of the pool, and—as Nell described them—incredible daybeds. Large enough for a small family, if needs be, and with soft mattresses and cerise-pink privacy curtains. Also, holding the "splash" early meant all the staff could be there to be a part of the celebration before they started work for the day.

Angus, our head chef had started breakfast half an hour earlier this morning, and Cherry, his partner, and assistant chef, had created fruit trays to go with the champagne cocktails. I could see the colourful array of tropical fruit lined up along the bar counter.

All our staff, present and former, were on the island this week. Evie and Jed had come across from their property south of Airlie Beach where Jed's rustic furniture business was doing very well. Evie, who had been our first landscaper, had helped Dylan—her replacement—with the final work over the past week. Like everyone else who'd been touched by Pentecost Island, she found it hard to stay away.

It was good to see Evie looking so happy since she and Jed had sorted out their marital misunderstanding. She and Dylan had done a superb job with the landscaping around the pool. Where there had once been a flat sandy area edged with dark rocks on the shore prior to the pool going in, full-grown tropical shrubs in bloom now created a lush backdrop edging the paths and surrounding the new pool bar. Jed had completed a rush job of furniture for us and the new timber outdoor tables and chairs had arrived late last week.

Guests were beginning to leave comments in the guest book saying how beautiful the gardens on our island were and how the landscaping had added to their overall five-star experience. I made a mental note to thank Dylan and Evie for their work.

I smiled again and my gaze swept over the assembled group waiting as Rafe and Zac walked to the edge of the infinity pool. Rafe was doing the official bit this morning; I'd been so emotional since I'd lost our baby, I still didn't trust myself to speak in public and keep it together. Zac, our new lifeguard was doing the honours for the "official opening".

I chuckled quietly as I thought back to the girls' sunset drinks on the beach last week. Friday night drinks and a debrief at the end of each week had become an institution that Tam, Nell and I had started at the end of our first week on the island.

'I have a task for you, ladies,' I'd said as I stood on the high rock and looked down at my group of friends. 'We need someone to do the official jump into the pool and the first lap next week. Do we need to vote who it should be?'

Odessa's plummy voice rose over the soft swishing of the waves on the sand. 'Really, Phillipa darling, that is a no-brainer.'

A few months ago, I would have bristled at her tone, but I knew Odessa well enough now not to take any offence. 'A no-brainer? Does that mean you vote for your Dylan?'

She waved a languid hand, and I noticed that she was wearing some of the new pieces of jewellery she'd made to stock in our new boutique. 'As much as I think Dylan is the best-looking man on the island, it has to be Zac, as the lifeguard.'

Tess, Nell's relatively new assistant in the office, blushed as everyone agreed and the winning vote was cast for Zac.

Zac had brought Tess back over to the island two weeks ago, the day before I flew to Brisbane with Nell and Tamsin to select our dresses for Nell's wedding. Rafe and I had been on our balcony when he drew my attention to the couple who had come in by tender to our wharf.

I looked down as Zac took Tess into his arms and kissed her thoroughly, and then my gaze lifted to the white cruiser moored outside the bay.

A soft sigh had escaped my lips. 'Another happy couple on our island.'

'The "island of love" hashtag that the guest created is pretty accurate,' Rafe said.

Zac and Tess had been inseparable ever since, and Zac's boat was now a permanent feature moored outside our bay. To our surprise once he'd sorted the past misunderstandings with Tess, Zac had asked if he could stay on and continue with the lifeguard and bar job.

'We both want to stay here, Pip,' Tess said. 'That is, if you're happy to have us. We love Pentecost Island.'

'Of course, we are,' I assured them. 'We don't want you to go anywhere. But Zac are you really sure you want to *work* here?'

Zac taking the job had originally been to track Tess down and convince her that he loved her. He had been successful, and they were now a happy couple, but considering he was a very wealthy man, I was surprised that he wanted to be our pool lifeguard and that they were going to stay.

'I want to be a part of your venture, Pippa. It's such a special place. We'll cruise around the islands on our days off,' Zac said. 'Eliza and Phillipe have told us about some of the great spots to moor. We've got seventy-four islands to explore.' He looked at me intently. 'And if you ever want to expand and need a silent partner, I'd like to put my hand up.'

Eliza, who had also bought into the island, and her partner, Phillipe, were spending less time cruising the islands these days, and I suspected that they were going to build a house on our island.

I glanced across to my two best friends beside me. Nell and Tamsin had been busy looking at house plans with our builders, the Riccardos, as well as both preparing for their babies who were due in the middle of the year. I pushed away that little bit of sadness that was always in my heart, and my sigh didn't get past eagle-eyed Tamsin.

'Why the sigh, Pip?' Tamsin's gaze was intent. No one apart from Rafe knew about the miscarriage.

'A happy sigh,' I forced a smile. 'Another love story on our island. Look at the way Tess is looking at Zac.'

Tam's voice was dry. 'Any living, breathing woman would look at Zac Montgomery like that. He's extremely easy on the eye.'

'Zac looks a bit self-conscious,' Nell said.

'And Tess looks smitten,' I added.

Tess and Cherry faced each other across the pool each holding an end of the bright pink ribbon. Rafe was going to cut the ribbon, and then Zac—looking very tanned and muscular—was to dive into the pool and swim the short lap. Phillipe was taking the photos for us to mark the occasion.

My brief melancholy lifted, and happiness filled me again as I looked around at the staff.

My friends. Each and every one of them.

Gabe and Nat came across to stand beside Tam and Nell. Eliza, Evie and Jed, Odessa and Dylan, Sienna and Danny stood together across from us. Angus was behind the bar, ready to pop the champagne corks, when Zac hit the water. Renzo Riccardo, our builder and his wife were chatting to Angus; they'd come across from their home on Hamilton Island, so they'd be here for the opening, too. As I thought about it, I realised that the love that everyone had for our island was the key to it being a huge success. And we would celebrate that again today.

One thing we did well on Pentecost Island was put on a celebration.

I was very pleased with the camaraderie between the staff. Even Odessa had settled in, and to my surprise, was becoming a close and loyal friend. Her wicked sense of humour had lifted my spirits a few times lately.

Our island was almost complete.

I was almost complete.

I had recovered physically and emotionally from my miscarriage and was looking forward to being pregnant again soon. I had faith that it would happen, and I had managed to shed my doubts with Rafe's love and support. I believed that a baby, the first in our future family would be the next step to strengthening our life on this island.

As far as the development of the business side of things

went, the island was buzzing. Plans were well underway, and we were all looking forward to Nell and Nat's wedding in two weeks, not to mention the two babies on the way.

We would have a full complement of staff by then. I'd interviewed Isla O'Sullivan by phone, and Sienna's glowing praise of her work skills had been enough for me to offer her a twelve-month contract. I was still wary of the unknown though, and there was a month-long probation period. Sienna was excited about the arrival of her friend who was due to arrive on Jiminy's launch this morning.

'Excited, Pip?' Tamsin leaned in and interrupted my thoughts. 'Or daydreaming again?'

'Excited. And content.' I said, meeting her gaze steadily. I glanced down at her pregnant bump, which seemed to be growing bigger every day.

'Good.'

'What about you?'

'Tired, but I'm good too.'

Nell nudged us to be quiet. 'Ssh, you pair, Rafe's about to start the official stuff.'

Rafe held the microphone up and a delicious shiver ran down my spine as my husband's deep voice, with his sexy posh accent, interrupted the happy conversations around us.

'Are we ready?' Rafe spoke over the portable PA system we'd brought in from the restaurant bar. He and Zac stood in the middle of the narrow walkway between the pool and the bar.

I flashed a thank-you smile at him; being an author—a famous author, I must add—he was excellent with the written word, but Rafe hated speaking in public. I knew his speech would be short and sweet.

'Good morning all, on this beautiful Whitsunday morning. Welcome to our guests, and our staff.'

The crowd quietened.

'I know you're all keen to try out our incredible new infinity pool, not to mention those inviting day beds, so it gives me great pleasure to declare Ma Carmichael's pool open. Zac, over to you.'

Yep, he was short and sweet, and I loved him for it.

I glanced over at Tess as Zac stepped up onto the short

springboard. The love on her face kept the smile on my lips.

Zac walked to the end of the board and stood on his toes. He looked up and lifted a hand to his mouth and blew a kiss to Tess. I nodded as a sigh came from most of the women in the crowd. He sure *was* a fine-looking man. Zac's bronze tan was accentuated by his white boardshorts, but despite the collective admiration, his eyes sought only Tess's as he stood, poised on his toes on the edge of the walkway.

As Zac executed a perfect dive into the pool, a cheer went up and the popping of champagne corks came from the bar. We'd all agreed it wasn't too early to celebrate the pool opening with mimosas, and each guest was being given a complimentary drink in honour of the occasion. Dylan, Nat and Angus were soon walking around with trays of orange juice and champagne, and Cherry placed a tray of tropical fruit on each of the tables.

A horn sounded and I looked across to the east of the bay. Jiminy's launch was in earlier than usual.

I stared at the tall girl with dark curly hair who stood on the top of Jiminy's wheelhouse and waved madly, yelling out at the top of her voice. 'Helloooo, I'm here.'

'Sienna,' I called over the noise of conversations, 'Isla's arrived.'

Chapter One

Isla moved from the front of the boat where she'd kept a running commentary going since Pentecost Island had come into view.

'Oh, my sweet Lord, what a glorious island.' Taking a deep breath, she tried to fill her energy well so she could keep going when she greeted Sienna, and when she finally met the famous Pippa of Pentecost Island. Last night on Hamilton Island her sleep had been fractured by those old dreams, and each time she woke, self-doubt had gripped hold of her.

When they had been on Esculanta island, Sienna had commented on her confidence and wisdom. Isla rolled her eyes; she could have set Sienna straight, but no one would ever know the truth; she was far from wise. If she had half the wisdom and experience she pretended to have, her life choices would have been very different and her life would have been a lot easier. The *Isla* presented to the world was very different to the Isla within. It had been more than nine years since her world had shattered and she was beginning to think she would never get over it.

So, Isla had to keep the flamboyance going. She would be Sienna's wise and exuberant friend from Esculanta Island, and Pippa would think she was truly as wonderful as the performance she'd put on during the phone interview.

One day, who knew, maybe one day she could be herself again.

Oh, there was no doubt she could do this job. That was the one area of her life where Isla excelled. She was a very good therapist, and she enjoyed her work. The course on Esculanta Island had honed her deep tissue massage skills and she flexed her fingers as she thought of some of the new techniques she'd learned.

After they passed a luxurious white motor cruiser moored in the bay, they approached the wharf ahead where a huge black boat was secured to the end of the jetty, and Isla took another breath.

'Jesus, Mary, and Joseph! Will you look at that luxurious boat!' She put one hand to her chest and fanned her face with the other, broadening her Irish accent. She lifted her face to the sun and closed her eyes. 'Have I died and gone to heaven? A tropical island, palm trees and the boats of my dreams.'

When she was met with silence, Isla cracked one eye open, pleased to see that the rest of the passengers on the launch were focused on the island looming ahead of them, and the skipper—Jiminy, not a bad-looking buff Aussie bloke wearing a wedding ring—was ignoring her, and concentrating on the narrow approach to the bay.

Being loud and getting in people's faces was a sure way to get ignored. Isla had tried the quiet and mysterious persona, but that just made observers more curious about you. Be an obnoxious loudmouth and people tended to steer clear and that suited her just fine. They didn't ask questions she didn't want to answer.

With a determined breath, she climbed onto the seat at the front of the boat and put her arms out, pretending Leonardo di Caprio was behind her as they approached the wharf.

'I'm flying,' she called out.

No one replied, continuing to ignore her as they paid more attention to the island ahead. As the launch approached the jetty, Isla managed to distinguish Sienna's bright auburn hair among the crowd gathered together by a divine swimming pool.

'Helloooo, I'm here.' she called out, satisfied when heads turned.

***

Ronan Doyle stood beside the skipper of the launch and looked down at his watch. As soon as they'd disembarked, and he'd checked into his room, he was going to keep a low profile. He didn't want to come under the radar of the woman he'd been watching.

It would be better to disappear quietly and keep to himself until he had had a chance to check out the island, do some more research and figure out the best approach.

He still couldn't believe his luck. He'd searched for her for a long time, and in the end, the answer had fallen into his lap. Three countries, eight months and much investigation, and what had ensued was obviously meant to be. Serendipity, coincidence or just pure luck?

A chance meeting in Mission Beach, an overheard conversation, and he'd looked into the face of the woman he'd been hired to locate.

Call it what you like, but Ronan was sure in that moment he'd found the woman he'd been searching for over the past year.

The hardest thing was not reacting. He'd turned away in that Blues Bar in Mission Beach and pretended to be focused on the music. His connection had delivered, but he hadn't expected it to be so easy once he'd left Alaska. After he'd traced her there, she'd left and dropped off the radar for a few months. She'd changed her name—slightly—but this woman was a dead spit for the woman in the photo he carried in his wallet. The photo her sister had given him.

His biggest dilemma was not letting Isla O'Sullivan guess he was interested in her, because, as he well knew, she was a mistress of disappearing. He'd gone so close to tracking her down again in Cairns, and then the trail had run cold when he'd followed her to the resort on Esculanta Island. One day, she'd been there; the next, she was gone, and as far as he knew, she hadn't caught either the plane or the launch to the mainland that day.

He would put his head down and not open his mouth in front of her because as soon as Isla heard his Irish accent, she would be on her guard. The last thing he needed was for her to do a runner again.

He looked away as she squealed and waved to a red-headed woman waiting on the wharf.

Chapter Two

Dublin. Ten years earlier.

Aisling O'Sullivan jumped off the school bus without a backward glance. In the space of fifteen minutes, since she'd boarded the bus in Castleknock, one of the posh suburbs of Dublin, she'd managed to change her clothes, trace her eyes with black kohl, load her lashes with mascara, and paint her lips with black lipstick.

The other girls had to dye their hair black, but Aisling was lucky. Her shoulder-length hair was naturally jet black, and her eyes didn't really need the kohl to tip them up at the corners. Having a Sri Lankan great-grandmother had given her a genetic advantage, but she still needed the clothes and the lipstick to fit in with her new group of friends.

'Well, look what we have here,' Brigid McGuire said as she pushed herself off the low whitewashed fence at the bus stop. The tall girl stubbed her cigarette against the wall before dropping the stub to the footpath.

'Aisling, you came.' Celia, Aisling's friend, grabbed her arm. 'You look gorgeous.' She lowered her voice to a whisper. 'A word of advice. Maybe don't look so good next time. Brigid won't like it.'

Aisling lifted her head and stared over tiny Celia's head to Brigid. 'Brigid will just have to get used to it, won't you, sweetie? You invited me to be a part of your group. You take me how I am. Or you don't take me at all. What do you have to say to that, girlfriend?'

Brigid shrugged and gestured to the other girl beside her. 'Something smells around here since the bus arrived. Come on, Dory, let's leave them to their boring selves.'

To her credit, Celia stayed with Aisling after the other two girls also dressed in black from head to toe disappeared around the corner.

'Oh, God, Aisling, what are we going to do now? They were going to take us to that club. Should we go back to school?'

'Looking like this? Can you imagine what Sister Mary would do? She'd have our parents in there in a flash. Besides, my sister already rang up and pretended to be my mam and said I was home with period cramps.' Aisling stared at Celia and reached into her pocket and pulled out a cigarette. 'You can go back to school if you want to. I'm going to look for some fun. You can come or you can go. Your choice.'

Celia pulled herself up straight; she barely reached Aisling's shoulder. 'I'm coming. So where are we going?'

Aisling grinned at the tiny girl who had been her friend since the first day of prep school. '*Sanity* have a sale on and Da happened to leave fifty quid lying around this morning. Let's go buy some music.' The bitterly cold wind whistled down Tower Road and she pulled her black hoodie around her shoulders as she blew out cigarette smoke. 'And then we might go and look for some new Doc Martens.'

'I haven't got any money,' Celia said with a frown.

'There's ways to get around that,' Aisling said. She strode ahead as the wind blew rubbish around the street. Her parents and her sister, Marlene, deserved everything they got. She'd teach them to treat her as a second-class citizen.

Grounded, because she'd failed her stupid mathematics exam. Hauled over the coals and told she wasn't half the good girl that boring Marlene was. Although to be fair, Marlene had covered for her today. Aisling didn't care what trouble she got into. What were they going to do about it? She was their daughter. They'd chosen to have her, and if they didn't like what they got, they could live with it.

Same as the bitches who'd just left.

She was going to have fun, and she was going to do whatever she wanted.

Chapter Three

Pippa

I stood on the path at the side of the beach where Sienna had asked me to meet Isla when she got off the boat. As I watched them chatting, Jiminy spotted me and walked across the sand.

'Hey, Pippa. How's it going?'

I leaned over and kissed his cheek. Jiminy, the launch captain, had been my friend since high school when I lived up here on the island with Aunty Vi. 'Really good. You missed the pool opening. I was just standing over there thinking how well everything's going.'

'That's great. You've got some interesting guests just arrived on the launch.'

'Interesting?'

'Yeah, I guess you're bound to get some strange ones every now and then.'

'Interesting and strange? You have me intrigued.' I watched as two middle-aged couples and a guy by himself headed towards reception in the old house to check in. Tess had hotfooted it over there as soon as Zac had climbed out of the pool. 'Which ones? I'll let the staff know.'

He inclined his head towards the edge of the forest where the arriving guests had stepped onto the path. 'That guy's by himself. Couldn't get a peep out of him, not even a hello or an answer, just a nod when I held out my hand and introduced myself. He's bloody strange. Spent most of the trip perving on the other strange one. I even wondered if they were together and had had a fight.'

I shook my head. It was the most words I'd ever heard Jiminy say in one conversation, so I knew I'd better take heed. 'Which is the other strange one you're talking about?'

'The one who thought she was on the Titanic and never shut up the whole way. The two couples moved away and ended up ignoring her. That's her over there, she's waylaid Sienna.'

I groaned. 'Not that girl with the dark curly hair?'

'Yeah, that one.'

'That, my friend, is our new beauty therapist.' I rolled my eyes and stepped back towards the path. 'Thanks for the heads-up. I'll take close notice.'

'Good luck.' Jiminy grinned and headed over to the office to collect the guests who were departing this morning. I plastered a welcoming smile on my face and headed over to meet our newest staff member. If Jiminy was right and she didn't fit into our team she'd be gone after the month, even if Sienna didn't like it. I was surprised to hear what he'd had to say because Sienna had spoken so highly of Isla.

I would make my own judgment.

'Welcome to Pentecost Island, Isla.' I greeted her as she followed Sienna down the steps from the wharf. I held out my hand and held Isla's gaze steadily. 'I'm Pippa Rendell.'

A pair of intent dark eyes held mine just as steadily, and my first impression was of self-confidence. A warm and soft hand took mine in a firm grip and she smiled.

'Hello Pippa, it's lovely to meet you in person. I was just telling Sienna that the beauty of the island has rendered me speechless.' Her words seemed sincere, and her laugh was warm and attractive. If Jiminy hadn't warned me I would have been sucked right in then and there. Tam always told me I was a poor judge of character.

'I am just beside myself that I am going to be working here,' she said with a broad smile.

'We're very pleased to have you here.' I could lay it on thick too. Dropping her hand, I stepped back as Isla reached down to pick up a small suitcase.

'Do you have any other luggage, Isla?' Sienna asked.

'Just my big suitcase, and a couple of boxes of a new product I thought you might like to try in the spa, but Jim said not to worry because he would get them unloaded for me.'

As she answered Sienna, I checked Isla O'Sullivan out. She was certainly a stunning-looking woman. Her dark eyes were tipped up at the corners, but I suspected that look was enhanced by eyeliner, but it was hard to tell. Jet-black curls tumbled over her shoulders in wild abandon. Fair skin and rosy cheeks gave her a Snow White appearance; she was very beautiful.

'You'll be sharing my room in the old house just for a few days. I hope that's okay,' Sienna said as we crossed the beach to the path leading to the house. 'The new staff accommodation lodge up the hill is almost ready. Danny said he'd take us up to look at the rooms later today.' Sienna turned to me. 'If that's okay, Pippa?'

'Of course. I was up there yesterday, and the Riccardos have done a fine job. They're good enough to be used as resort rooms.'

Isla stopped and put one hand to her chest as we stepped out of the glade. 'Oh my lordy, what a sweet house. It reminds me of our little house in Dingle.'

'Dingle?' I asked.

'Yes, where I grew up in Ireland. The house wasn't as big as that one, and there were nine of us living there back in those days. I tell you what, it was a pleasure some days to go to school for peace and quiet. Oh Pippa, I haven't told you yet, but if I blather on too much, do tell me to put a sock in it. I'm used to trying to talk over my family, and sometimes I can run off at the mouth. I won't be offended.'

'I'll note that,' I said drily. I wondered how Odessa would take to our new arrival. Isla was certainly going to be an interesting addition to our team. Despite Jiminy's warning, I didn't see a problem . . . yet.

Chapter Four

Ronan

'Dinner is served in the restaurant from six p.m. but it's wise to let the staff know what time you'd like to eat.' The receptionist—Tess, according to her name tag—handed over a small pack of brochures along with his key. 'Now, Mr Doyle, you're in hut number ten, which is close to our new pool. You've arrived on the right day. The infinity pool was only opened this morning. I dipped my toe in and it's lovely and warm. There are beach towels in your hut if you'd like a swim.'

'Thank you.' Ronan pulled his handkerchief from his pocket and dabbed at his forehead. It was stifling hot on the island. 'I think that's the first thing I'll do.'

'Make sure you read your compendium and take heed of the warnings about stingers and crocodiles in the ocean. We may be in paradise here, but you still have to be careful.'

'I will.'

'We'll bring your suitcase to your hut once they're offloaded from the launch. I hope you have an enjoyable stay with us, and don't hesitate to ask if there's anything you need.'

Ronan nodded and lifted his laptop case from where he'd rested it on the floor to check in. 'One question, Tess. Wi-Fi?'

She nodded and as she spoke the door opened behind them. 'Yes, all the details are in the compendium in your room. If you require extra data or any assistance, our two IT guys live on the island after hours. Just leave a message at reception, and either Nat or Gabe will get back to you.'

'Thank—'

'Oh my goodness, it's as sweet inside as out. Look at those gorgeous curtains. Oh my God, and the view.'

Ronan froze as the Irish accent filled the small space. He flashed a smile at Tess, nodded and hurried from reception, hoping that the receptionist wouldn't comment about an Irishman being in the resort. Walking away quickly, he followed the signs directing him through a small rainforest to the huts. He was pleasantly surprised by the absolute quiet that surrounded him. If he had to be here working, it was certainly one of the nicer places he'd been to during the past three years. Once this assignment was over, he was going back home to retire from investigative work. If he'd finally tracked down his quarry—and he was pretty sure he had— the bonus alone would be enough to allow him to buy into his brother-in-law's commercial photography business in Dublin.

Ronan shrugged off the thought that working in the one location every day would be dull. Being in one room working with digital images could possibly be boring after his work travels of the past few years. He'd just have to get used to it. Granted, Patrick had contracts with some of the biggest firms in the UK and he still worked with film for some of the more detailed jobs, but strangely the thought of being back in the industry Ronan had worked in for ten years before moving into this present work didn't excite him anymore.

A bird squawked in the spreading tree above and Ronan lifted his face to the sun as he stepped out of the rainforest. Following the sign to hut ten, he thought about going back to the cold and grey of Dublin in winter. Living somewhere like this was much more appealing.

He'd been unsettled since Briony had dumped him a couple of years back.

'Boring, Ronan. All you think about is your job and a pint at the pub on Friday nights. I don't want my life to be like that. He'd had a rethink, and realised she was right. Taking on the investigative work had given him the opportunity to see the world outside of Dingle. Problem was, now that he had, he didn't know if he could face going back.

Ronan pulled his thoughts back to the present. He couldn't afford to lose focus. This assignment was a delicate one; when he'd lost his target before, he had begun to doubt his ability and worry that he'd lost his edge. This time he'd take it slow and carefully; if it took a few weeks to achieve his goal, so be it. Apparently, she'd taken a job here. He'd booked the hut for a month to give himself plenty of time to set the trap.

Forget home and the future. The best thing was, he was on

a tropical island, in a beautiful location, the weather was hot and clear—no misty rain that chilled you to the bone here. Maybe he should consider emigrating. Ronan frowned as he put the key in the door of hut ten; the door opened smoothly, and he stepped inside.

Where had that thought come from?

He looked around the room and let out a contented sigh. A floor to ceiling window provided an uninterrupted view of sapphire-blue water, and the gentle breeze ruffled the fronds of two palm trees framing the scene.

Maybe the idea wasn't so foolish after all. He had the skills to take up a few different careers. Maybe later, he'd open his laptop and see what was available in North Queensland.

Ronan put his laptop case on the luggage rack and slipped his shoes off. The white tiles were cool beneath his feet as he crossed the spacious room to the window. For what was classed as a hut, the room was pretty impressive. A king-size bed sat beneath the window with two white towels in a roll on the white coverlet. A posy of yellow and white flowers sat on top of the towels.

Wasted on a single guy here for work, he thought, but he appreciated the romantic touch. Leaning forward a little, he looked through the window. To the left he could just see the edge of the swimming pool the receptionist had mentioned. Past the pool was an expanse of water, broken only by the white sail of a lone yacht. To the right, a hut identical to his sat at the end of a short white stone path edged with colourful flowers.

Paradise, to be sure.

The only noise was the soft swish of the cane blades of the fan above and the low hum of the refrigerator in the small kitchenette in the corner. Ronan walked across to the door at the end of the kitchen counter, and opened it, peering inside at a compact bathroom tiled in white from floor to ceiling

Relaxation seeped through him. He'd keep a low profile today, maybe have a swim, boot up his laptop, email his client and do some more research on the life and movements of the O'Sullivan woman. Sometime in the next day or so he'd try to get a photo of her and send it to his client.

Chapter Five

Dublin. Ten years earlier.

'Aisling, I don't know if I want to go down there.' Celia grabbed her arm as Aisling turned into a back street three blocks from *Sanity.* 'It looks a bit dodgy.'

'It's fine. Robbie in the music store said there's a tattoo parlour down here who'll do the first small tat for free.'

Celia drew her breath in and her gasp annoyed Aisling. 'Jesus, Celia, what's wrong now?'

'A tat? That's permanent.'

'So?' Aisling stopped walking and stared at her friend. 'You don't have to get one. You can watch while I get mine.'

'You're going to get a tattoo? What will your parents say?'

'They won't see it.'

Another gasp. 'Where?'

'On my butt. A butterfly. I saw one on TV the other night. It looked friggin' cool.'

Aisling looked down the street and she knew Celia was right; it was the dodgy end of the city but she wasn't going to let Celia see her hesitate. Two homeless guys lounged in a doorway, one covered with a ragged coat, the other staring at them as he sat on the doorstep sucking on a cigarette. A shopping trolley filled with their possessions lay on an angle in the gutter. On the opposite side of the street, a young guy with a pock-marked face leaned on the bonnet of an old, rusted car watching them.

Aisling wrapped her black coat around her; the wind whistling down the street was fecking freezing. 'There's the tattoo shop down there. Are you going to come with me or wimp out?'

'I guess I'll come with you. I'm not walking back by myself. But I'm not going to watch. I'd spew.'

'Suit yourself.' Aisling took off, stepping onto the road as she passed the old guys and flicking a finger at the young guy as he yelled out to them.

'Wanna have some fun, ladies? I can handle two of you at once.'

'In your dreams, boyo,' Aisling yelled back, but she picked up the pace, they'd already spent two hours wandering around the shops. 'Come on Celia, we haven't got all day.'
##

'Bloody Nora, that hurts.'

'Just lie still, love. I'm almost done.' The tattoo guy paused for a few seconds before starting to ink her again. Aisling bit her lip. It would be worth it.

It would. Another sign of rebellion; even if they didn't see it, she'd know it was there.

In the end, Celia had decided to come in and watch; Aisling knew it was because she was too scared to sit out in the waiting room by herself.

'It's really pretty, Ash.' Celia sounded surprised.

'Are you going to get one too, lovey?'

'Oh, no. My parents'd kill me.'

'They don't have to see it.'

Her friend shook her head. 'No. I don't want to.'

'Whatever.'

A few minutes later the tattooist straightened. 'You're done, love. You want to see it?'

'Of course I bloody do.'

He shrugged and walked away and picked up two round mirrors from the cluttered bench. Handing her one, he moved to her side and held the other mirror above her backside. Aisling propped herself up on her elbows and adjusted the angle of the mirror, and nodded. 'It's cool. Thanks.'

With a shrug, he took the mirror from her. 'Ten quid, love.'

'I thought the first one was free.'

'In your dreams. A man has to make a living. Come out when you're dressed.'

As soon as the door closed, Celia widened her eyes and whispered. 'Ten pounds! Didn't you spend all your money at *Sanity?*'

Aisling slipped off the bench and pulled her black jeans up over the new tat. She grimaced as the fabric touched her tender skin. 'Nuh, I slipped those CDs into my coat.'

Celia stared at her and then giggled. 'Gosh, you're bad, Ash. But I love it.'

'Bad?' Aisling buttoned up her coat. 'Stick with me, kid. You ain't seen nothing yet.'

Bad? she thought to herself. Sometimes it was all too hard, but it was the only payback Aisling knew. Some nights she lay there in bed dreaming of being in a normal family where there were happy people and love. Not this constant pressure to perform, and turn into a clone of her parents and her sister.

Bloody Marlene had enrolled in her law degree, and Da had the same plans for Aisling. To come into the family law firm: O'Sullivan and O'Sullivan. Mam and Da, whoops, Mother and Father, were both solicitors. Aisling grinned, wondering whether it would be called O'Sullivan, O'Sullivan and O'Sullivan when Marlene joined them. It certainly wouldn't be any longer because she had no intention of doing law.

'I know you've still got a few months before your university entrance exams, but you cannot afford to fail one thing, Aisling,' he'd said when she failed her exam. 'You can spend the next two weeks in your room brushing up on your mathematics.'

There was no need to do that. She would have been able to blitz that exam if she'd wanted, but rebellion had kicked in when her mother had told her the morning of the exam that she'd booked her in for a beauty treatment for the coming weekend.

'No. I'm going to a rock concert with Celia this weekend.'

'No, Aisling. Your hair and eyebrows need attention, and I saw a pimple on your face yesterday.'

'I squeezed it.'

She might as well as said she'd murdered someone by the look on Mam's face.

'All the more reason to have a facial treatment. I'll talk to Celia's mother and pay for Celia to go with you for the weekend.'

'No. If I have to go to the stupid place, I'll go by myself. Anyway, Mrs Donohue would be embarrassed if you said that. There's no need to flaunt how rich you are, *Mam.*'

'Mother.'

'Bloody hell,' Aisling said. '*Mother.*'

She turned to Celia as they stepped out of the tattoo parlour. 'Come on, I need a drink.'

Chapter Six

Pippa

The Friday after Isla arrived on the island, I was late getting down to our regular sunset drinks on the shore. Eliza and I had an afternoon meeting with Renzo and Danny Riccardo, getting ready for the handover of the staff lodge. We'd toured the building, checked out the final tiling jobs in each of the ensuites, and looked over the large kitchen and other communal areas. All that was waiting was the new furniture for each room arriving by barge early next week. Ten single rooms ran along the western side of the building looking over the island, and five doubles to cater for couples who worked on the island, both now and in the future and overlooked the water. A wide verandah facing north provided an outdoor relaxation area and a barbeque.

I turned to Eliza with a huge grin. 'They are going to love this.'

'I can't get over how spacious the rooms are. Bigger than our cabin on Phillipe's boat.' She pulled a face.

'You're quite welcome to take one of the doubles, you know.'

'Don't tempt me.'

Tamsin and Gabe, and Nat and Nell were going to move into two of the double suites while their houses were being built. Angus and Cherry were moving across too. Odessa and Dylan had asked to stay in the building behind the old house close to where she had set up her jewellery making studio. Having the single rooms meant that we could have kitchen hands and housemaids living at the resort now rather than having to come across on the launch each day. Sienna and Isla would take a single room each.

'Absolutely fantastic, guys. Love, love, love it.' I turned back to Eliza. 'You did a great job with the colour scheme.'

Muted blues and greens in the bedrooms replicated the hues of the sea and forest, and the communal rooms: kitchen, games room and living room were painted white, with charcoal benchtops in the kitchen.

'I'm 'ere to please,' she said with a grin, putting on her Cockney accent. I'd smothered a grin a few times lately. Eliza put on a stronger accent and dropped her aitches in front of Odessa to get a rise out of her, and Odessa took the bait every time. Mind you, Odessa put on her plummy tones to stir Eliza too.

Renzo shook his head and held his hands up. 'You should be using this building for guests. Too good for workers.'

I shook my head. 'We look after our staff.'

'And they love you,' Danny chimed in with a smile.

'It's so good, I'll talk to Phillipe,' Eliza said. 'I could live here.'

'You'll never get him off his boat, sweets,' I said with a grin.

'I know. Just as well I like living on the water.' Eliza looked down at her phone. 'We're late for sunset drinks, Pip. I'm happy to sign off, are you?'

'I am. Great job, guys. Thank you.'

'Okay,' Renzo said. 'We'll get the last of the building gear out of here tomorrow, get the furniture in place on Monday, and your lucky staff should be right to move up around Tuesday.'

'Excellent. And then you will start on Aunty Vi's house?'

'Yes, we're ready to keep going.'

Eliza and I walked down the hill and she flicked a glance at me. 'Why the frown?'

'You know me. I always worry when things go too well. It's like tempting fate.'

A loud voice and laughter drifted across as we approached the beach. Isla was holding court and stood in the centre of the group with her hands on her hips. 'And Paulie told Ma he wanted to have ten kids, and Ma told him off. "Think of your poor wife, boy," she said. We all laughed but it was seeing Ma chasing him down the path with a broom that set us all off.'

I rolled my eyes and Eliza caught me.

'Not happy?'

'She's got an over the top personality.'

'She seems to be keeping everyone entertained.'

'Maybe I'm turning into an old cranky pants.'

Eliza chuckled and shook her head. 'We're getting older.'

As we got closer, Sienna interrupted Isla, the teller of the tale. Her musical accent was soft after the Irish brogue. 'But tell us, why would she chase him with the broom? I do not understand.'

'She always did with Paulie. He was always the naughtiest when we were growing up.'

Cherry's smile was wistful. 'I envy your big family. It sounds like a happy family despite the broom!'

'Oh, we were when we were growing up, and now with all the grandchildren, it's starting all over again.'

'How many grandchildren?' Nell asked.

'Oh, I do lose track,' Isla said. 'Let me see.' She counted off on her fingers. 'Paulie has Morag, and Johnnie, Johnnie has Susie and Paulie, Archie has Ian and Aisling, and Barrie's wife, Jennifer is expecting their first. So that makes almost seven'

'What about your other brother?' Sienna asked.

Isla shook her head. 'I only have four brothers.'

'I thought you had five?'

'No, thank goodness. Only four.' Isla looked away from Sienna.

'Do you miss them?' Nell asked as Eliza and I settled on a rock. Cherry poured two glasses of champagne and handed them to us.

'Thanks, love,' Eliza said as we clinked the glasses.

'Bloody hell, no. Screaming whinging kids. I had enough of that growing up in our tiny house. We Facetime once a month when they all go home for Sunday lunch. That's enough for me!' Isla looked across to Eliza and I. 'Hello, there, you pair. I love this idea of sunset drinks, Pippa.'

'It's a good way to wind down,' I said quietly. It was interesting to see the change in dynamic down here on the beach. We usually had a few quiet conversations going, but tonight Isla was centre stage; she was a very charismatic person. I wondered how she was going in the day spa. If she was so vocal with her clients, it might be a bit off-putting. I'd check in with Sienna later.

I sipped my champagne and enjoyed the fizz of the bubbles on my tongue. Isla was still holding court, talking about her primary school days in a place called Dingle. I shook off the annoyance that surfaced briefly. As Isla kept speaking to her seemingly spellbound audience, Sienna stood and moved across to stand at the edge of the water. I rose and followed her.

She turned to me with a smile, but I had seen the frown before I approached. 'Hi Pippa, have you had a good day?'

'I have. How about you?'

'Busy. We've been fully booked all week since Isla arrived.' Her glance swivelled back to the rocks where the rest of the girls were sitting.

'How's Isla fitting in?'

Sienna nodded slowly. 'Really well. In the treatment rooms, she is quiet and professional, and the feedback from the guests who have seen her this week has been excellent.'

'But?' I prompted.

Her delicate arched eyebrows rose as she turned to look at me. 'But what?'

'I sense some hesitation there.' I lowered my voice. 'As you know, each staff member comes on a one-month probation period. If you don't think she's going to work out, you need to let me know.'

Sienna's fair skin coloured slightly. 'Oh no, it's nothing like that. I've just been tired this week, and sharing a room with Isla has been—shall I say—a *leetle* bit full on. But please ignore me. I'm used to my quiet time at night, and I just have to get used to sharing a room.'

'That's fine, but if you have any issues, you make sure you let me know. Friendship can't get in the way of us having the best staff on Pentecost Island. And the good news is, that the staff lodge is ready, and you'll probably be able to move up in a few days. Eliza and I just gave it the tick of approval. The Riccardo boys have done an excellent job.'

'Danny is a very talented builder. He's shown me some of their projects on Hamilton Island.'

'You both look very happy together. How's it all going?'

'We are, and things are moving well. The solicitor who is helping Danny to leave his marriage has made excellent progress.'

'That's good news.'

Sienna and Danny had had a rocky start to their relationship, but it had all been resolved on another island when she had gone away to do some training. Coincidentally, Isla had been at the training course at the upmarket resort on Esculanta Island and her employment with us had come from their meeting there.

Another burst of laughter came from the group, and I stood. 'I'll go and let everyone know that the move up the hill is imminent.'

An hour later, I walked back to the old house with Tamsin and Nell. Tamsin had been quiet on the shore, and I had a feeling that she wasn't too impressed with Isla either. When we stepped out of the glade and approached the house, I paused.

'So, what do you think of Isla?'

Nell chuckled. 'She's like a breath of fresh air. I love that accent.'

'Tam?'

Tamsin put one hand to her back, and I frowned.

'You were quiet over there,' I said. 'You're not impressed?'

'I didn't take much notice.' Tam's voice was quiet and strained. 'I'm actually not feeling very good.'

Nell and I moved quickly across the path to her side.

'What's wrong?' Nell asked urgently as Tamsin grabbed at our hands as her knees buckled under her.

'I have a pain in my back, and I think I'm going to faint.' Her face lost all its colour and Nell and I supported her across to the steps, and sat her down on the bottom one, and she put her head between her knees.

'Can you call Gabe, please. He's still over on Hamo.' Her breath sounded short. 'He and Nat had a late job there.'

I nodded and made sure that Nell was right with Tamsin before I hurried into the office. This was the only downside to being on our island.

Medical emergencies.

Tess had stayed in the office tonight; she'd insisted on staying back and doing the end of week run, as she and Zac were going cruising south to the Shaw group of islands for the weekend.

'Tess, can you please look up the number for Prossie hospital for me, and get them on the line. Tam's not well.' She heard the urgency in my request and typed into her keyboard immediately. Luckily, I had Gabe's number in my phone and I pressed speed dial.

He picked up immediately. 'Pippa?'

'Gabe, don't panic, but Tamsin's not feeling very well.'

'God, is the baby coming? It's way too early.'

'No, at least I don't think so.' I knew nothing about babies and birth, apart from the pain and distress of my recent miscarriage. 'She's a bit lightheaded and her back's hurting. I'm just going to ring the hospital and see what they say. I think the medical centre on Hamo will be closed by now.'

'I'm on my way. I'll swing by the centre and see if anyone's still there on the way to the marina.'

'Do that but wait a short while before you come back. Depending on what the hospital says, we might bring her straight over to Hamo on Rafe's boat. I'll call you straight back after I talk to them. Do you have Nell's number? Give her a call. She's out there with Tam now. You can talk to Tam.'

'No, I don't, but Nat's here. I'll get the number off him.'

'Okay, I'll call you back in five.'

I was worried and on edge as Tess passed me the office mobile. I'd jinxed Tam by worrying that something was going to happen when I'd said that everything was going too well. 'Can you call Rafe and get him down here too, please Tess.'

My call to Proserpine Hospital was brief.

Chapter Seven

Aisling

Dublin. Ten years earlier.

Aisling took pity on Celia, and they walked three blocks before she found a likely looking bar. One that Celia would be comfortable in. Sometimes, Aisling wondered how they had stayed friends. She gestured with a short jerk of her head, and Celia followed her into the dark pub without a word.

A group of elderly men sitting at a table in the corner were the only other patrons, but an appetising aroma drifted out from the kitchen, masking the stale smell of beer and smoke. Aisling pulled out her phone and checked the time, ignoring three text message notifications from her mother.

Shit, obviously sprung. Bloody Marlene.

She pulled a face.

'What's wrong?' Celia's voice held its usual lack of confidence and Aisling wondered why she had even asked her to come to the city with her.

'Nothing.' She rolled her eyes. 'It's almost one. Drink, then food. I'll go and get a menu; you grab that table. What do you want to drink?'

'Ginger ale, please.'

As always, Celia did as Aisling instructed. With a shrug she waited until Celia was sitting at the table in the far corner, and she headed to the bar.

The barman had his back to her washing glasses, and she waited for him to turn around.

When he finally turned and put the cloth on the bar, Aisling drew a breath.

Mother of God, he was a fine thing. She was in instant lust.

She fluttered her mascara-enhanced lashes at him and smiled. 'Hello.'

'Good morning, lovely. What can I get you?' Deep blue

eyes surrounded by lush—unenhanced—lashes sat in a beautiful face. Pale white skin, high cheekbones and a lock of dark hair falling across a high brow got her attention. A slow and sexy smile tilted his lips as he retuned her gaze. He looked just like she imagined Dylan Thomas would have looked. She adored his poetry, and when things were really bad at home, she'd lie on her bed with her earphones blocking out any interruptions and listen to Dylan Thomas reading his poetry.

The only thing this guy didn't have was the Welsh accent, but Aisling was in instant love. She'd been going to order an ale for herself, but suddenly it didn't seem sophisticated enough.

'I'll have a glass of white wine, please, and a ginger ale for my friend.'

He didn't move and held her eyes with his for what seemed like minutes. Heat filled her cheeks as he kept staring.

'You don't remember me, do you?' he finally said.

'Remember you?' Her voice was breathless. 'Should I?'

'I was two years above you at Castleknock College.'

'Oh.' Aisling narrowed her eyes and stared at him. 'I don't remember you.'

Was it a pick-up line or was he for real? She was smitten, but smart enough to be careful.

'I always thought what a pretty little thing you were, but you've grown up. And you've obviously spread your wings. Have you left school?'

A pretty little thing? Okay, could be better, but she could live with that.

What to say?

'I'm thinking about it.' That was vague enough.

Reaching across to the shelf he took down a bottle of wine and opened it. 'Half or full?' Those glorious eyes met hers as he held the glass up.

'Full please.'

His voice was deep and melodious, and a memory tugged as he stared at her.

'Oh my love is like a red, red rose
That's newly sprung in June;
So fair art thou, my bonnie lass,
So deep in love am I,' he recited in that sexy voice. The

penny dropped.

'You spoke at the school assembly when Mr Laidlaw died, didn't you? I do remember you now. You read a poem you'd written about him.'

'Ah, thank you, God. She remembers me.' He put one hand to his chest as he poured the wine.

'I remember your voice, and I always remembered those beautiful words you wrote about him. I loved Mr Laidlaw.' Guilt trickled through Aisling as she thought what that fine teacher would have said about her bunking off from school, and her lack of ambition, if he'd still been alive.

'He was a brilliant teacher, and he inspired me to keep writing poetry.' He filled the glass and took a small bottle of ginger ale from the shelf.

'And you were in that student production of *Under Milkwood*. You played Captain Cat.'

'Ah, she remembers more.'

'I remember your voice, but I can't remember your name.'

'Now I'm heartbroken. Never once did I forget your pretty face, Rose Red, and *you* don't even recall my name.'

'What's your name?'

'Niall Buckley. I'm very pleased you remember me though, if not my name.' His dark eyes stayed on hers. 'Perhaps we could have a drink when I finish work and raise a glass to Mr Laidlaw? How long will you be in town for?'

'Long enough. I'd like that.' Aisling could have drowned in those eyes, and that voice, *oh my freakin' God*. 'I'd like that very much.'

##

Aisling and Celia rode the bus home from the city so that they'd arrive in Castleknock at the normal end of school time. For Celia's benefit that was; it didn't matter when Aisling got home because her parents would have some dinner or meeting in the city. She wondered why they bothered living out at Castleknock when they could have had an apartment in town close to the office.

As the bus headed the eight kilometres out of town, she found it hard to keep still. As she wriggled on the seat, the tender skin on her backside reminded her of the tattoo. Her head had been so full of Niall, and the meeting they'd planned, she'd totally forgotten about her act of rebellion, but now the tenderness of her skin reminded her. It had been important to her at the start of the day, but once she'd met Niall, she'd not even thought of it.

She'd said not a word to Celia about him, and when she'd put their drinks on the table, Celia had been intent on her phone and obviously hadn't noticed her chatting.

As they'd sat there in the dark corner Aisling had taken a hefty sip of her wine and pulled her phone out to look at the messages from her mother, trying not to return her gaze to the bar. She knew he was looking at her, she could feel the pull of Niall's gaze from across the room.

She dropped her eyes to her phone.

Shite. Sprung.

Why aren't you at school? Where are you? Your father is livid. AND I mean LIVID. Sister Mary rang.

Aisling grinned as she typed the reply. She would show them she didn't care. What could they do?

I had better things to do today than listen to Sister Mary rave on about geography. I'll be home late.

Hopefully very late, she thought an hour later after she'd left Celia at the bus stop and then walked around the corner to catch the bus back into town. She wasn't prepared to take the risk of going home to freshen up, in case her mother had gone home to wait for her.

Pigs might fly too. She'd go into the restroom at the railway station and redo her makeup.

Niall was knocking off at five and they were meeting at another bar in the city.

I can't be all bad, Aisling thought. *I saw Celia home safely.* A twinge of guilt tugged at her and for a brief second, she wondered if she should go home and face the music.

No, the appeal of spending time with a boy—a man—who quoted poetry to her and called her Rose Red, was much more enticing than the prospect of confronting her father. Maybe it was time to think about getting a job and leaving home. Leaving school. The last thing she wanted was to go to university.

Aisling knew she was smart enough, but the thought of following in her parents' and her sister's footsteps filled her with dread. Maybe she could get a job in a bar. Her excitement built as she stepped off the bus in Marlborough Street. Her hands were clammy, and there was an unfamiliar warm and hollow feeling in her chest. Anticipation built as she looked around. A smile tugged as she spotted Niall leaning against the sun-drenched building beside *The Confession Box* bar.

So much for freshening up.

He held a small book in one hand, and she could see his lips moving as he read the words. The last rays of the setting sun highlighted blue lights in his black hair. Aisling shivered as that strange feeling spread through her. A feeling that this man was going to be a part of her life. There was no need to put on her tough act; she could be herself with Niall. Maybe even she could be the pretty little thing he remembered.

But did she want to take that step towards him? The strong feeling that consumed her made her hesitate. This man would change her life; she was as sure of that as she was that the sun was going to drop over Killiney Hill in half an hour.

She took a step towards him, and then hesitated, but he must have caught her movement from the corner of his eye, or maybe he simply sensed her presence.

Slowly, Niall lifted his head, and when their eyes connected, Aisling stepped towards him.

No hesitation, no doubt. This was her path. This was where she wanted to be.

If it was a different path to that of her parents, then that's the way it would be.

She walked over to him, her confidence growing with each step. It might be too fast, but, she was sure.

A smile spread over his face as she reached him, and his eyes stayed on hers.

'I knew you'd come.' Niall leaned forward and took her hand, moving closer. Aisling held her breath as he lowered his head to hers and his whisper warmed her cheek.

'Shall I compare thee to a summer's day? Thou art more lovely . . . '

Chapter Eight

Ronan

The magic of being on a tropical island in the Down Under summer, when he knew it would be bleak and sleeting at home in Dublin, buoyed Ronan's spirits. As did his certainty that he was on the right track and that he had finally hit pay dirt. He was sure the new beauty therapist on the island was indeed the woman he'd been searching for over the past year. O'Sullivan was a common surname, but the photo he'd taken of her from the top of the hill with his telephoto lens this morning which he'd sent to his client had come back with an affirmative.

This was the closest and the longest he had been near her, and Ronan had managed to get a clear headshot when he'd been up on the track above the resort under the pretext of bird watching. He'd sent the photo to his client and had had a reply within minutes.

Yes, that is my sister.

The confirmation from Ireland that he had finally found the O'Sullivan woman was the easy part. The second part of his assignment—to get her back to Dublin—was going to be way more problematic. At least being on an island with only two ferries a day arriving and departing, meant he could keep a closer eye on her. With any luck she couldn't disappear into the night. He wondered if that was why he had lost her before, that she had been aware of him looking for her.

As he walked along the beach at sunset on his fifth day on the island, he considered the various ways he could go about it.

His first option was to tell her exactly what was going on and hope that she would be reasonable and listen to him. Ronan shook his head. Anyone who'd covered their tracks for so long didn't want to be found, and certainly wasn't going to listen to him and follow him happily back to Dublin.

Second option? Find out why she was hiding and try to find

a way that might convince her that she needed to go home. Show some empathy and get her to trust him. Again, it was clear that she didn't want to be found, and she wasn't going to trust a stranger with her deep secrets. The whole assignment was top secret, and apart from a few details, he'd been employed to find her and bring her back to Ireland. There had been some mention of an inheritance, and that the woman was required to attend a solicitor's office in person. He got the impression there was a large amount of money involved.

Third option? There wasn't one, apart from kidnapping her. Until he got to know her and made a judgment call on her likely response, Ronan knew he was working in the dark.

As he looked away from the water, a movement over towards the huts caught his attention. The beauty therapist with the red hair walked down the steps of the day spa towards the path and then disappeared into the forest. There was no sign of the Irish one, but a light was glowing from the hut,

Ronan narrowed his eyes; he'd kept a low profile on the island, hadn't got into any conversations with other guests or the staff, apart from the occasional please and thank you. He'd been totally focused on trying to figure out what to do, now that he'd found her.

A glimmer of light shone from the back window as another light was switched on. She was still in there.

Alone.

An idea formed and Ronan quickened his pace as he walked towards the day spa.

Chapter Nine

Isla

Isla had sensed a couple of days ago that Sienna needed space. They'd both had a day of back-to-back appointments, and when the last client left Sienna flopped into the chair behind the reception counter

'Oh my goodness, what a busy day that was. I'm so pleased that you're here now, Isla. Pippa and Eliza will be very pleased with the business we've done today. It's a record day for *Hebe*.' She put her head back and rested one hand on her forehead and Isla wondered how Sienna managed to look fresh and cool after such a busy day.

Isla reached up and tucked her hair up beneath the white bandanna. Her curls had come loose, as they always did, and she knew her makeup had run in the heat today. 'Yes, all of my clients went for the top of the range package. One of the women said she'd heard about us down in Sydney.' Isla sat in the cane chair by the window where the clients waited.

'Yes, the word is really spreading about Pentecost Island, and about *Hebe*. I am very pleased to be here,' Sienna said. 'Are you liking it here already? Do you think you will stay for a while before you move on?'

Isla put her head back and rested it against the smooth timber wall. 'I'll be honest with you. I'm sorry I've been so social this week. I know I've been a bit tiring for you.'

'No, no, not at all. It is a pleasure to have you here.'

'Come on, lovely, be honest. I think you are pleased that we now have our own rooms.'

'Okay. Well maybe just a little bit. I do like my own company.'

'I can't help being how I am. I guess it covers up what I'm lacking.'

'Lacking? What do you mean?'

Isla shrugged. She'd said too much already. This island was working its spell on her, and she was relaxing her guard. She knew she'd already slipped up the other night when she'd accidentally forgotten one of her "brothers", and Sienna had picked up on it.

'I guess I blather on and run away at the mouth so—'

'So that you are liked by new friends?' Sienna's voice was soft. 'I like you, Isla and I know the others do too. You have fitted in already, but I will say that there is no need to try so hard. You are a good person.'

Isla's eyes stung as tears threatened; she blinked. For the first time in five years of travelling, she'd found somewhere she'd like to stay. A beautiful island where she had good employment with fabulous pay, a great room, and—for a change—other women close by, who she was sure she could become friends with.

Women, she sensed, she could trust and who would back her if she needed support.

She cleared her throat. 'Thank you, Sienna. That means a lot to me. More than you can ever know. And that's all I'm saying.' She jumped to her feet. 'Now lovely, I know that gorgeous man of yours will be waiting to see you before he goes back to his island, so get yourself over to the bar. I'll put the towels in the machine and have a tidy up. We've got another busy day tomorrow. You're fully booked, and I have one space first thing.'

Sienna stood slowly and stretched. 'Thank you, I'll accept that very kind offer. Don't worry too much, we can tidy up in the morning.'

'No, I'll be happy to potter around here for an hour or so while the towels dry. You go, and I'll be over to the kitchen for dinner in a while.'

Sienna shook her head. 'I think we should celebrate tonight. Danny has to go back to Hamo after I see him. He's flying to Port Douglas tomorrow for a meeting with his solicitor. I think you and I should have dinner at the restaurant—if they can fit us in.'

'That would be grand,' Isla said. 'I'd like that very much. So, shoo. Go and see your man, and I'll tidy up here. I feel manky; I need a shower before dinner. I'll see you in a while.'

After Sienna left, Isla changed the music on the iPod to something more upbeat than soothing rainforest bird calls and muted music. She gathered up the used towels and facecloths from both treatment rooms and took them to the compact laundry at the back of the hut. Starting the hot wash cycle, she added a capful of bleach to the machine, and set it for a quick wash. As she topped up products from the storage cupboard in the hall between the two rooms, she hummed along with the music. Now that she was here, she'd ease back on the loud and extroverted personality. She'd been accepted by the staff, and apart from clients in *Hebe*, she'd keep herself separate from the guests.

Most clients preferred peace and quiet while they had their treatments, not someone blathering away in an Irish accent. Isla had watched how calm and focused Sienna was as she worked and knew she would take a leaf out of her book.

Picking up the spray bottle and a clean cloth, she walked into the reception area, singing along with the Corrs *Summer Sunshine* and trying not to let the lyrics make her sad. That part of her life was over.

She'd moved on.

Isla leaned down behind the counter and wiped down the shelves.

'Hello.'

She jumped as the screen door clicked shut and a tall man filled the doorway.

'I wasn't sure if you were still open.' The voice with a strong Irish accent had her heart rate leaping.

'We're done for the day,' she said softy, as she put the bottle and cloth on the floor behind the counter. 'What can I do for you?'

As she stood, she looked up into a serious face, a frown marring a broad forehead.

'Ah, I'm sorry to come after hours, but Nell in reception said it might be best if I came here to make an appointment direct.' He gestured to the mobile on the counter. 'She did try to call, but there was no answer, and she thought you might both still be busy.'

Isla picked up the phone and checked it. 'Ah, it was still on mute.'

He nodded without speaking as she flicked off the mute button on the side of the mobile.

'Is the appointment for you? Or—'

'Yes, it is for me.' His face coloured as she looked back at him. The poor guy looked very much out of place in a day spa.

'I . . . ah . . . I feel like an eejit. I slipped on some loose rocks when I was walking this morning and I noticed in the compendium you do a hot stone massage, and ah,'— he cleared his throat—'do you have any free appointments tomorrow?'

'You're in luck. I do have one open at eight thirty tomorrow morning. Is that too early?'

'Oh, no not at all. I'm usually up walking a couple of hours before that.' He lifted his hand and for the first time she noticed he was holding a camera with a huge telephoto lens. 'I'm a nature photographer. And early morning is the best time to come across creatures feeding, and with brilliant light too.'

His cheeks were pink as she stared back at him, and Isla wondered if it was due to his fair complexion, or embarrassment at being in a day spa.

'Where did you hurt? Your back?'

He nodded and gestured to his lower back. 'Ay. It's not too bad, but I can't afford to miss the early start to the day, and I think I might come up sore tomorrow.'

Isla opened the booking screen on the laptop. 'I'll book you in for eight-thirty then. For a hot stone massage?'

'Yes, please.'

She hesitated and then looked up at him again. He was staring at her, and it made her feel uncomfortable.

'Your name, sir?'

'Oh, sorry. My name is Ronan Doyle.'

Chapter Ten

Pippa

I was walking past the office on my way to the new staff building when Nell ran out of the office holding the phone.

'Whoa, slow down, or you'll be over on the mainland in the hospital with Tam.'

Nell's grin was wide, and she shoved the office phone at me. 'Tam's on the phone. She has news.'

'Everything okay?' I said, taking the phone. 'She was good when I talked to her last night.'

'She's coming home. Gabe's with her now and they're catching the eleven o'clock ferry back from the mainland to Hamo.'

'Great. I'll send Rafe over to pick them up.' I took the phone and Nell stood there still grinning as I answered.

'Hey, Tamsin. Great news Nell tells me.'

Nell was clapping her hands and jumping around.

'What did she tell you?' Tam's voice was as dry as ever. She'd been in the hospital on the mainland while they ran some tests, and up until last night, everything had come back fine. I'd not been as worried as I had been a few days earlier when she'd been taken ill, because she was in the right place, and at six months along, all the tests had come back as they should. Her self-diagnosis was that she was simply overtired from doing too much, and the doctors had agreed with her.

'That you're on your way home today. And when you're home, you're going to put your feet up and knit baby booties. No more helping out in the restaurant or running up the hill to look at your block of land.'

'Yes, Mum,' she said with a chuckle. 'Are you quite finished?'

'I am. We'll see you later. I'll send Rafe over to Hamo.'

'Phillipa!' I could hear the exasperation in your voice.

419

'Will you listen to me. I have some news. I had another scan.'

'And you know now if you need pink or blue booties?' I grinned at Nell. She was still squirming with excitement. 'By the look on Nell's face, I'd say it's a girl.'

Nell rolled her eyes and mouthed at me. 'Listen to Tamsin!'

'I do know,' Tam said. 'And I think you'll need to get your knitting needles out too.'

'I can't knit,' I said. 'Hang on a minute.' I turned to Nell. 'Are you okay. Do you need the loo?'

Nell folded her arms and gestured to the phone. 'Listen!'

With a shrug, I turned back to the call. 'Nell told me to listen to you.'

'I've been waiting. What I want to tell you is that we need both pink and blue booties.' Tamsin's voice broke as my mouth dropped open. 'We're having twins. A boy and a girl.'

'Oh my God.' I stood there as Nell flung her arms around me.

'Twins!' she squealed. 'We're going to have three babies on the island.' Nell grabbed the phone from me. 'Celebration tonight? Or are you too tired?'

I stood there, feeling happy for Tam and Gabe, and surprised that my sadness stayed away as I processed the news.

Life on our island was going to change this year.
##
It didn't take long for Tam and Gabe's news to spread through the staff, and when Rafe and I sat in *Violet's*, our main restaurant, with Nell and Nat, and Tam and Gabe that evening, there was a constant stream of friends stopping at the table to say congratulations.

Rafe held my hand under the table, and the occasional squeeze of his fingers soothed me, and kept me smiling.

At one stage Cherry came out of the kitchen, with a small bunch of pink and blue balloons and tied them to the back of Tam's chair.

'Where on earth did you find them?' I asked.

'We are prepared for any occasion in *Violet's* restaurant,' she said. Leaning down to brush a kiss on Tam's cheek, Cherry caught my eye. 'Angus has excelled himself tonight. He's put on a special menu for this table. You're not allowed to order, he said.'

'Angus excels himself every night,' Rafe said with a nod.

'He does, 'I agreed. 'We'll wait to see what he's created for us tonight.'

When Cherry had gone back into the kitchen, Tam sat back in her chair and placed her hands on top of her large stomach. She'd grown bigger in the week she'd been away. She must have read my thoughts because she nodded. 'And I'm going to get way bigger than this by June.'

It was a happy night, with lots of soda water consumed by the girls, and Angus did excel himself with a new beef dish that he'd created.

I hugged Tam as we said goodnight, but I frowned as I looked up the hill to the staff lodge. 'Are you right to walk up there?'

'I have to be,' she said. 'But yes. If I take it easy, I'll be fine.'

I was thoughtful as Rafe and I climbed up the steps to our house on the hill.

'Okay, love?' he said putting his arm around me.

'I am. I'm happy for them. Both of them. Tamsin and Nell. I wasn't thinking about us. I was thinking about talking to Eliza tomorrow. We need a road up to the staff building and we need to buy a couple of electric buggies.'

'For Tam? A couple? Or one for Nell too?'

I leaned into him as he pulled me closer. No, silly. I've been thinking about Zac's offer. But yes, one to get Tam up there for the next few months. And Nell. But as for a bigger picture, I think we could build a lookout up there, and then—' I paused as we reached our gate and looked across the island to the opposite hill where the lights glowed in the staff building on the opposite hill.

'And then?' my patient husband prompted me.

'And then, the road could go further, and we could build some exclusive huts up on the hill. Maybe two- and three-bedroom huts. We're starting to get groups of rock climbers and birdwatching groups book in, and we haven't had enough room to meet the demand.'

Rafe's arms went around me, and I rested my head on his

shoulder as happiness seeped through me.

'Have I told you recently how happy I am that your Aunty Vi left her island to her great niece?'

I reached up and brushed my lips across his. 'Not this week, I don't think.'

'Well, I am, and I think she knew what an entrepreneur you would turn into. She always told me how special you were.' His lips rested against my forehead. 'Just so I'm prepared. How many extra huts are we talking about?'

The moon was bright, and I knew my eyes would be alight with laughter as I moved back and held his.

'Hmm, I think we have room to build another twenty or so. I'll see Eliza tomorrow and see what she thinks about talking to Zac.'

I turned to go through the gate, but Rafe's hand caught my arm. 'Phillipa?'

I turned as I picked up the concern in his voice.

'This isn't just to fill that gap in our life, is it?'

I shook my head. 'No, sweetheart, that gap will be filled when the time is right. This is Phillipa, the businesswoman thinking; not Phillipa who will one day be a mother too.' I turned to him as he moved closer, and I slipped my hand beneath my husband's shirt, my fingers playing along the silken skin of his back. 'Maybe we should go practise a little bit, what do you think?'

'Are we talking business or pleasure now?' His lips moved to mine and it was quite a while before I answered.

'Pleasure, definitely pleasure.'

Chapter Eleven

Aisling
Dublin. Ten years earlier.

Aisling had always known that one day her happiness would come to an end. Trying to juggle school, and meeting Niall at night and on weekends had the inevitable effect on her grades because she had little time to study. Her parents had been in London for three weeks involved in some important big case, so her freedom was much more than it would have been if they'd been home.

After the stoush when she was caught bunking off—that wonderful day when she'd met Niall—she'd promised faithfully she wouldn't do it again. Mother had forgiven her for being rude on the phone, but only because they were so preoccupied with their work, not from any motherly concern. Her next school report would be a catalyst for more trouble because she hadn't handed in most of the work that was due. As for the exams, she didn't even know if it was worth turning up for them.

She hadn't bunked off again, but she did get the bus straight into town every afternoon, and then back home late at night after spending time with Niall.

After the first few afternoons, when they'd either gone to a park or a coffee shop if it was raining, he'd looked at her with those sexy eyes.

'Would you think I was forward if I invited you back to my bedsit tomorrow afternoon?' His deep voice sent a shiver down her back, as did the thought of being alone with him. Niall had been a perfect gentleman, with a chaste goodnight kiss on her cheek each night when he put her on the bus. 'Not for any nefarious reason, of course, but just so we can spend time alone together.'

'Say that again,' she said.

'What?'

'Nefarious. I love the way your voice wraps around those

syllables.' Aisling loved every word that came out of his mouth.

'Nefarious,' he said slowly with a smile. 'Perhaps I may not have been quite honest, as I do have some nefarious designs on you, but it is too soon yet.'

They were waiting at the bus stop and the heavy fog from the River Liffey shrouded them in its damp blanket.

Aisling reached up and pressed her mouth against Niall's. The taste of whiskey on his breath lingered on her lips when she moved away. 'I don't think it's too soon,' she whispered. 'And this weekend is perfect. My sister is going away on a uni field trip to London. I will be home alone.'

She straightened as the idea came to her. 'I have a better idea. Why don't you come to my place? The cook will have left all my meals for the weekend, and my father has a wonderfully stocked bar.'

'Would it be the right thing to do?'

'Yes, you are my friend and I'm inviting you to my house.'

##

Niall had agreed, and that weekend stayed in Aisling's memory long after everything went to shite. The weather cleared, and they were alone for two whole days and two nights before Niall took the bus back to the city on Sunday night. True to his word, he had not slept in her bed, even though Aisling had been willing.

'No, my sweet red rose. I don't want you to think this is about sex. I want to get to know you. I want to lie in the sun and read poetry to you. I want to get a true vision of you, so I can write a poem about you.'

They spent many hours on the sofa, her feet in his lap as he'd read his poetry to her. For the time it was enough for her, but she knew that one day soon there would be more.

As the bus taking him back to the city trundled down the rough cobblestones of the village street, she stood looking after it.

Next weekend.

Next weekend, she would go to Dublin, and in Niall's bedsit it would be time to take their relationship to the next level.

Aisling smiled all the way back to the house. As she turned the corner into their street, she drew in a breath as her father's green Jaguar approached the house from the other end of the narrow road.

Shite, what state had they left the house in?

Narrowing her eyes, she tried to think as she whipped out her phone and called Celia.

'Ceels, a favour. If anyone asks, you stayed at my house this weekend. Okay?'

'Did I?'

'Yes. Okay?'

'Okay, Ash. But can we catch up for a coffee after school one day this week? We haven't talked properly for ages.'

'Sure. And thanks, love, I owe you.'

'How's your tat? Did you get into trouble?'

'Nah, they've been away. I've been busy. Look I've got to go and clean up the house. They've just got home.'

'Okay. See you at school.'

Aisling hurried down the street and was through the front door before Da's Jag was in the garage. By the time the back door closed, and footsteps approached she'd whipped around the living room, and taken the dirty dishes and glasses into the kitchen. As she loaded the dishwasher, her father walked in.

'Hello, Da. I thought you and Mother were away for another week.'

His brows beetled over his narrowed eyes. 'We are. I had to come home for a file we left in the office. I'm very pleased to see you home and not out gallivanting around. I trust you've been studying?'

'Yes. Yes, I have.' Aisling nodded and crossed her fingers behind her back. 'All weekend.'

'Good, because I had a call from Sister Mary this week.'

She bit the inside of her cheek, before she could ask what the stupid old cow wanted. 'Yes?

'I was pleased to hear you've not missed a day of school, but Sister is concerned about how you've fallen behind in your work. She can't understand why.'

'The work's hard, Da. I've been working all weekend. I'm almost caught up.'

'Excellent. Your mother and I were talking, and we've had an offer from Charles Caul for you to begin an internship in his law firm before university starts. We think it's best if you don't come into the family law firm straight after your final school examinations. You're a very different person to Marlene, and shall we say, perhaps not as amenable. I think you would be more likely to take instruction from Charles and his son, rather than your mother and I.'

Aisling couldn't hold her temper back. 'Roger? Roger Caul? He's a bloody pervert. I've lost count of the number of times he's tried to grope me under the table at family dinners.'

'Aisling. Just stop it.' Her father's cheeks were red, and a vein pulsed in his temple. 'I am very tired of you twisting the truth, so you don't have to do things you don't want to do. You need to learn responsibility and learn to tell the truth. And stop taking money from my wallet. All you have to do is ask.'

'Yeah, and all you'd say would be no. Feckin' hell, Da. I know I'm not good enough for this family, but a bit of trust now and then would be nice.'

His eyes were hard. 'You have to earn that, Aisling.'

She closed her eyes, and thought of Niall's voice, and of the admiration he held for her. Niall saw the good in her, and he thought she was a fine person. She would not be going to university, and she would not be working with the bloody Cauls in their dark and depressing office. Her voice was cold when she opened her eyes and stared at her father. 'Yes, Da, you're right. I shall do my best to be responsible, and to earn your trust as you say.'

Aisling turned and walked up the stairs to her room. Five minutes later the back door closed, and the purr of her father's car faded as he drove out of town.

Chapter Twelve

Isla

Isla was preoccupied as she sat in the resort restaurant having dinner with Sienna. Staff were given a fifty percent discount on meals but were only able to eat in once the bookings were checked and there were spare tables. Some of the guests preferred to dine on the verandah of their huts. Angus and Cherry had also started an evening picnic deal where an exotic cold picnic was packed into a basket and delivered to a couple of grassy areas on the island. The guests pre-ordered and chose the location, and the meal was delivered by one of the waiters, along with a bottle of the finest champagne.

According to Sienna, it was a popular choice for proposals.

Island of love. It wouldn't be for her.

Isla sighed and stared out into the night as they waited for their main courses. Meeting that Irish guy this afternoon had rocked her a little bit. She knew that her family were trying to track her down; she'd changed her email address a few times, and she had a dummy profile on Facebook and Instagram to get tabs on them.

Of course, her parents didn't do social media, but the occasional time she'd logged into her old account, there had been dozens of messages from Marlene.

Where are you?

We need to talk to you.

Call home.

Urgent. Please call.

Not a snowball's chance in hell.

As far as Isla was concerned, she had no family.

'Are you tired, Isla?' Sienna's soft voice broke into her musings. Gawd, if she let every Irish voice remind her of home and upset her, she had no chance of making a life for herself.

She plastered a smile on her face. 'I am, but a good night's sleep and a jog up to the wall in the morning will have me as right as rain.'

'You be careful up there. Apparently, there are wild goats.'

'They don't hurt you. I'm more worried about those huge birds that fly over the peak. Have you seen their wingspan? They're the size of a feckin' truck.'

Sienna giggled. 'I love listening to your accent, and your words. One day I will go to your Ireland.'

'Darlin', trust me. You don't want to. Grey skies, dense fog and sad faces. Stay in this gorgeous country. Or get Danny to take you to Italy. Now that is beautiful.'

'I've been to Italy. Eliza and I had a holiday there. It wasn't a very happy time.' Sienna's fair cheeks coloured. 'I think I will be staying here though. Danny has booked a picnic over at Back Bay on Saturday night. It's a full moon, and he told me he has something to ask me.' She reached over and grabbed Isla's hand. 'Do you think I am reading too much into it? Maybe it's just a simple picnic.'

Isla squeezed Sienna's fingers. 'Didn't you say this solicitor was about to sort out his ex?'

Sienna leaned back in her chair and smiled up at the new waiter as he held up the half bottle of wine they were sharing. 'Thank you, just a top up please.'

Isla put her hand over her glass. 'Not for me, thanks.'

When they were alone again, Sienna nodded. 'I think so.'

'No point worrying until things go pear-shaped, darlin'. Trust me, I'm an expert on that.'

And I should take my own advice, she thought.

The Irish guy was harmless. A bit of a nerd, and lacking self-confidence. She had to stop being suspicious.

It was still early by the time they finished their meals, and Sienna gestured to the bar where a group of off duty staff had gathered. 'I'm going to have a quick coffee. Do you want one too? You can have a sleep-in tomorrow before your run. Your first appointment's not until ten.'

Isla shook her head. 'My early one filled up after you left. An Irish guy, as shy as, with a bad back is coming in at eight-thirty so I'll be up at sparrow's fart.'

Sienna's eyes widened. 'What?'

'Don't worry, he just asked for the hot stone massage, even

though I can do remedial, I know we don't offer that, so don't worry, I'm not doing the wrong thing.' Isla's words were clipped. It was the first time Sienna had challenged her.

Sienna waved her hand. 'Don't be silly. I said *what*, meaning what is that thing you talk about the sparrow?'

Isla giggled. 'Sorry, I was being precious. Just take my word for it. Sparrow's fart means very early in the day. I grew up with that expression, and I've heard it used Down Under too. Do you know what fart means?'

Sienna shook her head. 'No.'

'Okay, we'll leave it at that. Thanks for the great company, Sienna. I'll see you in the morning.'

Sienna reached over and hugged her goodnight. Isla knew she had made good friends here already. Life was on the up and up. She walked up the hill to her room, her self-confidence returning.

Chapter Thirteen

Aisling
Dublin. Ten years earlier.

'I don't care what you think, Niall. It's not too soon. I'm ready. I've never met anyone in my life I've cared about so much.' Aisling's voice shook as she sat in front of the small gas heater in Niall's tiny bedsit. 'I'm eighteen years old and I love you,' she added quietly. 'I know my mind.'

Warm hands took hers and when she didn't look up, he let go of one of her hands and tipped her chin up so she was looking into warm blue eyes.

'Did you really say that, Aisling? Or did I imagine it? Was it wishful thinking?'

'No. I said it. I love you, Niall.' Her head shook from side to side. 'I can't imagine being without you.'

Six weeks had passed since that afternoon when Aisling and Celia had walked into that old pub and Aisling had fallen head over heels in love. In those six weeks, Niall had treated her with respect, even on the nights she had stayed over in his bedsit, and the weekend he had come to Castleknock to stay in her family home—when her parents were away of course.

Six weeks of reading together, listening to poetry and falling in love with the English language. Her insightful comments at school, in the weeks after she had met Niall and spent all those afternoons and nights talking poetry and literature had not only awakened new knowledge in her but had surprised the dour Sister Mary.

Her English marks had gone off the scale for the final examinations, but that was not enough to make up for her dismal performance in all the other subjects.

'I don't care,' she protested vehemently when Sister Mary called her to the office one day. 'I don't want to be a lawyer, and I don't want to go to university. I just want—'

'What do you want, child?' The concern in the nun's voice

had surprised Aisling. Six years in the school and she'd never once seen a glimmer of interest in the woman's face, but now that Niall had introduced her to the beauty of literature, a connection had been forged with the elderly nun.

'I am going to have to speak to your father. If you fail your examinations—and I am sure that that will happen, he will not be impressed that I haven't warned him.'

'I don't care. He is trying to live his life through me. I don't want to go to university, I just want—'

'What do you want, Aisling?'

I want Niall.

But of course, she wouldn't say that to the nun.

Now Niall's hands cupped her cheeks, and his voice was intense.

'Love is too young to know what conscience
is. Yet who knows not conscience is born of love?'

Aisling stamped her foot. 'Stop it. Just stop it. I know what I want, Niall. I am not too young. I want you.' Her shaking hands went to her school shirt, and she began to unbutton the heavy cotton. When it was open, she slid down the zip of her serge skirt and as it fell to the threadbare carpet, she kicked it aside.

Niall's groan as he reached for her told her all she wanted to hear.

To hear, to feel, to experience.

Aisling's lip tipped up in a satisfied smile as Niall's lips trailed a warm path down her neck.

##

Later that night, Niall walked her to the bus stop. It was a Friday night, and her parents would be home from the city after they had been to dinner.

She knew she should be on top of the world and all she wanted to do was stay in Niall's bed. Sometimes Aisling wondered what right her parents had to direct her life, when she was very much on the periphery of all that mattered to them. If she disappeared, would they even notice? Or care?

'What's wrong? You seem unhappy tonight,' he said. 'You should be happy.'

'Oh Niall, I am. I don't want to leave you tonight. I worry about what's going to happen. My father is so bloody minded, he's likely to do anything. Promise me that if anything happens you'll come and find me?'

'Nothing's going to happen, sweetheart. The worst that can happen is that he'll throw you out and you know you have a place with me.' He pulled her close and his lips were hard against hers. 'I love you, Aisling, and I will not let you go. Trust me.'

A group of young boys walking past the bus stop catcalled them. 'Get a room, boyo,' one of them called out.

That afternoon was the last time she ever saw Niall. Her father was waiting for her when she walked in at nine o'clock. In the months to come, Aisling knew that if she'd known what was going to happen, she would never have left Niall that night.

Her life would have been different.

It would have been happy.

She would not have had to run away.

##

'You are leaving school. And you will have a live-in tutor. You are grounded until you resit your examinations and pass them.'

Aisling twisted out of her father's cruel grasp and looked to her mother for support, but there was nothing in her expression that gave her hope. 'No. That will not happen.'

'Oh, yes it will. You are not leaving this house. Jennifer, go and ask Sean to come in please.'

When Mam left the study her father's eyes glittered with dark malevolence and Aisling swore that she would leave the house tonight and go to Niall.

'And before you even consider running away, you will be confined to your room. Sean, your tutor, will teach you at your desk, and Cook will deliver your meals to your room. I will take you myself for a daily exercise in the fresh air. You will do as we expect, Aisling. I am over your rebellion. I will teach you what it expected of an O'Sullivan.'

'No!' she screamed like a banshee. 'Disown me. Throw me out. I will not do it.'

'You will.' Her father turned as the door opened and her mother walked in with a stranger.

'Aisling, this is Sean Roberts. He will be your tutor and

will prepare you for your examinations.'

Suddenly, Aisling realised that rebellion was not the way to achieve what she wanted; complacency would earn trust, and trust would mean escape.

She lifted her eyes to meet those of her tutor and revulsion ran through her as his eyes settled on her breasts.

'It's a pleasure to be your tutor, Aisling. I'm sure we can bring your mathematics up to the required standard.

Aisling stared at him and waved a hand. 'Whatever.'

Her father nodded and her mother looked away.

Chapter Fourteen

Isla

At six-thirty the following morning Isla reached the top of the track where the path to the mountain and Red Wave Wall crossed the beach track. She bent double and caught her breath; the jog up the mountain was challenging but her fitness was improving each morning. It was a grand start to the day and put her in a good frame of mind.

She drew in a deep breath and her fingertips tingled with excitement as she turned to survey the vista below. Her new home, and by the way she was feeling, it was a new start. A chance to heal, and finally an opportunity to put the past behind her. Maybe she could come to terms with her life and become Aisling again. Be honest about her past and stop hiding behind an imaginary family where happiness was the norm.

Maybe soon.

Maybe then, she'd sit down with Sienna and tell her the truth about her family. Forget the imaginary brothers and sweet Ma and Da, and the tribe of nephews and nieces. Maybe telling someone the truth for the first time would take the pain of loss away. Maybe telling about her cold and cruel family would help her heal.

Isla sat on a rock already warm from the early sun. Even if she got over what had happened, she would never forget the day she had found Niall five years ago. It had been too late, way too late and she knew that well. The reach of bloody social media. She would have been better off not looking, of not knowing. It had sealed a lid on the coffin of her happy future.

Too late for her, and too late to do anything about it. With a sigh, Isla tried to put those thoughts away; she could not live the rest of her life like this. Skipping from place to place, never putting roots down. Never forming relationships. Witnessing the happiness on the island, she knew it was time to settle down. She'd heard a little about the history of each of the women here, and she knew she had to try to move on from her past too. They had overcome difficulties, and they had forged new lives for themselves. She let her gaze linger on the beauty in front of her.

It was too early for much water traffic out on the Whitsunday Passage, but in the distance two catamarans headed south, their sails white and billowing in the wind.

She put her hands on her hips and her breathing returned to normal. She had been in Australia long enough to think about emigrating, and this morning she promised herself that she would explore that path.

Whatever had to be done, she would do it.

Maybe she should also make contact with her family and let them know she was all right.

No. With a frown, Aisling shook her head. No, of course she wouldn't. She had no family. They had ensured she wanted nothing to do with them.

The future would have to happen without contact; she could not forget or forgive. Her parents had talked about responsibility when she was eighteen, but it was their lack of responsibility, and a lack of parental love that had ruined her life.

Sure she had been responsible for some of her choices, but each of those had been in direct response to how she had been treated.

She could not forgive. Closing her eyes, she made herself think about the time when her chance of a life with Niall had come to an end.

It had probably been a dream, but she'd never know now.

Chapter Fifteen

Aisling

Dublin. Ten years earlier.

Six weeks after Aisling had last seen Niall, she woke up one morning and grimaced as she rolled over. Her breasts hurt when she lay on her stomach.

With a frown she rolled over again and ran her fingers over the tender skin, and it still hurt.

Her mouth dried as she realised that her period was overdue.

Oh shit.

Could she be pregnant, or was it simply her hormones responding to the bizarre and stressful situation her bloody father had created with the damn tutor. He wanted her to go into law. If—when—she got out of this stupid predicament, she'd sue him for everything she could.

Aisling touched her stomach in wonder and looked down, but then worry wrapped its insidious fingers around her.

Yes, she most certainly could be pregnant. Niall didn't believe in contraception and because she was so smitten with him, she had listened.

What was he thinking? Did he wonder why she hadn't been back to see him? Did he wonder why she hadn't called? Why hadn't he come looking for her? He knew where she lived.

Had he called her? Da had taken her phone from her, and as he had threatened, he would, and she had been a prisoner in her room.

Doubt began to creep in. Had she fallen for Niall too quickly? He had been the first person to show her any love, and he'd made her believe in herself. That the person she was, was a good person and could be loved. With him, she didn't need the stuff that made her look different and rebellious.

Of course, he loved her: they had connected on an intellectual level and a spiritual level.

Don't forget the sexual level, a nagging voice reminded her. What if that was all it had been?

Had she been naïve?

No, she wouldn't doubt him.

She would trust.

The only person she'd seen since her parents had gone back to the city last Monday had been the slimy Sean as he had tried to teach her, and she'd hated every minute that she had to spend in his company. His constant brushing against her, and the way he looked at her breasts rather than her face made her feel ill.

Sean had taken to lying on her bed as she had completed the tasks that he gave her each morning—there was no explicit teaching taking place—and she was very wary of him and kept her distance. The smell of his deodorant lingered each afternoon when he left.

'Use the chair,' she finally snapped that morning as she worked her way through a mathematics exercise he'd put on her desk. Her temper had been much shorter than usual as she worried about the non-arrival of her period and her tender breasts.

'Make me,' he said with a leer.

Rolling her eyes Aisling turned back to the stupid maths exercise. At least the work filled the days even though she had to put up with Sean being in her room with her. Aisling had tried everything to escape her imprisonment. One day when Sean had been using *her* bathroom, she had moved silently to the door and tried to open it. As she expected it was locked, as were her windows. The next morning, she took notice as he came in and watched as he'd locked the door and put the key in his trouser pocket.

Last weekend after three weeks of being locked in her room, she had begged Da for a reprieve when they had come home for the weekend.

His eyes had been cold as they had walked around the back garden for her exercise. 'When you sit your examinations, we shall see.'

Aisling had been tempted to retort that her civil liberties

were being breached but had realised just in time that she would not be doing herself any favours.

She had put her head down meekly and said, 'Yes, Da,' as she vowed to herself that she would find a way out.

Today fear almost pushed her over the edge. She knew she had to get out, she had to find Niall.

Her life was turning into a Thomas Hardy novel, and Aisling knew she had to take control. Niall had been a huge fan of Hardy's work and they had had several vigorous conversations in his bedsit about Hardy's portrayal of women. It was the only time they had disagreed.

'Due to their humanity, suffering is inevitable, and guilt is a common compassion of his heroines,' Niall had said.

'No.' Aisling closed her eyes as she remembered how she had sat cross-legged on his bed and Niall had laughed and put his arms around her. 'He presents women as sensual creatures, but he portrays us as weak. No woman would have put up with the circumstances that he portrayed,' she had argued. 'Hardy portrays women affected by the pressure exerted on them by their environment and heredity.'

'I disagree,' Niall said to her surprise. 'Your sensuality and your weakness are what appeals.'

'What!' Aisling's mouth dropped open as she stared at him, unable to believe what he was saying. 'Are you talking about me or is that a stereotypical comment?' She had sat up straight on the old sofa and shaken her head. 'I can't believe you said that.'

All she got in return was a shrug and his gentle smile. So, she still hadn't known if he really meant was he said.

As she thought about that night, her chest ached. Despite their disagreement over Hardy's themes, it had also been the night she had first shared Niall's bed, and the night she had felt loved for the first time in her eighteen years. Aisling's vision blurred as tears ran down her face.

She was in the same weak position they had discussed. Pregnant, isolated from the man she loved, and imprisoned in her room. Her father couldn't keep her here forever. She wondered what he would do if she told him she was pregnant.

Tomorrow, she would somehow get the door key from Sean. No matter what she had to do. No matter what it took.

Oh Niall, please come and find me. Don't think I have left you.

Chapter Sixteen

Pippa

'Slow down, love.' Rafe reached out and grabbed me as I hurried through the kitchen, a piece of toast in one hand and a coffee in the other. The last few mornings I had woken up starving and had eaten a full breakfast but today I had too much to do.

'I can't.' My mouth was full as I replied. 'I have to meet Zac and Eliza in the office for a meeting in five minutes, and then after that, I have to talk to Cherry about the setup for the wedding on Saturday week, and then I have to go over to the day spa because there is a problem with—'

His lips swooped on mine, and I couldn't finish telling about the problem in *Hebe.* I grinned as he pulled straight back and wiped the back of his hand across his mouth. He took my coffee and swallowed a huge gulp.

'Oh yuk. Vegemite.'

'Hey, that's my coffee. And serves you right for kissing me when I'm in a hurry.'

'Phillipa.' My husband's voice was calm as he put his arms around me. 'Slow down.'

'I can't. I have a huge day.'

'I'll go and sort out the problem in the day spa for you.'

'You can't. You have to get your book in by the end of the week.'

'Sweetheart, an hour checking out a problem, and sorting it out is not going to impact on my deadline. It's the least I can do after you read those chapters for me all week. That put you behind in your work.'

I went to kiss him, and he moved away.

'Go and brush your teeth and then I'll kiss you after you do.'

Indignantly, I put my hands on my hips but I grinned up at him. Rafe hadn't shaved yet and his fair skin with the night stubble shadowing his jaw line and the black David Bowie T-shirt would have had me dragging him back to bed if I didn't have an appointment.

'Thank you, my love. But I have to go because Zac has to be at the pool at nine.'

He put his hands up in surrender and kissed my neck instead of my Vegemite-flavoured lips. 'Okay, go. I'll see you later.'

'Love you. And thank you, don't forget to go to *Hebe*. I know what you're like when your computer boots up.'

'I'll go now.' His grin was slow and sexy as he took my coffee from me again. 'As soon as I finish *your* coffee. You can get one in the restaurant.'

As I moved away my tummy let out a huge gurgle. 'I'll get breakfast down there too. I'm starving.'

Rafe narrowed his eyes, and we exchanged a significant look. 'That's not like you. You usually can't face breakfast.'

'It's not, is it?' My spirits sang and hope filled me as I hurried down to the restaurant to discuss the next stage of development of Ma Carmichael's resort.

It was not like me at all.

***

Isla

Isla was as nervous as a cat on a hot tin roof. She'd had a quick shower after her run, trying to tell herself that she'd be sure to have more Irish clients while she worked here, and there was nothing to stress about. There was no way Ronan Doyle would know her family or why she was hiding in Australia. Ireland was a big place.

Australia was an even bigger place.

Deep breath in, she told herself.

She'd arrived at *Hebe* before Sienna and then Rafe had turned up to look at the steriliser unit. She'd fumbled and dropped things as he'd checked the power and the cable and felt totally useless when he'd glanced across at her.

'Sorry,' she apologised. 'I'm still a bit shaky from my run. It'll be gone by my eight-thirty appointment.'

Rafe had chuckled. The problem with the steriliser was fixed and she got the room ready and set the stones to heat. Sienna was already in her room with her first client.

The appointment with the Irish guy had started well and it

didn't take Isla long to relax into her usual routine. He was quieter than any client she'd ever had, no questions, no conversation, and no incessant I-have-to-fill-the-silence with words. As soon as he was settled face down on the table, the lower half of his torso covered with a towel, she placed the hot granite stones on his lower back and then asked him to reach around and touch where his back was sore.

As soon as she touched his lower back where he'd indicated, she could feel where the twisted muscle was.

'I'll do the hot stone massage to start with, and then if you're happy I can do some remedial massage as part of the package.'

He nodded, and she got to work.

***

Ronan

Ronan tapped on the door of the day spa hut and waited for the door to open.

'Come in.' The Irish-accented voice was brisk as she stepped back to let him enter the dimly lit treatment room. A strong smell of massage oil wafted over to him as she pointed to the privacy screen.

'Strip down to your jocks and lie face down on the table. Give me a call when you're all settled, and we'll get your back sorted.'

She stepped outside as he walked over to the screen and stripped down, folding his shorts and T-shirt and placing them neatly on the chair provided. He was way out of his comfort zone. He'd never had a massage like this before; the last massage he could remember was a rub with liniment after a rugby game when he was at college.

'Research, man,' he muttered to himself. He wasn't looking forward to this, but hopefully he'd pick up some information.

'I'm ready,' he called quietly as he settled face down on the table and put his face into the soft vinyl ring and looked down at the floor. A click was followed by the sound of birds calling and water running.

'Rightio. We'll get started and have you as good as gold at the end of the hour.' He closed his eyes as two smooth warm hands gripped his calves and pulled his legs straight. Embarrassment warmed his face.

'Ah.' Her voice was soft.

Ronan tried to lift his head and look around, wondering what she was exclaiming about, but his face down position on the massage table made it impossible to see. He grimaced as she stretched his left leg back and then his right.

'Yes, you have a twisted muscle in your lower right quadrant. Not a drama.'

Ronan closed his eyes and let his mind drift as she placed hot stones on his lower back. He tried to focus on the remedial aspect of the massage, and then he tried to think about his certainty that she was the woman he was searching for, but her firm hands sliding up and down the backs of his calves and thighs, and the smooth sensation of the massage oil on his skin sent tingles up to his groin. He swallowed and focused on the smooth polished floorboards beneath the table. *Think about why you're here, boyo.*

Bloody inappropriate his reaction was. The tightness building in his groin began to lessen, until her warm hands reached his lower back.

Embarrassment flooded through him at the thought of her turning him over when she finished with the hot stones. He shouldn't have done it this way; the privacy issue was off the scale. But then all thoughts fled the window as her firm fingers hit a nerve at the base of his back and she pressed.

Hard. Freakin' hard.

Shite that hurt. He grunted in pain.

'Can you take that again?'

'Okay.' The two syllables were almost a squeak.

By the time, her fingers had worked their way from the base of his back to his shoulders, Ronan was in great discomfort. Did she know why he was here and it was payback time?

'This might hurt a little,' the melodious voice warned him.

Bloody hell! The points of her elbows were walking down his back now.

What would she do next? Bloody walk on him? But strangely the more pressure she applied and the greater the pain, the better he began to feel.

'Okay.' She lifted the stones from his lower back and a sensation of wellbeing swept over him. He was finding it hard to keep his eyes open, let alone keep his thoughts in order. 'Roll over for me, please.'

Ronan obliged and she adjusted the towel to cover him. He settled his head on the low pillow she eased beneath his neck, unable to figure out what she'd done and why he was suddenly feeling so good. Hell, he was so relaxed he would have told her anything she asked, so he jammed his lips together.

He closed his eyes again as she started on his feet and worked her way up his legs, kneading muscles.

'I'm not hurting your lower back?'

He shook his head, and kept his eyes closed.

Her hands left him for a moment, and he let his mind drift.

Gradually his doze lifted as relaxation took over his entire body.

He opened his eyes just in time to see her lift her hands and lightly rest one finger on his knees, his lower stomach, his chest, and his throat before lightly touching the top of his head.

'Just relax for a while. We have ten minutes left so enjoy the peace and when you're ready to get up, there is a glass of iced water for you beside the chair.'

He watched as she walked to the door, but she didn't turn before the door clicked slowly shut behind her. Well, he'd worked out one thing this morning; Isla O'Sullivan was freakin' good at what she did. He'd never felt so relaxed in his life.

Ronan shook his head as he pushed himself up from the massage bed. He couldn't afford to feel like this and lower his guard. He had a job to do; he had to prove that this woman was the one whose sister was desperate to contact her back in Dublin.

And he'd wasted the hour. He hadn't learned one damn thing about it.

As he slipped his shorts back on, and bent over without his back catching, he realised that the appointment had been worthwhile in that aspect.

He wasn't in pain anymore.

Ronan drank the iced water and stood in front of the mirror and smoothed his hand over his ruffled hair.

Okay he was going to have to get out of his comfort zone. Time was running out.

He stood straight and headed for the door, digging for

Annie Seaton

courage.

Chapter Seventeen

Isla

As Isla waited for the Irish guy to come out of the treatment room, she checked the appointment book and ran her finger down the bookings for the day. Thank goodness it was mostly facials; she'd gone in hard with the massage, and her fingers were tired from the extra pressure she'd used. But she knew that she'd been successful; he'd relaxed as she'd worked.

The door opened. Ronan came out of the treatment room and pulled his wallet out of his pocket.

Isla shook her head and held her hand up. 'No need. The treatment is added to your resort bill. You just have to sign for it here.'

He put his wallet away, and his smile was slow. Ronan Doyle seemed like a nice guy, but she felt sorry for him; he seemed very quiet.

'You seem to be moving a lot more easily. Is your back less tight?' she asked as she pushed the slip over for him to sign.

He lifted his head and stared at her, and she held his gaze. He was a fine-looking guy. She hadn't looked past the shy demeanour before. Now his dark brown eyes glowed with warmth and laughter crinkles appeared around his eyes.

'You have magic hands.'

This time, she was the one whose cheeks coloured. 'Thank you. As long as you feel better. It probably wouldn't hurt to come back in another couple of days. Until then, keep your back warm.'

He chuckled. 'Warm? I don't think I'll ever be cool again. It's very different to home.'

He looked down again, obviously embarrassed that he was talking too much. Isla felt sorry for him.

'Where is home?'

'A little town in the south-west of Ireland. I doubt if you've even heard of it.' He looked up again. 'Almost as far from Dublin as you can get.'

'Dublin?' She drew herself up. 'What makes you think I'm from Dublin?'

'Your accent. I have an ear for accents, and yours is posh Dublin.'

Isla couldn't help smiling. 'Posh Dublin, you say?'

He nodded and smiled back at her. 'It is. Am I right?'

She put one finger to her lips and shook her head. 'Maybe, maybe not. It's been a long time since I lived in Ireland. My posh as you say is probably a combination of the places I've been and worked over the past ten years. The world has been a bit of a melting pot for me.'

He stood there for a moment, and looked down, and then up again meeting her eyes, and then dropped his head again before he finally spoke. 'Ah, look I'm way out of practice at this and it might be inappropriate, or you may not even want to, but I was wondering, if ah, maybe if you'd like to have a drink with me tonight.' He took a deep breath and kept talking, this time, lifting his head and holding her gaze. 'Or another night. There's no rush. I'm having a long holiday here. Or look, you might even have a partner or be married, I'm sorry, forget I asked.'

Isla looked back at him, trying to figure him out. Was he really that shy or was it the pickup spiel that he used to get a woman to feel sorry for him?

Because she did. He seemed so out of his comfort zone, he had to be for real.

'Sure, I'll have a drink with you in the bar. You can tell me all about the village you say I won't have heard of.'

His eyes widened and his cheeks flushed. 'Oh, that is excellent. Not the village, I mean, but that you will have a drink with me. I won't push it and say dinner would be good, but we both have to eat, don't we?'

Isla couldn't help smiling. 'We do. But let's play it by ear. I have no idea what time I'll finish today. So, we'll make plans for a drink and see what happens from there.'

Having a normal conversation with a guy felt good. Letting her guard down felt good. Tonight she would be a normal almost thirty-year-old having a drink with an interesting man.

Because even though he was shy, she did find him

interesting. She didn't have to talk about herself, she'd get Ronan talking about himself.

Tonight would be her first step to getting back to a normal life. A life where she would be honest, and a life where she'd feel comfortable without putting on all that false exuberance.

His smile was as wide as hers as he signed the docket and passed it back to her. 'Thank you. You've made my day.' He stumbled over his words again. 'Not with the fixing my back, I mean. Although that was really good too. But by agreeing to meet me for a drink. My holiday is looking up. Oh, please don't feel as—'

'Ronan? Stop stressing and stop talking. You can talk to me all you want tonight, but for now, get going. Go out and have a great day and keep that back warm. I'll see you tonight. Okay?'

'Okay.' He nodded vigorously and turned so quickly, she thought he was going to fall over on the way to the door.

Shaking her head, Isla went back into the treatment room to tidy up, ready for the next client. Warmth settled in her chest, and she felt good. It was a step in the right direction.

What could go wrong on an island far removed from her old life by both time and distance?

Chapter Eighteen

Aisling - Dublin. Ten years earlier.

The day of reckoning came sooner than Aisling had hoped for. There had been no sign of Niall unless he'd come for her and been turned away without her knowing.

Sean had tried to become more familiar with her as the days passed and he was really starting to annoy her. Sometimes, a tingle of fear would thrum through her, but she was too preoccupied with her situation to let it take hold.

She had more things to worry about than a tutor who liked to perve on her. Every time she stood to stretch, Sean would be up in a flash, and press himself close behind her, his breath hot on her neck while he asked after her wellbeing. She'd soon learned to move away, and not say anything. On the few early occasions she'd told him to piss off, his fingers would tug at her hair until he'd turned her head to meet his eyes.

She didn't like what she saw in them.

He was a cruel and nasty man, but no one seemed to care. He'd been put with her so that she would pass her exams.

Occasionally Mrs Smithers, the cook, would throw her a sympathetic glance when she brought a hot lunch up for them each day.

Aisling's emotional strength declined as the days passed, and she tried to tell herself this situation could not last forever. She made sure that she ate properly; she had to look after her health and keep her energy up for when she finally escaped this hell, found Niall and made a life with him.

The week before the end of year examinations, her father arrived home unexpectedly one afternoon. Relief flooded through Aisling when he appeared in the doorway and gestured for Sean to come downstairs with him.

The Aisling of old would have had a rude comment to make to her father about how ignorant he was, but her courage had diminished; he had killed her spark and she no longer had the will to be objectionable.

Niall had been right when she had argued against his view that no woman would have put up with the circumstances that Hardy portrayed in his novels.

Aisling lay on her bed wondering what was being discussed downstairs. She knew she should have ranted and raved and told her father to release her immediately.

Maybe Sean would tell him how well she had worked and how compliant she'd been, and she would be freed from her room, the room that had become a prison.

Looking down, Aisling spread her fingers over her flat stomach. Was that all in her imagination?

Had she ever met Niall, or had he been a dream? This was doing her head in.

The door opened and Sean walked back in and locked the door. Aisling stood, disappointed that her father hadn't come back up to say it was over. As much as she hated him, he was the only one who would say she could go. There had been no sign of her mother for the whole six weeks she'd been in this stupid situation.

'Does Da want me to go downstairs now?' She looked at the key in Sean's hand.

Sean ignored her question and followed her gaze down to the key and he'd held it up. 'You'd really like to have this, wouldn't you?'

Aisling nodded. 'I would.'

'Maybe we can come to an arrangement?' He reached over and pressed his thumb against her lips. 'But it will have to be our secret.'

Aisling nodded as hope trickled in. 'I can keep a secret. I won't tell anyone you gave it to me.'

He shook his head. 'That's not what I meant.'

She frowned and tried to move back away from him but came up hard against the desk. He followed her and dangled the key in front of her nose as he pressed against her. 'That's not what I meant. You have to keep quiet about our arrangement.'

'What arrangement? We don't have one.' Fear iced her veins as he pressed harder against her.

'Do you want the key?'

'You know I do.'

'Then my dear, it's simple. We have an arrangement.'

Sean took her hand and unclenched the fingers that Aisling hadn't realised were fisted against his chest. He put the key in her hand and closed her fingers around it. 'I've kept my end of the deal, now it's all up to you, Aisling. You're not going to tell anyone about this, are you?'

Her eyes widened in horror as he began to remove the belt from his trousers.

Chapter Nineteen

Pippa

The morning of Nell and Nat's wedding, Rafe stood beside me in our ensuite and held my hand as we both stared at the white pregnancy test stick lying flat on the bench beside the basin.

'How long has it been now?' My voice shook as he looked at his phone.

'Two minutes and thirty seconds.'

'Thirty seconds to go,' I said.

He rested his forehead against mine and I could feel his tension. 'The longest thirty seconds of our lives, do you think?'

'Maybe, but as soon as they are over, I have to go down to the restaurant and make sure Tamsin doesn't overdo it. She wants the catering to be perfect this afternoon, and I know she'll be down there already.'

Rafe held his phone up. 'Time's up, sweetheart.'

I closed my eyes. 'Are you going to look, or am I?'

'How about we look together?' He was as shaky as I was.

'Okay.' I reached out and picked up the stick and held it up so we could both read it together.

When I saw the result on the little screen, I looked up at Rafe with tears in my eyes.

He was smiling too, but his tears matched mine.

'We did it, my darling Pip. We're having a baby.'

***

I walked on air down the steps to the resort, Rafe holding my hand tightly. Every couple of steps we would look at each other and grin. When we reached the bottom step, he took me into his arms and kissed me soundly before he headed to the pool to supervise the lights that were going up today, and I headed to the restaurant to check on Tamsin.

'Are we going to keep it a secret, or do you want to tell the girls?' he said against my mouth as I looped my arms around his neck.

'What do you think?' I was beside myself with excitement, but strangely, I wasn't focused on the fear of miscarrying, even though I had lost our first child.

'I'll leave it up to you, Pip. One look at your face today and anyone will guess you are excited.'

'And yours too,' I said kissing him back.

'Yes, and mine too,' he admitted. 'When will you be back at the house?'

'Once I check on Tam, I'll chase Nell up. We're due over at the day spa for Sienna to do our hair and makeup. I'll get dressed up at the house, so I'll see you late morning.'

His lips found mine again. 'You be careful, Mrs Rendell.'

'I will. And Rafe?' I tipped my head to the side and smiled at him. 'We could have a problem.'

'Yes? What's wrong?'

'Have you checked your clothes are ready for the ceremony? Last time I noticed your dress shirt was in the laundry basket.'

'Oh shit, I'd better get that sorted.'

'You'd better. Can't have the MC looking like a derro.'

'Why do I keep getting these microphone jobs?' He pulled a face. 'And what's a derro?'

'Because you have such a gorgeous sexy voice, my dear. And a derro is what you'll look like if you don't iron your shirt for the wedding.'

'Never fear, my dear. I won't let you down.'

He kissed me again and I reluctantly stepped away. 'I have to go. I love you.'

'Love you too, sweetheart.'

He let go of my hands and I hurried through the glade towards the restaurant. I was bursting with the news that I was pregnant, but I didn't want to take the shine off Nell's wedding day.

Chapter Twenty

Isla

Isla called into *Hebe* briefly before she headed over to the restaurant to help set up for the lunch. Sienna was doing the makeup for the bride and her two attendants, Pippa and Tamsin, for the noon wedding, which was to be followed by a casual luncheon.

Being with brides and bridesmaids and getting caught up in that sort of celebration was the last place she wanted to be. Sienna was doing Nell's hair, and Pippa and Tamsin were sitting with towels wrapped turban-like around their heads.

'All good here, Sienna? Or do you need an extra pair of hands?' Isla crossed her fingers behind her back.

'We're fine, you go and take some time for you. You've been working hard.'

'Okay. Have a great day, ladies,' she said with a cheery smile. The three of them had huge smiles on their faces, and a niggle of envy gripped Isla briefly.

Last night, when she had swung by the restaurant to collect a takeaway curry, as she'd rung up her meal, Cherry had asked Sienna if she could help set the tables in the restaurant mid-morning.

'I wouldn't ask but Tess is off for the weekend, and my usual kitchen hand is filling in at the reception.'

'Of course,' she agreed happily. The drink with Ronan could wait. 'I'm not needed in the day spa, and I've got the whole afternoon off. We closed *Hebe* to guests today, because of the wedding.'

'That's why Nell decided to have her wedding in the middle of the day,' Cherry said. 'She wanted to be married on the island, but she didn't want it to disrupt the guests.'

Isla smiled. 'They won't be disrupted. A wedding on the

island of love!'

Cherry chuckled. 'Pentecost Island sure is getting that reputation. Watch out, or you'll find you lose your heart here too. The rest of us have.'

'No fear of that. My heart is ironclad.' Isla put a hand on her chest and fluttered her lashes to soften her words.

'We'll see. We all fall eventually, even if there can be difficulties. Angus and I wasted a whole year due to misunderstandings.'

Isla nodded. She didn't want to know the details. 'So, what's the plan for lunch?'

'The reception is in *Violet's* restaurant. Lunch will be served from the pool bar for the guests, and then the restaurant will be open for dinner as usual tonight. Once the meal and speeches are over the wedding guests are going up to Pippa and Rafe's house to continue the celebration. It's a very small wedding so there's not many tables to set up.'

'Do you need a hand in the restaurant at night?' Isla offered.

'Thanks anyway, but we're all good. Take some time for yourself. I've seen how busy you and Sienna have been. You've been putting in some long days.'

'I will. After the ceremony, I'm going to head up to the rock-climbing wall to have a look.' Nell had invited all the staff to witness the ceremony if they wanted to, but the wedding reception was for close friends and family.

The resort had to keep functioning despite one of the partners getting married. The huts were at full capacity—some with Nat and Nell's families—but the rest were fully booked by holidaymakers.

'You're into climbing rocks?'

Isla shook her head and grinned. 'Gosh, no. I hate heights. But so many of my clients have been talking about the view from up there this week, I thought I'd go up and take a look.'

'It's pretty spectacular. You can see Indian Head from up there. The rock climbers have started climbing that rock too. Angus wanted me to do it with him, but I said no way! When I have time off, I want to spend it lying around the pool.'

'I'll check it out,' Isla said. 'I'm getting to love this island.'

As she left, her Irish client gave her a half-smile from the table near the counter. She walked over and his cheeks coloured.

'I'll have to take a rain check on our drink. I've been rostered on some extra duties.'

'Oaky, Thanks for letting me know.' Isla had worried about hurting his feelings as she'd walked back to her room.

After the tables were set, and Isla had watched Nat and Nell make their wedding vows, she went back to her room to get changed to go for a walk up to Red Wave Wall.

The ceremony had been short and sweet, but it had left her feeling unsettled. The island seemed to be full of love and romance—the bridal couple and the other girls with partners set off a small niggle of envy in Isla's chest.

She shook her head and stamped down on that thought.

Just think back, girl, and look where it got you. She had vowed to stay alone for her whole life. She had been hurt too badly by people she should have been able to trust, and like she had told Cherry, her heart was ironclad.

So, being unsettled emotionally, watching the happiness of those around her was stupid. It did not—and would not—tempt her at all.

Pulling on her walking boots, Isla focused on the walk ahead. She picked up a small backpack and grabbed a couple of bottles of water out of the communal fridge in the staff lodge. The staff here were looked after so well; it was the best working conditions she'd ever had. Adding a couple of muesli bars and an apple to her bag, she slipped it onto her back, looking forward to an afternoon by herself exploring this wonderful island.

As she purposefully stepped out of the lodge, halfway up the hill towards the walking track, music and laughter drifted up from below.

She ignored it and strode up the track. Soon, the only sounds were the rustling of the leaves in the hoop pine forests and the occasional call of a bird.

Peace began to seep through her skin as she stared out over the glorious blue vista that spread out below her the higher she climbed. The sounds, the smell of the sea, and the feel of the warm air caressing her skin surrounded her with serenity.

She had climbed so high now that the resort was only the occasional glimpse of buildings peeking through the rainforest canopy below.

She was almost on top of the world, and she was up here by herself. Isla enjoyed her own company; she didn't need to be with anyone to appreciate the beauty of nature surrounding her.

She didn't need to talk incessantly to a companion, or to seek their opinions or their agreement on anything. Her life was good the way it was, and she was happy being that way.

In those dark months in Dublin after she'd left the hospital, retreating into her own company and her own thoughts had been her salvation.

That was the last time she'd ever seen her father. Her mother had been absent since Sean Roberts had first turned up at the house.

Isla had made no contact with them and had cut herself off from her family.

'And I'm happy,' she thought as she reached the place where the path split. One way led to the mountain path which led to Red Wave Wall. Unscrewing the top of her bottle, Isla took a good drink of water before she began to climb the path. Half an hour later she was perspiring freely and reached up to wipe her forehead with her forearm. The sun was high in the February sky, and high thunderclouds sat above the horizon to the east as they did each afternoon, but so far had not delivered any rain.

She drew in a deep breath and her fingertips tingled with excitement as Isla turned to survey the vista in front of her.

In the distance, a fleet of sailing boats headed south, their headsails white and billowing in the wind.

The sky and the sea melded together in a deep turquoise, and she drew in a deep sigh of contentment. Isla was pretty sure she'd found the place she was going to stay.

With a determined step she followed the path that led to the climbing wall.

Chapter Twenty-One

Ronan

Ronan leaned back against the hot rock of the steep wall. The patch of shade he was sitting in had lessened as the sun had sunk lower in the afternoon sky. He'd drunk all of his water and his handkerchief was soaked from where he'd been mopping the sweat from his head and neck since he'd started the climb two hours ago. If he stayed up here much longer, he knew he'd end up dehydrated. There was a large spreading tree a little bit further up the track, but he didn't have the energy to keep going. He'd sit here for a while longer and then go up to the tree. It looked like his quarry wasn't coming up the mountain after all.

He looked down at his watch; he'd move to the shady tree and give her another fifteen minutes and then he'd head back down. He was sure that he'd heard the conversation correctly in the restaurant last night. Isla had told Cherry she was going to climb up to the climbing wall early afternoon. She hadn't turned up for a drink with him the night he'd had his treatment, and he hadn't pursued it. He didn't want to seem too keen and get her wondering about his motivation.

He'd made a plan, grabbed some hiking gear, and his walking sticks, and—foolishly—only one bottle of water, and headed up the hill towards the rock face at eleven o'clock.

Now four hours later, he was hot, sunburned, cranky and probably dehydrated; honestly this case was doing his head in. Maybe it was time to give up and decide what he was going to do.

Whether he was going to go back and work with Patrick, or if he was going to stay in Australia for a while. Do some travelling and not have to skulk around tailing people who didn't want to be found.

Now it looked as though the one he had been going to "bump" into accidentally this afternoon had changed her mind about climbing the hill, and he'd wasted his time. And got a good dose of sunburn as well.

As Ronan sat there feeling cranky and trying to summon up the energy to move, a small rockfall tumbled down the cliff below him and to his left.

More freakin' goats, he thought. He'd encountered a couple of large feral goats on the track halfway up and they had given him a scare. They were three times the size of the cute goats on his Pa's farm. And not only were they bloody ugly, they were also curious.

He leaned his head back and closed his eyes to summon up the energy to go back down. His head was starting to ache and his vision flickered a bit.

Five more minutes and he'd move. At least when he started off down the track it would be faster than coming up. As long as a bloody goat didn't push him off the path into the sea.

He'd be adding some danger money to his bill this week.

'Jaysus, Mary and bloody Joseph. You're not dead, are you?'

His eyes flew open, and Isla O'Sullivan suddenly appeared in front of him.

'No, I'm not dead. I'm just bloody hot and cranky,' he said before he could think.

She crouched beside him and rocked back on her heels and a cool hand touched his forehead.

'Jaysus, man, you're burning up. Your skin's hotter than Hades. Are you sick? Did you fall?'

He struggled to get up, but a firm hand pushed him back down. 'Stay there while I get my water out.'

'I won't say no to that,' he said with a weak smile.

A minute later a cool bottle of water was thrust into his hand. He unscrewed the lid and put the plastic bottle to his lips.

'Slowly, go slowly,' she said.

'Don't worry, I won't drink all your water. You'll need some too.'

'It's all right. I've got another bottle in my pack.'

As the welcome liquid quenched his thirst, and the bottle cooled his skin, Ronan began to feel better and then realised that here was the perfect opportunity to find out what he needed. Then he could get the hell off this island.

He looked up to encounter a pair of dark eyes full of

concern. 'I'm sorry if I gave you a fright. I sat down because I got hot, and I must have drifted off to sleep. And I'm sorry I was a cranky bugger.'

'Feckin' hell, Ronan. I thought you were dead. I was even looking up to see if the vultures were circling.'

'Do you get vultures on a tropical island?'

'I wouldn't know' she said. 'I haven't been here long enough.'

Ronan moved across as Isla sat beside him. There was just enough shade left for both of them.

'Ah, I see. How long have you been here?'

'Are you taking the Mickey out of me?' She looked at him with her eyes that were screwed up to match her forehead.

'Me?' he said. 'What do you mean?'

'We arrived on the same boat, man. So you know exactly how long I've been here.' Her eyes narrowed with suspicion and Ronan cursed inwardly. Here was his perfect opportunity to do some digging and he was bloody sunstruck and couldn't even get his thoughts in order.

'Ah. I thought you might have been away visiting another island.'

Again, she looked suspicious. 'No. That was the day I moved to the island. Why did you want to know how long I'd been here?'

'No, I just wondered.' His neck heated. 'Sorry, it's none of my business. I'll go back down now and leave you to your walk.'

'Don't be an eejit. You're in no fit state to walk down there by yourself yet. Have some more water, and then we're going to go and sit under that big shady tree.'

'Are you always so bossy? You were quiet and kind when you fixed my back.'

'Ah, so fixed it is, is it? Just as well because walking up that hill wouldn't have done you much good. Especially if you'd slipped on those loose rocks.'

Ronan felt guilty; it had been a ruse to speak to check her out. His injury hadn't been that bad, although the tight muscle in his lower back had been better since the treatment.

'It's been very good. Whatever it was, you fixed it.'

'Well, I'm pleased to be hearing that,' she said. 'Now can

you get yourself up, or do I have to help you? We need to get out of this westering sun.'

'I'm fine,' he muttered and put one hand down on the rocky ground to push himself up.

She was nimble and up on her feet before he was, and as she stood beside him, her eyes fixed on him, Ronan's head spun, and he tottered on his feet.

'You're not, you know. Silly man, getting too much sun. What if I hadn't come up and found you? How would it be for the guests to stumble upon a dead Irishman when all they wanted was to see the sun rise over the sea? That would be the end of the island of love, wouldn't it, boyo? Although I suppose it doesn't matter to you, because you are a guest.'

'Do you always talk this much?' he asked as she led him over to the shade.

'Only when I'm trying to stop a silly Irishman from flaking out on me. You've broken the saying, you know.'

'What saying?' He went to shake his head but decided against it as the world tilted.

'Mad dogs and Englishmen. If you'd died up here, it would have been mad dogs and an Irishman. I'm sure Pippa wouldn't have liked that.'

Ronan sat down gingerly, appreciating the shade of the wide spreading tree as she leaned back on the trunk. 'Probably not, although her husband could have written it into a book.'

'Her husband?' She screwed up her face and looked at him. 'What would Rafe be doin' writing that down.'

'Jack Smith.'

Her brow creased in a frown, and she moved closer, peering into his eyes to check if he was delirious or something. 'Look into my eyes, please.'

'He's Jack Smith, *the* Jack Smith who wrote that book that was made into *The Legacy* movie a couple of years ago.'

'Get away with you! Are you sure? You're not dreaming?' She looked at him suspiciously. 'Or pulling my leg because I'm prattling on?'

Ronan couldn't help the smile that tugged at his mouth. He pulled out his phone and was pleased to see he had five bars of service up here. He quickly Googled the book on Amazon and flicked to the second image of the paperback where the author's photo was on the back of the book. He held the phone out. 'Look.'

Before she took it, her eyes widened, and she screeched. 'Jesus, get away from that tree.'

Ronan dropped the phone and scrambled to his feet as she lunged at him and started hitting his shoulders. This time his head didn't spin as he stared at her, and she continued hitting and brushing at his shoulders and neck.

'Is that some sort of beautician treatment for sunstroke?' he asked bemused.

'No, it's me saving you from the army of green tree ants that were marching down your shoulder ready to attack that pink skin on your neck.'

'Jesus!' Ronan lifted the bottom of his T-shirt and pulled it over his head. 'Quick, did you miss any?'

Chapter Twenty-Two

Isla

'No, I think they were only on the outside of your shirt, but there is one in your hair still.' Isla reached up and flicked the almost transparent green and brown ant to kingdom come with her finger.

'And here I was starting to think about emigrating to Australia. I think the bloody feral goats and the giant tree ants have changed my mind. There's a lot to be said for the pouring rain and cold of our Emerald Isle where there's no nasty creatures to disturb a man's peace.'

'Hmph.' Isla couldn't help the nasty sound that escaped her lips before she could stop it. She'd had enough nasty experiences in his Emerald Isle to keep her away from there forever.

He looked at her curiously. 'Not a fan of rain and cold, I guess, then.'

'You could say that. Now sit back down, *away* from that tree trunk, and you can tell me about yourself and why you think Jack Smith lives on the island.' If she was stuck up here on the mountain with him until he was rehydrated, they would talk about him, not her.

He picked up his phone, flicked the screen, and handed it to her without a word. Then he vigorously shook his T-shirt, turned it inside out, and then back again before he pulled it over his head. Once he was finished, Isla looked down at the phone and frowned.

'That's Rafe,' she said. 'It *is* Rafe.'

He nodded at her. 'Yes, Pippa's husband, Rafe, is Jack Smith, the famous English author. I read about him moving to some island after I read his second book.'

'Well, I never.' She sat on the grass and looked up at him. 'Sit beside me and drink the rest of that water.'

'Yes, ma'am.' He did as she asked.

'Okay. Now you've told me about Rafe, tell me about yourself, Ronan Doyle. What do you do when you're not having yourself a holiday on an ant-infested goat island.' Isla knew she was in full blather mode but she didn't want to give him the chance to ask her any questions. She figured if she gave him ten minutes or so, and he drank both her bottles of water, he'd be right to get down the hill.

'Me? I'm pretty boring.' He sat close to her, so close that when he moved, his legs brushed against hers. She didn't want to move away and make it look too obvious, but she was still uncomfortable so close to a man, especially one she didn't know.

'What sort of work, do you do?'

'A bit of commercial photography.' He gestured to the camera bag on the ground across from them. She'd been so worried about him that she hadn't noticed it before. 'Birds.'

'Commercial bird photography. What does that mean?'

'You know, nature stuff. And landscapes. Tourist brochures and the like. Magazines, ads, all sorts of things.'

'Is there money in it? Enough to live on?' She swallowed a smile as he gawked at her. It was not the done thing to talk about money, but Isla had learned that doing the right thing never got you anywhere.

'Enough to get by.'

'And why do you want to move to Oz?' She tipped her head to the side as she looked at him. He had unusual eyes—flecks of gold in the brown. Very trustworthy eyes.

He stared back, and Isla shivered as she saw curiosity in his expression. She rushed on, 'Do you not have family over there? A wife, brothers, and sisters who'll miss you.'

'I do have family there,' he replied. 'But they all have their own busy lives. My sister's husband wants me to join up my business with his, but I'm only just startin' to think about it now.' As he spoke, he dropped back into the deep burr of the southwest.

'The southwest you said you were from. Even if you hadn't said that I would have picked it from the way you said "goat".'

'Goat? I don't say it any different to you.'

'Yes, you did. One syllable. So, tell me where exactly are you from?'

He shook his head. 'Not from Dublin, like you. I'm from Dingle.'

Isla froze. 'Dingle?'

'What's wrong with me coming from Dingle?'

'You really and truly came from Dingle?'

'I do.'

'Tell me about it.'

'Tell you what?'

'Tell me about Dingle.' Isla had a feeling that Ronan Doyle was telling the truth and she'd run into the only person she'd ever met who came from Dingle. Dingle, the village she'd chosen on the map, as far away from Dublin as she could pick and where she'd pretended she'd grown up, to everyone who had asked about her past over the last nine years.

He looked at her curiously again. 'Well, I was born and grew up in Dingle. I lived there until five years ago when I went to work for—when I changed my career to follow my love of . . . um . . . photography of birds.'

'What sort of birds are there in Dingle?' she asked trying to catch him out. Him coming from Dingle was too much of a coincidence for her peace of mind. Suspicion tinged her tone, but he still held her gaze steadily.

'The Dingle Peninsula is one of the best birdwatching areas in Ireland, and famous for its seabird colonies. My da used to take me birdwatching when I was a little fella. I asked for a camera one Christmas, and I got one. That's where it all started.'

'What sort of birds?' she repeated. He looked at her as though she was the one with sunstroke.

'Okay, there's many different varieties. The Blasket and the Maharee islands together have tens of thousands of nesting birds every summer.'

'What sort, I asked?'

He shook his head. 'Where do I start? Storm petrels, shearwaters, terns, gulls and auks, and the colourful puffins. Before I moved away, I used to work on the eco-marine tours on Blasket Island.'

Isla widened her eyes as relief flooded through her. No one could have made all that up on the spur of the moment. He was telling the truth. It was a coincidence! She couldn't help the laugh that began to bubble up from her chest. 'You really do come from Dingle?'

'I do. That's what I said. What's the joke? It's not that sad a town.'

'How big is your family?

'I have a younger sister and four brothers older than me.'

Isla snorted. 'Tell me their names aren't Paulie, Johnny, Archie and Barrie, please.'

'No,' he said cautiously, looking at her as though she'd well and truly lost the plot. 'Declan, Liam, Tony and Kevin. Why?'

'Did your grandparents live with you?' Isla giggled again. 'And did you go to the village school?'

'The village school? Have you never been to Dingle?' he asked. 'It's not a village, and there is no "village" school. My brothers and I went to school in Ballyduff.'

'Well, I got that part wrong,' she said half to herself.

Ronan sat up straight and his gaze was intense. 'Isla, are you feeling all right? What are you talking about?'

'You know, it's an absolute hoot. I've done some serious thinking since I arrived on the island, I'm pretty sure I'm going to settle and make a new life here. An honest one.' She snorted again. 'And who comes along? An Irishman who grew up in feckin' Dingle! I have to tell the girls first that it's been a sham.'

Ronan scratched his head as he kept looking at her. He looked confused—and she couldn't blame him—but there was a flare of interest in his eyes too. The sort of interest she usually ignored or talked over until the guy's eyes glazed over.

'Do you want to tell me what you're talking about,' he asked softly. 'Or do you want me to play a guessing game?'

'No, I'll be honest with you. I think you arriving on Pentecost Island in my first week is a sign.'

'A sign from who? The Almighty?'

'Hell, no! Not *the* Almighty that you're probably talking about. I lost my faith in that one when I stopped being myself.'

He leaned over and put his hand on her arm, and she looked down at the long, tanned fingers against her still-fair skin. 'Look, I'm feeling a lot better now thanks to you rescuing me, and your bottles of water. Before it gets any hotter how about we head back down, grab a couple of beers and find a shady spot and you can tell me your story.'

Isla nodded slowly as he looked at her earnestly, and on a totally out of character impulse, she decided to trust him. 'Yes. I think I'd like that.'

Chapter Twenty-Three

Ronan

Ronan didn't know whether to be excited because he was getting close to wrapping up this job or whether he felt like a total shit. The Isla who had rescued him from the hill, and the Isla of the competent massage treatment was very different to the loudmouthed and brash woman on the boat on the way to the island.

She obviously trusted him and getting up close and personal with her didn't sit comfortably with him in terms of the assignment. The last few jobs he'd completed for clients had not involved speaking to or getting close to the person he was searching for.

Not that he wouldn't like to get up close and personal with Isla O'Sullivan. He enjoyed her company, she had a wicked sense of humour and a quirky turn of phrase, not to mention being one of the most beautiful women he had ever seen. Her dark eyes had an exotic slant to them, and her black hair tumbled past her shoulders in a riot of curls. Her beautiful lips were a natural rosy colour. Even though he's been feeling so woozy up on the hill, he still hadn't been able to take his eyes off her. The photos his client had given him didn't do her justice.

Ronan was caught between a rock and a hard place, and as he walked back to his hut to take a cool shower after he left her at the bottom of the hill, he wondered if he'd done the wrong thing by organising to have a beer with Isla.

He stood under the shower and let the hard jets of cold water soothe his overheated and sunburnt face. As he tipped his head back, he tried to figure out how to approach this. Reaching for the soft white bath sheet he patted his red face dry before digging out some clean clothes.

As he went to lock the door of the hut behind him, he wondered if he should take his camera, so he'd look like a bona fide photographer.

Huh, he thought. This was a drink and chat date; she wouldn't expect him to be working.

Isla was waiting for him at the pool bar where they had organised to meet. She was chatting to a barman he hadn't seen before and when she put her head back and laughed at something the guy said, a flash of jealousy hit Ronan.

How stupid. He had no reason—or right—to feel like that.

'Where's your camera?' Isla asked when he crossed the outdoor area to the bar. 'There's going to be a ripper of a sunset.'

'Ah, I was in too much of rush to meet you.' He stumbled over his words. 'Plus, I thought it was probably rude to bring it.'

She looked at him curiously. 'I wouldn't mind.'

'Okay, I'll get our drinks and I'll collect it and my tripod'—that sounded professional—'on our way. What would you like to drink? A beer or a wine? I'm a lot cooler now.'

'You're nowhere near as red-faced. You had me worried there for a while.' She'd obviously had a quick shower too. Her hair was damp, and the curls were hanging in tight ringlets. 'How about we get a bottle of wine, or are you a beer sort of guy?'

'A cold white wine would be refreshing.' Ronan nodded as the barman passed him the wine list, and he ran his finger down. 'An NZ sauvignon blanc? Is that okay?'

'Sounds good. You grab the wine and I'll get some water and glasses. And maybe some nibbles. Do you have anything here, Larry?'

The barman hadn't taken his eyes off her as she'd chattered away, and he reached down and took out a readymade plate of cheese, olives, and cold meat from the fridge beneath the counter.

'All ready for the evening rush, but you're the first, Isla.' He flicked a glance at Ronan. 'Later tonight after I knock off, how about we have a drink up in the staff quarters?'

The hide of the gobshite, Ronan thought as he gave him a death glare.

'Thanks, Larry, but I have a rule not to socialise with the staff. And I need an early night too. A full day of bookings again tomorrow.'

With a shrug, he grinned. 'Nothing ventured, nothing gained.' Ronan couldn't help looking smug as they left the bar.

Isla led the way to a grassy point on the northern side of the jetty. There were a couple of rustic tables with bench seats overlooking the sea, but there was no one else making use of them.

Ronan opened the bottle of wine and filled the two glasses and passed one over to Isla. She uncovered the plate of cheese and pushed it over to him. 'You're probably hungry after your big adventure. And you forgot to get your camera again.'

He shook his head. 'No, I decided to give my whole attention to you while you tell me your story.'

'Oh.'

'You don't sound as enthusiastic anymore,' he commented.

'I am. It's going to be good to talk about why I am the way I am. Or the way I was. I think it's going to be cathartic for me. Strangers passing in the night. You don't know me, and you won't judge me. I'll stay here on the island, and you'll move on to your next adventure.' Her grin was cheeky as she looked up at him, and again he was stuck by her exotic beauty.

'I guess it was the Dingle connection that did it.'

Isla laughed and put one hand on her chest. She'd changed and was wearing a bright red T-shirt with *Love Hard, Live Longer* on the front. 'It was. I absolutely thought you were taking the Mickey out of me, and you knew what my background was. Or the one I used.'

Ronan picked up his glass and held it up for her to clink hers on. 'Here's to Dingle and old and new pasts, and to a mysterious woman who has crossed my path.'

Her smile was sweet, but there was tension around her pretty eyes.

'So, Isla Sullivan, tell me about the real you. I know you are definitely a massage therapist, because of the awesome job you did on my back. What else are you?'

She reached over and carefully put a piece of cheese on one of the crackers. 'I'll start at the beginning.'

'Always a good place to start.' Ronan immediately knew his tone was too flippant. He reached over and placed his hand on hers. 'I'll listen and I won't judge.'

'Thank you.' Isla stared over his shoulder looking towards the sunset as she began to speak. 'I was born in Dublin almost thirty years ago into a high-achieving family. My name was Isla

Aisling O'Sullivan, and I was called Aisling—Ash for short—until I chose to leave. My grandmother's name was Isla and I preferred Aisling then. My da and my mam were both lawyers and I often wondered why they ever had me. All my memories of my childhood were of nannies and cooks.' She picked up the glass and took a big sip. 'And a mean bully of a big sister. Her name was Marlene, and I haven't seen her for ten years. Or my parents.' Her voice dropped to a whisper. 'And I don't want to.'

Ronan froze. Marlene was the name of his client. Hearing the name of the woman who'd hired him from Isla's lips made him very uncomfortable. Later, he knew that that's when he should have stopped her and told her why he was there and what he knew, but this afternoon, he was transfixed by the look on her face. A combination of sadness and regret, but there was also strength. Her mouth was set in a straight line and her fingers clenched the stem of the wine glass, but Isla continued.

He could tell that she *needed* to talk. Now that she had started, it seemed as though it was hard for her to stop.

'I started high school, and I hit adolescence with a vengeance. All my father—and I guess my mother too—wanted was for another smart daughter, a daughter who would be biddable and follow her sister into the family law firm. I hated the thought of it. The only thing I loved at school were my English lessons, and if I'd gone up to university it would have been to study literature.'

She continued to look past him, and her eyes were sad. 'We'll cut to the year I was supposed to finish my schooling and get my university entry. I thought I was pretty cool.' She turned her gaze to him for a moment. 'I did everything I could to get their attention, but nothing worked. I wagged school, I smoked, I stole money from Da's wallet, it changed nothing.'

She took a deep breath. 'Until one day when I met a man—I guess he would have been a boy, but I was too smitten to take much notice. He loved literature and he understood me.' Her hand shook as she put the glass down. 'At least I thought he did. I guess I saw what I was wanting to see.

'Anyway, to cut a long story short, I fell pregnant, as many Irish girls did in those days. Being good Catholics and all.'

Ronan drew a quick breath and she flicked him an amused

glance.

'You think that got my parents' attention?'

He shook his head. 'I guess not, or you wouldn't be here telling me this story.'

'Got it in one, boyo. Now we get to the nasty bit.' She sipped her wine this time. Ronan ignored his glass, he was riveted by her story, and as she spoke, he knew that he would not be completing this job. She had been treated badly, and it wasn't up to him to deliver her to the sister who was looking for her. He would email her tonight, and say he was mistaken about finding her, and terminate the contract.

'My da was still determined I would pass my exams, and he hired a tutor to get me there. I was locked in my room for six hellish weeks with this pervert of a tutor who would arrive every morning and lock the door behind him at night.'

Ronan felt sick as he listened. 'That's against the law.'

'Probably, but all my da wanted was the top exam marks. Marlene topped the school and got the university medal the year she graduated.' Her voice shook as her eyes brimmed with tears. 'I got what I deserved.'

Chapter Twenty-Four

Aisling

'Are you absolutely sure?' The counsellor in the private clinic in London stared at Aisling after her father left the room.

Aisling nodded, unable to bring herself to speak because she knew she'd start crying, and if she started, there would be no stopping her.

She looked up at the counsellor and the nurse sitting across the coffee table from her, where papers sat waiting for her to sign.

'I sensed a tension between you and your father. It is most unusual for a father to bring his daughter to the clinic, so I want to be absolutely sure that it is you who wants this termination, and it's not simply your father's—or your parents'—wishes. The initial consultation is usually done with the patient alone, to make sure she's happy with her decision. Your father was most insistent on coming in with you.'

Aisling dug deep as she stared at the woman's hair. She couldn't bring herself to look at her eyes, and she spoke by rote.

'It is my choice. My parents support me. My father came across to London with me from Dublin as my mother is working on an important case. They are both solicitors, you know.' She swallowed. 'I never knew that we couldn't have an abortion in Ireland. How naïve was I?'

'Not naïve, at all. It's not the sort of thing that an eighteen-year old would pay much attention to. You are aware of the other options?'

'I think so.'

'Now according to your GP who referred you, you are ten weeks pregnant.'

Aisling nodded. She knew the baby was Niall's, but once she had told Da about Sean assaulting her, and the test had indeed confirmed a pregnancy, she had let her parents make the assumption that Sean was the father.

She was tired, distressed and more emotional than she had ever been in her life.

Consumed by hatred, and distress that Niall had not tried to find her, Aisling followed her parents' wishes. She tried very hard not to think about the tiny little thing inside her ever being a person.

'The three choices are abortion, becoming a parent, or adoption.' The nurse's voice was soft, and the kindness in her tone almost brought Aisling to tears.

'I know. That's why we're at the clinic.'

'Very well. If you would just sign here, and here, please Miss O'Sullivan.'

She quickly did as she was told and looked down at her hands clenched on her lap.

'Tomorrow morning, you will be placed under a general anaesthetic and the procedure will only take ten to fifteen minutes,' the nurse continued. 'Most women don't experience any problems after this procedure. But there are some risks, such as infection of the womb, damage to the womb and excessive bleeding. We will give you painkillers and an aftercare phone line so you can call us any time of the day or night if you are worried.'

'When are you going back to Dublin?' the counsellor asked.

Aisling lifted her head, and her steely determination kicked in. 'I'm not.'

##

Two days later, Aisling stood outside the private clinic beside her father.

He insisted that she come home with him, but despite her weak physical condition and her confused emotional state, she had found the strength to stand up to him.

'I will never set foot in that house again. Not after what happened there in *my* bedroom. It is all on your head.' She couldn't even bring herself to say *Da*.

'Now, now,' he'd huffed as he'd tried to get her into the Jag. 'Don't be like that. I'll admit that I was wrong.'

Aisling's laugh was bitter as she pushed away his hand.

'But that is in the past now. We've sorted it out—'

'Have we?' she finally yelled. 'How have we done that?'

'Sean Roberts will never work in teaching again, and medically we've got you sorted.'

Bile rose in her throat at her father's attitude. 'I'm so pleased for your peace of mind that you have me all "sorted" in your head.' She fought back the tears that were always there. She would not cry in front of her father. 'Goodbye. Have a nice life.'

Chapter Twenty-Five

Isla

'What did you do?' Somehow, Ronan had moved around to her side of the table, and his arms were around her, and her head was resting on his shoulder. Isla blinked, surprised to feel her cheeks wet. She had blocked the thought of those two days, and the following weeks for a long time.

'I waited until he was in the car and went to his window. I held my hand out and told him I wanted money. He must have known I was serious because he pulled his wallet out. Before he opened it, he looked at me and his eyes were like flint.

'"If you take this, you will no longer be our daughter," he said to me. "It is the last I will ever give you. You have been a constant disappointment to your mother and I, your whole life."'

'Jaysus!' Ronan's voice vibrated against her cheek. 'What the hell did you do?'

'He gave me five hundred pounds, and I was still clutching it in my hand when I was taken to emergency. Someone found me crying in the gutter, and I was incoherent. I spent six weeks in a mental health ward. I'm not proud to say I had a total breakdown; it took me five years to get my self-confidence back. When I was in hospital, I would sit in the garden and invent the family I wanted to have.' She lifted her head and smiled through her tears. 'My Dingle family. All my lovely brothers and my parents and my grandparents. For a while there, they all became very real to me.'

'If you had really been in Dingle, I would have been your friend, Isla.' His eyes held hers and they were full of kindness. 'What about the father of your baby? The boy you met?'

Her laugh was bitter. 'I found Niall on Facebook a few years back. He's a tutor at Trinity now, and he has a lovely wife and two young children. I wonder if he ever thinks of the girl he thought of as one of his Thomas Hardy heroines?'

'What about your sister? Were you ever in contact with

her?'

'No, but I keep tabs on her through Facebook. She's married now and has her own law firm.'

'You wouldn't ever want to talk to her, or your parents?'

'No. I don't have any family. Or rather I choose not to. I realise that it wasn't my fault. I was a normal teenager, and I was treated very badly. My life is my own, and I am going to make it a good life.' She reached out and took Ronan's hand. 'Thank you so much for listening to me. I'm very pleased you chose Pentecost Island for your holiday. You were meant to pass through my life.'

To her surprise he looked quite distressed, and he moved away from her and then stood suddenly.

'Do you mind if I leave you here for a few minutes? Please don't go, but there is something I have to do. Would you like me to bring anything back? More wine? Or how about I order some dinner at the bar?'

She nodded. 'That would be good, thank you. Pizza?'

Even though she smiled up at him, Ronan looked very serious, and she wondered if she had gone too far, telling her life story to a stranger.

'Pizza, it is. Give me ten minutes.'

As Isla watched Ronan stride across the grass towards the path laughter drifted down from Pippa and Rafe's house, making her smile. An unfamiliar feeling of lightness had descended on her when she had shared her story with Ronan. He had been very kind to her, and she had to admit that when his arms had gone around her, it had felt right.

***

Ronan cursed himself in all manner of ways as he hurried back to his hut. How the hell did this get so complicated? He detoured via the bar and ordered two medium pizzas, and another bottle of wine from a sour Larry, but he didn't give a shit about that guy's problem. All he was focused on was getting back to his laptop and sending an email off to England to his client—Isla's bloody sister. The one who had treated her like dirt.

After hearing what Isla had been through Ronan didn't want anything to do with this job anymore. He pulled out his laptop, powered it up and connected to the Wi-Fi and thought carefully about the wording of his email.

In the end he kept it brief and formal.

Dear Marlene

Please note that I was mistaken in identifying the woman I emailed you about as your sister. That person is not Aisling O'Sullivan. I apologise for my error. As the trail seems to be cold I will now remove myself from this assignment. There is no account outstanding. Thank you for your patience. I am sorry that I could not assist you. Sincerely, Ronan Doyle.

Listening to Isla's story had been harrowing. He could not comprehend that a family—a mother and father—could treat their child as she had been treated. Granted, she had made mistakes, but they should have supported her. Trying to relate to how parents could be like that was impossible for him. His parents and his siblings would have been supportive and caring.

With a disgusted shrug, he composed himself and after he pressed send, he locked the door behind him and headed back to the beach where he had left Isla.

He was surprised to see Pippa and Rafe standing at the table and hurried across hoping that everything was okay. He was reassured when he heard Isla's distinctive laugh.

'Hi there,' he said. 'How did the wedding go?'

Pippa's smile was wide. 'It was beautiful We've just taken Nell and Nat down to the wharf to Rafe's boat. We were on our way back when we noticed Isla sitting here.'

Isla turned to him. 'Pippa and Rafe gave the happy couple a week in a penthouse on Hamilton Island.'

Pippa shook her head. 'As grateful as they were, would you believe that Nell said she'd rather be here on the island!'

Isla chuckled. 'It is known as the island of love.'

'There's no way I'd let them spend their wedding week in the staff lodge! The huts are at full capacity for the next two months.'

Ronan pulled a face. 'I was hoping to extend my stay, but it looks as though that won't be possible.'

'Actually, I was going to come and see you tomorrow,' Pippa said. 'Tess told me that Zac told her—nothing like the island grapevine—that you're a commercial photographer.'

'He is,' Isla exclaimed. 'He's done work for magazines and brochures promoting Dingle in southwest Ireland.'

Ronan nodded. 'I am and I have.' He flicked a smile to Isla, pleased that she sounded so upbeat now.

'Do you have a portfolio I could look at?' Pippa pulled a face at Rafe. 'I know. It's not work time, but you know me, when I get an idea, I'm ready to run with it.'

Her husband put his arm around her and dropped a kiss on top of her head. 'I know and I wouldn't have you any other way, love.'

'I have a digital portfolio. I can give you the link.'

'Great, send it to the email address in your compendium,'—she patted the pockets of her dress—'I don't carry a business card in my wedding finery.'

'What sort of photography are you looking for?'

'A bit of everything, but mainly up at Red Wave Wall, and up in the hills. We're looking at really developing the climbing and birdwatching market.'

Ronan caught Isla's eye and could see the mirth on her face. He put a hand on her shoulder.

'Don't you say a word, Ms O'Sullivan.'

'My lips are sealed,' she said with a giggle.

Pippa looked from Ronan to Isla and a satisfied smile lit up her face. 'Sounds like you two Irish are hitting it off. Good to see.'

Rafe tugged at his wife's hand. 'As much as we'd love to stay and chat, we still have about twenty guests up at the house. Good to catch up with you both. Have a good evening.'

They walked off together towards the step leading up to the house on the top of the hill and as Ronan turned back, Isla put one hand to her chest.

'Oh my God, now I know he's Jack Smith too, I'm even more smitten.'

'He seems like a nice guy. Hey, and thanks for the photography plug too.'

'My pleasure. As long as you remember to wear sunscreen and take water with you if you get the assignment. And I'm sure you will. Get it, I mean. Pippa seemed pretty keen before you came back.'

'She hasn't seen any of my work, and besides, there's nowhere to stay. I can't extend my booking.' Ronan tried not to get excited about the possibility of a job with the island.

'I'm sure she'll figure something out.'

He held his hand out to pull Isla up from the bench seat. 'Now before you go puttin' the cart in front of the horse, *macushla*, we have two pizzas to eat, and wine to drink. Are you ready?'

'I am. Are we going to eat at the bar?'

'If you're happy to.'

'Yes. As long as you and Larry don't look daggers at each other. It might ruin my appetite.'

Ronan laughed as he pulled her up. 'How about you take it as a compliment. And Isla?'

'Yes?' Those beautiful dark eyes held his.

'I am so pleased to see you smiling. That was a big story you told me before.'

'Thank you for listening.' Before he realised what she intended, soft lips brushed his cheek. 'I really appreciated it. I feel so good. Now I'm starving, let's go eat.'

Ronan smiled as she held his hand all the way back to the bar.

Chapter Twenty-Six

Pippa -Three weeks later

I dressed quickly, came out of the medical rooms, and hurried across to Rafe who was waiting in the foyer. He'd been in the room with me when the sonographer held the wand thing on my bare tummy, and he had held my gaze as we both heard the rapid little heartbeat. Excitement had taken over when the obstetrician had met with us and confirmed that not only was the baby fine and growing quickly, but I was four weeks out in my dates, and was a month further along than I thought.

Our baby was due in late winter. And by then, we would have four babies on the island.

Rafe put his arm around my shoulders as we walked to the car he kept in an underground garage near the marina at Port of Airlie. Neither of us said a word until we were heading along Shute Harbour Road.

I put both hands up to my face, and Rafe glanced over at me, and then put his hand on my knee. 'We've been given a gift of four weeks, Rafe. I can't believe it. Four weeks when I didn't have to worry about reaching the twelve-week mark, and now we're there.'

'I couldn't believe it when the doctor said that.'

'And everything is going perfectly, and he's really happy. Do you think I'll be tempting fate if I'm a little bit happy too?'

'A little bit happy?' He shook his head. 'No, we are both going to let ourselves be very happy. Not only happy, but . . . ecstatic. Overjoyed. Thrilled. Elated and—'

'Okay, stop showing off, Mr Author,' I said as he turned the car off the roundabout leading to the apartment block where the car was garaged.

I put my hand on my stomach and looked down. 'He sure had a strong little heartbeat, didn't he?'

'*She* sure did,' Rafe said with a chuckle. 'And she looked

very comfortable all curled up inside you.' He parked the car and came around to my side and opened the door. 'Now that we're past twelve weeks, can we break the news?'

I nodded. 'First thing we'll do as soon as we get back.'

'Great timing because everyone's home.'

'Jed and Evie too?' I linked my arm through his as we walked to his boat.

'Yes, Jed called when you were getting changed. They're on the way over now with the new furniture for the top glade.'

'Oh, that's fabulous. And Zac and Tess came back last night, and Philippe and Eliza sailed around the point as we were heading across the Passage this morning.' I leaned into him. 'But I think there's one call you should make before we tell everyone.'

He looked down at me and squeezed my fingers. 'You don't mind?'

'Of course not, and as soon as we tell everyone Odessa will be on the phone to Jenny and Bryant, so you need to call them first.'

'How about now? As soon as we get on the boat?' He glanced at his watch. 'We should just catch them before they retire for the night.'

I giggled. 'Have I told you how much I love you today, Rafe?'

'Not in the last half hour.' He leaned down and caught me in a kiss. 'You have been very remiss.'

'As you would be *remiss* if you didn't catch them before they *retired for the night*.'

He kissed me again to stop me from giggling.

'Okay, I shall do the right thing and ring them before they go to bed, you wench. You do realise that I shall be teaching our daughter to speak properly. None of this casual Aussie lingo.'

'Oh, will you just?' I nudged him with my shoulder and received another kiss.

As soon as we were on Rafe's boat, he called Jenny and Bryant, and the joy on his face as he broke our news to his best friends in England had me blinking away happy tears.

##

When we walked from the wharf to the office, our island was buzzing. On the way back, we decided it would be too hard to get everyone together, so we called in and delivered our news to everyone wherever they happened to be as we walked around the resort.

The last three weeks had seen some changes at Ma Carmichael's. Nell had dropped back to three hours a day in the office. Eliza was working with the Riccardos on the design of the new accommodation up the hill for the birdwatching and climbing groups and was more often than not in the office with Tess using the computers. The renovations of Aunty Vi's house were almost complete, and I couldn't believe how fast the builder's crews worked.

They were about to start work on the new buildings up past the staff lodge, and I had hired Ronan Doyle as our onsite photographer, both for advertising photos, as well as to record images for the development of the resort. Isla had given me the idea when she mentioned in passing one day that Esculanta Island had a history montage of photographs in the main restaurant. I'd managed to dig out a lot of Aunty Vi's old photos too. I smiled to myself as I remembered how pleased Isla had been when she had heard that Ronan was staying on the island for a while and moving into a room up at the staff lodge. They seemed to have developed a strong friendship over the past month, and I often saw them walking along the shore in the early evening.

As we approached the house I paused and looked around. 'I wonder what Aunty Vi would have made of all this?' I said to Rafe.

'She had no doubt that you would live here—she told me that on more than one occasion—but I don't know that she ever thought that you'd turn it into one of the most sought-after resorts in the country. And trust me, she'd be delighted with what you achieved, Pip. You were like a daughter to her.'

'She was a good old stick.' I looked up to the verandah. There was a group sitting at the table on the verandah facing the sea.

'Oh look, we're in luck.' The butterflies in my tummy fluttered with anticipation. 'Nell and Tam are having lunch with Tess and Eliza.'

'And there's Evie and Cherry walking across to the house.'

'Oh yay! And Odessa will be in the boutique too. There's only Sienna and Isla missing.'

'I'm feeling rather outnumbered here. Do you want me to go and you can tell the girls?'

'No. You're coming too. But sweetie, will you go and get Odessa to come out before we tell them, please?'

He ran up the steps ahead of me to the new resort boutique that Odessa had taken over. As well as her handcrafted jewellery, we were stocking some gorgeous sarongs and scarves created by a local designer over on Hamo. It seemed to be a first stop for a lot of the guests as soon as they checked in. And Odessa had turned out to be an incredible salesperson.

'Hey, Pip. What are you pair up to? A romantic lunch? I thought you went over to Hamo this morning,' Nell said leaning back in her chair. My eyes dropped to the hand she placed on her pregnant stomach, before I moved my gaze to Tamsin. She was sitting on one of the sofas against the wall. She seemed to be bigger every day. Since she'd found out she was carrying twins Tam had stopped working in the catering side of things. Angus had taken over all the ordering and the accounts, and it was going well.

'No,' I said slowly, making a huge effort not to put my hand on my stomach too. Not that there was any bump there yet, although Rafe said this morning that he could see a little rise, low on my tummy. I had stood at the mirror front on, and side on and twisted from side to side until Rafe chuckled.

'We have some news.'

Tam's eyes narrowed, and she nudged Nell, who smiled and nodded.

Eliza moaned. 'Not more new buildings?'

Evie looked up from the drawings she had put on the table before she'd sat down. 'More gardens?'

'A new computer system?' Tess asked.

'Another restaurant?' Cherry said hopefully.

Odessa walked out of the boutique with Rafe. She leaned on the wall next to the door and her smile was wide. I raised my eyebrows at Rafe, and he shook his head.

'It wasn't me. Jenny and Bryant called Odessa,' he said.

'What's going on, Pippa?' Tamsin's smile was hopeful.

I couldn't keep the smile from my face as I stood there.

'Well, there's no new buildings, Eliza, and sorry, Cherry, you won't get your own restaurant yet. Evie, no, not gardens. And Tess, we just put in a new computer system, didn't we?'

Rafe walked across to me and put his arm around my shoulders. 'What my darling wife is trying to tell you all, is that in spring, there will be a new addition to Pentecost Island. We're having a baby.'

You never would have guessed that Tam and Nell were pregnant; they both jumped out of their chairs and ran over to me.

I couldn't help myself. I burst into tears as they hugged me and was instantly a blubbering mess.

Tam never cried, but when she spoke her voice trembled. 'Hey, Pip. All for one, and one for all, hey?'

'You got it, sister,' Nell said, joining in the three-way hug.

A flurry of kisses and congratulations followed and eventually Rafe passed me his handkerchief. As I wiped my eyes, I looked at the group of women who were making the island the wonderful place it was, and who I did love as sisters. 'Thanks, everyone. We're pretty excited. Come on, Rafe. We'll go over to *Hebe*, now.' I shook my head. 'We didn't expect to find you all here.'

We left the excited buzz of conversation behind as we headed though the forest to the day spa hut.

'They're probably both in appointments,' I said as we approached *Hebe*.

'It's only ten minutes before the hour so they should be free soon.'

Rafe was right and soon Sienna and Isla knew our news as well.

Isla waited until we were about to leave, and she looked nervous as she spoke to me quietly. 'Pippa, could I come and see you when we finish this afternoon?'

'Sure, come on up to the house. We'll be there.'

'Thanks. I'll see you later.'

Rafe waited for me at the top of the stairs. 'May I take you out for a celebratory lunch now, Mrs Rendell.'

'You may.'

He took my hand, and we walked through the glade together.

Chapter Twenty-Seven

Isla

Isla pounded on Ronan's door. His room was at the other end of the staff lodge from hers. She'd hurried back from her last appointment because they had a sunset date, that is if you could call racing up to the top of the mountain with him a date. Over the past two weeks since Ronan had moved out of the guest accommodation and taken a three-month contract on Pentecost Island to produce a whole new range of brochures for Pippa, Isla had spent most afternoons with him in various locations on the island—including underwater, clad in a head-to-toe stinger suit as he took photos of green turtles.

'Ronan, if you don't get a move on, you're going to miss the light.' She pounded on the door again.

'Okay, okay, I'm coming.' He opened the door and stood there, water running down his bare chest and his hair slicked back. 'I just have to get dressed. Can you come in and grab my camera bag, and check the batteries are in there? And the tripod,' he called over his shoulder as he disappeared into the bathroom.

Isla shook her head as she went inside. One thing she'd discovered about Ronan over the past few weeks was that he had no sense of time.

'Sheesh,' she yelled after his departing back. 'I'm the one who's been at work all day, and what have you been doing? Sitting at the computer, I'd say.'

His head appeared around the door. 'I have, and wait till you see those underwater photos we got last weekend. They are bloody incredible.' He burst out laughing. 'Especially the one of you in your elegant stinger suit.'

'Ronan, hurry up!' She checked the batteries were both there, and then looked at her phone. 'We have fourteen minutes to get up the hill.'

'I'm ready,' he raced out pulling a T-shirt over his wet hair.

'Can you see my thongs?'

'They're out on the veranda.'

'Okay, let's go.'

Isla grinned as she hurried down the steps after Ronan. She'd had the best few weeks since she had spilled her guts to Ronan that night.

They were good mates, as Pippa would say.

'Oh, feckin' hell.' She stopped dead at the bottom of the stairs.

'What's wrong?'

'I totally forgot I arranged to see Pippa at five.'

'Should you go now?' Ronan hoisted the camera bag higher on his shoulder and held his hand out for the tripod she was carrying.

'No. It's a bit late. I said straight after work. I'll leave it until tomorrow. If I'm going to lose my job, one day's not going to make a difference.'

His eyes widened. 'Lose your job? Why?'

'Keep going, we can talk on the way up.'

'What happened?' Ronan asked when they started walking again.

'Nothing. I'm just a bit worried because I'm in my sixth week here, and there's been no mention of permanency or a contract. I was on four weeks probation, and Pippa hasn't mentioned a thing, so I took matters into my own hands and asked her if I could see her this afternoon, and then I forgot all about it. It's your fault.'

'My fault? How can it be my fault?'

'You and your sunsets. I was worried that you'd get involved in your graphics program and you'd lose track of the time and miss this afternoon. You said it was special because the yacht race is on, and the sails with the sun setting would be an awesome shot.'

'Okay. My fault. I can live with that. You're very good to me, Isla.'

'I'm good *for* you. You're starting to learn what a clock is for.'

'Come on then, let's pick up the pace. You're right, they are going to be great shots. The light is perfect already. And don't worry about Pippa and our contract. She loves you, and she probably didn't give it a thought because she's so busy with everything else.'

'And the baby,' Isla added.

'What baby?'

'Didn't you hear? You must be the only one on the island who doesn't know. Pippa and Rafe are having a baby.'

'That's great news.' Ronan stopped as they reached the first gap above Indian Head. 'The island is a great place, isn't it? I'll be sorry to leave. It's worked its magic on me. I've never been so relaxed.'

'And I've never felt this happy. Ever I don't think.'

The look that Ronan flicked her way was hard to fathom. They'd spent hours together in her time off, and the thought of him not being here made her feel strange. Just good mates, no hint of anything else.

For the first time in her life, Isla felt comfortable in her own skin. She was herself and not trying to be anybody else, and every day was a discovery for her as she relaxed and let herself be natural.

The problem was that, being relaxed and letting down her guard, she had let feelings creep in, and that was going to make it hard when Ronan did move on.

Never in a trillion years would she give him any sign that she was interested in him in *that* way.

That would be a surefire way to lose him as a friend. He'd be embarrassed. He was a good man, and a good friend, and she would make the most of that while he was here.

When he left, she'd fill the gap somehow.

When she looked up, he was still looking at her and she handed the tripod to him. 'Sorry, I was miles away.'

'Don't worry about your job, *macushla.* I'm one hundred percent sure you have nothing to worry about.' He put his camera bag down, came a step closer, took the tripod from her, and put it on the ground beside the bag.

Tipping his finger beneath her chin he tilted her head up. 'Give me a smile.'

'You'll miss the sunset.'

'There'll be another one tomorrow. You're more important.

You look sad. What else is bothering you?'

'Take your photos here and I'll tell you when we get to the top of the path.' Heat ran up from Isla's chest; he stood so close she could feel the warmth of his body against hers.

He flicked her cheek with his finger and smiled. 'Good.'

Within seconds the camera was on the tripod, and the continuous click of the shutter filled the air.

Isla sat on a flat rock and watched as Ronan repositioned the camera a few times. The sun was still well above the mountains and the yachts were still a good distance from the island, but Ronan seemed happy enough. As he focused on the viewfinder, she let her gaze run over his body. He had a stocky build, and he was strong. When he'd held her close that one time, as she'd told him of her past, Isla had felt the corded muscles beneath his shirt, and as she got to know him better, she'd heard about his teenage years spent working on the family farm in Dingle.

A smile crossed her face. *Dingle.*

As she sat there grinning, all was quiet, and she realised that the camera noise had stopped. Ronan was looking at her, and a jolt ran through her as she saw the hunger in his gaze. He looked away quickly and picked up the tripod.

'Come on, let's get to the top of the hill. The yachts will be close enough just in time.' His voice was a bit gruff.

Feckin' hell, now I'm imagining things. Wishful thinking, girl. Get over it.

Chapter Twenty-Eight

Ronan

Spending so much time with Isla, and being close to her was doing Ronan's head in. The more time he spent with her the harder it was to keep his distance. After what she'd been through, and how she'd opened up to him, the last thing he wanted to do was destroy the trust between them.

He would be her friend no matter how hard it was. Leaving Isla at the end of the three months, when he'd completed his contract here was something he tried not to think about.

The crest of the hill appeared ahead, and Ronan paused to let her catch up. She seemed to be in a strange mood this afternoon, but he put that down to her worry about her job.

He had no doubt she was worrying needlessly, but after having watched her over the last few months in various locations, he knew that if anything did happen here, she'd be sure to move on and settle in somewhere else. There was only one thing worrying him. It had been a few weeks since he'd emailed her sister, and there'd not been a reply from her. He was hoping it was because she'd accepted what he'd said and was looking elsewhere.

Isla caught up to him, barely out of breath after the long climb. 'How's the light?'

'Almost there. Come and sit for a while, and you can tell me what else you're worrying about.'

Her teeth flashed in the fading light as she cracked a big grin at him. 'What are you now, my father confessor?'

He nudged her with his shoulder. 'If you have something to confess, I can be.'

'Nope. I never did like going to confession anyway.'

'Come and sit over here, while I set up the remote, then the camera can do its own work while we talk.'

She followed him to the edge of the cliff and sat away from the edge while he secured the tripod, screwed the camera to the top and set it to remote.

He walked over and sat beside her and opened the app on his phone that would control the camera. 'Okay, all set. Now tell Father Ronan what's bothering you. I know something is.'

Isla looked down and wouldn't meet his eyes, and a horrible thought gripped him.

'Jaysus, is it because you don't want to be up here? Am I presuming too much expecting you to traipse around after me after you've been at work all day?'

'Hell no. I totally enjoy being with you.' Finally, she looked up. 'If I'm going to be honest, maybe too much. I'm getting used to you bein' around, and when you go, I'm going to miss you.'

Relief flooded through him. 'You'll miss me?'

'I will.'

Ronan leaned back and lifted the phone and pressed the shutter button on the app as the first of the yachts slipped in the golden glow of the sunset.

'Beautiful,' he said. 'Every time I see that photo, I'll think about you missing me. You know what? If you didn't get your contract renewed, it wouldn't be a bad thing. You could come with me. I need a camera assistant.'

Her laugh was soft. 'That's a consolation, anyway.'

As she stared up at him, Ronan forgot all about the yachts and the sunset. Her eyes held his and her lips were softly parted, and he reached out and cupped her cheek. 'And if your contract does get renewed, I might only go as far as Hamilton Island, and then I could see you on weekends. What would you say about that?'

Her lips tilted in a little smile. 'I would say that was an excellent idea.'

'Ah, and what would you say about this?' He leaned forward and touched his lips to hers. The feel of Isla's soft rosy lips beneath his was everything Ronan had dreamed about for the past few weeks. She turned her head slightly and the gentle slide of her moist lips sent need rushing through him. She gripped his T-shirt and held him close. 'I would say that's another excellent idea. There's only one problem.' Her lips vibrated beneath his as she spoke.

'A problem?' he asked.

'The photos.'

'They can wait. This can't. I love touching you.' He slipped his hands beneath her T-shirt and was pleased to hear her moan softly. 'Your lips are like honey and your skin is like silk. You've been in my dreams since the first time I saw you.'

'Do you think we should pack the gear up and go back down to your room. It might be a bit embarrassing for any birdwatcher or rock climber to come across you without your shirt on.'

Ronan frowned and looked down. 'But I've still got my shirt on.'

'Not for much longer, boyo,' she said with a sultry smile.

Chapter Twenty-Nine

Isla

There were degrees of happiness, and Isla realised the next morning, as she sat on the side of Ronan's bed, that she had only scratched the surface over the past few weeks. The feeling that consumed her now was hard to define but it was one she didn't want to let go.

Ronan rolled over and sat up so that he was beside her on the edge of the bed. He yawned. 'What are you doing?'

'Ah, so you're finally awake.'

'That I am,' he said stretching his arms above his head. 'Although, I could do with a bit more sleep.'

'You can sleep after you feed me. I'm going to take a shower while you get me some food, and then you can sleep the day away while I work.'

'Are you really hungry? We had bacon and eggs at midnight!'

'I'm starving again. All that strenuous activity.' She looked at him through half-closed lids and moved away as he went to put his arms around her.

'As much as I'd love to stay, I have to go to work. My first appointment is at eight-thirty. I have forty-five minutes.'

'Okay. I'll go cook you a big breakfast while you shower.' Ronan climbed out of bed and pulled on a pair of jeans.

'You're a good man.'

He came back to her and leaned down and kissed her thoroughly. 'Hold that thought.'

Five minutes later, Isla was showered and dressed. All she had to do was go via her room and put on her *Hebe* uniform.

She crossed the room to the small table where the dishes from their midnight feast sat congealed with remnants of egg and bacon fat. Ronan's camera was sitting on the table, and she picked it up while she waited for him.

If the photo of her in the stinger suit was as awful as he'd said, she'd delete it. Flicking the screen to play, she scrolled through the photos. The one he'd captured last night of the yachts in the golden sunlight was spectacular. Hitting the back button she scrolled though some photos and realised she was going the wrong way. As she went to scroll forward again to search for the turtle photos, her breath caught.

Confusion filled Isla as she looked at photos of herself. Photos of her at the lodge in Alaska. She frowned and kept scrolling. A photo of her at the blues bar in Mission Beach a few months ago. Another photo of her on Esculanta Island, with half of Sienna's face in the background.

What. The. Hell.

The creep, the lowlife bastard.

And she'd fallen for it.

Ronan Doyle from Dingle. Just another man she couldn't trust. And she'd spilled her guts to him.

Isla knew she was going to have to run again. He'd been sent to find her. That was the only reason he'd have photos of her all over the world.

What a fool she'd been to think Ronan was any different to every other man who had been in her life.

It was hard to say whether it was anger or disappointment that was making her hands and legs shake.

She had to get out of here. She had to get off the island. She had to run from the man she loved.

Dropping the camera on the table, not caring if it broke, she grabbed her bag and ran for the door.

***

Ronan was fully awake now, so he'd ended up cooking himself a feed too. It hadn't taken any longer to cook for two, than for Isla. He sang along with the radio as he'd stood at the stove flipping the eggs and waiting for the toast to come up.

Dylan walked in and opened the fridge. 'You're sounding chirpy this morning, Ronan.' His glance was knowing. 'Had a good night, did you?'

Ronan flicked him a look. 'A good night?'

'Yeah, I just saw a certain pretty Irish girl sneak out of your room. She was in a hurry; she took off like a rocket.'

Ronan frowned and switched the stove off. 'Where to? She hasn't had her breakfast yet.'

Dylan poured a glass of milk and then drank it before he shrugged. 'I thought Isla must have been late for work, because she went down the steps really fast.'

Ronan lifted the pan onto the table and quickly transferred the toast to one plate, and then tipped the eggs on. 'Have a good day,' he said as he hurried from the kitchen wondering where Isla had gone.

Maybe she'd had second thoughts, although she'd been a willing participant all night.

With a frown he headed back to his room, carrying the plate of eggs and toast.

Chapter Thirty

Isla

By the time Isla reached the spa hut, she had her emotions under a semblance of control. Her anger was bubbling under the surface, and she knew she was going to have to work very hard to keep it under control.

She wasn't going to run from Pentecost Island. As crazy as it was, even though she knew that Ronan wasn't who he had pretended to be, he had still helped her face her demons.

She drew in a shaky breath as she unlocked the door and went inside.

And he had turned out to be one of her demons. Another man who had proved he couldn't be trusted.

But she no longer had any fear of the past. Her first thought was that Ronan had been following her to get information for her father. Although she couldn't understand why it had taken almost ten years for him to look for her. Even if her father turned up here, she was a grown woman heading for thirty, for feck's sake. And why would he anyway? Da had made it quite clear that she was no longer his daughter or a member of their family.

And that suits me just fine.

It was hard to hold in her emotions as she thought of the way her parents had treated her when she was eighteen. Locked away with a man who had turned out to be untrustworthy, her parents then forced her to have an abortion and then Da had abandoned her on a street in London. It was unforgivable. If they *had* sent someone to find her and bring her home, they—and bloody Ronan Doyle—could go take a flying leap.

Her second thought was that Ronan was some sort of creepy stalker, but she dismissed that as soon as the possibility came to her. Before she knew that he had been secretly taking photographs of her, she'd got to know him, and she'd liked him. More than liked him, if she was honest. She would have preferred it if he had asked her outright why she was here, rather than gradually gaining her trust and finding out about her dishonestly.

With a sigh, Isla crossed to the desk. That wasn't quite true, because if he had simply asked her about her past, for sure she would have given him the whole happy family spiel.

But she'd foolishly trusted him and opened her heart and soul to him and told him the truth. Stuff she'd never told anyone before.

Not even Sienna.

If he'd been any sort of decent and honest human being, he would have told her then that he already knew all about her, and why he was here. If he'd been honest, maybe she could have tried to understand.

But, no.

Instead, he'd reached out and held her, and for feck's sake, she'd burrowed into his shoulder and lapped the attention up like a needy child.

Well, never again. That just showed her what happened when she took down her barriers and trusted someone.

As Isla's anger faded, disappointment kicked in. She'd really *liked* Ronan, and she'd just spent the night in his bed. An incredible night, and she was sure she had seen the true Ronan, either that or he was a bloody good actor.

As she crossed the room, she spotted a note on the reception desk in Sienna's loopy writing.

'Tess called. Your nine-thirty has cancelled, but now you have a ten-thirty after that. Hut Seven, but I didn't catch the name.'

As Isla prepared the room for her first client, she tried to push Ronan from her thoughts.

Deep breaths, think of good things. The psychologist in the mental health ward in London had taught her those strategies, and she'd tried to practise them every time the blackness descended.

For the first few years, it had been hard to think of good things. As Isla had travelled the world, she had banked a store of beautiful images in her mind and was able to run them through her thoughts like a slide show when she needed to. The huge lemons on the trees growing on the steep hills on the Amalfi coast, the beautiful untouched canvas of blinding-white snow around the lodge in Alaska, the faces of the beautiful children in Bali; the images and memories always calmed her.

Closing her eyes, she tried to summon the scenes to her thoughts, but all she could see were the photos on Ronan's camera, and her anger came rushing back.

Why? Why had he let her down too? Like everyone else did. Why did he have to be the same?

Isla wondered if he'd come looking for her, or if he'd stay away from her now that she was on to him. He'd noticed the camera had been moved, and he'd realise she'd seen the photos on it.

She didn't care what Ronan's reaction was; he couldn't be trusted to tell the truth. She couldn't trust him. She was incapable of trust.

As Isla stood at the window, her hands clenched by her side, Sienna opened the door and walked in with a wide smile.

'Good morning, you look tired, *liebling*. Did you have a late night?'

'Have you been talking to Dylan?' Isla couldn't help her snappish reply.

'No? Should I have?' Sienna's smooth brow creased in a frown and guilt trickled though Isla. It wasn't Sienna's fault.

'Sorry I was short tempered. I'm tired.' Isla closed her eyes briefly. She felt as though anyone who looked at her today would know she'd spent the night in Ronan's bed. She looked up and cleared her throat. 'What about Ronan? Was he there?'

'I didn't see him; I was only to have a quick piece of toast and a coffee. Are you okay? You don't look very happy.' Her voice held concern. 'What's wrong?'

'I'm not very happy at all, but don't worry. I won't let my bad mood impact on the clients today. I'm going to go over and see Pippa after the first appointment.'

Sienna's frown deepened. 'Tell me what's wrong, Isla. You're not thinking about leaving the island, are you?'

'No. I won't do that. If I did, I'd let you know first.'

'Good. I was worried for a moment.' Sienna moved towards the door and hesitated. 'You know, Isla, if there's anything you need to talk about, I'm happy to listen.'

A lump rose in Isla's throat as she heard the sympathy in

her friend's voice.

'Thank you.' She unclenched her fingers and tried to relax. 'I appreciate that. But I'm all good. I'll get over it. And I won't let you down.'

'Okay, but I have offered that I am here if you would like to talk. Remember that.'

'I will.'

'Isla? I wanted to—' Sienna hesitated and then opened the door to her treatment room. 'It doesn't matter. I'll talk to you later.' She closed the door quietly behind her, and Isla frowned, wondering what she had been going to say.

With a shrug, she began to prepare for her first client. There was a clean uniform in the cupboard in her treatment room, and once she had changed, she lit the candles on the bench under the window. With a deep sigh, Isla looked out the window, and wondered why her life had gone to shite again.

Worst of all, she knew was going to miss Ronan like crazy, the Ronan she thought she'd knew. Not the lowlife, conniving, dishonest man he really was.

Chapter Thirty-One

An hour later, Isla had one satisfied client leave the treatment room.

'Best hot stone massage I've ever had. You've got good hands, love.'

'Thank you. We aim to please here on Pentecost Island.' She managed to keep her voice upbeat, and she smiled as the woman left a hundred-dollar tip on the counter.

'I'll be telling all my friends about you. The resort's great, but *Hebe* is the best part of it for me.'

Isla slipped the money into their shared tip jar before she headed out to go and find Pippa to apologise for not turning up last night.

Her first stop was the office to see if the girls knew what Pippa's schedule was. She was in luck. Pippa was in the office talking to Sienna's Danny.

'Tess, can you tell Pippa I'd like a word when she's free?'

'Sure, love.' Tess gave her a coy look, but Isla pretended not to notice.

For fecks' sake, is nothing private on this island? Or am I imagining that everyone knows how I spent the night?

Isla went into the kitchen and made herself a cup of tea to take to the veranda while she waited for Pippa. Focusing on her work for the past hour had calmed her, but she yawned as she pulled out a chair. She hadn't had much sleep last night in Ronan's bed. Her face heated as she remembered what an incredible night they had spent together. Never in her life had she felt so close to another human being.

But it had all been a lie.

She closed her eyes trying to deal with the knowledge that Ronan had used her, but hurt pierced her heart. He'd be gone from the island as soon as he finished his contract, and she would just have to deal with him being here until then. She would stay away from him and ignore him.

I am not running again, she vowed to herself. *Unless I have to.*

As Isla lifted the teacup, a cross voice come from the office. 'Yes, I need to know now. It is *extremely* important.'

Her heart thudded and her whole body tensed. She dropped her cup into the saucer with a clatter as the flight instinct took over, and coffee splashed down the front of her white uniform.

No way. She was just on edge.

'How exactly can I help you?' Tess's voice was quiet and patient, totally at odds with the crazy feelings that were taking over Isla.

It couldn't be. Her hands were like ice, and she couldn't stop shaking as disbelief flooded through her. It was just a woman with an Irish accent.

'I'd like to know if you have a guest on the island by the name of Ronan Doyle, please.'

That voice took Isla back many years. Whining at the kitchen table when Isla was too slow eating her breakfast, and they were running late for the school bus. Teasing her when she didn't get invited to Mary Malone's birthday party because she wasn't in the cool group at school. And then later, only hearing her sister's voice when she talked to their parents, because Marlene was a cool university student who didn't waste her breath on a teenage sister.

A multitude of feelings surfaced in Isla as she sat there glued to the chair. She gripped the table as Tess answered. 'I'm sorry, Mrs Kendall, but Mr Doyle is no longer a guest here. But I can get a message to him if you would like to leave one.'

Mrs Kendall? *Good, it wasn't her.* Her mind was doing her head in since Ronan had shown his true colours.

'Thank you. Please tell him that Marlene Kendall is on the island and needs to speak to him as a matter of urgency.'

Isla gagged. She managed to stand and walk along the veranda to the back of the house before running down the steps.

God, the last person she wanted to see was her sister. Despite the fast-building heat of the morning her hands stayed cold and her legs barely supported her as she hurried across the lawn, no destination in mind. She just needed to get away, out of sight somewhere.

'Isla!' Pippa's voice followed her, and Isla closed her eyes.

'Isla, wait up!'

Isla stopped in the middle of the lawn at the back of the house and waited for Pippa to reach her.

'Sorry, Isla, I wanted to catch you before you went back to work. I'm sorry I wasn't available last night. We had some issues with the computer system and Gabe needed me in the office.'

Isla put her hand on her chest. 'Oh, that makes me feel better. To be honest, I forgot. We—I—was busy and didn't give it a thought. It doesn't matter, I have to go now.'

'That worked out well then. You haven't got time to come back to the office now?'

'No. I mean, yes.' Isla shook her head. 'But not the office. Can we just talk here?' She spoke quickly and her words ran together. Distracted by Pippa, she glanced over her shoulder to make sure no one else was coming. Pippa gently took her arm and steered her towards the low building in front of them.

Isla hadn't been in there before and looked around nervously. 'Do the guests come in here?'

'No, it's Odessa's studio.' Pippa frowned. 'Isla, what's wrong? You're as tense as anything.'

Isla was embarrassed when tears filled her eyes. She wasn't used to anyone worrying about her, or how she was feeling. She sniffed and pulled a tissue out of her uniform pocket. 'I'm sorry. I just didn't want that woman to see me. I don't want her to know that I work here.'

'Is there a problem? I noticed her Irish accent. Do you know her?'

'Unfortunately, I do.' Isla nodded and dabbed at her eyes. 'Marlene's my sister but I haven't seen her since I left Ireland almost ten years ago. And I don't want to.'

'Do you think she knows you're here? Or could it be a coincidence?'

'Not if she was looking for Ronan, like she said.' Her voice was bitter. 'I'm sorry, Pippa. You don't want to get involved in my problems. I'll be fine. I'll keep a very low profile while she's on the island.'

'Is that what you wanted to see me about?'

'Oh, no. Of course not. I wouldn't involve you. Just forget about it.'

They walked through the workshop to a small sitting room at the back, and Pippa gestured to the low sofa under the window. 'Sit down, Isla.' She smiled and her voice was quiet. 'This sofa was the original from my great aunt's house back in the 1930s or 40s. I'm not sure exactly how old it is, but it's seen lots of tears and heard many secrets.' She reached out and Isla looked down when Pippa took her hand. 'You're really pale, love. Please tell me how I can help. That's what we do here. We all look out for each other, and we take care of each other when there's a problem. And you obviously have something difficult that you're dealing with. I'd like to be able to help.'

'Please don't worry about my . . . my family stuff.' Isla sniffed and wiped her nose. 'I just wanted to know if I've passed my probationary month. I was getting a bit worried.'

'Oh, no need to. My brain seems to have gone to mush the last couple of weeks. That totally slipped my mind. Of course, you're staying. We love having you here and the feedback from the *Hebe* clients has been awesome. I'm so sorry. With the wedding and then sharing our baby news, I've been preoccupied.'

'Thank you.'

'You will stay, won't you? We'd like you to.'

'I'd like to as well.' Isla looked around. 'I'll be honest. It does depend on a few things though.' She didn't know what that might be, but if things got too hard, she would leave the island if she had to. But she didn't want to.

'Well, if there's anything I can do, just let me know. Do you know why your sister was looking for Ronan? Does she know him?'

'Apparently, she does, but I don't know how. Time will tell.'

'I've been really pleased to see you and Ronan spending time together.'

'No more,' Isla said fiercely and jumped to her feet. 'I'm sorry. I have to go. I have a client due in soon.'

'Okay. Now if you want to talk some more, you know where to find me.' Pippa's eyes were full of concern. 'I mean that. You come and find me. At the house. Any time of the day or night.'

Chapter Thirty-Two

Ronan

Sienna's face held no expression as she stood by *Hebe's* counter. She'd been with a client but had come out to see who had opened the sliding door. Ronan stood in the doorway and looked around the foyer of the day spa.

'Good morning, Ronan. Do you wish to make another appointment?'

He shook his head. 'No, thank you. Not yet. I'm looking for Isla. Is she here?'

'No, she's gone over to the main office.'

'Thanks, I'll go and catch her on the way back.'

As he turned to go Sienna caught his arm. 'Just so you know, Isla looked very upset when she arrived this morning.'

'I thought she might have been, that's why I need to talk to her. As soon as I can.'

Before she can disappear again, he thought. But this time it had nothing to do with the assignment he'd been given; it was because Ronan couldn't bear the thought of losing Isla. And knowing that she thought badly of him.

Jesus, what had she thought when she'd scrolled through his camera? There were dozens and dozens of photos of her. Most were taken with his telephoto lens. In about three different locations that she would recognise.

Did Isla have any idea that her sister was searching for her? When Isla had been honest with him about her difficult past, he should have opened up then and told her the truth.

Sienna's eyes were full of sympathy as she reached out and lightly touched his arm. 'Go and find her. Whatever the problem is, be truthful. Don't let there be any room for misunderstanding.' She looked down at her left hand and smiled, and Ronan noticed the flash of diamonds, but he didn't comment.

'I will, thank you. And I'll sort it out.'

'She won't be long. She has an appointment shortly.'

Ronan nodded and headed out the door. There was no sign of anyone coming along the path, so he sat on one of the garden bench seats that had been built around the tree trunks. From where he sat in the sun-dappled glade, he could see the front steps of *Hebe* as well as back along the path to the house where the office was located. Only a few minutes passed before the sound of someone walking along the track reached him. He stood and waited, and when the sunlight shone on the white uniform, he knew it was Isla.

Her head was down as she approached, and the last thing he wanted to do was spook her. He rose and stood still and quiet as she got closer.

When she had almost reached him, Ronan stepped forward. 'Isla, I need to talk to you.'

She lifted her chin and scowled at him. Regret pummelled his chest as her cold stare suggested he had just crawled out from under a rock.

'Cop onto yourself, you scut. See these?' Isla placed both hands over her ears. 'I don't want to hear a word from your lying mouth. You feckin' jackeen.'

'I'm sorry, I've never heard that term before.' He tried to keep his voice quiet.

'You haven't? Well, let me enlighten you. It means an obnoxious piece of shite.' She pushed past him, and her cold stare almost broke his heart. The warm and loving woman who had laughed with him through the most glorious night of his life had morphed into someone who hated him.

And he couldn't blame her, but he needed to explain.

'Now let me through. *I* have to go to work. But I guess you're on holiday now. Your job here is done, hey boyo?'

'Isla, please listen to me. Once I was sure who you were, and realised you didn't want to be found, I emailed my client and told them it wasn't you, and I quit. I—'

'Ronan, didn't you hear what I said? I don't want to talk to you and I don't want to hear your lies.'

'I'm not lying. I need to explain. Isla, I—'

'You're not lying? Bollocks! Poor little Irishman who didn't take enough water on his walk so I felt sorry for you. The loving family boyo who made up a whole family in Dingle just to get my interest. And then, and then you had the gall to entice me into your bloody bed. You say you're not lying, then why the feck is my sister in reception asking for you? I can't imagine anyone except for my family who would have put you up to this.'

'Your sister?' Ronan's hope of making her listen disintegrated with those two words.

'Yes, my sister.' Isla turned on her heel and ran towards the day spa hut. 'Just feck off out of my life!'

Chapter Thirty-Three

Isla drew in a deep shuddering breath as she pushed open the front door of the day spa. Sienna's treatment room was in use, and she let out her breath with a sigh of relief. She didn't want to talk to anyone. She couldn't talk to anyone without cracking. Not until she came to grips with her feelings. Could this day get any worse?

It had been bloody hard not to give in and listen to Ronan, and hear his feeble excuses, but she knew to survive she had to be strong. As much as she wanted to give in and let him hold her, she couldn't.

She couldn't *trust* him. Like everyone else in her life, Ronan had let her down, and in the worst way possible. He had lied to her.

Even though Niall had let her down, he had always been truthful, and as for Da? Well, Isla had always known where she stood with him.

The lowest of the low. The daughter who was a disappointment and never good enough. She blinked away tears. Maybe she shouldn't have given in and let her parents organise the termination of her pregnancy. Maybe she should have told the counsellor, no, I want to have a child! Someone who would love her, and someone who she could care about.

Maybe if she had, and had sought out Niall back then, her life would have been very different.

Maybe he would have married her, and she would be the wife who lived with him in that beautiful house in Dublin and she would have had more of his children. They would have lived in the house with the happy family she had seen when she had found him on Facebook five years ago.

Isla couldn't even remember where she had been when she had seen it. The image had stayed in her mind and had sent her into a downward spiral for months.

But since she had met Sienna on Esculanta Island, she had been happy and was looking forward to staying and working on

Pentecost Island. She *loved* it here, and she wasn't going anywhere. She felt valued for the first time in her life.

The sooner Ronan Doyle removed himself from the island and her life, and left her in peace the better, she told herself.

But a small part of her heart disagreed.

'Isla?'

Isla lifted her head quickly. Sienna had come out of her room, and Isla hadn't even heard the door open.

'Sorry. I was miles away.'

'Are you all right?' Sienna's voice was soft.

Isla nodded. 'I'm okay. I have to get organised now. I have a client in a few minutes.'

'Okay, as long as you're fine.'

'I am. But I tell you what, I could sure do with a sunset drink on the beach tonight.'

Sienna reached up and pushed her hair back from her forehead.

Isla widened her eyes. 'My God, Sienna! Is that an engagement ring on your hand? It is! Why didn't you tell me?'

Sienna's cheeks flushed and she nodded. 'I thought you were unhappy, and I didn't want to make you feel worse.'

Isla stepped over and hugged her friend. 'Don't be silly. I'm so happy for you. I'm fine. My little hiccup is over. Done and dusted. Time to move on. But tell me, when did this happen?' She picked up Sienna's left hand and looked at the ring. 'It's beautiful.'

'The other night.' Sienna's smile was wide, and a tiny burst of jealousy bloomed in Isla's heart, but she pushed it down. 'When I was hoping that's what Danny had planned. And he did.'

'All the more reason for a celebration tonight!' Isla kept her voice bright and upbeat.

'Let's talk to the others this afternoon, and see if they have plans,' Sienna said. 'There's a lot happening on the island at the moment.'

'Sure, let's do that.'

The door of the treatment room opened and Sienna's client stepped out.

'Back to work,' Isla said quietly.

The front door slid open and she looked up. Her heart thudded and her legs shook as she looked into the face of the sister she hadn't seen for over ten years.

Unable to speak, Isla nodded briefly and opened the door of her room. Sienna frowned and crossed to the reception counter, and as Isla closed the door and leaned her back against it, she closed her eyes listening to Sienna welcoming the "client".

'Please take a seat, Isla is just preparing the room, and will be with you shortly.'

Panic gripped her, and Isla looked to the small window opposite the massage table wondering if she could climb out and simply disappear into the forest.

This was all Ronan's fault.

A light tap on the door had her jumping forward.

'Isla? That is your client waiting.'

'Yes, thank you. Please tell her I will only be a moment.' Isla crossed to the sink and ran a flannel under the hot water. She placed it over her eyes for a few seconds and then when it cooled, she pressed the flannel against her hot cheeks.

Crossing to the mirror beside the table, she pulled her hair back and tightened the clip securing her curls, and then smoothed her uniform with shaking hands.

Taking a deep breath, she opened the door and stepped out.

'Hello Marlene, I won't lie and say it's been too long, but it has been a long time. Come in. and we'll get this over and done with.'

Her older sister followed her into the room.

Chapter Thirty-Four

Pippa

Sometimes, the days went by so quickly that I didn't know how we got everything done on the island. Guests came and went every day, and there was always something new to focus on. This week, Eliza and I worked closely with Ronan to put the finishing touches on our new promotion package. Eliza had the crazy idea of entering us in the state tourism awards.

'It's too soon,' I had protested. 'We'll be a laughingstock of the industry.'

But I couldn't budge her, and Ronan had agreed it was a good idea too. As I walked back to the office after Isla had left me, I consciously focused on my breathing. A visit to the bathroom was an essential stop first; I had been drinking lots of water as the late summer sun—and my pregnancy—sapped my energy.

Seeing Isla upset had worried me, and I'd make sure that I found her later when she had finished her appointments for the day. Not only had her sister turned up here, but it seemed as though her close friendship with Ronan—or more, according to the island grapevine—had hit a rocky patch.

I was happy, and I wanted everyone on the island to be happy. Eliza and I had a meeting with him now to discuss the progress of his photographic work for the current promotion, and I'd dig gently and see what I could do to help. After I came out of the newly renovated bathroom—oh, how I wished Aunty Vi could have seen it—he and Eliza were waiting in the small office that Renzo had added to the back of the veranda. Even though the layout of the rooms and the décor had changed—I still caught myself walking towards doorways that were no longer there—the house had retained its beautiful character. Sometimes I would walk up the steps and half expect Aunty Vi to be waiting there for me.

'Hi Pip. We were just getting a coffee. Would you like

one?' Eliza stood behind Ronan who was sitting on the small sofa in the office. She gestured down to him and frowned.

'No, thanks,' I said catching her eye and giving a small nod. 'I'm drinking herbal tea now. Smells and tastes foul, but it's better for the baby. If there's a herbal tea bag in the kitchen, I'll have one of those, please.'

'I'll get it for you. White tea with two for you, Ronan?'

'Yes, please.' His voice was dull, and his hands were clenched between his knees as he looked down.

I sat in the low chair on the other side of the coffee table and leaned back. 'So, Ronan, how are the photos going? Every time I've been somewhere on the island, I've seen you there with your camera. And your camera assistant.' I looked sideways at him.

'Yeah, it's going well.' He sat up straight and finally looked over at me. The poor guy looked totally miserable, and I couldn't let it go.

'You don't look very happy. Is there anything I can do?'

He shook his head and colour crept up his neck. 'Thanks, but no. I've done enough as it is. I'm going to get this contract finished quickly and I'll hand the photographs over to you. I think it would be best if I leave the island as soon as I can.'

'Is it because of Isla?' I hurried on to explain myself. 'Look, I'm not worried about your photos or her work. I'm worried about her. And you too, Ronan. For the past month you pair have seemed inseparable, and you looked so happy together.'

'We were, but I stuffed it up. Big time.'

I smiled at him. 'Men are good at doing that. Just give her a few days, and then make a peace offering.'

He shook his head again. 'I'll be gone by then. And it's not that easy. She'll never forgive me for what I did, and that's what I deserve. I should have been honest with her from the get-go.'

'Rubbish, don't be a wimp. The last thing you need to do is take off. Would it help to talk about it? Maybe I can help you sort it out?'

Eliza was standing in the doorway with a tray holding our drinks. 'Sorry to eavesdrop, but I agree with Pippa. I think we can help. That's if you want us to.'

For the first time, Ronan's expression brightened. 'Do you

think you could talk to her?'

'How about you tell us your story and we'll see what we can do to help,' I said.

Chapter Thirty-Five

Isla

'You didn't know?' Isla sat across from her sister where she sat with clients before she left them to prepare for their treatment. 'You really and truly didn't know?' Her hand shook as she picked up the glass of water.

'Isla, I had no idea. All I was ever told was that Da took you over to London because you'd decided to go to university there.'

'Bloody liar.' Isla snorted. 'He kept up the façade that I would go to university, did he?'

'That's what he told me, and then after that when I would ask, he would say you had made your choice and you didn't want anything more to do with the family. I should have tried harder to contact you. I'm so sorry. What you've told me is just dreadful. But he was a hard man, always.'

Isla's throat closed. 'He left me in a London street, outside the abortion clinic with five hundred pounds clutched in my hand. I spent weeks in a mental health facility.' Isla put her hand over her eyes as she spoke. 'Why can't he just leave me to get on with my life? Why is he chasing me now? I'm a strong woman these days, but this week has been absolute shite.' The feel of her sister's hand on her other arm had her lifting her hand away from her face.

'Isla, you don't know—' Marlene's fingers gripped her wrist. 'Da and Mam are both gone.'

'Gone? Gone where?' she asked.

'They've both passed on.'

Isla opened her mouth in shock. 'You mean they died?'

'Yes. That's why I've been looking for you. And that's why I hired Ronan Doyle to find you. He had a good reputation, and when he sent me your photo, and I knew he'd found you here on this island, I was really pleased. And then he emailed and said it wasn't you, that he was mistaken, and he was ending our contract.

And I had no idea what was going on, because I knew it was you from the photo.'

'He did that?' Isla couldn't help the little spurt of joy.

'Yes, and I have no idea why. Because I knew it was you. So, I decided to travel here and see for myself.'

'I don't understand why you needed to.'

Marlene looked away. 'It started off as a legal matter, but Isla, I need to tell you that I'm really pleased to have found you, and to have learned the truth. I hope you can forgive me for abandoning you for all of those years.'

Isla waved her hand. 'We were never close, Marlene, so why should you have worried?'

'Because I knew what Da could be like and how Mam followed him blindly, no matter what he did. You were treated horrendously, and I hope I can make it up to you.'

'It's not your responsibility.'

'It is. And I have to tell you why I needed to find you. It might upset you, but I'd rather you knew the truth.'

Isla sighed but she sat up straighter. 'Upset me? I don't think anything could make the day worse. Hit me with it.'

'Two years ago, Da had a stroke while he was driving back from the office one night and the car was a wreck. He only lived for a couple of days, but Mam was in the car with him, and although she was badly hurt, she recovered. But never fully. To be honest, I think she was so used to being bossed around by him and doing as he wanted; without him, she was lost.'

Isla stared at her sister.

'Da had cut you out of his will, but not long before she died, Mam redid her will, and she told me that she had made sure that you were to get half of the estate. She was really sad and said the way you had been treated wasn't fair. I thought she meant in the will. I didn't know any of that other stuff.'

'I don't want it.'

'It's been bequeathed to you.

'I don't want it. I don't want any memory of those days. I'm happy enough here and I have enough money for what I need. I've supported myself around the world for the past ten years, and I can keep doing that.'

But do I want to keep doing it? Isla wondered.

Her sister shook her head. 'You have to. The estate can't be finalised until you do. Take it and do whatever you want with it.'

'Because until I do you can't get your share? Is that why you travelled halfway across the world to find me? Why you hired an Irishman to find me?'

Her sister had the grace to look embarrassed. 'That's part of it. But Isla, honestly, I am so pleased to have found you. I'd like . . . I'd like for us to stay in touch.'

Isla lifted her chin. 'Why?'

Marlene reached out again. 'I'd like my two girls to meet their Aunty Aisling. I'd like you to be a part of our family. I know it might be hard to forgive, but I'd like to make it up to you.' As she held Isla's hand, a smile crept over her face. 'I think you would get on very well with Claire, my youngest. She is very much like you were when you were a teenager.' Marlene chuckled. 'She's doing my head in.'

'Poor kid,' Isla said.

'No. I used to envy you. You were so strong and you knew what you wanted. You wouldn't take any of Da's bullying. I didn't want to do law, but I did as I was told.' She held Isla's gaze. 'I haven't practised since I had the girls. Please come home and meet them. There's nothing there to hurt you anymore. If you don't I'll bring them Down Under later in the year.'

'I'll think about it. I have some things to do here first. How long are you on the island for?' Isla looked up at the clock. 'I have another client due in, and I'm busy all afternoon.' She took a breath. 'Perhaps we could have dinner together.'

Marlene smiled at her. 'I'd like that very much.'

Chapter Thirty-Six

Ronan

Ronan felt more hopeful as he left the office after talking to Pippa and Eliza. He walked along the path to his hut, wondering how long it would be before Isla would listen to him. It was so hot he could see the waves of heat shimmering above the sand on the beach. He pulled his handkerchief from his shorts pocket and mopped at his brow. How did anyone live in this heat?

Pippa and Eliza had reassured him. Both women had listened sympathetically as he'd told them the story of being hired to find Isla.

'Yes, you stuffed up,' Pippa said.

Eliza nodded. 'And at least you recognise that yourself. It takes a big man to admit that he made a mistake.'

'But Isla won't listen to me. She won't believe me that I told her sister that the woman I found wasn't her.'

Pippa had put one finger to her lips. 'You have strong feelings for her? For Isla, I mean.'

'Of course I do. If I didn't care about her, I would have left as soon as I told her sister she was here.'

Pippa nodded. 'Yes, the sister. Another complication to be overcome. Isla told me she was here, and I could see she was worried. Okay, if she won't talk to you, leave it with us. I don't want to see anyone unhappy on our island.'

Eliza had reached over and squeezed his hand reassuringly. 'Trust us, Ronan. Okay? They don't call Pentecost Island the "Island of Love" for nothing.'

Perspiration trickled down his neck as he approached his hut. He would get his camera and take some more shots of the rainforest; it might be cooler in there. Then again, he could stay in the air-conditioned bar, and try to figure out how to convince Isla that he *had* told the truth. It was good of Pippa and Eliza to offer to help, but it was up to him.

As Ronan wrestled with a decision, he turned onto the path towards the bar.

'About feckin' time you came back, boyo.'

His head flew up and he stopped as he stared into the dim forest. Isla was sitting in the shade on the seat underneath the spreading tree before the pool area.

'Hello,' he said cautiously. 'I'm pleased to see you. I think.'

'Make up your mind.'

He nodded. 'I am. Very pleased. Were you taking a rest in the heat, or could I dare hope you were waiting for me?'

'I was waiting for you.'

'I thought you had appointments all day?'

'Sienna took my next one for me. She had a cancellation. Come and sit by me. I need to talk to you.'

Ronan sat beside her and, as he looked at Isla, he realised she was as nervous as he was.

'I owe you an apology,' she said. 'I should have listened to you, but I was upset. I'm sorry for yelling at you and calling you all those names.'

'No. It's me who must apologise. I should have told you the truth. I should have told you that I had emailed your sister. I really did, Isla.'

'I know. She told me.'

'Thank the heavens for that.'

'I should have trusted you, but I'm not very good at trusting.'

'Maybe it's time you had someone in your life who could teach you how to trust.'

'Do you think so?' She moved closer to him. 'Maybe it is.'

Ronan lifted his arm and put it around Isla's shoulder. 'There's just one thing you need to know before you make up your mind.'

'What's that?' Isla turned her face up to his and put one hand on his cheek.

He lowered his head so that his lips hovered over hers. 'I really do come from Dingle, and if you decide to accept me as a part of your life, you'll have to put up with my family. A large family.'

'You'll have to teach me how to be a part of a family.'

Ronan closed his eyes as happiness and relief surged through him.

'And Ronan? I've found *my* family today,' she said.

He smiled against her lips as Isla's arms went around his neck and pulled him close. There would be plenty of time later for her to find out that her island family was watching out for her too.

'*Macushla,*' he said softly before his lips claimed hers.

Epilogue

Pippa – Five months later

Even though my childhood in Brisbane, before I had moved up to live with Aunty Vi, had been tragic and difficult, I had some special memories that I cherished. My friendship with Tam and Nell since that swimming carnival when I had won a ribbon in Grade 4, and the memories of my special times with my mum. For the twelve short years of my life, I had a mother, and I adored her. We spent a lot of time home alone because Dad worked down on the oil rigs in Bass Strait; he was one of the first fly-in-fly-out workers before it became commonplace.

One lovely Sunday afternoon in the winter before she . . . died, Mum took me to where the old Cloudland ballroom had been in Bowen Hills. It had been demolished without a permit one night before I was born, but Mum had shared with me how she had met my father there. We had danced along the footpath and she had sung me a whole set of seventies songs, and the memory of that day was as clear as if it had been yesterday, twenty years later.

A new Cloudland had been created not far from the original site, and the annual state tourism awards were being held at the venue. So, I guess being here tonight for the awards ceremony has brought me full circle.

Now that I had Rafe and I was going to be a mother, I could understand a little more of what had made my mum the way she was.

The week before Dad came home every second month, there was always a mad flurry in the house. The rooms all smelled like furniture polish and baby violets filled tiny little vases on every space. The kitchen benches were covered with fresh-baked bikkies and cakes cooling on wire racks.

I loved that week because the rest of the time, we lived in chaos and made do with bought biscuits and takeaway food.

I guess I did get more from Mum than the ginger hair. I

vowed that I would show our child how much I loved him . . . or her.

'Are you okay, Pip?' Rafe held my hand tightly as we walked behind Nat and Nell. 'You're very quiet. No pains or anything.'

My pregnancy was too advanced for flying down to Brisbane—there was only a week before our baby was due to arrive—so Rafe and I had taken two days to drive down. I wasn't going to miss this ceremony for anything. Ma Carmichael's Resort had been nominated in three categories.

I squeezed his hand back. 'Just thinking about growing up in Brisbane.' I grinned as I looked ahead at Tam and Gabe, who were pushing a double stroller holding their three-month-old twins, Harriet and Thomas, and at Nell and Nat, who were holding their six-week-old daughter, Lee-Anne, who had the loudest cry I had ever heard. 'And thinking how grateful I am to our friends who've all contributed to bringing our resort this far. I just wish they could have all come tonight.'

'Someone has to run Ma Carmichael's.' he said.

'True,' I said.

'We'll take lots of photos, and I think Ronan is going to video the parts we're nominated for,' Eliza said as she and Phillipe caught up to us.

We caught up to the rest of our group and Dylan pointed to the large circular table we were all sitting at. I was pleased that Odessa had been able to come as they were flying to England in the morning to show off her engagement ring to Jenny and Bryant, her parents.

I had asked for a table near the exit, so Tam and Nell could make an easy exit if the babies needed attention. It was also close to the ladies' room for me; I'd seemed to live in the loo the past week.

'Are you excited, Pippa?' Isla asked as she stood next to Ronan at the table.

'I am,' I said with a smile for them both. 'Our nominations are because of the wonderful work your man did, Isla.'

'Don't sell yourself short, Pippa. The nominations are because of the wonderful resort you created. I just took the photos of what you created.' Ronan held Isla close to him. They had moved in together to one of the double rooms in the staff lodge and they both seemed very happy. Ronan had agreed to work with us part time on promotion, and he'd picked up some more photographic work with the local tourism body at Airlie Beach.

Before I could reply to Ronan, Tamsin turned to me with a grin. 'Nice evening dress, girlfriend. If you didn't know you were pregnant . . .'

'Ha ha. If they didn't know, anyone could guess by taking one look at my huge belly.' I put my hand on the olive-green silk that was straining across my stomach. The dress had fitted last week, when I had picked it up, but I had expanded in those five days.

'You look gorgeous, Pip.' Nell reached across and hugged me. 'My God, is that baby still kicking?'

We all sat down at the table as the MC on the stage asked everyone to take their seats, and we were soon eating our meal and watching a slideshow of all the nominated resorts, restaurants and tourist attractions.

'Look, there we are!' I clapped my hands together as a fabulous drone shot of Pentecost Island filled the screen. The oohs and ahs from the audience sent a thrill through me.

Rafe leaned over and kissed my cheek. 'You've done very well, sweetheart.'

'We've all done very well.' I drew in my breath as a sudden ache gripped my lower back, but I didn't say anything. It went away slowly and didn't come back.

After dessert was served, the presentation of the awards began, and Tamsin and Nell's little cherubs stayed fast asleep. Motherhood was going to be a breeze, I thought.

I was chuffed when *Violet's,* our restaurant, received the highly commended award in Excellence in Customer Experience - Restaurants

I was astounded when *Hebe,* our day spa was runner up in the Excellence in Customer Experience Boutique Service category. Eliza accepted the silver award for us.

As I leaned closer to Rafe, another ache held me in its vice briefly, and I paused before I spoke to him. He was looking at the small, carved award that Eliza had passed around the table and didn't notice me hesitate.

'I am so proud,' I finally managed to get out. 'I can't believe we've won two awards and we're just coming up to our second anniversary.'

'It's not over yet,' my husband said.

The lights dimmed and there was a drum roll as the Minister for Tourism held up the envelope for the highest award for the night.

'I have much pleasure in announcing the winner for Excellence in Customer Experience, Hotel and Resort Accommodation.' Opening the envelope, he read it and leaned towards the microphone. 'And the winner is Ma Carmichael's Resort on Pentecost Island in our beautiful Whitsunday region.'

I don't recall how I got to the stage, but when I got there, I was flanked by my best friends, Tamsin, Nell and Eliza. We were all in shock, and as we stood there, the spotlight hit our table and tears rolled down my cheeks when I saw the look on Rafe's face. He stood proudly beside Nat and Gabe—who were each holding a baby, and on his other side was Odessa, holding Tam and Gabe's other twin.

The Minister shook my hand, and I was asked to say a few words.

I stood in front of the microphone ignoring the ache building in my lower back.

'Two years ago, three friends came to Pentecost Island,'—I smiled through my tears—'now also known as the "Island of Love". Together we worked hard, and our friendship circle grew as more good people joined us. It is the love and commitment of each one of those people I am proud to call my friends that has created the wonderful resort that we now have. Thank you.' I held the gold trophy aloft and leaned closer to the microphone as I clutched my stomach. 'I just have one more thing to say. Rafe, I think we need to find a hospital.'

Our perfect little daughter, Violet Adele Rendell arrived safely just over an hour later.

I watched Rafe as he stared down at her face, his expression full of awe. 'I told you we were going to have a little girl and she's beautiful, just like her mother.' He leaned down and brushed his lips over mine, and then on our daughter's forehead. 'And look, her hair is the same apricot colour as yours.'

'And look at her eyes,' I whispered. 'She has her father's eyes.'

##

Two weeks later, on a warm afternoon in spring, Tasmin, Nell, Eliza and I stood on the beach as the sun hovered over the mountains in the west. The sky faded from that deep indigo blue into an array of pinks shot with gold, and the only sound was the small waves breaking on the shingly sand.

I lifted my glass of soda water. 'To friendship, girls. To the unbreakable bond that has seen us stay together through the ups and downs of our lives. And the friendships and love that has created our wonderful resort. All for one and one for all.'

'All for one, and one for all,' they replied.

As the sun slipped slowly towards the sea, we sat there in silence, each lost in our own thoughts of the past two years. All that we had achieved, the love that we had found—our partners, our children, and together, the resort we had created thanks to my dear Aunty Vi—Ma Carmichael's Resort.

I looked up at the fading sky and the first star of the evening twinkled at me. I smiled and raised my glass to Aunty Vi.

THE END

OTHER BOOKS from ANNIE

Daughters of the Darling
From Across the Sea
Over the River (2024)
Porter Sisters Series
Kakadu Sunset
Daintree
Diamond Sky
Hidden Valley
Larapinta
Kakadu Dawn

Pentecost Island Series
Pippa
Eliza
Nell
Tamsin
Evie
Cherry
Odessa
Sienna
Tess
Isla

The Augathella Girls Series
Outback Roads
Outback Sky
Outback Escape
Outback Wind
Outback Dawn
Outback Moonlight
Outback Dust
Outback Hope

Augathella Short and Sweet Series

Annie Seaton

An Augathella Surprise
An Augathella Baby
An Augathella Spring
An Augathella Christmas
An Augathella Wedding
An Augathella Easter
An Augathella Masquerade Ball

Sunshine Coast Series
Waiting for Ana
The Trouble with Jack
Healing His Heart
Sunshine Coast Boxed Set

The Richards Brothers Series
The Trouble with Paradise
Marry in Haste
Outback Sunrise
Richards Brothers Boxed Set

Bondi Beach Love Series
Beach House
Beach Music
Beach Walk
Beach Dreams
The House on the Hill

Second Chance Bay Series
Her Outback Playboy
Her Outback Protector
Her Outback Haven
Her Outback Paradise
The McDougalls of Second Chance Bay Boxed Set

Love Across Time Series
Come Back to Me
Follow Me

Finding Home
The Threads that Bind
Love Across Time 1-4 Boxed Set

Bindarra Creek
Worth the Wait
Full Circle
Secrets of River Cottage
A Clever Christmas
A Place to Belong

Others
Whitsunday Dawn
Undara
Osprey Reef
East of Alice
Four Seasons Short and Sweet
Follow the Sun
Ten Days in Paradise
Deadly Secrets
Adventures in Time
Silver Valley Witch
The Emerald Necklace
A Clever Christmas
Christmas with the Boss
Her Christmas Star

About the Author

Annie lives in Australia, on the beautiful north coast of New South Wales. She sits in her writing chair and looks out over the tranquil Pacific Ocean.

She writes contemporary romance and loves telling stories that always have a happily ever after. She lives with her very own hero of many years and they share their home with Barney, the ragdoll puss, who hides when the four grandchildren come to visit.

Stay up to date with her latest releases at her website: http://www.annieseaton.net

Awards

2023: Winner of the long contemporary RUBY award for Larapinta

Finalist for the NZ KORU Award 2018 and 2020.

Winner ...Best Established Author of the Year 2017 AUSROM

Longlisted for the Sisters in Crime Davitt Awards 2016, 2017, 2018, 2019

Best Established Author, Ausrom Readers' Choice 2017

Finalist in Book of the Year, Long Romance, RWA Ruby Awards 2016 Kakadu Sunset

Winner, Best Established Author of the Year 2015 AUSOM

Winner, Author of the Year 2014 AUSROM